Everyone is talking about
Kari Lynn Dell's Texas Rodeo

"A fun, wild ride! You need to pick up a Kari Lynn Dell."

—**B.J. Daniels**, *New York Times* and
USA Today bestselling author

"An extraordinarily gifted writer."

—**Karen Templeton**, three-time RITA
Award–winning author, for *Reckless in Texas*

"Real ranchers. Real rodeo. Real romance."

—**Laura Drake**, RITA Award–winning author,
for *Reckless in Texas*

"Look out, world! There's a new cowboy in town."

—**Carolyn Brown**, *New York Times*
bestselling author, for *Tangled in Texas*

"Dell's writing is notable, and her rodeo setting is fascinating, with characters that leap off the page and an intriguing series of actions, conflicts, and backstory elements that keep the plot moving... A sexy, engaging romance set in the captivating world of rodeo."

—*Kirkus Reviews* for *Reckless in Texas*

"A standout in Western romance."

—*Publishers Weekly* for *Reckless in Texas*

"This well-written tale includes strong characters and a detailed view of the world of bullfighting... Readers

Also by Kari Lynn Dell

FEARLESS *in* TEXAS

KARI LYNN DELL

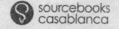
sourcebooks
casablanca

Published by Sourcebooks Casablanca, an imprint of Sourcebooks, Inc.
P.O. Box 4410, Naperville, Illinois 60567-4410
(630) 961-3900
Fax: (630) 961-2168
sourcebooks.com

Printed and bound in the United States of America.
OPM 10 9 8 7 6 5 4 3 2 1

To my husband, who's still cheering me on even though this writing gig takes longer to turn a profit than the cattle business.

Chapter 1

THE INSTANT WYATT'S FINGERS CAME TO REST ON MELANIE'S bare skin, they both cursed—a mutual, almost silent hiss, too quiet for any of the crowd encircling the nearly empty dance floor to hear over the music. Their steps didn't falter. They didn't blink. But he didn't pretend he couldn't feel the jolt at the inevitable, unavoidable contact…and neither did Melanie.

He smiled—a generic, *just making conversation* smile that would fool anyone besides the woman looking him directly in the eye. "Well. This is inconvenient."

"Extremely," Melanie agreed.

He didn't bother to move his hand. The cut of her emerald-green halter-top bridesmaid dress left him with no alternatives other than her exposed back or her satin-covered butt. Her long, straight chestnut hair had been pinned into a tousled updo with tendrils that trailed down her neck, begging a man to twirl them around his fingers.

Damn Violet for being the one woman on earth determined to make her maid of honor look as hot as sin.

As they circled the floor, eyebrows were raised and glances exchanged. He was aware of the picture they made—him blond and elegant, at ease in the tuxedo that made the other cowboys tug at neckties and fidget with cummerbunds; her following his lead as effortlessly as if they'd been dancing together for years. They were sleek and athletic, glowing with the pheromones that had been accumulating, molecule by molecule, over the enforced proximity created by two days of the standard pre-wedding hullabaloo.

Wyatt flicked a glance toward the bride and groom, so wrapped up in each other they wouldn't have noticed if their attendants had broken into a tango. "Joe is the closest thing I have to a brother."

Even though he did *have* a male sibling.

"Violet *is* my sister," Melanie countered. "Her family is my family."

Even though her own parents were sitting at a table only a few feet away, pointedly ignoring each other.

He studied the circle of faces that surrounded them, let his gaze settle for a beat on Joe and Violet, then focused on Melanie again, his voice hardening. "I'm not giving them up."

"I was here first."

Which was why his position was so much more precarious. He had only just found this weird and wonderful extended family that was more about loyalty than blood. Melanie's ties to them were forever.

"So this"—his fingers flexed, creating a slight, dangerous increase in pressure—"would be incredibly stupid. Especially for us."

She tilted her head in question.

"You don't like me. You certainly don't trust me," he said.

"Depending on the circumstances. You are a good friend to them. If you hadn't forced Joe to come to Texas in the first place, he'd still be in Oregon instead of over there trying not to fall face-first into Violet's cleavage— which is pretty damn impressive in that dress." Melanie smiled fondly at the two of them, then brought her gaze back to meet Wyatt's. "I've seen you risk life and limb for him in the arena."

He shrugged. "I'm a bullfighter. You do what it takes to make sure the cowboy and your partner walk away."

He didn't have to explain. She'd been on the rodeo trail long before she took her first steps, and her brother was also a bullfighter. But she shook her head. "You'd do the same for a complete stranger in a back alley. If I ever got caught in the middle of a convenience store robbery, you'd be the person I wanted standing at the Slurpee machine."

"But not sitting across the breakfast table."

She pursed glossy red lips as she considered the question. "It would be too crowded with you, me, and whatever agenda you're currently working. I'd have a hard time deciding where I fit into the scheme of the day."

"Says the woman who makes a living parting the unsuspecting public from their hard-earned dollars."

"Ouch." But the edge in her voice was more amusement than offense. "I'll have to tell Human Resources to add that to the job description."

"And this conversation is a perfect example of why we would be a disaster. Despite this." He traced a featherlight arc across her skin with his thumb.

She let her lashes flutter lower, to match her voice. "We could sneak off for a single night of depraved sex. Get it out of our systems."

For a moment, the possibility hovered between them like a heat mirage. They both inhaled sharply, then exhaled slowly.

"Been there, tried that, have the divorce papers to prove it." And he would not let his dick lead him into that steel-jawed trap again. Not when he had so much more than a simple broken heart on the line. He flashed a smile, bright and lethal. "I have it on good authority that you can—and will—hold a grudge."

"Every girl needs a superpower," she said with an equally toothy grin.

"Yours could make future Thanksgiving dinners a little awkward, don't you think?"

Her eyes narrowed. "I *think* I am both reasonable and mature enough to handle myself."

"History begs to differ."

Color flared in her cheeks, a visible gauge of her rising temper. "Are you trying to irritate me?"

"Yes."

She blinked. Then laughed in disbelief. "You really think that's going to help?"

"Can't hurt. And it comes so naturally to both of us." He twirled her, then pulled her close again, nearly eye to eye with her in heels. "We can't be friends."

The song was winding down. One more chorus, and he would have to step away to dutifully tap the father of the bride on the shoulder and cut in for the traditional dance with the bride's mother.

"We also can't avoid each other completely," she said.

"Close enough. I live in Oregon; you live in Amarillo. I visit a few times a year, and even when I am here, you're usually working. It's been over a year since Joe and Violet got together, and we've barely crossed paths, except at holidays."

"Then we should be safe. I've had plenty of practice behaving myself at Miz Iris's house."

He raised his eyebrows. "Also not what I've heard."

"Hey, it was all at least half Violet's fault." Her soft laugh was laced with affection. Then her eyes narrowed again. "So we agree on one thing." She dragged a fingernail lightly down his neck on the pretense of flicking off a speck of the infernal glitter Violet's son had blasted them with upon arrival at the reception hall. "This—"

"—is not worth the risk." Wyatt kept his voice cool, despite the hot pulse of his blood.

"And we swear never to speak of it to any of them." Her gaze sharpened on his face. "Ever."

He curled his lip. "Would you like to spit on our hands and shake to seal the deal?"

"Sunshine," she drawled. "If I decide to swap spit with you, I guarantee it'll get a lot messier than that."

He gave a strangled laugh, dropped his hands, and took a step back as a passing waiter shoved plastic champagne flutes at them for the latest in an endless series of toasts.

Ignoring the drunken ramblings of some distant cousin, Melanie lifted her glass. "Here's to no lovin' between *this* man and *this* woman."

"For as long as we both shall live," he agreed mockingly.

They tapped their glasses together, and both tossed back the champagne.

She handed him her empty glass before sauntering over to join Joe and Violet. Wyatt rocked back on his heels, appreciating the view…as he was sure she had intended. He took two full steps in pursuit before he caught himself, turned, and walked in the opposite direction.

A decision he would live to regret for a very, *very* long time.

Chapter 2

JUST. SAY. NO.

Melanie had been practicing for days, knowing this moment would come, and still the damn word wouldn't fall out of her mouth—just like every other time her boss had shoved work off his desk and into her lap.

Leachman smirked at her as he massaged his chest, two fat little fingers slipping between the buttons of his shirt in a way that was downright obscene. "I'll need that back from you first thing Monday morning."

She paged through the proposal, fingers trembling with the urge to ball it up and toss it in his face. Only two of the sections he'd highlighted had any direct correlation to marketing. The rest were all technical or financial. In other words...*not her job*.

"It's Wednesday afternoon," she pointed out in a miraculously level voice. "I'm in the middle of putting together the monthly client newsletter, and I have to spend most of tomorrow with the graphic designer, working on packaging for the new line of probiotics."

"Our last marketing director didn't mind logging a few extra hours when we were in a pinch." He let his gaze make a leisurely trip over her severely cut suit, past the pencil skirt to linger on her legs. "But then, I don't imagine he had your, um, social life."

What social life? This was the third week in a row her evenings and weekend would be consumed by a last-minute project the Leech had dumped on her desk, and for a month before that she'd been on the road, traveling across the country to trade shows and seminars. This was the first spring in her life that she hadn't been able to get out to the ranch, saddle up a horse, and spend hours meandering through the Canadian River breaks, admiring the wildflowers and the flush of new grass. The yearning for wide, open spaces, the thud of hooves on red dirt, and the musky scent of horse and sweat-stained leather was a low, permanent ache lodged behind her breastbone. And just when she'd finally had a whole Sunday to break loose.

"If you can't handle it…" Leachman half extended a hand in what they both knew was a token gesture. He wouldn't take the application back unless she crammed it down his throat.

Hell. She could already hear Violet's disgust when she called to say she wouldn't make Sunday dinner after all. But dammit, the competition for this grant would be stiff, and the team down in research and development needed every penny.

And that's where the bastard knew he had her. Their odds of acceptance were at least doubled if Melanie wrote the proposal. With the extra funding, Westwind could accelerate their research and development of the next generation of livestock supplements, greatly reducing the need for antibiotics and the related risk of triggering the emergence of drug-resistant bacteria. Melanie could rattle the whole spiel right off the top of her head. After all, she had written the press releases.

And once again, she would have to take one for the team.

She tucked the grant application under her arm, and her heart gave a single, painful squeeze as images of endless blue skies and this year's crop of slick, rambunctious calves faded away. "I'd better get cracking if I'm going to—"

She turned sharply at the rap of knuckles on the doorframe. The man who stood there smiled apologetically from beneath the brim of a well-shaped white straw cowboy hat. "I don't mean to interrupt. The receptionist said to come on back, and the door was open…"

"No, no, come on in!" Leachman lunged to his feet. "Good to see you."

Melanie stepped aside to allow the newcomer to accept the proffered handshake.

"Glad I could make it." He paused, angling a glance at Melanie from warm, hazel eyes. "Michael Miller, from Great Plains Feeders."

"Oh! I wasn't expecting you until tomorrow morning." Her smile was genuine as his hand closed around hers, firm and callused. "I'm Melanie Brookman. We spoke on the phone. I'm so glad you agreed to come down and take a closer look at what we have to offer."

"Me too."

Her face started to heat as she realized how her words could be misinterpreted, but Michael's smile didn't waver, and his gaze didn't wander from her face. He was the prototype of cowboy, with his close-cropped brown hair and a body that did wonderful things for a sage-colored, pearl snap shirt and starched jeans. "It took a hell of a sales pitch to make my boss agree to even consider working with anyone besides our usual feed company."

"Well, I was glad to make the trip to Pueblo so we could sit down and iron things out," the Leech declared. "I've always believed business should be done in person."

Michael made an apologetic face. "With all due respect, it was the data that won him over. Miz Brookman is a genius at translating all that science into what you can do for our bottom line."

Melanie felt like the Grinch, her heart swelling three sizes at the unsolicited praise. Leachman stuck out his chin and ran a hand over sparse silver hair—classic signs of repressed anger. Even if Melanie hadn't made a point of becoming an expert interpreter of body language, he would've been an easy read. A *danger, danger* signal dinged in her head. His ego had been pricked, and he certainly couldn't take it out on the client. Melanie, on the other hand…

Then suddenly, he was the soul of benevolence. "Since the two of you are already on the same page, I'll let Melanie give you the full tour of our facilities. She doesn't have anything on her desk that can't wait."

She sucked in a breath so sharp that Michael flinched. Leachman beamed, pleased to draw a visible response.

"I can wait until tomorrow." Michael gestured toward her skirt. "She's not really dressed for slogging around a feed mill."

Leachman waved him off. "She doesn't mind getting a little dirty, do you, sweetheart?"

She forced her lips into a tight smile that eased slightly when she turned it on Michael. "Give me a couple of minutes to throw on jeans and boots, and I'll meet you out front."

—◊—

When they returned from the mill two hours later, she was shocked to see Leachman's car still in its assigned spot. She'd assumed he'd pawned Michael off on her so he wouldn't have to break his weekly golf date with Jimmy Ray Towler, the head of Sagebrush Feeders and the second biggest slimeball in the Panhandle. Did either of the wives realize that their husbands' traditional post-golf meal had less to do with the truck stop's famous chicken-fried steak than with the services offered by women who prowled the parking lot in search of drivers who'd been alone on the road a little too long?

Melanie blocked that grotesque vision as she escorted Michael inside, unable to ignore the excellent fit of his bootcut jeans when he walked ahead into the Leech's office. If she was gonna picture anyone naked...

She glanced up and caught Leachman narrowing his eyes, his expression more shrewd than normal. Damn. She had to be careful. He wasn't as dumb as she let herself believe.

Then he blinked, and he was once again his usual smarmy self. "Well, what do you think?" he asked Michael.

"Your people are doing some really interesting stuff. I'd love to be a part of it, but I'll have to convince my boss it's worth the extra hassle to sign on as a test site." He gave a self-deprecating smile. "It's a lot of information. I'll need time to process everything."

"Take all you need. In fact..." Leachman's expression was so bland it made Melanie's antennae quiver.

"Since Melanie is so good at *translating*, I'll let the two of you continue your conversation over dinner while I catch up on a few other things."

That son of a bitch. It wasn't enough that he'd robbed her of most of the afternoon. Leachman was going to milk every precious hour he could out of this visit, knowing what it would cost her to have to make them up.

And, no doubt, use the planned dinner as an excuse to get home very late tonight. *I had a meeting, honey…*

Melanie ruthlessly wiped any reaction from her face. "Of course. I'll see if any of the R&D team can join us so they can answer his questions."

And so she wouldn't be alone with him. Michael Miller looked a little too much like a possible antidote to her stubborn fascination with a certain fair-haired boy, and even though consorting with the clients wasn't expressly prohibited, it wasn't exactly smart, either.

Conversation at dinner centered on nutritive values of different grains, nutrient availability and absorption, and how bioactive compounds could improve health and feed efficiency. By the time they finished, Melanie was happily stuffed with both information and excellent barbecued brisket. They'd been joined by Anna from the lab and Tyler from production, so she'd teased out and made note of nearly everything she needed to kick ass on that grant application, which would save her hours of weeding through reports.

Take that, you slimy Leech.

She was feeling especially pleased with herself as she waved good night to the others and strolled with Michael to where he'd parked beside her SUV after following her to the restaurant. The night air was fresh, but with a soft-edged promise of spring. She drew in a deep, appreciative breath and caught a whiff of Michael's scent, hints of citrus and sage underpinned by warm male.

Yum. But sadly, not on the menu.

She beeped open her door, then turned, startled to find him closer to her than she'd expected in the narrow, shadowy space between their vehicles. When he smiled this time, he made no attempt to keep it professional.

"Can I talk you into coming by my hotel for a drink?" he asked.

"I can't." Shaking her head regretfully, Melanie reached for her door handle. "I don't date business associates."

His eyebrows lifted. "Who do you date? As far as I can tell, your boss keeps you too busy for anything but business."

Which would account for why it had been far too long since a man had gotten this close. Her breath caught when he reached up and brushed a fingertip beneath her chin.

"You need to take some time for yourself now and then. I'm sure Leachman didn't put in fourteen hours today."

Resentment flared, gasoline on the flame of attraction she'd been trying to squelch. No, Leachman definitely would not be the one staying up until the wee hours, converting those notes she'd taken into persuasive language for the grant application. But she shook her head again. "Very tempting, but way too complicated."

"Not really. We can keep it just between you and me."

She frowned. "I'm not a fan of sneaking around."

"Not sneaking. Just being discreet." As if realizing he'd pushed his luck as far as he dared, he stepped back, giving her space. "No rush. I intend to convince *my* boss that it's worth our while to work with you—which means I'll be making regular trips down here." His eyes warmed as they met hers. "I definitely like what I see at Westwind."

Ever the gentleman, he waited for her to drive away first, giving a short, good-night beep of his horn as she turned in the opposite direction from his hotel. When she reached her apartment, Melanie dumped her briefcase and purse on the couch and went straight to her laptop, pulling up an Internet browser and typing in *Michael Miller, Pueblo, Colorado*.

Because seriously. A man like that still running around single was too good to be true.

There were plenty of Michael Millers, but none of the men posting photos of their kids' soccer games online looked anything the one who'd brightened her day, and the only mention she found was related to his work at the feedlot. He was obviously not a fan of social media, and didn't blog or maintain a website. And unlike certain people, searching his name didn't bring up reams of highlight videos from rodeos across the country.

Her fingers hovered over the keys for a tempting moment, but then she slapped the laptop shut. Wyatt had put himself firmly out of reach. She *would* find a way to drive him out her mind.

—∾—

Two months later, Michael perched on the edge of her desk, pretending to study the chart on her computer monitor. As he leaned in, he lowered his voice and let his leg rub against her thigh behind the desk. "I don't suppose we could spend some extra time going over these at lunch tomorrow before I leave?"

She felt a warm tingle at the contact—a side effect of the late *lunch* they'd just wrapped up—but also a niggle of irritation. He'd worn her down in part because he'd promised to be one hundred percent professional at the office, and to a greater degree because Leachman had pawned off the entire project on her, putting her and Michael in constant contact.

Hearing the thud of boots in the hallway, she scooted away and touched a finger to the screen. "As you can see, your rate of gain should continue to increase with the tweaks we're making to improve palatability."

"Looks good." Michael straightened and turned as Leachman walked in the door. "How soon can we have a batch of the latest mix delivered? I've got five loads of calves coming in next week."

Leachman glanced at Melanie in question.

"It'll be tight," she said.

The Leech puffed out his chest. "We can make it happen. Let's go twist some arms down in production."

Her phone rang as the front doors whooshed shut behind Michael and the Leech. She checked the number and winced. *Damn.* Melanie heaved a sigh and answered. "Hey, Violet."

"I don't like that tone," Violet said. "You're going to tell me you're not coming tonight, aren't you?"

Melanie propped an elbow on the desk and pressed

her forehead into her hand. "I'm sorry. I just… Michael's in town."

"So bring him. It's about time we met the mystery man."

Her mind instantly rejected the idea. But why? An elementary science fair might not be the most romantic date, but Michael was a small-town, ranch-raised boy. He should fit right in with her friends. Why did she keep making excuses not to introduce them?

Possibly, she admitted reluctantly, for the same reason she hadn't pressed him to move beyond moments snatched during his visits and infrequent texts in between, mostly about work. She didn't have a burning desire to share random thoughts or ridiculous moments with him. Her desire for him didn't really burn at all. It was more of a warm tingle, unlike…

A vision of taut muscles and Caribbean-blue eyes swam into her head. She tried to harpoon it, but the damn thing was slippery as always, even though she knew Wyatt was a non-option, and getting more so all the time. At the beginning, she'd assumed they'd eventually act on the attraction that sizzled between them, despite that idiotic vow. They were all—Violet and Joe included—reasonable, intelligent adults. Those friendships were strong enough to weather any fallout. But Wyatt obviously hadn't considered her worth the risk—and then he'd started picking on Hank.

Her heart clenched at the thought of her brother. *Dammit, Hank. Where are you?*

"Excuse me," Violet broke in. "We were having a conversation here?"

"Sorry," Melanie said again. "I'm not ready to drag Michael in front of the jury yet."

"Uh-huh. Who are you ashamed of, Mel…us, or him?"

"I am *not* ashamed, so don't try the guilt angle." She already felt bad enough for canceling…again. "It's just…"

That her last argument with Wyatt had been more of a rush than the very adequate orgasm Michael had served up at lunch.

Damn him. Wyatt Darrington was the itch she'd never had a chance to scratch, a perennial *what-if* that wormed its way into every potential relationship. The physical comparison was stupid, and grossly unfair. Hat and boots aside, Michael was a businessman, while as a bullfighter, Wyatt's life literally depended on keeping his body tuned to perfection. Mentally…

Well, you didn't stumble over Ivy League–educated cowboys every day. Wyatt forced her to up her game, and she'd always loved a challenge. On the other hand, for all the dinners they'd shared, she hadn't once been tempted to stab Michael with her fork.

"It's just…?" Violet echoed.

"It's your fault," Melanie said, shoving Wyatt firmly out of her mind. "You and Tori and Shawnee—you're all so freakishly happy that I can't settle for anything less than total bliss."

"I'm sorry," Violet said, smug as all get out.

"No, you are not. And I have to go. Unlike you, I am not the boss of things around here."

"Fine. But you and I are going to talk, even if I have to make an appointment."

Melanie glanced at her overflowing schedule. "I'll pencil in the CFO of Jacobs Livestock for lunch on Friday."

"I will be there."

"Tell Beni good luck tonight, and try not to blow up the school."

Violet's tone went grim. "Don't even joke about that."

Melanie laughed and hung up.

She was frowning at an email from one of their longest-running customers when she heard Leachman clomp through the front door. Leaning out and craning her neck, she watched him disappear into his office… alone. He must have left Michael down at the plant. Well, then. No time like the present. She picked up her paper copy of the email and dragged herself across the reception area to his open door, where she rapped on the frame.

"Do you have a few minutes?" she asked when he looked up.

"Is it important?"

No. I'm here because I treasure your company. She held up the email. "I just got this from the manager at the H Bar C Ranch. He is not pleased that he was sold the wrong mineral for their operation."

She walked over and handed him the email. Leachman barely glanced at it before tossing it aside. "So fix it."

"I smoothed things over, but it's going to cost us two tons of replacement mineral and a lot of goodwill." She paused for breath, stepping cautiously. "This was Jeffery again. He can't seem to get a handle on the correct applications for each formula."

And refused to consult anyone else before making recommendations. If it had been any other sales associate—especially Kimberly—they would have been booted out the door after the first mistake. But Jeffery was Leachman's pet, and a major suck-up. The surly, overconfident ass Melanie dealt with could turn on the charm in the blink of an eye when the boss was watching.

"You said you were going to give him additional training," Leachman said.

"And I did. It doesn't seem to have made any difference."

"Maybe he needs a better teacher."

Melanie bit down on her rising temper. "He has alienated so many of the staff that I'm not sure I can persuade anyone else to work with him. Plus, he's already had more training than the rest of the sales team combined. Pulling someone out of production to go over it again would be a waste of time."

Leachman stiffened, his mottled cheeks reddening as he leaned forward and stabbed a finger into the top of his desk. "*I* decide what's a waste of time around here. And if we're talking about unprofessional behavior, maybe you'd like to discuss this thing with you and Michael."

The sucker punch caught her right in the kidneys. Shit. *Shit*. Hadn't she known it was a bad idea? She'd told Michael, over and over, until even she'd stopped listening.

But she refused to cower, or to make excuses. She stood square and kept her gaze and voice level. "That has no bearing on this conversation. Michael and I are unattached, consenting adults who happen to work together."

"Are you now?" Unease trickled down her rigid spine as Leachman tilted back in his chair and laced his hands over his potbelly, oozing malice. "I'll bet Mrs. Miller would be surprised to hear that. What's her name? Ah, that's right. Sara. Sweet little thing."

"He's...*married*?" The walls tilted and the floor

swayed, as if the building had been hit by an earthquake. He had to be wrong. Michael couldn't have—

"Of course. Why wouldn't he be?" Leachman snorted in contempt. "Women are so gullible, especially when they get to your age and haven't snagged a man. As soon as I saw how he was buttering you up, I knew this deal was in the bag as long as I put you in charge of *servicing* the client."

"You…you…" The words jammed up in her throat, trying to elbow one another aside. "You *used* me."

He lifted both hands, but the triumphant glitter in his eyes made a lie of the innocent gesture. "I just asked two consenting adults to work together. The rest was all you."

Rage tore through her, so all-consuming she couldn't breathe, let alone speak. Her gaze skittered over his desk. There must be a paperweight, a letter opener, a shotgun left conveniently loaded…

She spun around and walked out before she could make a grab for the putter leaning in the corner. Assault and battery would *not* look good on her résumé. Her breath roared in her ears as she stalked to her office to grab her purse and the phone she'd left on her desk. She was already dialing when she burst out the side door.

"Jacobs Livestock, Violet speaking."

"That son of a bitch," Melanie hissed, her voice shaking.

She set out on foot, sweating through her white blouse in the June heat as the words poured out of her, laced with the bile that had gathered at the back of her throat. She tried to draw a breath, calm herself, but that only made her stomach clench because, *God*, she could still smell him on her—sage, citrus, and horribly tainted sex. It was all she could do not to claw at her own skin. "Geezus, Violet. I'm the *other woman*."

"It doesn't count if you didn't know!"

"I *should* have! Me, who's supposed to be such an expert at reading people, and I let him play me like a used car salesman."

Violet made a noise that was probably meant to be soothing, but came out more like a growl. "Obviously he's a pro if he pulled one over on you. And he had help. Who would think that he'd dare when the Leech had met his wife?"

Michael would dare, because he knew fellow scum when he saw it. And maybe Melanie *was* that desperate, sex-deprived thirtysomething Leachman had mocked, closing her eyes to the signs that now glowed neon red. She mashed her hands over her ears, as if she could unhear that snide voice. Those ugly words. "I could just… just…*aighh!*"

"Do not go back in there, Mel," Violet ordered. "Come out to our place, *right now*."

Melanie was on the verge of agreeing when her gaze fell on Michael's pickup. The one she'd ridden in when he'd taken her to his hotel for *lunch*. Her hands fisted. Keying his pickup was too clichéd. Ditto puncturing tires. She could cut a few important wires, though. Or a brake line.

Keys.

She stopped dead, her thoughts snapping into focus. As she took one centering breath, then another, she turned it over in her mind. Finally, she said, "I'd rather be alone tonight."

"Melanie." Violet stretched her name into three distinct, warning syllables. "You sound awfully calm all of the sudden. That's never a good sign."

Crap. It was hard to slip anything past a woman who'd known you since before you'd thrown your first punch—Jeffrey Dillard, wannabe kindergarten bully. Melanie smoothed out her voice, injecting a note of fatigue. "I just ran out of steam. I'm going home to burn these clothes and scrub myself under the shower until every inch of skin that man touched falls off."

"You won't do anything—"

"Trust me."

"Hah! Who do you think you're talking to? Get your ass out here, Melanie Brookman, or I swear to God, I will come in there and duct-tape you to your couch until I'm sure he's long gone."

She probably wasn't kidding, but… "You have to go to the science fair." Melanie added a pleading note. "Just let me wallow, okay? I can't face everyone right now. But keep Friday night open—a meeting of the ladies' club is definitely in order."

She hung up on Violet's protest, then silenced the immediate ring of her phone. Melanie studied the pickup for a moment, typed in a text, made a minor adjustment to strike just the right note, and hit Send.

I think I lost an earring in your pickup. Any chance I can get your keys?

It seemed like hours before his answer popped up. Yep. Just as she'd expected. Michael was the type to always have a fallback plan, which included being sure no incriminating evidence was left where the little woman might find it.

There's an emergency key stashed inside the rear bumper, but don't let anyone see you.

With a grim smile she replied: Don't worry. I never leave witnesses.

Chapter 3

WHERE MELANIE WAS CONCERNED, WYATT HAD SCREWED UP so many times, in so many ways, he supposed she would consider *creepy stalker* just another entry on his rap sheet, between *arrogant prick* and *manipulative bastard*.

It was five twenty-nine in the morning, and he'd been sitting at Gene's All-Night Diner for almost four hours. In that time, he had discovered its only redeeming feature was location—immediately across the street from Melanie's apartment complex. The bar next door had kicked him out at closing time, consigning him to this fluorescent-lighted, vinyl-coated hell that reeked of the ghosts of greasy burgers long past. And the coffee... He picked up his cup, grimaced, and set it aside. From the smell of it, the percolator had last been cleaned during the first Bush administration. The pie was even worse.

But the alternative was to go pound on Michael Miller's hotel room door. And then pound on his head.

Wyatt fished a soggy lump of apple out of the sea of brown-flecked slime and mashed it with his fork, imagining it was Michael's face. That lying son of a bitch had touched Melanie. Been with her in ways that Wyatt wasn't allowed. Hurt her without a second thought.

And Wyatt couldn't even offer her his shoulder to cry on. His knuckles went white around the fork as he fought the urge to jump out of the grimy booth. How could he just sit here when she needed... He shook his

head with a quiet laugh. *Not* a hug. Right now, she'd
smack anyone who tried to offer her sympathy.

Maybe Violet wasn't crazy for sending Wyatt to play
punching bag. He'd had a lot of practice. But didn't she
realize that seeing Melanie in pain, being close to her
and forced to know that some other bastard had been so
much closer, would slice his guts into ribbons?

No. Of course she didn't. He'd made damn sure no
one—including Melanie—knew how hard he struggled
to keep his precious distance. Except those times when
he couldn't resist getting close, then picked a fight with
her in the time-honored tradition of juvenile pigtail-
pullers everywhere.

And every Thanksgiving and Easter he'd held his
breath, bracing himself for the inevitable day when she
brought a man. *The* man.

But that day hadn't come. Wyatt continued to live off
the crumbs she tossed across the table, along with those
barbed smiles that had grown razor-sharp since he'd
made the colossal error in judgment that had contrib-
uted to her brother's downward spiral. He didn't blame
her for blaming him. It was better than blaming Joe or,
worse, Violet.

And it saved Wyatt from having to work at alienat-
ing her.

He mutilated another piece of apple, then pushed the
plate away in disgust and checked the time on his phone.
Five thirty-seven. If Melanie was going to commit an act
of retribution, surely she would have done it by now.
And he still had no idea what he could do to stop her.

"You know she won't listen to me," he'd warned
Violet. "Why don't you go sit on her?"

Then Violet had grinned, cocking her eyebrows. "Friends don't let friends' wives get arrested. And if worst comes to worst, *you* won't have to borrow money for her bail."

Yet another perk of being a trust fund brat, along with perfect teeth and generations of ruthlessly wielded rich, white privilege. And since he was already here, he might as well give Melanie until sunup before calling this stakeout a bust.

He grabbed his tablet and tapped to replay one of a series of rodeo videos to distract himself. On-screen, a bull rider nodded his head. The gate swung open, and the bull made an immediate, devastating left, ripping the cowboy's hand out of the rope and slamming him into the front of the adjacent chute where he fell—knocked half senseless with no escape route. As the bull whipped around to finish him off, a man stepped into the gap and swatted the Brahma on the head. The bull took a nasty swipe at him. The bullfighter grabbed the top rail of the chute and jumped, so the stubby horn caught him under the hip and tossed him up and over the gate, out of reach.

Meanwhile, the other two bullfighters had closed in— one on either side. The taller yelled and slapped at the bull's head, distracting it while the second bullfighter grabbed the cowboy and helped him scramble to safety.

Perfect position, perfect execution. Wyatt hit Pause, freezing the scene.

"That's insane," someone said from over his shoulder. He glanced back to see the waitress, a carafe of steaming poison in one hand. She gestured at the video. "Tryin' to ride one of those things is crazy enough, but what kind of idiot would want to be a bullfighter?"

"Me." He held up the tablet to give her a closer look, adding helpfully, "I'm the one in yellow."

Her jaw dropped, and hot color flared into her cheeks. "Well, I-I didn't mean… You don't look…"

What? Crazy? Or like a cowboy? He was neither, though members of his family would beg to differ on the first point. He had stumbled into this career by accident, from a world so far away it might as well be Mars. Unlike everyone he worked with, he'd learned to ride English style, in custom-fitted knee-high boots that cost more than this waitress would take home in a month. Now his uniform consisted of a soccer-style jersey and shorts, baseball cleats, and body armor. A cowboy hat was mandatory, but he took it off the first chance he got. Even after close to fifteen years on the circuit, wearing western gear made him feel like a city boy playing dress-up.

Sort of like tonight, in his black, long-sleeved T-shirt, dark-blue jeans, and a black cap to cover his short blond hair. All he needed was a camera with a phallic-sized telephoto lens, and his creepy stalker costume would be complete.

He could argue that Violet had twisted his arm—but that would only spread the blame.

A flash of yellow caught his eye as a taxi pulled to a stop across the street. In a blink, Melanie was across the sidewalk and into the back seat, a swift-moving shadow also in dark jeans, a black hoodie, and a baseball cap, with a backpack slung over her shoulder. *Hell*. That didn't look good. Wyatt fumbled for his wallet, tossed a twenty onto the table, and charged out past the startled waitress, but by the time he got to his rental car, the cab had disappeared around the corner. He made an educated guess as to her destination and was rewarded when he saw the taxi several blocks ahead on the four-lane avenue, aimed toward Michael's hotel.

He could follow. Or he could attempt to cut her off. He chose the latter, passing on the left in the generic sedan he'd rented for the occasion, and parked under the hotel's portico just ahead of the taxi. Then he waited, braced to do whatever was necessary…and hoping she didn't do any permanent bodily damage.

The yellow cab sailed past the front entrance and around to the side lot. *Crap!* She was going in the back. He should have known she'd have a key card to Michael's room. Wyatt bailed out of his car and started for the front entrance, intending to meet her at the rear door, but instead of heading for the hotel, she hopped out of the taxi at the far end of the lot and paused for an instant to reach under the rear bumper of a Ford pickup. Before he could change directions, she'd climbed in and fired up the engine. Wyatt ducked behind a bush as she roared past and onto the street.

The pickup had Colorado plates.

Oh hell. Her version of *Don't get mad, get even* was going to involve $60,000 worth of prime American steel. What was in that backpack? Too small for a Louisville Slugger, but there was plenty of room for a can of lighter fluid. Or dynamite.

His crappy rental didn't even have enough oomph to lay rubber when he jumped in and hit the gas. He spotted her immediately, driving well within speed limit, but he had to hang back several blocks, thanks to the deserted streets. They headed for an industrial section on the edge of Amarillo and…Westwind Feeds? He swore as she jumped out, unlocked the single bar that barricaded the entrance to the parking lot, and swung it aside, her movements as swift and precise as a covert operative on a well-planned mission. Before Wyatt got within a block, she was inside—and he was locked out. The street that fronted the property was marked *No Parking*. If he left his car there to go after her, it would draw the attention of any passing cop.

He swore again, then made a left to circle around the block opposite Westwind, killing his headlights as he pulled into an alley between two warehouses. He left the car halfway down and made like a ninja, creeping through the shadows until he had a clear view of where Melanie had pulled the Ford into a slot marked *Executive Parking*, next to one of the Westwind company pickups. Wyatt paused, then gagged when he made the mistake of inhaling. He pulled his T-shirt up over his nose to filter out some of the dirty-diaper and rotting-fish stench of the nearby Dumpster. If tonight was any indication, it was just as well he'd crossed *undercover cop* and *spy* off the list when he'd decided against Yale Divinity and gone in search of a less holier-than-thou career.

Across the road, Melanie was crouched beside the pickup, scrawling blocky neon-green letters all the way down the side of the Ford with a can of spray paint.

She finished, stepped back to admire her work for a second, then grabbed her open backpack and circled around to duck out of sight between the vehicles and go to work on the Westwind pickup. Well, hell. Once again he'd failed miserably, because once again he had badly underestimated her.

A hard lesson Michael Miller was about to learn. You didn't mess with Melanie and stroll away whistling.

Wyatt flattened his reluctant smile and contemplated the situation. The damage was already well in progress. The best he could do now was to get her out of here as quickly and quietly as possible. He looked both ways and, seeing no sign of life in either direction, sprinted across the street. The hissing of the spray can stopped. He eased up and peeked over the tailgate of Michael's pickup as she pulled a long security cable from the backpack. Heavy duty, impervious to bolt cutters. Damn. She had thought of everything. She threaded an end through the front wheel of each pickup and wrapped it twice around the *Executive Parking* sign, anchoring both vehicles in place.

As she snapped a padlock through the looped ends, Wyatt said, "Your *P* is running."

She yelped, snatched the nearest paint can, and spun around. Only Wyatt's superior reflexes kept him from getting a blast of orange square in the face. He counted to ten, then cautiously peered over the tailgate again.

She snarled up at him. "Violet sent *you*?"

"No sense getting you all pissed off at someone else." He tapped the Ford, then cocked his head toward the Westwind pickup. "*ADULTERER* goes without saying, but *PIMP*?"

"My boss knew Michael was married. He met the wife." Her face twisted, a combination of fury and disgust. "Then he saw Michael giving me the eye and threw me in with the deal like I was one of his truck-stop hookers."

So she'd been deceived, exploited, and undermined in one fell swoop. Wyatt squelched the urge to kick a dent into the side of the Ford, opting to survey the parking lot instead. "How were you planning to get out of here?"

She waved a hand at her running shoes. "It's not that far back to my place."

And at this time in the morning she would be just another jogger, getting in a few miles before work. Actually, her timing was brilliant all around. In the middle of the night her presence would be suspicious, but if a passerby did see her in the lot at this time of the morning, they'd assume someone was getting an early start on the day—unless they spotted her artwork.

Headlights flickered in Wyatt's peripheral vision. He lunged forward, throwing his arms around her and turning so he bore the brunt of slamming into the pavement between the pickups.

"What the hell?" She jabbed an elbow into his side, putting some serious intent behind it.

He grunted and tightened his hold, rolling both of them underneath the Ford and losing some skin from his forearm in the process. She squirmed, but she was pinned by his weight, and he'd taken advantage of her surprise to angle his hips between her knees so she couldn't inflict any serious pain. "Cop!" he hissed.

She froze.

Chapter 4

WYATT EASED SOME OF HIS WEIGHT ONTO HIS ELBOWS TO avoid crushing her, but they were still pressed so tightly together that he could feel her rib cage expand when she sucked in a breath. His own lungs hitched as he watched the Amarillo police cruiser idle down the street. *Don't stop, don't stop, don't stop…*

Thankfully, the pickups were parked at an angle that made the neon spray paint invisible from the street—yet another detail she'd managed brilliantly. The cop kept moving, but at a snail's pace. The quiet swish of the tires on pavement, the hum of the engine, and the pain from the piece of gravel digging into his right elbow faded away as Wyatt's senses filled with warm, firm woman.

And if they stayed in this position much longer, his hips pressed hard between her thighs, he wasn't going to be able to pretend that his ragged breathing was entirely due to adrenaline. His senses painted in all the details he'd only been able to imagine before—the taut curve of her waist under his hand, the way their breathing instinctively fell into rhythm, creating a micro-friction that brought every nerve ending to tingling life. The sunshine and wild prairie scent of her hair tickled his nose as he craned his head to watch the cop turn the corner at the end of the street.

Melanie's breath *whooshed* out, a hot caress against his neck, and her lips brushed the bare skin just above the collar of his T-shirt when she twisted again, pushing at his shoulders. He rolled off of her onto his back, taking a moment to regroup as she scooted out from under the pickup. *Deep breath*. He grimaced. Nothing like the aroma of engine fluid and asphalt to bring him back to earth. He slid out after her and snatched the backpack before she could get a hand on it.

"What—"

"I assume you either have mace or a .45 if you were planning to jog in this neighborhood. I'd rather you didn't use either of them on me." He hitched the pack over his shoulder, took a moment to look and listen for traffic, then set off for the gate. "Let's get out of here before that cop circles back."

She hesitated, swore again, but followed. The sky was brightening fast as they jogged across the lot, ducked under the locked driveway barrier and into the alley. Wyatt glanced at his watch. Six fifteen. All of that had taken less than five minutes. When they reached his rental, he tossed her backpack in the trunk.

"Hey! My house keys and my wallet are in there."

"So I assumed." Wyatt climbed into the driver's seat and waited while she kicked the nearest tire and cursed some more.

Then she got in and slammed the door hard enough to rock the car. "Where are you taking me?"

"To breakfast."

He, for one, was dying for a cup of decent coffee. Melanie sat in stubborn silence as he drove clear around the 335 Loop to the Waffle House off the I-27 exit, on the opposite side of the city. Had they ever been alone together? Not that he could recall—and he remembered every word they'd ever exchanged. His body was so intensely aware of hers in the closed space of the car that it was a relief to escape into the Waffle House. Neither of them spoke as they nodded yes to coffee and retreated behind their menus.

Wyatt ordered blueberry waffles with bacon on the side. He waited for Melanie to declare she wasn't hungry, but she flashed him a bright smile instead.

"As long as you're buying…" And proceeded to order a ten-ounce T-bone smothered in onions with eggs and bacon and a large orange juice. She winked at the waiter as she handed over her menu. "He can afford it, and he's a great tipper. It makes him feel better about himself if he shares the wealth with us less-fortunates."

Zing! Direct hit. Wyatt just smiled. "Now, honey. Don't be cranky. I know you're disappointed that the Turners didn't turn out to be as…um, *aggressive* as you like, but I promise the next couple will be much more experienced."

The waiter's mouth dropped open, and his wide-eyed gaze jumped from Wyatt to Melanie before he scurried off.

"Nice." She leaned back and folded her arms. "But I'm already a home-wrecker, so masochistic swinger doesn't make much of a dent in my reputation."

"That stunt you just pulled will." Wyatt took a sip of coffee as he studied her over the table, trying to pretend he wasn't drinking her in, too. "You did it anyway."

She angled forward, her body straining against her arms as if they were the only thing holding her back. "I am so *tired* of watching men like that strut away while women like me slink off in shame. Screw that. This time I made sure the boys are gonna get burned, too."

But she would pay the bigger price. The *boys* would do everything in their power to make sure she never worked in Texas agribusiness again. Or any other state, if they had enough reach. And Melanie might have a temper, but she wasn't delusional.

"Bullshit," Wyatt said calmly.

She gaped at him. "*Excuse* me?"

"What I said. You had all night to think about the consequences. This wasn't your temper going off." He cocked his head, studying the tightly drawn lines of her face. "So that leaves us with the question: Why *did* you decide to blow up your career?"

"I did not—" She sucked in air between her teeth and spit out a curse before continuing in a mocking imitation of a talk show host. "And now, ladies and gentlemen, we welcome renowned amateur psychologist Wyatt Darrington, who sees all and knows even more."

He raised a lazy eyebrow. "I'm not a doctor, but I watch them on television every afternoon."

And he'd been watching Melanie for years. Like Violet and Joe and all her other friends, he'd seen how this damn job had sucked the joy out of her. Dragged her away from too many of the things that had always mattered most to her. For what? Ambition? Money? The same driving need to win that had made her a champion roper?

Possible. Take away the rodeos, and that intensely competitive spirit would have to find another outlet.

"So? What's the diagnosis?" she asked, applying the sarcasm with a trowel.

He shook his head. "As you say, I'm not qualified to make that call. I'm just pointing out the obvious."

"Which is?"

"There are other, less-damaging outlets for revenge. You've got to ask yourself why you took the nuclear option."

"The hell I do," she muttered into her coffee cup.

Okay then. Definitely not ready to discuss her choices. Wyatt wondered how long it would be before she realized that she'd acted from a deeply buried sense of self-preservation. And being Melanie, she'd made sure she got in a few good licks on the way out.

He continued to study her while she dosed her second cup of coffee with sugar and cream, wondering yet again what it was about her that he found so irresistible. He knew plenty of beautiful women—breathtaking, eye-poppingly gorgeous women. Melanie wasn't one of them. Yes, she was attractive, but there wasn't anything truly remarkable about her looks. Strong bones, a hint of freckles—the kind of face that smiled from the back row of every small-town basketball team photo, feet braced, a ball tucked under one arm and a *just try me* set to her shoulders. The player sports reporters invariably called *scrappy*.

In his fifteen-plus years on the rodeo circuit, Wyatt had met dozens of them. Ranch-raised, cowgirls to the bone, with a thin layer of sophistication on top. But none were quite like Melanie. She had a way of looking into him, making him feel exposed, as if he'd spent his entire life playing the Wizard, and she was the only one who could see straight through the curtain.

If this were Oz, he could wave his hands and make

it all better—call in a favor or two and line up another job for her at a better company, with no awkward questions asked—but he knew exactly how that offer would be received. His stomach burned with the frustration of being forced to stand aside and twiddle his thumbs, and the hot coffee wasn't doing much to soothe his ulcer.

She tilted her cup toward him in invitation. "Go ahead. I'm sure you're dying to analyze why I let myself be a complete fool."

"Were you?"

"Obviously, or we wouldn't be having this delightful encounter. Here…*Exhibit A*." She pulled her phone from her pocket and set it in the middle of the table, displaying a series of texts. "Read them if you want. Michael never said anything that couldn't be explained away as business if the little woman checked his messages. Never called me outside of office hours. And the real kicker…" She gave a short, bitter laugh. "On the phone, he always called me Mel."

"So it sounded like he was talking to a man."

She tapped a finger to her nose, then pointed it at him. "You got it."

"Most of your friends call you Mel at least some of the time. Why would it strike you as odd?"

Her straight, dark brows lifted. "What, you're not going to question how I, of all people, fell for the scam?"

"From what Violet told me, it sounds like you were the victim of a master manipulator." The instant *victim* popped out of his mouth, Wyatt wanted to snatch it back. *Wrong, wrong, wrong…*

Her eyes flashed, and her voice took on the silky edge of a razor. "Well, you would know."

Zing! Another bull's-eye. This time he refused to return fire or defend himself. *But I'm not like that... I would never... I only do what's necessary...*

None of which made him any less guilty of her accusation.

"Right. I forgot your ironclad moral code." She leaned back again, her lip curling. "*You* only scheme and lie and deliver judgment in the name of all that is righteous...by your definition."

Again, he had no defense. He could tell her the truth about what had happened between him and her brother, but what difference did it make that it had all been an act on Wyatt's part? He'd threatened to use his influence to blackball Hank at the biggest pro rodeos, hoping to scare some sense into the kid. Instead, Hank had gone completely off the rails—and Wyatt had helped push him. If he'd listened to Joe, let him tackle the situation head on instead of trying to be so damned smart...

Hank might be back at work for Jacobs Livestock by now. He might not have made one increasingly bad decision after another, as if he was determined to destroy his life—and doing a damn good job of it.

But Hank hadn't failed at everything. Before slamming out of the hotel in Fort Worth, he'd jabbed a finger at Wyatt. "Someday I'll make you pay for this. I swear it."

Mission accomplished. Wyatt was definitely paying the price for Hank's implosion. Hank just didn't know it.

And thankfully, neither did his sister. Yet.

Chapter 5

As if Melanie's disgrace wasn't quite complete, Violet had sent Wyatt to bear witness. *Thanks a lot, good buddy*. But then, of all the people in their circle, Wyatt had always been the one Melanie had pretended to care least about, so she supposed he would seem like the obvious choice.

"Violet didn't tell me you were visiting," she said. "Don't you have baby bullfighters to torture back in Pendleton?"

He shrugged at her snide reference to his training program, yet another of Wyatt's rescue missions. Besides athletic ability, the only prerequisite for his clinic was a diploma from the school of hard knocks. "They got a break while Joe and I worked the rodeo in Redding, California. We flew home Sunday night, and I stayed a few days to catch up with rest of the family."

But he hadn't shown up at Easter, a point Melanie had been determined not to ponder. Was it because of her? Over the past year, he'd gone from keeping her at arm's length to actively avoiding her, and she couldn't for the life of her figure out what had changed. He didn't seem to be all that put off by her presence now.

But then, Wyatt never got ruffled. He was like the James Bond of rodeo, popping up here and there in his airplane, always the coolest dude in the room. Even after a sleepless night, with the bright globe lamp above the table picking out the lines of fatigue around his eyes and mouth, he was still so inhumanly pretty he could have been photoshopped into the booth. But she had smudged him up a little. His shirt was dusty from rolling around on the pavement, and the streak of orange paint on the back of his hand gave her an absurd amount of satisfaction, along with the oil stain on his jeans. Teach him to tackle her.

He frowned, catching the direction of her gaze, and rubbed at the paint. She debated leaving him to it, then dunked a paper napkin into her water glass and handed it to him. He dabbed at the paint, then shot her a questioning glance when it dissolved.

"It's washable—the stuff they use on store windows for homecoming and Valentine's Day—so no destruction of property charges for me! Contrary to what you may think, I'm not bent on total self-destruction. Or a complete idiot."

She just played one occasionally, when the right man flashed her a killer smile.

Michael wouldn't be smiling once the plant manager unlocked the gate and let in the morning shift. She wanted to be there to savor his reaction—especially the panic. Almost as much as she never wanted to lay eyes on him again.

Wyatt glanced at the clock on a nearby wall. "What time will people show up for work?"

"Production starts at seven. Administration at eight. The boss doesn't usually wander in until around nine."

Even if he hauled his sorry ass down there as soon as he got the call, dozens of plant workers would drive past those pickups before they figured out what to do with that burglar-proof cable. It had been damn tempting to hang around and enjoy the show, but her good sense had prevailed. Or would have—probably—if she'd been given a choice.

Instead she was trapped here with Wyatt, waiting for the proverbial shit to hit the fan.

After the others were gone for the day, she'd hustled into the empty office to grab all her personal possessions and leave her letter of resignation on her desk, but she couldn't just fade away. She felt too violated. They'd smeared her soul with a black, indelible stain, and they would do it to someone else without a second thought. The hell with Wyatt's *less-damaging options*. She'd seen how well those worked for other women…and all the men who'd skated away untouched.

The server set their plates in front of them, and Melanie tackled her steak, grateful for something to focus on instead of the man across the table or the ticking of the clock. After a moment, she looked up to see Wyatt watching her shovel in food with something between amusement and awe.

"What?" she demanded.

He just shook his head.

She stuffed a hunk of steak in her mouth and chewed belligerently. Yes, she had a tendency to eat her anger and stress, a habit she'd had to rein in sharply since going to work at Westwind, or her Thai food budget alone would've bankrupted her.

Wyatt took another sip of coffee. He'd barely touched his pancakes. She'd just started to cut another piece of her steak when her phone rang, startling her. She fumbled her knife, giving Wyatt time to snatch her cell, crank the volume, and hit the speaker.

"Melanie!" Michael's voice exploded from the phone. "What the *fuck*?"

Heads snapped around at the adjacent tables and booths. Melanie stared at Wyatt, stupefied, as he kept one hand on the phone, ready to pull it out of reach if she tried to mute it.

Damn him! Was he determined to shred every fiber of her dignity? Or was this his idea of entertainment?

He didn't look amused, watching her with that diamond-hard glitter in his eyes.

"Melanie? Are you there?" Michael demanded.

Wyatt raised his eyebrows. *Well?*

Going after him across the table wasn't an option—immediately anyway—so she set down her silverware, scraped up her wits, and injected confusion and concern into her voice, as if she had *no* idea what he was talking about. "Michael? Is something wrong?"

"You know damn well… Are you insane?"

"Is this about me not coming over last night? Didn't you get my message? I was, like, puking sick." She paused, then purred, "Must've been something I had for *lunch*."

He swore again. "I swear to God, if my wife finds out about this—"

"*Wife?*" She widened her eyes and pressed a palm to her heart. As long as she was being forced to play this out for a growing audience—which now included their server and two others, all with coffeepots in hand and wide, fascinated eyes—she might as put on a good show. "You didn't tell me you were married! I would never have—"

"Bull*shit*. You must have known, or you would have been pushing me to get serious."

"Wow. That's some ego you've got there. I don't suppose it occurred to you that I had as much of you as I wanted?"

"Sure. You say that now."

She refrained from smashing the phone with her plate—doubly tempting since it was in Wyatt's hand. "Don't you feel even a little bit guilty?"

"I treat my wife like a queen. I'm just not cut out to be a one-woman man." He made an angry, huffing noise. "I don't know how you found out, or why you had to make such a goddamn fuss. If it hadn't been you, it would've been someone else."

Ouch. Melanie's face went hot as a murmur rippled through the gawkers. Shame washed through her. She beat it down and summoned up ice from deep in her gut.

"Well, too bad for you that it *was* me. As you are now aware, I have a bit of a temper." She braced her elbows on the table and leaned closer to the phone, lowering her voice so the onlookers couldn't hear. "You know those annoying ads that magically appear online, trying to sell whatever you were just talking about on Facebook? My friend can make one that says *Serial Adulterer Michael Miller Discovers the Secret to Driving Women Crazy.* There will be pictures. It will latch on to your email contacts and pop up every time one of your friends or business associates opens their web browser. And then attach itself to everyone in *their* email contacts. And so on, and so on…"

There was a moment of dead silence. Then he blustered, his outrage muted because Wyatt had turned down the volume. "That's…hacking. Or stalking. Or something. I could have you arrested…if I didn't think you were bluffing."

"She's not," Wyatt said.

Melanie shot him a startled glance.

His face was grim, his eyes several shades colder than their normal tropical blue. "Not only *can* she make it happen, but I guarantee no one will be able to track where it came from."

"But she's the only one who could—"

"Is she? How many people had an opportunity to take a picture of your pickup this morning?"

"That's..." Michael sputtered a few more curses. "Who are you, anyway?"

Now Wyatt did smile, and it was like coming face-to-face with a shark in deep water. "My name is Wyatt Darrington. Look it up. Ask around. Then keep in mind that if you retaliate against Melanie in any way, I *will* find out."

He reached out and tapped the end button. For a moment, it seemed as if the entire restaurant was frozen. Then someone started to clap, and it multiplied until a cheer rocked their section. Well, hell. What else could she do? Melanie turned in her seat and bowed from the waist. A few of the women gave her a standing ovation...but behind the sympathy she could swear she saw judgment. And in some cases, condemnation.

Home-wrecker.

She swallowed a new surge of bile and glared across the table at Wyatt. "Thanks so much for your *assistance*, but I had it handled."

"I know. I had my reasons." Wyatt always had his *reasons*. This time, she refused to play along and ask. He cocked his head. "Were you bluffing?"

"Maybe." Her hand clenched her knife as she rode

out another wave of rage. If there was any justice, she should be able to destroy Michael—if she could destroy *only* Michael. She sighed and relaxed back again. "He deserves it. His wife doesn't."

Wyatt pushed his empty plate aside and folded his hands on the table. "Now what?"

"You can take me home?"

He shook his head. "I wasn't asking what you're going to do after breakfast."

"I've been thinking about making a career change." She used the tines of her fork to draw lines in a smear of egg yolk on her plate. "Obviously, I'd planned to have a better exit strategy."

Now…well, she could head out to the ranch and lie low while she figured out her next move. Space, horses, and hard physical labor might help bleed off some of her anger, and her father could always use the extra help. Until she'd left for college, she'd been his number one hand, with Hank being almost ten years younger. She loved the ranch. She just hadn't been able to breathe in the toxic atmosphere between her parents.

So she'd run away and left Hank to suffocate. And now he was…what? She was afraid to even list the possibilities.

"You could come to work for me."

Her head jerked up, and she gaped at Wyatt. He seemed almost as startled as she was by the offer, as if he hadn't intended to blurt it out…but Wyatt was never impetuous.

"Doing what?" she asked, instantly suspicious.

He hesitated ever so slightly before the mask was back in place. "I bought a bar. I need someone to promote it."

She shook her head. "That's a freelance project, not a job. It'd take a month, tops."

"You haven't seen this bar," he said dryly.

Despite herself, her interest was piqued. But her, working for Wyatt? Now there was a recipe for maiming, at the very least. She scowled. "Assuming there's some convoluted reason you're actually serious, why would I even consider this offer?"

"Two reasons." Wyatt ran a deliberate gaze around the fellow patrons still sneaking curious glances at their booth. He looked back at Melanie. "My bar is in Oregon."

Okay. That was a major point in his favor. Once news of all this reached her hometown, she would have to barricade herself on the ranch to fend off the army of church ladies determined to salvage her mortal soul—or at least gather some juicy gossip in the attempt. She had a pretty good idea how her father would react. And her mother.

Supportive wasn't the first word that came to mind.

"And?" she asked.

For an instant she thought she detected a flicker of uncertainty in his eyes. Then he blinked, and it was gone. "If you accept…I'll find your brother."

Oh.

Melanie settled back and braced her hands on the table. How did he know Hank had disappeared? She hadn't even started really worrying until the past couple of months. During his brief Christmas visit, Hank had been, well, a real shit—sullen and defensive, impossible to talk to. When he'd left town without even saying goodbye, she'd vowed that this time she wouldn't be the one to break the silence. And because of her crazy travel schedule and even more insane workload, for once she had kept that promise. The weeks had slipped by, one after another, until suddenly it was spring and her birthday.

For the first time ever, Hank didn't call. No goofy email card, not even a text with some stupid GIF.

She'd waited another week, hoping he'd just lost track of the date. Then she'd broken down and dialed his number. The same number he'd had for as long as he'd owned a cell phone. It was out of service. She'd called the best friend he had left in Earnest. No, he hadn't heard from Hank either. As the new rodeo season kicked into gear, she'd begun scouring the Internet for any mention of him.

She'd found nothing.

She hadn't mentioned her growing fear to anyone, not even Violet. Saying it made the scary possibilities all too real. But somehow Wyatt knew…because he did seem to know everything. And he had resources—some more questionable than others—that she lacked.

The real question was, "Why?"

"Why not…since it's my fault he's gone."

If he was waiting for her to disagree, they were going to be here awhile. Not that she blamed Wyatt entirely, but he sure as hell hadn't helped. His suggestion was more tempting than she would have guessed. He no doubt *could* find Hank; this job *would* get her far, far away from the Panhandle; and with Wyatt, she wouldn't have to bother smiling and playing nice.

"There would have to be conditions," she said, and had the satisfaction of seeing his eyes widen. So that was it. He'd made the offer assuming she wouldn't accept. A free stroke for his guilty conscience. *See? I tried to help, but she turned me down*. Damned if she'd let him off that easy when she could make him sweat for a while.

"It would be a freelance job," she said. "I'd work *with* you, not for you."

He studied her for a beat. Then he nodded.

"Email me a description of what you have in mind, and I'll send you a proposal and a quote." She pushed out of the booth and stood. "If we agree to terms, I'll see how soon I can be there."

As she started to walk away, he reached out to catch her arm. She whirled, glaring down at him, their gazes tangling for an electric moment before he jerked his hand back. Even through her hoodie, her skin was dangerously sensitive to his touch. "Where are you going?" he asked.

"Wherever the fuck I want."

As she strode out of the restaurant, the muscles along her spine quivered, winding up to turn on him again when he came after her. He didn't. Glancing back as she stepped outside, she could see him through the window, still watching her from the booth. She looked away, studying her surroundings in the clear morning sunlight. She'd walk toward the city center until she got tired, then stop and call a cab. The cash in her pocket would get her close enough to home, and the building manager would let her into her apartment. Wyatt could hold her backpack hostage as long as he wanted.

But as she stepped off the curb and started across the lot, the trunk on his rental car popped open. She hesitated, then grabbed her pack and slammed the lid shut, refusing to look back again as she strode away. Her, working for Wyatt under any conditions? Impossible.

But she did owe him one dubious favor. Any lingering ghost of Michael's touch had been seared away by the hot, hard imprint of Wyatt's body…and the intense, flammable blue of his eyes.

Chapter 6

As she strode out of sight, Wyatt dropped his car keys on the table and allowed himself the luxury of swearing under his breath. *Hell*. Nothing like heaping more public humiliation onto her already overflowing plate.

But it had to be done.

He tightened his grip on the well-worn lines of restraint that had been placed in his hands at birth, even as he cursed his genetic predilection to callously milk every possible advantage from a situation.

The server cautiously approached with the check in one hand and a coffeepot in the other. "Can I get you anything else?"

"A refill, please. I could also use a piece of paper and a pen." Wyatt very deliberately set a stack of bills beside his cup. "And your name."

The boy's eyes widened, darting from Wyatt's face to the cash. "What for?"

"You *were* listening." Wyatt made it a statement, leaving no room for denial. "You and the two waitresses."

"Yes," the boy admitted reluctantly.

"That makes you witnesses. I need to know how to find all of you...just in case. You heard that guy. He was furious. There's no saying what he might do." When the server still hesitated, Wyatt tapped the bills with one finger. "I am a *very* good tipper."

The boy stared at the money for a beat, his Adam's apple bobbing as he swallowed his reservations. "Okay."

He hurried off, and Wyatt turned his attention to his next target, three twentysomethings at the table directly across from them. The smile he turned on them had been getting Darringtons whatever they wanted for generations. The nearest, a narrow-faced blond with dark roots and bad highlights, blinked, then offered a dazzled smile in return.

Wyatt nodded at the phone next to her plate. "You recorded most of that."

"I…uh." Her cheeks reddened. "Maybe."

Wyatt turned the full force of his intense blue gaze on her. "I'm worried about my friend. She may need protection—a restraining order or something—but the cops won't listen to us without some kind of proof. If you wouldn't mind sharing your video…"

"Oh!" She blinked again and put the phone on the palm he extended. "Of course. Anything I can do."

"Thanks. You have no idea how much I appreciate this." He turned slightly so she couldn't see the screen while he located the video and uploaded it to his cloud storage, then deleted the original from both the album file and the recycle bin before handing the phone back. At least he could save Melanie the embarrassment of having that show up on social media.

He flashed another blinding smile. "If you all wouldn't mind giving me your names and signing off on a statement about what you saw and heard—" He turned to the server, who had returned with a few sheets of blank copy paper and a pen. "Perfect. And bring me the check for the ladies, too."

Ten minutes later, he walked out of the restaurant with all the evidence he would need if Michael Miller was stupid enough to try to cause Melanie any more trouble. Instead of climbing into the car, Wyatt propped his hips against the hood and pulled a phone number up from his contacts. He dug a roll of antacids out of his pocket and thumbed two into his mouth, crunching them between his teeth as he listened to the phone ring *one, two, three…*

Gil Sanchez picked up and said, "I assume this isn't good news."

"I talked to Melanie. She hasn't heard from Hank, either…and she's worried enough to consider letting me help her find him."

Gil responded with a string of curses as another phone began to ring in the background. He ignored it. "Has it occurred to anyone that it'd be a lot less trouble to let him stay gone?"

"For us, maybe. Not for his sister."

Gil swore again. The second phone stopped ringing, only to immediately begin again. Without bothering to cover the mouthpiece, Gil yelled, "Dad! I'm on my cell. Could you pick up the damn phone?"

Obviously, Wyatt had caught him in the dispatcher's office at Sanchez Trucking.

"We have a deal," Wyatt reminded him. "You got me into this mess, and you said you'd handle Hank if I took care of the rest."

"The way you handled Melanie? Geezus. You were supposed to stop her, not drive the getaway car."

Wyatt nearly dropped his phone. "How do you know—"

"Spies. We have them everywhere. Did you give her a bag of cash and a ticket to the Bahamas, too?"

"No," Wyatt snapped, unnerved. "I offered her a job. In Oregon."

Silence. Then a low, amused whistle. "You get points for guts. I assume she turned you down flat?"

"Not yet."

There was a telling pause. Then, "Well, shit. That could make things interesting."

"No kidding." Which was something Wyatt should have given a lot more thought to before blurting out the fabulous idea that had popped into his head. But dammit, he couldn't just sit there and do nothing.

"If I know Melanie, she's just messing with your head," Gil said. "She'll let you stew for a few days before she says no. But on the off chance that she actually accepts, try not to let this turn into a complete clusterfuck. I'll spread the word among my drivers and have them ask around. Unless Hank's sleeping in a box under a bridge or has a sugar mama, he's gotta be working at something. With his commercial driver's license, he could've got on with someone I know."

Or one of thousands of other jobs that required a CDL and were outside Gil's network.

But not Wyatt's. He knew a guy…

Not yet. He'd run through every other possible option twice before he'd make that call.

"Keep in touch," he said brusquely.

"Bet yer ass. If Melanie does come to work for you, I'll call every night to see if you're still alive."

Wyatt hung up and turned to brace his elbows on the roof of the car, digging the heels of his hands into aching temples. This was Joe's fault. He had married into what Gil acidly referred to as the Earnest Brat Pack—the Brookman siblings, the Sanchez brothers, the Jacobs sisters and their cousin, Cole—and dragged Wyatt in with him. How in the *hell* had Wyatt ended up in cahoots with the most maddening and unpredictable of the whole damn bunch?

He heaved a sigh and climbed into the car. The temptation to turn north and track Melanie down was huge, but he fought it off. She wouldn't accept a ride any more than she was going to accept his ill-conceived job offer, but that didn't mean he was off the hook.

He still had to find Hank—and not just for Melanie's sake.

As he started the car, his mind snagged on something Melanie had said about Leachman. Now *there* was a matter that could provide serious leverage. He grabbed his phone and hit Redial.

Gil picked up before the first ring. "What—"

"Tell me everything you know about truck-stop prostitutes."

Gil was remarkably quick on the uptake. "Would this have something to do with Melanie's sleazebag boss?"

"It would."

Wyatt could picture Gil's savage grin as he said, "Just leave that to us."

Chapter 7

ON THURSDAY AFTERNOON, MELANIE TOOK A SEAT AT THE conference table in the offices of Leatherberry and Schnell, having been summoned by the legal counsel for Westwind Feeds. Janine—the only other woman in Westwind's administration wing—stared stonily down at the manila envelope on the polished mahogany in front of her and muttered a barely audible greeting.

Robert Schnell clasped his hands on the armrests of his plush leather chair and frowned at Melanie. "Let's keep this as straightforward and civilized as possible under the circumstances, shall we? Westwind Feeds has accepted your resignation, effective immediately. Janine has the paperwork regarding your 401(k) and the continuation of your health insurance coverage, should you choose."

Janine slid the envelope across, her gaze still firmly fixed on the wood grain. Melanie clasped her hands over the top of it without glancing inside. She kept her chin up, her feet planted firmly on the floor, projecting confidence and strength with every fiber of her being.

The attorney pushed another piece of paper toward her. "This letter outlines our position regarding Wednesday morning's incident. There will be no criminal charges. However, Westwind does reserve the right to file a defamation suit if negative publicity results in harm to the reputation of the company or the loss of business."

In other words, we're going to overlook this little

incident as long as you keep your mouth shut from here on out. She gave him a cool smile. "How will you prove it's not my absence that's causing the lost revenue? Westwind has seen a steady increase in visibility and profits since I was hired as marketing director. The newsletter I designed and produced was named last year's best digital campaign by the Texas Marketing Association, and our CEO bragged in a recent interview that our innovative approach to educating livestock producers has been the key to our success. I was solely responsible for developing and implementing that education plan, and I was the lead contact with all our larger clients. I am not going to be easy to replace."

His eyebrows rose. "You're awfully sure of yourself, Miz Brookman."

"Yes, I am," she agreed. "If Westwind wants to generate even more publicity by taking this matter to court, I'm happy to oblige."

"Is that a threat?"

"Just a little friendly advice. Before deciding how to proceed, you might want to consider who has the most to lose."

Robert Schnell narrowed his eyes and tried to stare her down. She didn't blink. Finally, he gave a curt nod and rose. "That's all, Miz Brookman. For now. I'll leave the two of you to deal with the paperwork."

Of course. Didn't the women always get stuck playing secretary? When he was gone, Melanie tried another smile at Janine. "I can fill these out right now and send them with you."

Janine stood abruptly, shoulders stiff. "Put them in the mail. I need to get back to the office."

What the hell? Melanie lowered her voice. "Janine! They can't fire you just for talking to me."

"I don't have anything to say."

"Excuse me?" Melanie took a couple of long, swift strides to cut her former coworker off at the door. "Are you *mad* at me?"

The woman shot a glare at Melanie, then dropped her gaze to a spot between them on the floor. "The past two days have been pure hell. The ruckus you caused, the embarrassment…all because Michael wouldn't leave his wife for you?"

Melanie gaped at her. "You believe I would knowingly sleep with a married man?"

"I don't know. Did you? Or are you pissed because he turned you down?"

Shit. How many different lies were they spreading?

"He made all the moves." Melanie had to make a determined effort to keep her voice down. "We were being discreet because he was a client."

"Exactly!" Janine jabbed a triumphant finger at the ceiling. "It was totally unprofessional."

Melanie's jaw dropped. "You dated the rep from our software vendor for six months!"

"That was different. It didn't affect the business when we broke up."

"Other than a two-week delay releasing the BIOGRO feed line because he *accidentally* forgot to order the new software for the mixing plant."

"That had nothing to do with me." Hard lines bracketed Janine's mouth. "Leachman was impossible before, but now you've gone and proved everything he says about women being too emotional to hack it in upper management. I guarantee the next marketing director will not be female, thanks to you."

"I..." Melanie was speechless. Her gut screamed that somebody had to put up a fight, or the parasites like Leachman and Michael would continue to thrive. During the long, dark hours that she'd paced her apartment, she had ultimately decided calling them out was worth the damage to her own career if, in the long run, it made life easier for the women who followed.

But her calculations had counted heavily on the goodwill of her coworkers. She knew they liked and respected her. Otherwise, they wouldn't have sought her out with their suggestions, thanked her for ensuring that their contributions were noted, shared the photos of their babies, grandbabies, and weddings...and poured their frustrations with Leachman into her ear. He was dead weight, they complained, nothing but an overpriced figurehead propped in a cushy chair. He was so out of date he dictated paper memos instead of sending emails. He made outrageously inappropriate comments about the warehouse manager's well-endowed wife. The list went on and on.

Melanie had stood in his office, going to bat on behalf of everyone from the forklift drivers in the warehouse to the lead researcher in the lab. Was it so naive to assume that they would jump to her defense? At worst, she'd figured some might swallow their tongues to protect their own butts.

She hadn't dreamed they would turn on her.

"I have to get back," Janine said again, and angled past Melanie to escape.

Melanie's hands were steady as she stacked the letter

neatly on top of the manila envelope, despite the fine tremble in her muscles. *Not here*.

She carved a smile onto her stiff face and added an aggressive tilt to her chin. Her stride was long and confident as she gave the receptionist a curt nod. Then she was out the door, down the street, and mercifully, around the corner. She ducked into a coffee shop and headed straight for the restroom, where she locked the stall door and collapsed onto the toilet.

Shit, shit, *shit*. She fisted her hands and beat them on her knees in time to the curses. Janine had exposed the fatal flaw in her plan. She'd put herself so firmly outside of Westwind that she had no chance to tell her side of the story.

But everything she'd said in that conference room was true. They *would* be hard put to replace her. In addition to her skills, she brought a lifetime of connections and the Brookman name to the table, and their mostly rural customers cared who your people were. Even if her coworkers didn't defend her, they would damn well miss her.

She sucked in a steadying breath—ugh, this place could use an air freshener and some decent ventilation—and pulled herself together. Janine was only one person. Why rush to the conclusion that hers was the prevailing opinion?

Melanie paused in front of the mirror to smooth a hand over her white blouse, tug her navy jacket straight, and check her makeup for any stray mascara. There. She looked composed, respectable, and totally professional.

Out in the coffee shop, she paused to study the menu board. An iced coffee sounded heavenly. *Hmm. Mocha, macchiato—*

"Melanie?"

She turned at the sound of her name and found herself face-to-face with a diminutive woman in straight-legged distressed jeans, boots, and a floaty, sleeveless turquoise top, her blond hair an artful mess of shoulder-length curls, her smile wide and genuine.

"Claudia!" The other girl's head barely came to Melanie's shoulder when they exchanged a hug. "You look great, as always."

"And you. Wow." Claudia stepped back to arm's length and made a head-to-toe gesture. "I barely recognized you in your business duds."

Beside Claudia's daisy-fresh femininity, Melanie felt stodgy and wilted. "I, um, just got out of a meeting. And you? Still tearing 'em up in the barrel racing, I assume?"

"You could say that. I finally found that horse I've been waiting for all my life. We won Denver and San Antone, and broke into the top ten in the world standings after the Memorial Day rodeos."

"Are you kidding me? That is so great!" And no one deserved it more than Claudia, as hard as she'd worked. "I can't believe I hadn't heard."

Claudia hitched one petite but well-toned shoulder, the result of hours on and around horses. "I suppose it's hard to keep track once you lose touch with the rodeo crowd. You're really not roping anymore?"

"No. I... It got to be too much, with work and all."

"Mmm. It's a shame, though. You were so good. But I guess it's worth it, if you really love what you're doing. And from what I hear..." Claudia's voice faltered, and color flooded her cheeks as if she'd just remembered what she'd heard about Melanie. "It, um, sounds like you've been keeping busy," she finished and blushed harder, obviously realizing how that might sound if she'd been the bitchy type.

Which she wasn't. Her green eyes held nothing but sympathy…and she might as well have slapped Melanie right across the face. Her cheeks stung with prickling heat. Geezus. Claudia felt *sorry* for her. Poor, pitiful Melanie who'd obviously lost her way.

"Things have been pretty crazy." Melanie's voice was tight to the verge of squeaking.

"Well. We all get a little, um…off track, right?" Claudia gave Melanie's hand a squeeze. "I'm sure you'll be back on your feet in no time."

Melanie nodded and began to root in her bag, an excuse to duck her head. She pulled out her phone, turning it so the other woman could see the alert on the screen. "Damn. I'd love to stay and catch up, but I've been waiting for this email…"

"I understand completely. Duty calls and all that." Claudia's words echoed with relief.

Melanie sidled toward the door. "It was great to see you. I'll be keeping an eye on the standings, rooting you on."

"Thanks. And you…take care now, you hear?"

Melanie made some kind of noise in response and spun around to leave, plowing into a man who was coming through the door. She muttered an apology as she stumbled past him and onto the sidewalk.

Her car was parked a block down. Once inside, she had to jab twice at the ignition button to start the engine. Then she cranked the air conditioner full blast and just sat, staring through the windshield. Shit. *Shit*. She'd been prepared to stare down the lawyer's scorn, to fight back against Janine's antagonism, but Claudia's genuine concern undid something vital in her chest. Her counterattack against Michael was supposed to be a show of strength. A public declaration of war on misogyny. *Vengeance, thy name is woman.*

She was not supposed to look pathetic.

She groaned and let her head drop until her forehead thumped against the steering wheel, turning the vents so they blasted directly in her face, then glanced down at her phone and got another jolt.

The email was from Wyatt. His proposal, or a note saying he'd changed his mind and what the hell was he thinking anyway? She dropped the phone on the passenger's seat. At this particular moment, she wanted to be anywhere else so desperately that if he had repeated the offer, she might say yes.

Exactly what she needed right now—to put herself in proximity to Wyatt with none of their friends to run interference.

She pushed herself up, put the car in drive, and pulled out, drawing a screech of brakes and the blast of a horn from a car she'd cut off. *Dammit!* She couldn't think, the doubts rattling off her brain like hailstones on a tin roof. Where was all that righteous anger when she needed it? The certainty that she could weather any storm? She raked a hand through her hair before she remembered it was pulled back in a barrette. The pain in her scalp snapped her back to the present. The traffic. And the sign on a familiar building three blocks ahead.

Panhandle Orthopedics.

Before she'd consciously made the decision to stop,

her car had swerved into the parking lot. It struck her as odd that it would be Tori she ran to for help. Melanie, Shawnee, and Violet had not treated her well back in college—and Melanie still cringed at the memory. But the prissy rich girl who'd taken too much of their crap had come back to the Panhandle a kick-ass woman.

Then she'd married Delon Sanchez—the father of Violet's son—and Shawnee had married Violet's cousin, Cole. And Melanie...

Melanie was a hot mess.

The receptionist looked up as she walked in. Beth took in the suit, and her eyes went wide. "Did you actually go to *work* today?"

Naturally the older woman would be in the gossip loop. She and Tori had become good friends, bonding over a shared lack of give-a-shit.

"No. I had an exit interview—" To Melanie's horror, her voice caught. She tried to clear her throat. "Is Tori..."

"I'll get her." Beth jumped up and hustled out into the clinic.

Melanie stood in the middle of the thankfully empty waiting room, incapable of deciding whether to take a seat.

The door opened, and Tori grimly looked her up and down. Then she tilted her head. "Come on."

Instead of the office, which Tori shared with two other therapists, she led Melanie to a private treatment room and waved her inside. "Give me two minutes to boot my last patient out the door."

Melanie nodded mutely. When Tori was gone, she went to the sink in the corner, wetted a paper towel and pressed it to her burning cheeks, then unclipped the barrette and finger-combed her hair so it slid forward, a long, brown curtain hiding her face as she leaned over the sink to douse the towel again and hold it to her forehead. She didn't move when the door opened, then closed with a quiet click.

"Did I just take a giant step backward on behalf of womankind?" she asked.

"Whoever told you that has been drinking the *Good girls keep quiet* Kool-Aid for too long."

No hesitation. No bullshit. Tori was rarely less than brutally honest. And that, Melanie realized, was why she'd come. To get an unbiased answer...and advice.

She straightened to meet Tori's steady, gray-blue gaze. "I need a good lawyer."

And who could give a better recommendation than the daughter of a former U.S. senator whose family owned, among God knew how many other things, a law firm?

Tori gestured toward a blinking light on the wall phone. "Line three. Beth has her on hold."

Chapter 8

MELANIE HAD BARELY KICKED HER SUIT INTO THE CORNER IN favor of ratty jeans and her last surviving West Texas A&M T-shirt before the knock came at her door. When she opened it, Tori strolled in with a six-pack of Dr. Pepper in one hand and three pizza boxes in the other.

"The ladies' club is meeting a day early." She dropped the pizzas on the coffee table and went into the kitchen to rummage for plates and paper towels.

Before Melanie could close the door, Violet appeared cradling a large covered cake pan, followed by Miz Iris with a double-decker pie carrier.

"Hey, sugar." Violet's mother paused to tip onto her toes and kiss Melanie's cheek. "I brought blueberry *and* apple."

A lump rose in Melanie's throat. Her personal cavalry had just come galloping over the hill. As she started to lean back against the door, it flew open, slamming into her shoulders. Violet stuck out an arm to keep her from face-planting into the red velvet cupcakes.

"What the hell?" Shawnee demanded, plunking a bottle of tequila down on the table to free up one hand, which she used to smack Melanie upside the head hard enough to make her ears ring. "You go out to commit grand theft auto *and* vandalism, and you don't even invite me?"

Melanie dodged out of reach behind the love seat. As

usual, Shawnee looked like she'd blown in on a tornado, her long, wildly curly hair a life force all its own.

"I was trying to be stealthy," Melanie said.

"I can do stealth," Shawnee protested.

Violet snorted. Then she squinted down toward Shawnee's legs. "You brought Katie?"

"Hey, she's a woman too." They all eyed the red heeler, who planted her butt squarely in the middle of the room and glared back at them. Shawnee scowled. "The rest of the crew left for the rodeo in Vernon this afternoon, and *somebody* thinks I am incapable of driving three whole hours all by my delicate little self."

"Hah!" Violet crowed, pointing. "You broke the man rule. Drink!"

"It doesn't go into effect until I put down the official glass. So…" She held up an opaque white shot glass emblazoned with the words *Here goes the last fuck I have to give*. "The *next* person who mentions one of them other than for purely business purposes takes the first shot."

She thumped the glass down beside the bottle of tequila. Then chaos broke out as everyone grabbed for plates and rifled through boxes. No one mentioned Michael, or the reason they were all here.

"I cannot believe Mariah Swift qualified for the College National Finals riding Butthead," Tori said as she snatched the last piece of pepperoni.

"Shocked the hell outta me," Shawnee said. "Who knew he just needed to go so fast he doesn't have time to be stupid?"

Melanie tried not to flinch at the mention of the name. It wasn't Mariah's fault that Hank's misplaced crush was the reason he was no longer a bullfighter at Jacobs Livestock's rodeos. Melanie pushed away the depressing thought and curled into an armchair, letting the chatter swirl around her as she sipped beer, munched pizza, and blessed Violet for the night she'd slammed into their college apartment brandishing a bottle of tequila, fresh off the latest in her epic series of dating disasters.

"I do *not* want to talk about it," she'd declared. "In fact, I so much don't want to talk about it that the first person who even mentions one of *them* has to drink."

They'd made a pact, sealed it with a round of shots — and the tradition had been set.

Everyone found a seat and tucked into their food. Katie stumped over and dropped to her belly in front of Shawnee, all sad, starving eyes. Shawnee ignored her, immune from long practice.

Miz Iris tossed the dog a pizza crust, then shifted her focus to Melanie. "What did the lawyer have to say?"

So much for small talk. The war council was now convened — and there wasn't a trace of pity on any of their faces. Thank God.

"She's drafting a response, stating that I also reserve the right to file suit if they slander or defame me." Melanie tossed the rest of her pizza slice onto her plate, her appetite ruined. "They have to prove that my *statements* were untrue and caused measurable damage to Westwind."

Violet made a thoughtful face as she licked cream-cheese frosting from her finger. "I wish we could hear the scuttlebutt around that place."

"We could break in and bug the office," Shawnee suggested.

"Or we could just ask," Tori said. When everyone

stared at her, she shrugged. "They're a Sanchez Trucking client, and I'm sure Gil would love to skulk around the warehouse while he's waiting to load."

Damn. Why hadn't Melanie thought of that? It was a banner day if either Gil or Delon was behind the wheel when a Sanchez truck backed up to the loading dock. Gil had been a star in his own right before the wreck that had crushed his pelvis and ended his bareback riding career, and the luster of Delon's two world championships had rubbed off on the whole family and their business. The elder, less-scrupulous Sanchez brother wouldn't hesitate to use it to his advantage.

"The guys will tell him anything he wants to know, no skulking necessary," Melanie said.

Tori made a face. "Well, that'll ruin Gil's fun."

No doubt. Melanie could remember a time when she—and every other adolescent girl within fifty miles of Earnest—had woven elaborate, happily-ever-after fantasies around the hotter-than-sin Sanchez boys. Even then, before he'd descended into the hell of chronic pain and addiction, there'd been a wildness in Gil that was a little bit scary…and sexy as hell. Since Tori had located a surgeon in Boston who'd successfully rebuilt his hip and left him almost good as new, Gil *had* lightened up some.

Now he was only moderately scary.

"Anything else we can do?" Shawnee cracked her knuckles. "Someone we can rough up in a dark alley?"

Melanie gave a sour half laugh. "Sure. And while we're at it, let's get Tori's daddy to buy Westwind and replace Leachman. Be sure the new CEO is a woman— that *would* kill him."

"Unfortunately, Daddy spent this month's paycheck on another new horse," Tori said dryly.

Miz Iris folded her hands and gave Melanie the same look she'd given a pair of eight-year-olds she'd caught skinny-dipping in the stock tank. *What* are *we going to do with you?* "You can't stay in Amarillo."

"It would be safer if I get out of town," Melanie agreed.

"Ya think?" Shawnee scooped up a piece of apple pie, took a bite, and moaned in approval. "Miz Iris, you are a genius. So how are you set for money, Mel? Got enough to pay the lawyer and tide you over until you find another job?"

Blunt, as always. Before she could answer, Violet chimed in. "We can always use extra help in the office at the rodeos." She shot a glare at Tori. "Especially since Sanchez Trucking stole my best secretary."

Tori raised both hands. "Don't look at me, I know better than to stick my nose in the family business. But Analise is one hell of a dispatcher...and *we* have dental."

"Like I don't have enough trouble—" Violet began.

"Oh my God!" Melanie straightened. "I forgot to ask about the science fair."

Tori, Miz Iris, and Shawnee exchanged a glance, then burst out laughing.

Violet's scowl deepened. "Beni insisted on doing his project on the breeding cycle of horses." She made an *I know, I know* gesture. "We made sure the posters were all PG-rated."

"But they forgot to search his backpack," Tori said.

"He brought models." Violet's expression went even darker. "Which he had altered to be anatomically correct."

"And…he used them…to demonstrate…*conception*!" Shawnee choked out, then spewed crumbs as she doubled over laughing.

"Just you wait." Violet stabbed finger at Tori. "Next year, you and Delon are in charge of the science fair."

Tori shrugged. "I'll pawn it off on my sister. The two of them can splice some genes or something."

"What about your parents?" Miz Iris asked.

All the laughter in the room died. Melanie grimaced. "I called them. Neither picked up, so I left messages with the gist of the story. Daddy hasn't called back… Big surprise. And Mama sent me a text saying not to worry, she didn't think it would cause any problems for her clear down in Lubbock, and I should thank God at least *I* didn't have two kids to worry about when my life went to hell."

There was a beat of stunned silence.

"Wow," Shawnee said. "I should be used to it, but the ability to make everything all about her still blows me away."

"It is a gift." And the reason Melanie hadn't asked if their mother had heard from Hank. She didn't need a daily "But I am *so* worried, I just can't stand it!" phone call to jack up her own fears. Or worse, *Have you seen my son?* plastered all over the Internet, the better to be the center of a storm of prayers and "Oh, you poor thing!" replies.

Silence fell again as if they were all waiting for someone else to speak up. Finally, Tori said, "I did talk to Daddy. He'd be happy to make a place for you in one of his companies."

"And Joe's stepfather will do the same in a heartbeat," Violet added. "You could go work in Japan or Brazil if you really want to get away."

A lump rose in Melanie's throat, even though she'd been expecting just this. Had, in fact, counted on it as a last resort. As she'd told Wyatt, she wasn't a complete idiot—all evidence to the contrary. These people would always come through for her. But first she had to make every effort to do this on her own. Anything else felt like cheating.

"I appreciate it," she said. "And I will take one of them up on it if it turns out my marketing career is reduced to stuffing flyers under windshield wipers at the Shop-n-Save. I don't want to jump into anything, though."

"What are you gonna do while you're sorting yourself out?" Shawnee asked.

Melanie thought of the proposal Wyatt had emailed—businesslike, professional, and very generous—which she'd read when she got home. The immediate rejection she'd planned to send was still in her outbox. He had managed to snag her interest, presenting both an opportunity and a challenge unlike anything she'd done at Westwind. The Bull Dancer Saloon. Even the name caught at her imagination. Pendleton was a charming town steeped in the history of the Oregon Trail, drowsing happily along except for that one week in September when fifty thousand rodeo fans poured in and tripled the population during the famous Roundup.

And best of all, it was located fourteen hundred miles from the Texas Panhandle.

Of course, there was still Wyatt. But he had his students, and when he wasn't busy with them, he'd be flying off to fight bulls at rodeos all over the country. They'd barely even see each other…right?

Before she'd fully completed the thought, Melanie

heard herself say, "I have another job lined up. Just a short-term, freelance thing, but it'll tide me over."

"Here?" Violet asked.

"No." Melanie inspected her abused manicure. "It's, um, in Oregon."

They all stared at her. Finally, Tori said, "*You* are going to work for *Wyatt*?"

"No! I mean, not really. Like I said, it's freelance. He bought a bar, and he wants me to develop a marketing plan." When they kept staring, she added defensively. "Y'all said I should get out of town. The pay is good."

Miz Iris gave a sly grin. "And the scenery is spectacular."

Violet winced. "Mom!"

"Man-rule infraction!" Shawnee grabbed the tequila and the glass.

"Oh please." Violet rolled her eyes. "She does it on purpose."

Miz Iris toasted her and tipped back the shot without a blink.

Shawnee frowned. "I don't think I like this. What if they hook up? It would be too weird."

Tori snorted. "Like, say, you and Cole?"

"Exactly!" Shawnee flicked pie crumbs off her boob. "I mean, how bizarre was *that*? It still sorta freaks me out."

Tori shook her head and looked back at Melanie. "When are you leaving?"

"I, um, haven't decided." First she would need to actually accept the job—and make sure there were paramedics on standby to resuscitate Wyatt when he got her email. She waved a hand to indicate her apartment. "I have to pack, tie up some loose ends, figure out what to do with this place."

Tori peeled back the paper on the last cupcake. "We have a temporary therapist who's filling in for a maternity leave. She's in an extended-stay hotel, so she could move in by this weekend."

"I can't be ready—" Melanie protested.

"Sure you can." Miz Iris set her plate on the floor so the dog could clean up the crumbs and stood. "Violet, you and Shawnee go find some boxes. I'll take the bathroom. Tori, you've got the kitchen. And Mel, you tackle the bedroom. Set aside what you want to take along. We'll haul everything else out and store it in the bunkhouse."

Melanie shoved out of her chair. "Hey! I didn't agree—"

They all ignored her, bustling off to tackle their assigned chores. Melanie looked at the dog. Katie gave her the canine version of a shrug and stuck her nose in one of the pizza boxes to pull out a slice they'd missed.

By nine o'clock, all of Melanie's worldly possessions besides what she would need in Oregon were loaded in Violet's pickup. The apartment was spotless, and her house sitter was scheduled to stop by before work in the morning to pick up the keys. Tori and Shawnee headed for the door, both facing an early-morning wake-up call. Miz Iris hugged Melanie and ordered her not to worry— they would keep an eye on things while she was gone.

Violet hung back, letting them disappear around the corner before she turned to face Melanie, folding her arms around her ribs. "Are you sure about this, Mel? I mean, you and Wyatt…"

"Are both capable of being professionals." She hoped.

"If you say so." Violet looked like she had her doubts.

"It's just…you're not exactly at your most reasonable right now. Which is totally understandable. And Wyatt…"

Melanie's antennae twitched at the odd note in Violet's voice. "What about him?"

"He's changed the last year or so. He's quieter. And sort of distant."

So it wasn't just Melanie. A finger of unwelcome concern poked her in the gut. She brushed it away. "It's probably a woman."

"I don't think so. Even if he fell for someone totally inappropriate—married, or too young, or whatever—he'd tell Joe." Violet hunched her shoulders. "There's something else."

Something to do with Hank? It would explain how Wyatt had known he'd dropped out of sight.

Melanie shook off the ridiculous thought. She was just projecting her own worries. Besides, if Wyatt knew terrible secrets about her brother, wouldn't he tell her instead of offering to find Hank?

She puffed out an impatient breath. "Are you saying I shouldn't go to Oregon?"

"It's too late now." Violet glanced around the empty apartment, frowning, then sighed. "Just try to play nice, okay? I don't want to see either of you get hurt."

"I didn't pack any weapons."

"Sweetie, when it comes to Wyatt, your fuse is always lit." Then she gave Melanie a hard hug and patted her back. "It's good that you're getting away. And don't worry, this was just the first battle. We'll make sure those bastards don't win the war."

Violet was gone before Melanie could decide whether she meant the fuse attached to her temper—or her desire.

Chapter 9

HE WAS SUCH A COWARD. AND NOW HE WAS GOING TO PAY... again.

In Wyatt's defense, he'd barely gotten accustomed to being welcomed into the Jacobs fold when Melanie had strolled in and bowled him over. His fear of losing his place—combined with a well-earned, knee-jerk mistrust of instantaneous attraction—had skewed his judgment. By the time he'd realized his mistake, he'd damn near obliterated the chance that she'd want anything to do with him.

Then Gil had come along and finished the job.

Now here he was, once again faced with the consequences of misjudging her. Even after she'd faxed him the signed contract, he'd been so sure she'd balk that he'd kept her imminent arrival to himself. Then she'd texted him from Mountain Home, Idaho, last night to say she'd be arriving around noon today.

Which meant he'd given Grace less than twenty-four hours' warning.

To say she wasn't happy with him was a massive understatement—a fact she was underlining by taking her time in arriving for the morning training session. She knew how he hated to wait.

He paced the dirt alley of his practice arena, pausing to stretch and check the highway that passed his small acreage east of Pendleton and trying to ignore the random skips of his heart. *She's coming. Melanie is really coming.*

He forced his scattered brain to focus on the here and now. Three young men lounged against the fence, dressed in shorts, kneepads, cleats, helmets, and Kevlar vests. Wyatt paused to study them, moving his focus from one to the next and noting how they reacted to his scrutiny.

They didn't trust him. They'd never had much reason to trust anyone. But in this profession, success—and occasionally survival—depended on teamwork. You had to have absolute faith in your partner...and be a partner who had earned the same faith.

He expected a lot from his students. In return, he offered an escape from grinding poverty, addiction, violence, hopelessness. All they had to contribute were desire, guts, and a willingness to put their lives on the line.

They all had the talent, but did they also have the drive and the discipline? Look at Hank Brookman. No one had had a straighter shot to the top—blessed with a crazy amount of athletic ability, and growing up a member of the Jacobs Livestock crew. He'd still managed to screw it up.

And now Wyatt was dragging Melanie to Oregon. Talk about your self-destructive urges.

Of course, a lot of people thought his entire career was suicidal. Wyatt disagreed. A rodeo bullfighter was no different from a Coast Guard swimmer. His job was to jump in and save a cowboy who was in over his head. If that meant putting himself in harm's way—well, in all of recorded history, there had been the rescuers.

Which was not the same thing as a savior, but Wyatt had never been able to stop himself from trying to be both.

Did any of these men have those all-important protective instincts? Bullfighting naturally attracted the adrenaline junkies, but if they only wanted thrills, they wouldn't last. The rodeo season was a marathon, and nobody gave a good goddamn if you were tired and aching. You either gutted it out because the cowboys needed you, or you walked away. If you could still walk.

Finally he spotted Grace's pickup coming down the highway and breathed a quiet thank-you that she hadn't stood him up completely. He ignored the ache in his right ankle—courtesy of three surgeries and the chill that lingered beneath the June sunshine—and strode to the gate that closed off the large, round corral from the wide alley beyond.

"We've practiced the basic moves using the dummy." He waved toward the set of horns and plastic body mounted on a wheelbarrow frame that functioned as a fake bull, then flipped the latch on the gate to the round pen. "It's time to work with live cattle. I need two guys. Who's first?"

There was a hesitation, glances exchanged, then Dante, the son of migrant farmworkers, stepped up. Three years earlier, at a cocky seventeen, he'd stayed behind in Pasco, Washington, while the rest of his family followed the harvest season to California. He'd immediately been sucked into the gang culture, and they'd had to notify his parole officer before Wyatt could bring him across the state line into Oregon.

Philip also stepped forward, lanky and solemn, with black hair worn in a single braid down his back. A member of the Blackfeet tribe on the windblown plains of northern Montana, he'd been a standout basketball player in high school who, like so many Native American athletes, hadn't bartered his ability into a college scholarship. With Wyatt's help, he might be able to turn it into a career.

Red-haired, baby-faced Scotty, the smallest and youngest of the three, hung back. Not out of fear, but from long, painful experience that had taught him to keep his head down until he'd seen exactly what he was getting into. When he'd turned eighteen and the foster care system had dumped him out in Pendleton, he had applied for a minimum-wage, part-time job scrubbing floors in the Bull Dancer—the only marketable skill he possessed. They were working on changing that.

Wyatt swung the gate open. His students exchanged more glances.

"What are *those*?" Dante asked.

"Cows."

"Ain't like no cows I've seen," Scotty said.

"You're used to beef cattle. These are mostly exotics." Wyatt gestured at the animals, identifying them cow by cow. "Brahma, Corriente, Brangus Cross, Longhorn, Gelbvieh. That gray one's called the Panther. And the black one on the end is Wild Woman."

"I thought we came to fight bulls," Dante said.

As if hearing the sneer in his voice, the cows threw their heads up, testing the wind. Their eyes glittered with evil intention. This was a game they had played often—and well. And unlike bulls, they weren't inclined to bust down fences to get at the sassy purebred Angus heifers across the road, a benefit Wyatt had embraced after fielding angry phone calls when his Brahmas paid them a midnight visit.

"We'll see how you do with these girls first." From the corner of his eye, Wyatt saw Grace take up her position outside the fence as he pointed at the cow on one end of the little herd. "See that brown, tiger-striped cow? One of you go in and hold her there while we let the rest go down the alley."

Dante gave a *no problem* shrug and strutted toward the cow. "I got this."

The brindle tossed her head, then lowered it as she flung a deliberate hoof full of sand against the fence. Dante hesitated ten strides in front of her, then flapped his hands. "Uh…shoo!"

The brindle backed a step, snorted, and flung more sand. As if on cue, the rest of the herd wheeled and bolted for the gate. Scotty had enough sense to jump clear, but as the Panther burst through the gap, she kicked out to the side, caught Philip's hip, and spun him around. He staggered, swore, and had barely gotten his feet under him when the brindle charged.

Dante made the fatal error of scrambling backward, getting caught on his heels. Her head slammed into his chest and sent him skidding like a turtle in his Kevlar shell. As the cow lunged for him, Wyatt leapt to intervene, but Philip was closer. He threw his body at the cow's face as her hooves slashed at Dante. She flung her head up, flipping Philip ass over heels to crash into the fence. Before she could decide which of the downed men to go after, Wyatt stepped in, slapping her ear as he circled past, and sprinted for the gate, giving her a clear target. She took the bait, blowing snot as she feinted at him, then bolted down the alley to join the rest of what Joe affectionately called the Hell Bitches.

Scotty raced over to Philip, who was crumpled against the fence. "Holy shit, man! You okay?"

"Don't touch him!" Grace commanded.

Scotty froze with one hand on Philip's arm. Grace swung over the fence and trotted across the corral, dropping a medical kit on the ground. Wyatt squatted beside her as she placed a hand on Philip's shoulder and began to talk to him, her voice low and calm.

"Just stay put for a minute. Get your breath. Can you tell me where you are? No…don't nod. Tell me."

He did. Philip's voice gained strength with every response, and after a quick check of head, neck, and back, Grace allowed him to sit up, arms braced on splayed knees. He drew a few deep, steadying breaths, then lifted his gaze, eyes clear. "I'm good. Just lost my air."

"Okay." Wyatt held out a hand and pulled the young man to his feet. Then he clapped the shoulder of the woman who had risen to stand beside him, the top of her head barely reaching his armpit. "Boys, this is Grace. She's our resident athletic trainer. Treat her right. You're going to need her before you're done."

She nodded in greeting, looking all of fifteen years old with her pert, freckled nose and her ginger curls pulled into a short, bushy ponytail.

Dante grabbed at his upper thigh and smirked. "Yeah, I think I pulled my groin."

"Wow. I've never heard that one before." Grace reached into the medical bag, pulled out an instant cold pack, and gave it a twist. Then she marched over and thrust it at him, the antithesis of her name with her brisk movements and the pugnacious tilt of her chin. "Stuff this in your shorts."

Dante grinned down at her. "How 'bout a massage instead?"

"Do it," Wyatt commanded.

The grin melted. "But I was just—"

"Now." Wyatt jerked his head toward the fence. "Out there. Fifteen minutes."

The kid tried a hard-ass stare. Wyatt turned it back on him, double strength. Dante scowled, took the ice pack, and shoved through the gate to flop on the ground, only to yelp and jump up again, swiping at a scatter of dark, triangular thorns stuck to his butt.

"Goatsheads," Grace declared in her sweetest Texas drawl. "Nasty buggers. Gotta watch your step."

Dante glared at her. She smiled. He crammed the ice pack into place and lowered himself carefully onto a bare patch of dirt.

Wyatt made a disgusted noise, but Grace only shrugged. "There's one in every crowd, and he's not gonna last. He's got no feel for it."

Wyatt had come to the same conclusion. Some things couldn't be taught, especially to a man who wasn't good at listening, but he would let Dante figure that out for himself.

"That one's a keeper…" Grace cocked her head toward Philip. "If he doesn't get himself killed before he gets a clue."

"We're going to work on that. Bring 'em back!" he called to the remaining pair.

When they were out of earshot, Grace said, "Sorry I'm late. I can't fathom how I let the time get away from me."

Her tone was as chilly as the ice pack currently frosting Dante's balls.

"I should have told you as soon as Melanie accepted the job." The words stuck a little. Wyatt wasn't accustomed to making apologies—or excuses.

She jerked a shoulder. "I assume you have your reasons. You always do."

"It was unexpected—"

She cut him off with a quick shake of her head. "I get it. She was in a bind; you had to help. I suppose it's time I dealt with this, and having Melanie around is as good a place to start as any. Maybe she can tell me what's wrong with my roping."

Wyatt made a sympathetic face. "Bad weekend?"

"I had a throw at both rodeos to win money and roped both calves around the ears instead of the neck. And I was being sarcastic, so don't even think about asking Melanie to coach me." Her tone was belligerent, but just beneath was a tremor of anxiety.

Way to go, Wyatt. And he hadn't even told her the worst yet.

"There's more." When Grace narrowed her eyes, it was all he could do not to shuffle his feet. "I promised to find Hank."

Her gaze dropped to the ground. She didn't move or speak for so long that Wyatt felt compelled to fill the dead air. "That's all I'm going to do, Grace. Just find him, so Melanie can stop worrying."

"Yeah, right." Her laugh was short and bitter.

"Whatever hole he crawled into, she won't be able to leave him there. And neither will you."

He didn't bother trying to deny it. "Even if we can drag him out, he won't come anywhere near you as long as you're here." *In the same zip code as me.*

She slanted him another of those sharp-edged glances. "But I'll know where he is."

"You'd rather be in the dark?"

"Yes." She hitched the strap of the medical bag higher on her shoulder and started for her usual post outside the gate. "Makes it easier to pretend he never existed."

Chapter 10

MELANIE STOPPED TO TEXT WYATT FROM A SCENIC PULLOUT halfway down Cabbage Hill, where the interstate crested the eastern edge of the mountains she'd been winding through since crossing the Idaho border. She stayed for the view.

She'd been here before, of course, in the wonder years when her daddy was tall, handsome Johnny Brookman, one of the most respected tie-down ropers and horsemen on the professional circuit. Back when Melanie was too young to pay much attention to the scenery.

Like everyone else, she'd assumed she would always be back the next year.

Far off in the distance—fifty miles, maybe a hundred for all this flatlander could judge—the tips of glistening white peaks speared up on the horizon. She identified them on her map...Mount Hood, Mount Adams, and several other slumbering volcanoes. Directly below her, an expanse of flat ground rose and folded to the west, acre upon acre of cropland cut by the winding course of the Umatilla River and the deep groove it had carved from the rich, volcanic topsoil.

And just off the foot of the mountains was Pendleton—one of the birthplaces of professional rodeo and maker of legends, from Yakima Canutt, to the bucking horse War Paint, to modern-day iron man Trevor Brazile. Cowboys dreamed their entire career of carrying home a championship saddle from the historic Pendleton Roundup.

Johnny Brookman was a member of that elite club, even if he had almost nothing to show for it.

Melanie couldn't see the arena from her vantage point. Only the fringes of town were visible, the bulk of it crammed into the narrow river valley. No sense wasting precious farmland on something as trivial as homes and businesses. Joe had warned her that these lowlands in the gap between the Blue Mountains and the coastal range were drier than the Panhandle. This was not the Oregon of *Portlandia* and webbed feet. Instead of rain forests and waterfalls, row upon row of green wheat undulated over every tillable surface, *tillable* being a generous description. There had to be some serious pucker factor involved in driving farm equipment across some of those hillsides. Anything that wasn't farmed or irrigated was already turning summer brown.

She texted Wyatt—*Be there in about fifteen*—then leaned against the hood of the car to take in her temporary home, a welcome respite from her yammering thoughts. The clamor was momentarily banished by the startling abundance of light and space. Yes, Texas was wide open, but you couldn't stand on the side of a mountain and see to the ends of the earth. And there was so much air. Infinite, unending air—above, below, and beyond. For the first time in days, she felt like she could breathe.

Reluctantly, she climbed back into the car and followed Wyatt's directions, taking an exit that dove off the south side of what Oregonians called a coulee. The steep street was flanked by houses stacked nearly on top of one another. A left turn, then a right, across the railroad tracks, and she found herself downtown—and immediately charmed. Each block was a row of stately brick buildings, either impeccably preserved or built to match the originals. Huge baskets of flowers hung from black iron streetlamps, and trees lined the sidewalks. The downtown section of Main Street ran only four blocks before it crossed the river and angled sharply up the North Hill. In the middle of the final block, she saw her destination.

She parked across the street from the old-fashioned sign—a stark, black silhouette of a bullfighter dodging a bull on a white background, ringed by round, yellow marquee-style lightbulbs. A classic red muscle car with a broad, white rally stripe rumbled across the bridge to idle in the spot in front of the bar. Her pulse gave a little blip at the sight of the famous Camaro. Joe claimed that car was Wyatt's one true love.

Melanie could see why.

She dragged in a deep breath and got out of her sensible SUV, rumpled and road weary in jeans and a T-shirt with a drizzle of coffee down the front. Wyatt emerged looking like a television ad for impeccably engineered Swiss watches.

"You're here," he said as if he was almost as amazed to see her as she was to be standing there.

"Sorry to disappoint you. I did consider making a U-turn south of Salt Lake City."

"If I didn't want you, I wouldn't have asked." Wyatt tapped his knuckles once on the roof of the Camaro, apparently oblivious to how his statement could be misinterpreted, and tilted his head toward the sign. "Welcome to the Bull Dancer Saloon."

She waited as he unlocked the heavy wood door, then followed him inside, pausing at the end of the short entry hall as he flipped on lights.

What the—

She closed her eyes. Opened them again. She was still blinded by a dazzle of red and gold, velvet and gilt. She stepped into the middle of the room and turned a full circle as she tilted her head back to study the wrought-iron scrollwork on a narrow second-floor balcony ringed with half a dozen doors.

"It's a whorehouse," she said.

"Originally." Lounging against the bar in a white button-down shirt, khakis, and loafers, his damp hair slicked back and that maddening smirk in place, Wyatt could have subbed for Paul Newman as Cool Hand Luke—pure trouble but possibly worth the consequences. "A couple of the rooms upstairs are still intact…furniture, clothes, even some photos and other personal items."

"Any of the original occupants hanging around?"

His teeth flashed in the low light. "There are stories."

Awesome. Melanie dropped her purse on a table and sank onto the red vinyl of one of the circular booths. A week ago, she'd been contemplating whether it was time to update her résumé and make the next move in her corporate climb. Now here she was, in a potentially haunted whorehouse with Wyatt Darrington. "Well, that answers one question."

"Which is?"

She hesitated, then shrugged. "I wondered if you really needed help, or just offered me the job because you felt sorry for me."

"Sorry? For you?" He sounded gratifyingly amazed at the idea. "Why?"

Was he serious? He *had* heard everything Michael said. "Oh, I don't know. Maybe because I was just duped and dumped by my lover?"

"Technically, you dumped him." A frown creased the space between Wyatt's brows. "And you weren't *in* love with him."

She gaped at his calm certainty. "What makes you so sure?"

"You said, *I had all of you I wanted*."

"*He* didn't believe me."

Wyatt shrugged. "He doesn't know you. If he'd mattered, you would've taken him to Earnest to see what your friends thought of him."

"Oh." *Damn*. When he laid it out that way, it sounded pretty cold. She narrowed her eyes at his pressed perfection. "I thought you said you'd be working out with your trainees today."

"In the morning. They have a Concepts of Computing class this afternoon at Blue Mountain Community College."

Melanie blinked. "That's a requirement for fighting bulls?"

"It's a requirement for life. There aren't many decent jobs for people who don't know basic computer operations, and how many do you know who make a living just at the rodeos?"

One out of hundreds. Melanie took a moment to absorb the information. She'd assumed that, like most rodeo clinics, Wyatt's classes lasted a few days, with a new batch of students each session. But if they were also enrolled at the college… "How long does this school of yours last?"

"All summer."

"And you organize and finance all of this?"

"The Bull Dancer Foundation does. It's a registered nonprofit. I have people to take care of the details."

People. A.k.a. minions. Wyatt had had hordes of flunkies all his life, from nannies to tax attorneys. Now Melanie was one of them…and didn't that just needle the ol' pride?

"What else?" she asked. "Do your boys learn how to use proper English and behave in public?"

His gaze was cool and level. "I try. Some are more coachable than others."

Like Hank. Melanie dropped her gaze to the floor. If she had a dollar for every time she'd heard, "*For Christ's sake, Hank, what were you thinking?*" she could start an advertising agency and hire her own damn minions.

"In the evenings, my crew heads to the athletic club to work out," Wyatt added, and something in his voice made her tense, like a warning whiff of smoke on the breeze. "The speed and agility program is Grace's department."

Melanie's heart clutched, then dropped. *Shit.* She'd been so wrapped up in her own drama, she hadn't thought about Grace McKenna, even though she'd known Wyatt had helped her find a job as an athletic trainer somewhere in Oregon. "I thought she worked at a high school."

"Yes. This one." Wyatt gestured toward what she guessed was the general location of Pendleton High School.

"So convenient of them to have a job opening." Melanie cocked an eyebrow at him. "How'd you pull that off?"

He shrugged lazily. "Their regular athletic trainer had been invited to work the Winter Games, but he had to take a whole school year off to prep at the Olympic Training Center ahead of time."

"What's she going to do now?"

"She's applied in some other places."

Like Texas? The Lone Star State was one of the best job markets, thanks to legislation that required schools to have a certified athletic trainer on staff. Had Grace recovered sufficiently from her public shaming to come back to the Panhandle?

Melanie gritted her teeth. *Damn it, Hank.*

It had been almost a year and a half since he'd been fired by Cole Jacobs and had gone rampaging off, vowing to make them all sorry. He'd rolled back into town a few days before Thanksgiving, still packing that massive chip on his shoulder, and immediately got into a pissing match with their dad in the Corral Café before taking off again. No big surprise that he'd chosen to spend Christmas in Lubbock with their mother, but it had been a shock when he'd staggered into the Lone Steer Saloon on New Year's Eve, falling-down drunk. Lord knew what had possessed Grace to even *want* to talk to him in that state, but it was no excuse for how he'd responded.

The one time in Hank's life that he'd been deliberately cruel, he'd chosen shy, smitten Grace as his target. Melanie still couldn't quite believe he'd humiliated the poor girl in front of a packed bar, then told the stunned onlookers to fuck off as his friends dragged him out the door.

Still, it hadn't seemed like enough to drive Grace clean out of the state. Then again, who was Melanie to talk, considering where she was standing.

Wyatt continued to watch her steadily. "Grace is very good at what she does. She'll be able to find a job almost anywhere she wants."

Melanie nodded mechanically, studying her hands. She really should scrub off the rest of her nail polish. French manicures were one more hassle of corporate life she could cross off the list—along with matching contributions to her 401(k), dental insurance, and a sizeable chunk of self-esteem.

And now here was Grace…one more reminder of how much of the rest of her life she'd let slide in the past two years. "She can't be happy about having me here."

At Wyatt's hesitation, Melanie looked up. The expression on his face was…pained? No. That was too simple. Like everything with Wyatt, there were shifting layers, but she'd caught the briefest glimpse of a real emotion before he decided what to put on display.

He went with a neutral shrug. "She has nothing against you."

"But the sins of the brother…?"

His eyes met hers, and there it was again. That complicated flash of…something. Unsettling enough to make Melanie's skin prickle. "Go easy on her," he said quietly.

Melanie lifted her eyebrows. "I'm not the one with an ax to grind."

"But you're a damned tempting target. She might not be able to resist taking a few whacks, and you're not exactly in the mood to take any shit." He'd switched on the intense gaze that was like being caught in a tractor beam. "She's tougher than she used to be, but she's still no match for you."

"And you want me to turn the other cheek, be the bigger woman, blah, blah, blah…"

"Please." A single, simple word, but his tone struck Melanie as more honest than anything he'd said so far.

Grace was important to him. *How* important? Just one in the long line of his rescue projects…or something more? Melanie brushed the suspicion aside. Wyatt was almost fifteen years and a lifetime of cynicism older than Grace, and if she was no match for Melanie, she certainly couldn't handle Wyatt.

"I can take a few shots without punching back," she said.

Wyatt's mouth quirked. "I'll have to take your word for it, since I've never experienced it personally."

"*You* are a special case."

"So I've been told."

Her gaze drifted past Wyatt, over the glittering rows of bottles lining the bar behind him and a mirror mottled with age. "What do you expect me to do with this place?"

"Make it profitable." He folded his arms, and it wasn't until his shoulders relaxed that Melanie realized how tense he'd been. "It's had three owners in eight years. The last was his own best customer and got shut down by the health department. We have to erase that reputation and find our niche, preferably without losing the essence of the place."

"So…BDSM parlor?" Melanie suggested.

Wyatt laughed, and the sound tickled parts of her that should not be feeling kindly toward any man right now. Especially this man. But old habits and all that.

"In a town this size, it's hard to maintain confidentiality, which I assume would be key to that venture," he said. "But we'll keep it in mind as a last resort."

"That doesn't sound very positive."

"The competition is stiff." This time, the wave of his hand encompassed the downtown area. "The Rainbow has been a local institution forever. Hamley's has the Old West ambiance and good food for the tourists. And the casino out on the Umatilla reservation has pulled a lot of business from town since they started serving alcohol and added a top-notch restaurant."

Melanie frowned. "Why did you buy this place if it's such a bad bet?"

"It's a historic landmark, and it'd been on the market for almost two years. I couldn't sit back and watch it rot."

"Ah. I see." She gave the bar another once-over, intensely aware that they were alone, and her body's cursed awareness of him ignited a flare of anger. Hadn't Michael taught her anything? She tossed Wyatt an insolent look. "Whorehouses, lost boys, wronged women… tell me something, Wyatt. How come my brother is the only thing you never figured was worth saving?"

Before he could respond, the front door swung open. Melanie blinked into the shaft of sunlight, then again as the door closed. Her body tensed, bracing for attack when she recognized the newcomer.

"Hello, Melanie," Grace said.

She didn't bother to add, "*Nice to see you.*"

Chapter 11

MELANIE STARED AT GRACE. GRACE STARED BACK. SHE had the same mop of rusty-brown curls and the same scatter of freckles, but her posture was ramrod straight, and her gaze was direct to the point of a challenge. Melanie offered a smile. Grace didn't return it.

Hoo-kay then. At least she had a pretty clear idea of where she stood.

And clarity was good, since this was the first time she'd spoken to Grace. Everything Melanie knew of the girl—woman now—was secondhand. Grace and Hank had been in the fourth grade when the McKennas settled their brood in Earnest. For reasons known only to Hank, he'd taken a liking to quiet, studious Grace. Lord knew, she hadn't been a part of his usual crowd. Forget carousing with Hank and company, her uber-religious parents hadn't even allowed television, movies, or pop music.

But somehow she had become what Hank called his little red-haired girl. She'd been the student trainer on the sidelines at football and basketball games, handing him water bottles and towels; taping his ankles better than any of the coaches, he'd bragged. And instead of the jocks or whatever girl Hank was romancing, he'd sat with Grace at lunch nearly every day until graduation. To be honest, without her help, he might not have been offered a diploma.

And all of that made the way he'd treated her more incomprehensible.

Wyatt's phone rang. He checked the number, hesitated, then said, "I should take this call. Grace, would you show Melanie the apartment? She can decide whether she'd rather stay there or out at a hotel."

Grace fired him a scorching look, then shrugged. "Sure."

She circled the bar and snagged a key from a hook near the cash register, then gestured Melanie to follow her out the front door. Grace made an immediate left beneath the *Bull Dancer Saloon* sign to an identical dark wood door. Behind it was a set of long, narrow stairs lit by skylights in a roof a full two stories above their heads. Grace trotted up and Melanie followed, surprised that she was barely out of breath at the top.

"What's the altitude here?" she asked.

"Eighteen hundred feet lower than Amarillo."

Huh. She never would've guessed from the proximity of the mountains. She sucked in a deep, appreciative breath of the oxygen-enriched air. The one thing she hadn't let slip was exercise—biweekly sessions with a personal trainer and pickup basketball games at her gym. Regular opportunities to sweat, curse, and throw elbows and body blocks were probably all that had kept her from throat-punching the Leech. If there was a summer league in Pendleton, maybe she could join...

She stopped dead.

Grace frowned at her. "Something wrong?"

"No, I...it just occurred to me that I can set my own schedule." She would have free time. On weekdays. The possibilities swelled inside her like shiny bubbles.

"I can jog outside in the daylight. Go to the post office. Do my banking *in person*." She laughed again, downright giddy. "I could even go riding. You know…if I had a horse."

Grace cocked her head. "Is that why you quit roping? No time?"

"Pretty much."

There hadn't been a specific moment when she'd thought, *I can't do this anymore*. If someone had told twenty-year-old Melanie that she would choose not to rodeo, she would have laughed in their face. She'd been a winner at every level from local junior rodeos to a national collegiate championship. Why would she quit? But with every month of squeezing in increasingly rushed practices, never spending the time with her horses that she should, and her mind always divided when she was there, it had become more of a burden and less of a joy. Of course her performance at the rodeos had suffered—and that *really* wasn't fun.

When her old horse had ambled into retirement, the colt that was supposed to be his replacement idled in the pasture until Shawnee had finally said, "If you're just gonna let him go to waste, I'm taking him."

It had been almost a relief. One less niggle on her conscience. Bad enough she couldn't find time for her brother or to help her father more out on the ranch when Hank was off fighting bulls; she didn't need to beat herself up over a horse, too. Or call home and listen to her dad complain about both of them. When Shawnee found a buyer for what had turned into an outstanding rope horse, Melanie had taken the check and her aging pickup and traded them for her shiny new SUV.

"I was busy," she added, defensive under the other woman's stony gaze. Grace, who'd had to manufacture her own opportunities in the arena, since her family had never owned a horse.

"Well, now you won't be so busy," Grace said. "For a while, anyway."

"What about you? Are you still roping?"

"Yeah." Abrupt. Conversation over. Grace paused to unlock the first door on the left and opened it with a flourish. "Welcome to the Madam's Suite."

Melanie stopped dead again, this time in shock. It was...*wow*.

The so-called suite was a single large room, the floor a dark polished hardwood with a gorgeous scalloped area rug, pink florals set off by black. The window hangings were layer upon layer of creamy sheers, draped and looped around oak rods in a way that was both airy and sensual. Every piece of furniture was a work of art. An elegant ladies' desk and chair stood between the windows, and the sunlight gleamed off a burnished-oak curio cabinet in one corner, filled with delicate crystal and china. By the opposite wall stood an honest-to-God swooning couch, the frame elaborately carved scrollwork with velvet upholstery the color of a dusty-pink rose.

And dear sweet heaven, just sleeping in that bed was probably sinful enough to send a girl straight to hell, let alone...

Melanie tore her gaze off the brass canopy, the silk drapes, and the acres of lace-and-satin comforter. She turned to find Grace trying not to smile. Melanie grinned back. For an instant, there was nothing between them but the perfect ridiculousness of this room.

Melanie threw her arms out. "Why?"

"Wyatt says he's going to rent it out for special occasions. Anniversaries, weddings…but honestly?" Grace shrugged. "I think he was just having fun."

Fun. Odd. It wasn't a word Melanie associated with Wyatt. Even when he was laughing on the surface, there was always a part of him held in reserve. Watching. Weighing. Separate. Joe and Hank threw themselves into their work with a kind of joyful exhilaration, but Wyatt was as cool as a sniper in the arena.

Completely at odds with the over-the-top extravagance of this room.

"The bathroom's back there," Grace said, gesturing to a silk-paneled trifold screen that mostly concealed the door, along with an old-fashioned sideboard that—on closer inspection—held a coffee maker, a small toaster oven, and a microwave.

The bathroom floor was black-and-white tile, with a huge, freestanding slipper tub and an antique, marble-topped dresser as a vanity. There was nothing practical here. It was all an elaborate but beautiful inside joke.

"So?" Grace asked. "Whaddaya think?"

"It's fabulous." Melanie hesitated, then added, "What's it going to cost me?"

"That's between you and Wyatt."

Grace dropped the key on the desk and started for the door, obviously done with the tour.

"Grace, wait. I just wanted to say—"

Grace stopped and threw up a warning hand. "Don't. That is not your apology to make."

"But I should have—"

"What? Handcuffed yourself to his wrist?" Grace's

poof of a ponytail bristled as she shook her head. "We've both been stupid about Hank. I got over it. You might want to give it a shot."

Melanie felt her face hardening. "He's my *brother*. My blood. That's forever."

Grace stared at her for a beat, something in her expression making Melanie's breath catch as if she'd stepped onto a ledge and felt it give beneath her weight. The younger girl turned away abruptly.

"Grace." Melanie reached out a hand, then pulled it back when Grace swung around. "Can we make a deal?"

"Like what?"

"I'll forget why you're in Oregon if you'll do the same for me." When Grace hesitated, she threw in a pleading smile. "I would really like to be friendly, even if we can't be friends."

Grace nodded stiffly. "I suppose I can try."

Okay. Points for honesty. "Thank you."

They stood for a few beats, neither knowing what came next. Then Grace said, "I need to talk to Wyatt. You coming?"

"Not right now." Melanie tucked the key into her pocket, checked her reflection in an ornate wall mirror, and wiped stray mascara from under one eye. She looked tired. Road worn. Forgettable.

Perfect.

She smiled at her reflection. "Tell Wyatt I'm going to have lunch and do some exploring."

And have a drink. Or three.

Chapter 12

SHE'S HERE. SHE'S HERE.

Wyatt gulped down the last of his protein drink, rinsed the glass, and set it in the drying rack beside the sink in his condo, trying to ignore the persistent drumbeat in his head. He couldn't erase the image of Melanie standing in the middle of his bar. His two worlds colliding—hopefully without triggering Armageddon.

Wyatt checked his email one last time—no new answers to any of the queries he'd scattered around the country regarding Hank. There was a text from Gil. Nothing new here. Heard Mel arrived safely. Text #OUCH if you need medical assistance, or #NICETRY if she turned right around and left again.

Wyatt did neither, slapping his phone onto the black-walnut butcher block harder than was healthy. Gil could afford to make jokes. His spot at Miz Iris's table was permanently reserved, even after spending years doing his damnedest to alienate everyone who got within striking distance. Gil was one of their own, like Melanie and Hank.

Wyatt was just a friend-in-law, included by the grace of Joe.

He stalked into the bedroom, yanking off his street clothes in favor of Lycra shorts and a lightweight nylon jersey. The hard plastic soles of his shoes clacked on the concrete as he lifted his custom-built ultralight bike down from the rack in his garage, an investment he'd made after the third surgery on his right ankle made jogging a poor choice. Today, he almost would have welcomed the distraction of pain.

The Cold Springs Highway wound north through gullies and over hills, bordered by mile after mile of grain fields, the rows of thigh-high wheat planted to within inches of the narrow strip of blacktop, no square foot of precious topsoil wasted. He took the turn onto Juniper Canyon Road and pushed hard, the burn in his lungs and legs searing away the sharpest edges of his thoughts. Melanie. Alone with Grace. What if…

No. Grace could handle it. He should worry more about leaving himself alone with Melanie. The way she tugged at him, mind and body, even though he knew that getting too close was the emotional equivalent of throwing himself off a bridge. The truth *would* come out, even if it was much later versus sooner. And when it did, everyone—even Joe—would be forced to choose a side.

Wyatt didn't have much doubt who they'd pick.

He shifted down a gear, winding through a landscape that had first intrigued and then captured him. Even after nearly twenty years, he didn't feel as if the sentiment was mutual. Pendleton could get by just fine without Wyatt Darrington.

The impression had been magnified tenfold since he'd bought the Bull Dancer. What was he thinking? *Buy it, and they will come?* Not for him, they wouldn't. He knew how to pull strings and push buttons. He knew how to sell himself to sponsors. He didn't know diddly about how to connect with his customers.

But now he had an exceptionally talented marketing

professional on retainer, so maybe offering Melanie the job wasn't entirely stupid.

He pushed his focus out, to the purpling heads of cheatgrass bobbing in the gentle breeze, between the mounds of Russian thistles that would bake into prickly tumbleweeds and roll away in the summer heat. The warm, bone-dry air carried the sweet scent of blooming greasewood and sucked the sweat off his skin.

Fourteen miles out, the high-tech watch on his wrist beeped that he'd reached the midpoint of his aerobic goal. As he turned around, Wyatt also deliberately changed the direction of his thoughts. He'd exhausted his usual sources of information, tossing subtlety aside to make dozens of calls and ask every cowboy, cowgirl, stock contractor, or rodeo announcer to spread the word. Had anyone seen Hank?

The answer was a resounding no. Hank hadn't fought bulls at a pro rodeo since the middle of last summer, when he'd rolled in a day late for a backwater show in Missouri and been fired on the spot. After that, one person recalled him working some amateur rodeos in South Dakota in August. Then…nothing.

People rarely disappeared by accident.

Hank had never been a loner. If he'd gone missing, someone should have been expecting to see him and reported his absence. His family would have been notified. His name hadn't shown up in any court records, so he wasn't in jail. He had no registered permanent address other than his parents' ranch. Not even a post office box. Worst-case scenario—if Hank Brookman was dead, his passing was not a matter of public record anywhere in the United States or Canada.

Which left Wyatt with only one last-ditch option. Every living person created some sort of trail—usually financial—and Wyatt could turn a bloodhound loose who was nearly guaranteed to pick up the scent.

He rolled down the final steep draw into Pendleton, past Blue Mountain Community College, then skirted the city aquatic center and the high school and turned straight up North Hill, his quads screaming as he climbed ten steep blocks before swinging into his driveway. Inside his garage, he scrubbed a towel over his damp hair, hung the bike and helmet on the rack, kicked off his shoes, and padded barefoot into the kitchen to guzzle water.

Then he reluctantly dialed the number of an old acquaintance who could track every swipe of a credit card, if he chose. Someone who believed he owed Wyatt a debt that could never be paid. On rare occasions, it served Wyatt's purposes to let the man try.

The telephone conversation dragged on much longer than Wyatt preferred, but he had to play the game. Pretend an interest in the world and the people he'd rejected with every fiber of his being. Yes, Wyatt had seen that his brother was now a prominent member of the House of Bishops and fully embraced the Episcopalian Church's progressive doctrines. At least publicly.

One did not let a small matter like complete disagreement with policy push you out of an institution in which your ancestors could trace a direct line of succession clear back to the apostles. The Episcopal Church had long been favored by wealthy, highly educated, and influential people, nowhere more so than in the traditional breeding grounds of old money where Wyatt had grown up. A quarter of all U.S. presidents had been Episcopalian, and there had always been a Darrington close enough to offer counsel and receive the blessing of insider status in return.

When he finally disconnected, he went straight to the shower, cranked up the multilevel jets, and stood, hands braced on the travertine tile and head bowed, letting the water pummel away the film of distaste that always settled over him when he reached back and touched his past.

He'd suffer the punishment to his ulcer if it led them to Hank. Despite what Melanie believed, he had always thought her brother was worth saving. He'd just never been able to figure out how.

But then, neither had Melanie.

━━◦◦◦━━

He tried to reach Melanie to arrange a time to introduce her to his bar manager, but his calls went straight to voicemail. No surprise. She'd driven almost straight through from Texas, and he doubted she'd been sleeping much even before she hit the road. Grace had said Melanie was staying in the Madam's Suite for now, at least. She'd probably turned her phone off to try to grab a nap.

And no, Wyatt was not going to let his mind paint pictures of her in that bed.

As usual, when he arrived at the Bull Dancer late that evening, only one person sat at the bar, his pear-shaped bulk a threat to the future health of the stool, his gray-streaked black hair pulled into a low ponytail that straggled down his broad back. Seeing Wyatt, he casually tilted his newspaper to hide the half-empty glass near his right hand.

Wyatt strolled over, picked up the glass, and tested the contents with the tip of one finger. "Coke?"

"Mostly ice. And the first one this week." Louie crossed his fingers and touched them to his heart with a quick twist of a grin. "Honest Injun."

Wyatt smiled despite a niggle of discomfort. Louie, a half-blood Umatilla, could crack those jokes, but Wyatt was never quite sure how to respond. He suspected Louie knew. It suited his sly sense of humor to make Wyatt squirm as often as possible.

"Have you had dinner?" Wyatt asked.

"I grabbed a sandwich right before I came in. And I got all my steps in today." He tapped the fitness tracker on his wrist, part of the exercise and nutrition program Wyatt and Grace closely monitored to help control his diabetes. Louie waved a hand toward the back corner booth. "If you wanna worry 'bout someone, maybe you should start with her."

Wyatt turned and squinted at the empty table. Then he saw a pair of running shoes, long, jean-clad legs, the too-familiar curve of a hip...and chestnut-brown hair spilling across the red seat.

"Came in a couple of hours ago." The stool creaked dangerously as Louie swiveled, folding meaty arms over his chest as he contemplated Melanie. "Introduced herself, friendly as can be, said she had some notes she wanted to go over, and could she get a cup of coffee? I went back to make a pot, and when I came out, she was like that."

Wyatt stepped gingerly toward the booth. A pocket-sized notebook, a pen, and a cold cup of coffee sat on the table. "And you just left her?"

"She was breathin'. And she looks pretty comfy."

She did. Her hands were pressed palm to palm, pillowing her cheek, and a strand of hair fluttered in front of her face as she exhaled. She looked so peaceful. So young. So much like—

He cut the thought dead. *Separate and compartmentalize.* It was the only way he would emerge with his sanity anywhere near intact. Wyatt leaned over and caught the unmistakable scent of alcohol. So much for innocence. "Was she drunk?"

"Not so's you could tell, but…" Louie jerked his chin toward her, the evidence speaking for itself.

Well…shit. Now what? Wake her? Wait until she came to on her own? There was the slim possibility other customers might wander in, and Wyatt was pretty sure having an unconscious woman sprawled in the back booth was some kind of violation. Health code? Liquor control? Something.

He touched a fingertip to her shoulder. "Melanie?"

Her eyes popped open. She remained perfectly still, taking a few slow blinks to orient herself. Then her gaze cut up toward Wyatt and Louie. She pushed into a seated position, glanced around the bar, then held a palm in front of her mouth, huffed out a breath, and grimaced. "Yuck."

The two men watched in fascination as she rummaged in her purse for a piece of gum and popped it in her mouth. Then she smoothed her hair back and smiled at them. "Was I snoring?"

"Uh, no. You were just…we were wondering…" Wyatt shoved his hands in the pockets of his chinos, unreasonably flustered by her steady gaze. "Are you okay?"

"Hunky-dory. I'm just a little short on sleep, and the bartenders in this town pour 'em pretty strong." She picked up the coffee, sniffed, and held it out to Louie. "I don't suppose you could freshen this up?"

"Yes, ma'am." He took the cup, a grin twitching at the corners of his mouth.

Wyatt hovered awkwardly for another couple of beats, then slid into the booth opposite her. She leaned back, folded her hands on the table, and watched him, her eyes alert. If it weren't for the crease on her cheek, he couldn't have guessed she'd been sound asleep a minute earlier.

"So…you took a tour of the town?" he asked.

"Market research." She tapped the notebook with one finger. "I wanted to check out the competition before word got around that I was working for you. Very friendly people. And informative."

Her words were crisp, clear—and Wyatt was too baffled to make sense of any of them.

"Something wrong?" she asked.

"No. I just thought you were…" Right. Accuse her of passing out. That was tactful.

"Oh, that?" She patted the booth she'd been using as a bed. "Sorry. Not very professional of me. I generally handle my booze pretty well, unless I'm really tired. Then I tend to keel over…but it's all good when I wake up. Which reminds me, what's the going rate for the room upstairs?"

"Consider it part of the package."

And why was he not surprised when she shook her head. "That's not in the contract. I'll pay you at least the going rate for an extended-stay hotel."

"That's too much. I haven't got around to setting it up as a rental, so it'll be vacant if you don't use it, and it costs me nothing if you do." Except the hours of sleep he would lose, picturing her sliding between the Egyptian sheets, hair spilling over the satin pillows. "It's a benefit to me because you're right here where you can soak up the atmosphere of the place."

She wrinkled her nose at an elaborate gilt-edged mirror. "I think it could use a little *less* atmosphere. But since you insist…how about five hundred a week?"

"That's a month's rent for a studio apartment in this town."

She laced her fingers together on the table and cocked her head, considering. He waited for her to insist that she wouldn't take a handout. Instead, she nodded. "I'll pay you five hundred for the duration of my stay…however long that ends up being."

"Deal," he said before she could reconsider.

Louie brought her a hot cup of coffee. She thanked him with a wide, genuine smile that made Wyatt want to kick something. And sure enough, as her gaze swung toward him, the smile tightened and he could see her take a mental step back. Always keeping a safe distance.

Then her dark lashes lifted, and for the space of a dozen heartbeats, their eyes locked. Around them, between them, the fabric of the universe shuddered with that *zing!* of connection he'd felt the first time they'd met. And as always, he was torn between leaning in and running away. His fingers itched to stroke that crease from her cheek. Comb through the silky length of her hair, lift it to his face and inhale…until his brain offered up a single, smiling image that was every reason he couldn't.

And then her stomach growled. Loudly.

She ducked her head, a slight flush rising on her cheeks. "I should have something more solid for lunch."

"I can fix that." Wyatt practically jumped from the booth and gestured to the door. "You can brief me on your *market research* over dinner."

Chapter 13

WELL, HELL. ONE DUMB-ASS, UNGUARDED LOOK, AND THEY might as well have been right back on that dance floor at Violet's wedding, the physical attraction between them a living, breathing entity that they'd only been able to drive into hibernation.

She should have said *no damn way* to his dinner invitation, but that would have been admitting the moment in the bar had rattled her.

So here they were, stepping out together into a twilight that had cooled enough to make Melanie shiver despite the hoodie she'd grabbed from her car. She expected Wyatt to lead her to any of the half-dozen restaurants within a block of the Bull Dancer. Instead, he unlocked the door of his Camaro and held it for her.

Great. After all the fantasies she'd tried not to have involving this car...

It gleamed under the newly awakened streetlight, a devil-red, four-wheeled aphrodisiac. When he closed the door, the leather-bound scent of privileged male wrapped around her—warm, spicy, mouthwatering. Too bad she was on a strict, no-Wyatt diet.

Tilting her head back, she let her eyelids drift nearly shut as he climbed in, but that only intensified all of her other senses. The engine growled to life, deep and just barely domesticated. The vibration worked its way up from the soles of her feet and set every nerve on high alert. The space separating them was so narrow his hand nearly brushed her thigh as he wrapped it around the gearshift knob.

She shifted away under the pretext of running a finger along the dashboard and inspecting it. No trace of dust. "Do you have this thing detailed once a week?"

"Every other. And I keep it covered, even in the garage." He angled her a look that sent another wave of prickling heat through her. "Some things are worth the effort."

She refused to let her breath catch. "I'm a low-maintenance kind of gal myself."

"I've noticed," he said, and left her to wonder if she'd been insulted or complimented.

He turned left onto the one-way that ran the long, narrow length of downtown. She was disappointed when he made another left after only four blocks and parked the Camaro across the street from what looked like a large, historic house. She'd been hoping they'd hit the highway and see what the car could do—as if she wasn't already half-dizzy from inhaling too much undiluted Wyatt.

She kicked open the door and got out. "We could've walked this far."

"I thought you might get cold."

His mild tone made her sound even bitchier. She realized she was hugging her arms across her chest and let them drop. Her stomach gave another audible growl at the aroma of grilled meat wafting in the air. And Lord, could she use that cup of coffee she hadn't gotten around to finishing before Wyatt hijacked her. She didn't get hangovers—a quirk that had annoyed the hell out of Shawnee and Violet in college—but she was in dire need of caffeine to finish the job of waking her up.

Not that she'd let Wyatt know she was still muzzy around the edges. She'd heard him come into the bar—four years of having Shawnee Pickett as a roommate had made her hard to sneak up on—and played possum on the off chance she might overhear something interesting. A girl didn't get many chances to catch Wyatt off guard.

"This place looks like it's been around a while." They climbed flagstone steps to a wide veranda that fronted the building, the steep, gabled roof braced by wooden columns.

"It was built in 1902 by the first president of the Pendleton Roundup, later converted to apartments, and now it's a restaurant." They stepped inside, and Wyatt held up two fingers for the hostess. "Consider this more research."

The weeknight crowd was sparse, but she and Wyatt still attracted a few glances as the hostess led them to a table by the front window. Obviously he was recognized, but no one waved or tried to chat. Melanie couldn't help but contrast it with walking into a cafe in Earnest with Joe, where they greeted him like a native son after only a few years.

Wyatt had lived in Pendleton for almost two decades. Was it the town…or was it him?

"What?" he asked as she frowned at him.

"I'm trying to understand why anyone would voluntarily wear a shirt that has to be ironed."

His gaze skimmed over her rumpled clothes. "I thought all Texans were addicted to starch."

"Not the ones who grew up doing their own laundry."
And Hank's.

And dammit, she really was soft in the head tonight,
making a glib comment that sharpened Wyatt's already
assessing gaze. He knew her family situation, but she
didn't need to advertise the lingering bitter taste.

The waitress came by to take their drink orders, forcing his attention away from Melanie while he listened to
a recitation of the microbrews on tap. Melanie breathed
a sigh of relief and tried to refrain from snatching the
coffee and drinking straight from the pot. She gave
her cup a meaningful shove. The woman grudgingly
peeled her eyes off Wyatt to fill it. The first sip scalded
Melanie's tongue, but her gray matter immediately
perked up.

The waitress departed, and Wyatt folded his arms
across his spotless white shirt. "You think I'm over-
dressed for the occasion?"

Melanie shrugged. "No criticism intended. I just
don't know many cowboys who wear tasseled loafers."

"I'm not a cowboy," he said flatly.

Melanie paused in the act of stirring cream into her
coffee. "You hold the record for the number of consecu-
tive appearances at the National Finals, which makes
you a shoo-in for the ProRodeo Hall of Fame."

"As a bullfighter. Not a cowboy. I've never worked
on a ranch. I've never competed in a rodeo. I put on my
gear, and I step into the arena the same way a football
player steps onto the field. The rest of the time..." A
flick of his fingers toward his chest invited her to take a
good look. "I'm this."

The waitress set his beer down, and he relaxed

into his chair as he thanked her. Once again, Melanie was struck by the unconscious release of tension. She would have pegged Wyatt as someone who didn't give a damn about popular opinion, but his body language was telling her otherwise — over something as trivial as how he dressed.

Which meant it wasn't trivial at all.

After they'd placed their meal orders, Melanie nursed her coffee, using it as an excuse to retreat into her thoughts. It was time to get serious about this job. If this was going to work on a professional level — and that was the *only* level she would consider — she had to stop thinking of him as Wyatt and start seeing him as a client.

And if she wanted to prove that Michael was an anomaly and not a sign that she'd gone people-blind, there was no better place to start.

She refused to believe she'd lost the insight that had been a lifetime in the making. At the tender age of eight, she'd realized she could predict how the day would go based on the way her father sawed at his pancakes and how loudly her mother's spoon clinked against the cup as she stirred her coffee. Those were the days she asked Daddy if she could ride with him when he went out to check the cows in the river breaks, and offered to pack the lunches they'd take along so her mother could leave early to meet with her study partners.

Little Melanie, the world's youngest PR specialist. A skill she'd honed in psychology classes and sales seminars taught by FBI interrogators. Everyone had tells, even Wyatt, and the longer she kept him talking, the more she would understand what he really wanted from that bar.

More than a successful business venture. Otherwise, it wouldn't still be sitting there in limbo—a shabby, woeful liability on his balance sheet. It struck her that as much time as she'd spent observing Wyatt in action, she had only the slightest grasp of what drove him. Loyalty, yes. A hero complex…possibly. But those were the *whats*.

She was only vaguely aware of his closely guarded *whys*. The real reasons he wasn't lounging on the terrace of a mansion on the Vineyard, sipping a rare vintage with heads of state and captains of industry. Back in Earnest, her life was an open book for anyone who bothered to read it, and she didn't like the advantage it gave him, knowing her better than she knew him.

She propped her elbow on the table, her chin on her fist, and gave him her rapt attention. "You witnessed my fall from grace. The least you can do is tell me about yours. Did you get disowned for using the wrong fork for the hors d'oeuvres?"

He turned the beer glass, seemingly admiring the perfect head of foam before taking the first sip. "You could say I refused to swallow whatever was put on my plate."

Whoa. A real answer. Now that was unexpected. And calculated, no doubt, but she was willing to risk whatever he hoped to gain. "What were they dishing up?"

"A version of morality I couldn't stomach."

"Such as?"

"Among other things…the unshakable belief that any version of religion, politics, or sexuality other than their own is a sin against God."

"Oh." Not that she would ever bring any of those up over breakfast with her own father, but no doubt the stakes would be a bit higher in the vaunted Darrington family. "I thought the Episcopal Church was one of the most progressive."

His eyebrows twitched in surprise. Yes, the Baptist girl actually read about these things. "The church as whole? Yes. My family in particular? Not so much."

She tried to read any nonverbal cues, but whatever emotions had been strong enough to drive him to rebellion were locked up behind that impenetrable blue gaze. "You couldn't just switch to a different…um, parish, or whatever?"

"It was a little more complicated than that." His mouth twisted, and for an instant his expression went bleak. "Let's just say I lost faith in more than my family."

Wow. That was…well, sad. Melanie was by no means a Bible-thumper, but her beliefs had always been a solid foundation in her life. An anchor when the world seemed to be one huge, ugly storm. Shattering that connection…

Would take more than an argument with her daddy. The *complication* that had caused Wyatt to lose his religion must've been a real doozy.

"Now I'm even more curious," she said. "I don't believe I've ever heard the story of your first rodeo. How did you end up in Pendleton?"

His expression barely seemed to change, but she could see him pulling on the mask he wore for reporters and fans. Friendly. Amused. Meaningless. "Call it a pilgrimage. I followed the Oregon Trail, and like a lot of the emigrants, this is where the wheels came off my wagon. Or in my case, the engine blew up in my Audi…which was no great loss. By the time I found the Camaro, I'd fallen in love with the town and decided not to move on."

A smooth, practiced line delivered with just the right touch of self-effacing humor, but not the whole story. He'd shifted as he spoke, and beneath the table he had crossed his ankles—classic signs he was holding something back. The trip hadn't been some rich boy's impulse, the decision to stay not so lightly made.

Melanie made an educated guess. "And who would ever expect to find someone like you holed up in this little cow town?"

"I didn't have a pack of bloodhounds on my trail." But he laced the fingers of both hands around his beer glass, a gesture she was beginning to recognize as his personal *No Trespassing* sign.

She ignored it and plowed on. "So you set up your homestead here, all by yourself?"

His fingers tightened a fraction before he lifted the glass and took a sip. When he lowered it, his slight smile was perfectly calibrated. "Why not? I was twenty-two years old, financially independent, and trying to *find* myself. This seemed like as good a place as any."

Liar. The best ones knew better than to look you directly in the eye.

"Do you own any other property in town?" she asked, shifting her angle of attack.

"The rest of my condo complex."

"Renters?" She lifted her eyebrows. "Seems like a hassle."

"A real estate agency manages them for me."

Just like the Bull Dancer Foundation. "You generally prefer hands-off investments."

"I travel a lot."

She let her eyes narrow just enough to indicate that

she wasn't buying his line. He took another sip of beer. She had another swallow of coffee. The moments began to weigh heavier, the strain of holding his stare without getting sucked into the blue, blue depths of his eyes growing exponentially with each beat of her heart.

She was insane, challenging him to a stare-down when her emotions were still so raw she felt as if she was carrying an armload of nitroglycerin bottles. One slip, and *kaboom!* Just like in those old western movies.

Wyatt broke first, circling a hand to indicate their surroundings. "What do you think? Would this suit the Bull Dancer?"

The Bull Dancer. A name that referred to both the bar and the man. She took her time examining the room— the way gleaming wood floors set off a seamless combination of clean lines and rich, contemporary color. A waitress passed with more plates, the food artfully arranged, magazine perfect.

Mentally comparing it to the shabby, degenerate glitz of the Bull Dancer, she had to squelch a laugh. Months after taking possession, Wyatt had changed almost nothing beyond cleaning and basic repairs, as if the place had him stymied. He wanted…something, but either didn't know exactly what it was or couldn't figure out how to accomplish it.

Since Wyatt was the most self-analytical person she'd ever met, she had to assume the second. Knowing what he really wanted and admitting it were two very different things, however. But he *would* tell her, if she kept asking the right questions and paying very close attention to his reactions.

The way you read Michael?

The hand on her lap fisted, grasping at her slippery control. *Damn him*. Of all the things Michael had fractured—her heart not included, but she'd been all too aware of that before the wreck—her previously steadfast faith in her own judgment was the most devastating. How did she get that back?

The same way she'd broken every rodeo slump of her career—with one big win. Many had tried, but all had failed to get to the true center of Wyatt Darrington. Even Violet and Joe accepted that there were parts of him they didn't really know. Given her damnable weakness where he was concerned—one that was at least somewhat mutual—getting too close would be a huge risk. But if she could succeed in fathoming the unfathomable…

He quirked an eyebrow, still waiting for her answer.

"If this was your goal, you would've already hired a designer and a fancy chef," she said. "Obviously it's not your heart's desire."

"What is?"

Melanie gave him a long, thorough appraisal, ignoring the rev of her pulse. "That's what I intend to find out."

"Should I be afraid?"

She smiled. He smiled. Their eyes locked again, and the tension level at the table ratcheted up several dangerous degrees.

Then the waitress arrived with their entrees, and they made the mutual, unspoken decision to back off, concentrate on their food, and limit interaction to how, yes, the grilled salmon special had been an excellent choice and the huckleberry glaze was perfect.

As Melanie was swabbing up the last of it, Wyatt frowned and pulled his vibrating phone out of his shirt pocket. A puzzled crease appeared between his eye-brows when he checked the screen, but he took the call. "This is Wyatt."

He listened for a few moments, then asked, "Did you find everything you need?"

Melanie's heart clutched. Was this about Hank? Wyatt's expression told her nothing.

He listened some more, then said, "That should be interesting. We'll see you in about fifteen minutes."

We? What did this have to do with her? Wyatt hung up and casually tucked the phone back into his pocket, but when he met her gaze, there was a gleam in his eyes that made her chin jerk up.

"What?" she demanded.

He gave her one of those irritating half smirks. "We need to swing by my arena when we're done here."

She wasn't going to like this. Otherwise, Wyatt wouldn't be so amused. Rather than peppering him with questions, she pushed her chair back and stood. "Let's go, then."

Before Wyatt slowed to turn into a gravel driveway, she spotted the rodeo rig parked beside his arena, but the outfit was fancier than anything her friends owned. Amber running lights outlined a modified, four-door semi-tractor attached to a massive, top-end horse trailer with a slide-out on the living quarters already extended. Someone was settling in for the night.

But who? And what did it have to do with her?

As she stepped out of the car, the scents and sounds hit her, loosing a wave of memories of nights just like this one. The cool air condensing the mingled smells of manure and fresh wood shavings from the trailer, dust and good clean hay, and amplifying the clomp and snuffle of horses. So many times this had been her and Shawnee making a pit stop between rodeos—minus the super-fancy rig.

A lanky figure ambled around the end of the trailer and paused as if he wasn't sure he wanted to get any closer. Melanie scrunched her face in confusion. "Brady?"

"Hi, Mel." Shawnee's sometime roping partner raised his hands in a gesture of both innocence and surrender, tossing a *help me* look in the direction of Wyatt, who opted to prop his elbows on his open car door and enjoy the show. "I swear," Brady said. "Shawnee didn't tell me you weren't expecting us until it was too late to turn around. And she swore you wouldn't murder the messenger."

"*Us?*"

"Me and, um, them." He gestured toward a large nearby pen where she could make out two bulky shadows.

Melanie's jaw dropped when she realized what he was saying, then snapped shut so hard she nearly chipped a tooth. "She sent *horses*? Without even asking me?"

"Uh, yeah. Seems like it."

Melanie gave her head a shake. Even for Shawnee... "What am I supposed to do with them? I don't have a saddle. Bridles. Anything."

Brady flattened a palm on the door to the rear tack compartment. "Everything you need is in here. She went out to your ranch and got it."

"It's...she...*what?*"

Brady took a step back, as if ready to make a run for it. Melanie caught the glint of Wyatt's smile.

Since he was closer, she turned on him. "Was this your idea?"

"Nope. First I heard of it was tonight."

Damn. She believed him. She'd seen his surprise at Brady's phone call, and besides, he wouldn't bother to lie. Which meant if she was going to vent…

She yanked out her phone and punched in the number, then paced in impatient circles as it rang, and rang, then went to voicemail. She immediately hit Redial. This time Shawnee picked up.

"It's after ten o'clock here. Do you have any idea what you're interrupting?"

"Yes. And I hope by the time I finish chewing your ass, Cole has rolled over and gone to sleep."

Shawnee gave a smug laugh. "You forget who I married. He's *way* too OCD to let a little interruption stop him from following through with the plan." There was a rumbled complaint in the background, and Shawnee's voice faded. "Hey, I meant that as a compliment, sweet cheeks."

"If you're trying to make me gag, it's not working." Melanie's circle had widened, taking her nearer where the horses were penned. In the faint glow from the trailer lights she could only see that one had dark mane and the other a white blaze. "What the hell, Shawnee?"

"From here on out, we'll be on the road almost straight through the summer. I can only take a couple of extra horses with me. No sense leaving those two standing in the pasture when you finally have time to rope."

"So…what? You sent me a couple of damn colts to train?"

"I wouldn't do that." A slight pause. "Well, not now, when you're so rusty. I figured you could use something more reliable."

More… Melanie stepped close to the fence. The nearest horse lifted his head, a chunk of hay sticking out the side of his mouth, his distinctive golden coat unmistakable even in the dim light.

Melanie sucked in a stunned breath. "That's…*Roy*."

Shawnee's treasured buckskin was still for a moment, looking Melanie over, then went back to munching calmly on the hay.

"The one and only. What you need right now is quality time with a man who'll never let you down."

"Are you sure you didn't mean to send Cole instead? You never let Roy out of your sight."

"It was a toss-up, but I can let you ride Roy without having to beat you to death. The other one is the heading horse Cole started over the winter, so you've got both ends covered if you want to do some team roping."

Melanie had a sudden need to sit down, but that wasn't possible, short of plopping her butt in the dirt, so she sagged against the fence. "You are out of your mind."

"Not yet, but if you'd shut up and let Cole finish—"

"Enough! Gah."

Shawnee laughed triumphantly. Melanie hung up. She started as Wyatt materialized out of the darkness to stand beside her, studying the horses.

"What am I going to do with them?"

"I've got plenty of room here." His smile glistened like a blade in the darkness. "And the saddle club where Grace practices is just down the road."

Melanie groaned, her stomach dropping even as her heart did a giddy swoop. *Damn* Shawnee. How was she supposed to make sensible choices about her future with the siren call of the arena ringing in her ears?

Chapter 14

SHE WAS WATCHING HIM AGAIN.

Wyatt could feel Melanie's gaze like a laser sight between his shoulder blades as he stood in the training ring, drilling Dante on how to step past a charging bull. For the moment, the part of the bull was being played by Scotty, pushing a wheelbarrow with a set of horns mounted on the front.

"On your toes!" Wyatt barked, sharper than he'd intended. That self-conscious itch was driving him nuts. He'd never had trouble focusing—until now. He glanced over his shoulder. She gave him a quick twist of a smile that said, *Yep, got my eye on you.*

He jerked his head around. *Why* was she watching him? Shouldn't she be defining their target demographic or developing their brand strategy, churning out spreadsheets and pie charts like all the other marketing professionals he'd ever dealt with? But no. She'd come out to feed the horses and stayed to watch, lounging against the fence beside Grace in a denim jacket and jeans, a West Texas A&M cap pulled low over her eyes and her hair in a single braid down her back—a long, tall drink of distilled cowgirl.

Watching him.

Dante rocked onto his toes, knees bent. Wyatt signaled and the "bull" charged. Dante immediately stepped backward, the loose sand catching his feet, throwing his shoulders back and his weight onto his heels. He stumbled, and the dummy bull plowed into his thighs, knocking him on his butt.

Wyatt swallowed another bark and reached down. Ignoring the hand he offered and Scotty's grin, Dante scrambled to his feet. Wyatt gestured for Scotty and the wheelbarrow to back off, then took Dante's place in front of it. "Imagine I'm a running back and the bull is a linebacker. If I move straight back, I'm toast. I have to take it to him with some kind of move that'll make him miss. Like this."

At Wyatt's gesture, Scotty charged again. Wyatt feinted left, then stepped back to the right, letting the wheelbarrow zip harmlessly past.

"It's like takin' the ball to the hoop," Philip said, miming a crossover dribble, two long steps, and a layup. "You gotta fake out the defense."

"Exactly." Wyatt gestured Dante forward. "Try it again."

They repeated the drill, each of the men taking his turn as the bull and the bullfighter, until they were all breathing hard and sporting at least a few bruises from well-timed swerves of the dummy bull's horns. They all seemed to be getting the gist of it, although Dante continued to struggle, having to think through every move.

If he was going to face real bulls, he had to learn to react. There was no time for thinking in bullfighting.

Dante braced his hands on his thighs as he sucked in air. "That's great when you're bein' chased by a wheelbarrow. But if it's a big-ass bull tryin' to run you down..."

Wyatt swiped an arm across his sweaty forehead. "First off, unlike linebackers or Scotty..." The redhead met his glare with a wide-eyed *Who, me?* look. "…a bull will hardly ever anticipate the fake. And second, they literally weigh a ton. That's a lot of momentum working in your favor."

Dante squinted at him. "Say what?"

"They can't turn on a dime," Melanie drawled. Every head swiveled in her direction. She grimaced and made a zipping motion in front of her mouth. "Sorry."

"You know as well as anyone," Wyatt said.

Dante cocked his head. "Your girlfriend is a bull-fighter?"

Wyatt opened his mouth to say no, she wasn't. A bullfighter. Or his girlfriend.

Melanie cut him short. "I used to step in once in a while at the Jacobs practice sessions."

Wyatt blinked. "Seriously?"

"Seriously." Her eyes gleamed, laughing at his aston-ishment. "I'm a pretty decent pickup man, too."

Now that wasn't a surprise. After all, she was Violet's best friend. They'd both grown up in front of and behind the chutes at Jacobs Livestock's weekly practices, where up-and-coming cowboys tested their mettle against the ranch's young horses and bulls. Violet had been fetching riders off of bucking horses since she was barely out of junior high. It was only natural that Melanie would give it a try.

But fighting bulls?

Her mouth dented in at one corner in answer to his silent question. "They dared me."

"Well, let's see your moves, mama." Scotty gave a wiggle of his hips.

She shook her head. "It's been a long time—"

"Ah, come on. We wanna see what you got," Dante chimed in, verging on a taunt.

"Ignore them," Wyatt said. "You don't want to—"

Big mistake. He knew better than to tell Melanie what she wanted. Her chin came up, and the glint in her eye turned steely. "Sure. Why not?"

Okay. Don't overreact. It was just a wheelbarrow dressed up a like a bull. How much trouble—

"But I'm not messing around with that thing." She curled her lip at Scotty. "*You* are a cheap-shot artist."

He smiled angelically, a freckle-faced Opie made of good intentions.

"Bring in the cows." Melanie shrugged out of her jacket and tossed it over the fence rail. "And hand me that sorting stick."

The boys grinned and trotted off down the alley to get the cows, and Grace went after the five-foot-long fiberglass stick with orange rubber tips, all of them acting as if Wyatt wasn't supposed to be in charge here. Melanie hopped up and down a few times, then dropped into a low lunge to stretch. Was he the only one who could see this was a terrible idea?

"How long has it been?" he asked.

"Since I got out of college and got a real job." She squinted, adding it up, as she switched legs and dropped into another lunge. Wyatt lost a few beats of conscious thought as the stretch pulled her jeans tight across her butt and emphasized the long, taut length of her legs. "So...twelve years? But it's not like I haven't been handling cows. Daddy drags me back to the ranch for all the big jobs—pregnancy testing, branding, weaning, and shipping."

"Regular cattle aren't quite the same thing."

"I agree." She angled him an amused look back over her shoulder. "I take it you don't know where Wild Woman and the Panther came from?"

"Joe picked them up…" In Texas. *Duh*. "They were yours?"

"Third generation. Those two were even more than Daddy could handle, and he's a firm believer in mama cows with protective instincts."

That explained why Hank was such a *natural*. Nothing like a lifetime of sheer survival to hone your moves.

She stood, then bent over and touched her toes, the view knocking Wyatt for another mental loop. Her hoodie and T-shirt slid up, revealing a stretch of smooth, taut skin. His heart gave a little sigh of disappointment when she straightened and tugged her shirt down as the cows came trotting into the ring, snorting and tossing their heads. Melanie jogged in place, then did a few side-to-side cuts to get a feel for the ground. Grace tossed her the sorting stick.

"You two." She pointed the stick at Scotty and Dante. "Watch the gate. Let everything out except Wild Woman. And you." She pointed at Philip. "Back Wyatt up if I get in trouble."

All three moved into position without question.

Shit. Wyatt yanked his jersey over his head, ripped off his protective vest, and shoved it into her free hand. Her gaze slid down to his chest and the nipples that hardened as the breeze danced over the sweat-damp polyester athletic shirt that fit him like a second skin. For an instant, she seemed to be struck dumb. Then her teeth snapped together with an audible click.

Wyatt pulled his jersey on. She shrugged into the vest, fastened the Velcro, and stepped toward the cows. As usual, the Longhorn made the first move. Melanie let her go, followed by two others. She paced closer, her gaze fixed on Wild Woman. The black cow threw up her head, shaking stubby horns that curled down and forward, broken off into blunt points just above her eyes. She looked left, saw Scotty and Dante blocking her path, then swung her head back and stood as if held by the force of Melanie's concentration. The Panther peeled off and broke for the gate. With a few quick steps and a wave of the sorting stick Melanie made sure Wild Woman didn't follow.

And just like that, the cows were sorted. If he hadn't been annoyed at how easy she made it look, Wyatt might have applauded.

She tossed the sorting stick back toward Grace without taking her eyes off the cow. "Hello, Sunshine. Miss me?"

The cow lowered her head and blew snot.

Melanie laughed. "Yeah. Me too."

She took three deliberate steps closer. The cow backed up a stride, then stopped, shaking her head again. A hoof-full of dirt clattered off the fence. Melanie grinned and stalked even closer. When there were no more than five yards between them, she made a sudden jab step to the left. As the cow lunged toward her, she dodged right and stepped past the charging animal's head with barely an inch to spare. Wild Woman swung around, dirt spewing from beneath her hooves as she circled. Melanie led her into a left turn, gave another fake, and reached back to put one hand on the cow's horn as she stopped hard, then did a pirouette to the right so flawless it damn near stopped Wyatt's heart.

Wild Woman bellowed, whirled around again, and charged. Melanie made another fake, but when she cut back, her foot slipped. The instant's hesitation was enough. The cow clipped one leg and brought her to her knees. Melanie swore and dropped into a roll, arms clasped over her head as Wild Woman rooted at her. Wyatt and Scotty jumped in from the front, slapping at the cow's head, while Philip yelled and grabbed her tail. The cow spun around and went after him. Philip sprinted for the gate, the cow on his heels, and vaulted over the fence to land in a pile on the other side as she tore past where Dante stood near the gate.

Before Grace could take a step toward her, Melanie was up, cursing as she swiped dirt-caked snot from under her nose. She had a smear across one cheek and a partial hoofprint where the cow had stepped on the back of one shoulder—on the vest, thank God—but she didn't seem to be injured. Wyatt blew out a huge breath of relief.

"Bring 'em back!" Melanie barked.

Wyatt spun around. "*What?*"

"I said, bring 'em back." When the men only gaped at her, she snatched up the sorting stick and started down the alley. "I'm not letting that bitch have the last shot."

The others sprang into motion, but Wyatt stood rooted to the ground, cursing even as his blood pounded with pure, adrenaline-laced awe.

God *damn*, she was something.

Chapter 15

MELANIE GROANED AS SHE EASED HER ACHING BODY INTO the slipper tub. Every scuff and scrape on her body sang out in angry protest at the sting of the hot water.

"I don't feel sorry for you," Violet said, via the speaker on the phone Melanie had brought in with her to listen to music while she soaked away the pain.

"I don't recall asking for sympathy." She lifted one foot and examined the purpling bruise on the side of her calf. Yep. That was gonna be pretty. "I can't believe Wyatt called Joe and tattled on me."

"He wasn't tattling. He was in shock. The man is used to pulling all the strings, and you ripped 'em right out of his hands."

Melanie slid a little lower in the water. Wyatt had a legitimate beef. Not only had she opened her big mouth when she'd intended to be seen and not heard, but by the time she was done screwing around, whatever plan he'd had for the morning had been totally shot. "I couldn't resist."

"And? How was it?"

Melanie grinned, admiring another well-earned bruise. "Awesome, even though I probably won't be able to get out of bed in the morning. Those are some muscles you do *not* use in the gym. But it felt good to go into battle mode and take it to 'em."

"Because you haven't been doing enough of that lately," Violet said dryly.

"It's not the same when you can't look the enemy in the eye. I prefer hand-to-hand combat."

"Says anyone who's ever played basketball against you."

Melanie laughed. "At least Wyatt can use me as a bad example."

"That's not what he said."

"Really?" She paused in the act of tucking a strand of hair back into the pile on top of her head, then cringed at how eager she sounded.

"I didn't get details." Violet made an irritated noise. "It was one of those *Don't tell her I said this* conversations, and I married a man who's big on keeping his word."

"Well, that's annoying."

"Only when I'm the one trying to compromise him. All Joe would say is that Wyatt was impressed at how well you handle cattle."

O-kay. That was…vaguely satisfying. Not that she'd set out to impress Wyatt. Had she?

No. It had been pure impulse. A challenge, and a physical outlet for the constant simmer of resentment in her gut. She wanted to attack. And—she cringed again when the thought struck—to be attacked, which gave her a chance to fight back.

An opportunity she didn't have at Westwind.

Damn. She was glad she didn't have to share that little gem with a shrink. Or Wyatt—although he'd probably already guessed. She scowled at the pressed-tin ceiling. He was probably kicked back in his condo on the hill, sipping a bottle of rarified water, analyzing her behavior, and reaching the same embarrassing conclusions.

While wearing one of those insanely sexy shirts.

She squeezed her eyes shut, but it didn't help. She could still see every detail of the extremely well-developed muscles in his chest and shoulders. Holy Toledo, he had an amazing set of shoulders. His prissy button-downs and polo shirts did not do them justice, unlike the sweaty second skin he'd been wearing this morning. Now she had a permanent impression of Wyatt's nipples on her gray matter and a whole new appreciation for wet T-shirt contests.

She growled in frustration and tried to reroute her thoughts. "Does Wyatt have any other friends or family out here?"

"Well...I assume you've seen Grace?"

"Yes. It's awkward, but we're managing." She lifted her foot to scrub dirt from under her toenails—her running shoes were full of the stuff—and once again wondered about Grace. She'd smiled when she offered Melanie an ice pack for the bruise on her shoulder. Then, almost as if she'd caught herself, she'd abruptly turned away. Her initial hostility was to be expected, but why would she consciously resist being too friendly?

"Did Joe ever meet anyone from the dark and mysterious days of Wyatt's past?" Melanie asked.

Violet paused, thinking. "Once. They were working...hmm. Molalla? St. Paul? One of those rodeos in that part of Oregon. A woman came to watch him. She stuck in Joe's mind because she was—his words—so gorgeous he couldn't even speak in whole sentences when Wyatt introduced them. He told Joe she was just an old friend who lived in Portland, and Joe got the distinct impression there were no benefits."

"Did Joe ever see her again?"

"Not after Wyatt married the stripper."

"*What?*" Melanie sat up so abruptly that water sloshed onto the floor.

"I told you about her," Violet said.

"You've mentioned his ex-wife." And that the union had been short and not very sweet. "You did *not* tell me she was a stripper."

"Oh. Well, we've never talked much about Wyatt. I thought you preferred it that way." When Melanie didn't jump to fill the pause, Violet made an exasperated noise. "We're not blind, Mel. It was obvious from day one that there were serious sparks between the two of you."

"And you never said anything?"

"It was just as obvious that both of you wanted to ignore it. And to be honest…we were sort of relieved."

Relieved? Ouch. Joe didn't want her dating his best friend? As usual, she reached for sarcasm to cover the sting. "What, you didn't want to be the BFFs who married BFFs and fantasized about how our kids could marry each other when they grow up?"

"Thank you for making my point. You can't even talk *about* him without turning into the Queen of Snark, let alone *to* him. And the minute you walk into the room, he goes all smug and arrogant and…*gah!*" Violet spit it out like a piece of black licorice. "I hate when he gets like that, and the way you've been…"

"I've been what?" Melanie demanded.

Violet was silent for a few beats, then heaved a

reluctant sigh. "Remember that day Joe's flight from Denver was delayed, and I borrowed a corner of your office to catch up on my emails while I waited? It was... wow. The last time I saw that much passive aggression in one place was your parent's twentieth wedding anniversary party."

"Yeah. The Leech brings it to a whole new level."

There was another long, weighty pause. Finally, quietly, Violet said, "I wasn't talking about him."

Melanie's chin nearly bounced off her chest. "Are you accusing me of turning into my mother?"

Whoever said a *picture* was worth a thousand words had never encountered one of Violet's strategic silences.

"I am *not* that bad." Melanie had to muster every ounce of control to keep from shrieking, *You take that back, my so-called friend.*

"Yet...but do you really want to risk it?" Violet persisted. "Is your career worth giving up *everything*, Mel? Your roping, your family, time at the ranch...your friends?"

There was hurt beneath Violet's words. An echo of dinners canceled, lunch dates broken, all the birthday parties, science fairs, and school plays Melanie had missed.

For what?

Violet's tone softened. "I realize that's the price you pay for success, especially as a woman, but I can't imagine that being enough of a life for you. Deep down, I think you know it, or you wouldn't have blown up every bridge in sight on your way out."

Melanie settled back into the water and gave a bitter laugh. "Joe's not the only one who's been talking to Wyatt."

"Why? Is that what he told you, too?"

Melanie glared at the phone. "Just because you agree doesn't make you right."

"It also doesn't make us wrong. At least take it into consideration while you're figuring out what to do next. And don't take it out on Wyatt. In fact, while you're out there, maybe the two of you could learn how to have a conversation without sniping at each other. It used to be entertaining. Now it's mostly just mean."

Melanie dipped her chin into the water and stared at her toes, trying to imagine having a normal, noncombative conversation with Wyatt. Just two people not attempting to draw blood. Though if she was honest, it was usually her taking the shots and Wyatt deflecting them—but he did have a killer backhand return.

"Tell me about the stripper," she blurted out.

"Gabrielle." The tension drained out of Violet's voice as she dived for the conversational escape hatch. "That was her *real* name. She went by Desiree onstage. One of the sponsors at Reno took Wyatt and Joe to the place she worked and paid for girls to hang with them. Turned out she was dancing her way to a master's degree in psychology. She and Wyatt ended up arguing nature versus nurture for two hours, and she went home with him that night."

Something disturbingly close to envy twinged in Melanie's chest. "Not your average buckle bunny."

"God, no. Joe said she was scary smart. And smoking hot, of course."

Of course. Melanie's gaze drifted downward, and she crossed her arms over her own not-so-spectacular chest. "So they hooked up during the Reno rodeo…"

"And stayed in touch afterward. It's not that far from

Pendleton to Reno, you know. You should take a road trip to Lake Tahoe while you're out there."

"Focus, Violet."

"Sorry. I'm not used to having a conversation for more than three minutes without being interrupted."

"Where are the critters?"

"Delon has Beni this week, and Rosie is down for the count. Cole came over and rolled around on the floor with her for an hour after dinner. She calls him her bubba bear."

Aw. Now that was adorable, imagining big, stoic Cole Jacobs putting himself at the mercy of Violet's rambunctious toddler. "That's great. Now, about how Wyatt acquired an ex-wife?"

"Right. One morning she called, seriously freaked out. She'd picked up a stalker at the club, and she'd come home from work and found a bunch of roses on her doorstep with, um, photos. Of stuff no woman wants to see, no matter what men think. She grabbed a few things, went to a friend's house, and called Wyatt."

"And he swooped in and saved the day."

"Literally. He jumped in his plane and flew down to get her. She'd finished school and was applying to doctoral programs, so she moved into his condo. About a month later, Wyatt informed Joe that they were married."

"Wow. That was…fast." And very uncalculated. Or so it appeared. Which made it very un-Wyatt-like. "Why the rush?"

"Believe me, after the divorce Wyatt spent a *lot* of time wondering the same thing. Out loud. Until Joe was ready to strangle him."

"What was his excuse?"

"Which one? He'd just turned thirty. Had his first major injury earlier that year. He was feeling his mortality. It was an early mid-life crisis. Finally Joe told him, 'Maybe you were just tired of being alone. *And* she was super hot.'" Violet giggled. "But at least Wyatt quit yammering on about it."

Melanie picked up a bar of soap that smelled like fresh spring rain and rubbed it between her hands. "They should've been a good match."

"You'd think." Violet's voice was muffled by what sounded suspiciously like cookie crumbs. "When they fought, Joe said it was like listening to Dr. Phil and Oprah throw down."

Melanie scrubbed a lily-white washcloth across the back of her neck. It came away brown with grime from getting rolled around in the dirt by the bitch squad. There was so much grit in her hair that it would turn the water the same color when she washed it. "What did they fight about?"

"*Everything.*" Violet's eye roll was audible. "Politics, religion, whether Freud was the worst thing that ever happened to mental health care, how many nuggets it takes to make a meal truly happy—you name it. Plus she was extremely independent…to the point that she refused to let him pay off her student loans. Not taking care of her drove him insane. He couldn't resist trying to help, and she did not want to be accepted into the doctoral program at the University of Oregon because Wyatt had *made a few calls*."

"He *did* that?" Melanie tossed aside the washcloth in disgust. "Geezus. He's supposed to be a student of human nature, and he didn't get that she would want to be admitted on her own merit?"

"Which is exactly what she said. And he said those things are always political, and she needed to learn to use whatever advantage she could get. She disagreed... loudly. It got so bad that she started packing. Wyatt talked her into giving it one last chance. He rented a cabin on Lake Pend Oreille—gorgeous scenery, secluded, romantic..." Violet gave an amused huff. "They didn't even make it to the lake. They started bickering, he pulled over at a rest area, and when he got out, she drove off and left him there."

Melanie sucked in a horrified breath. "In the *Camaro*?"

"I know. It's amazing he didn't have her arrested. Joe went and picked him up, and by the time they got back to Pendleton, the only thing she'd left at the condo was the car. She didn't even try to fleece him in the divorce. She just wanted out as fast as possible."

"Damn. That smarts."

"Yeah." They were both silent for a few moments. Then Violet said, "Joe said she could be a lot of fun when she wasn't frothing at the mouth, but there was Wyatt and his pathological need to save the world, with a woman who was incapable of accepting help of any kind." Violet hesitated, then added, "Actually, Joe says she was a lot like you."

Ouch.

Been there, tried that, have the divorce papers to prove it. There wasn't a chance in hell he was gonna give it another go—even if Melanie had been willing. So why did she have an insane urge to kick Gabrielle's smokin'-hot ass?

"Hey, Mel? Did you drown in there?"

Melanie made a sour face. "Tempting…but no."

"I'm sorry. I shouldn't have said…I'm not trying to be mean. I swear. I just don't want to see you get hurt anymore." Violet's voice caught, and Melanie could picture the tears welling in her eyes. For a seriously tough woman, Violet always had been a crier. "I miss my best friend, Mel. While you're doing all this soul-searching, could you try to track her down?"

Well, hell. Apparently Hank wasn't the only missing person in the Brookman family.

"Fine," she muttered. "But if you tell one person that I came to Oregon to *find myself*, you will pay."

Chapter 16

WHEN WYATT STROLLED INTO THE BULL DANCER ON Thursday evening, there was a customer sitting at the bar. Which, in itself, wasn't a complete shock. Tourists did occasionally wander in off the street. Wyatt got a vague impression of silver hair and a nylon sweat suit before his gaze caught on Melanie, who wore a high ponytail and an emerald-green racer-back tank top over calf-length leggings.

Tight. Black. Leggings.

Wyatt tore his gaze off her butt, which was planted on the stool next to the lone and—now that he managed to look past the leggings—familiar customer. Both were sipping tall glasses of ice water.

"Hey, boss man." Louie grinned from where he leaned against the back bar, arms folded, either participating or shamelessly eavesdropping on the conversation. "We got us a packed house."

Melanie swiveled on her stool and…smiled? His heart bumped up against his ribs at the unexpected warmth. "Wyatt! I was hoping you'd stop by. You know Mister Hadrich. We ran into each other on the river trail…which is lovely, by the way. He knows all kinds of interesting stories about this place."

Her Texas twang was in full bloom, along with that smile, which she transferred to the old man. Wyatt's heart plunked back into place. This wasn't personal.

This was Melanie in full PR mode. She wouldn't sneer at him in front of a potential…what? Did she have any idea that the man she'd dragged in off the street was no harmless senior citizen?

Wyatt extended a hand. "Nice to see you again, Mister Hadrich."

"Please. Just call me Gordon." His fingers felt brittle, but his grip was strong.

"Join us." With a subtle slant of her eyes, she indicated that Wyatt should take the seat on the other side of their guest. "Gordon has seen a lot of things come and go in this town. I've been picking his brain about what he thinks is missing."

Beneath wiry white brows, Gordon's eyes twinkled at Wyatt as he sat down. "Being a widower for the past nine years, I told her I wouldn't mind if you brought back the original menu."

Wyatt laughed, immediately charming as always. "City Hall informed me that they stopped issuing licenses for brothels back in the fifties."

"I know." Gordon sighed nostalgically. "But this place was something else until then. Especially for an eighteen-year-old ranch boy fresh in out of the hills."

Melanie pressed a shocked palm to her chest. "Gordon! You didn't tell me you were a client."

"Only when I could afford it," the old man said with a wink.

"What else do you miss?" Wyatt asked.

Gordon gave a slight, sad smile. "My wife, most of all. Did you ever meet her?"

"I did. She was a lovely lady."

"From Tennessee. I miss that most of all, I think.

Her voice." The smile widened slightly as he patted Melanie's arm. "Talking to this one…"

He stopped, pressing his lips together as if he couldn't put the sentiment into words. Then he visibly shook off his melancholy and took a look around the bar. "There were plenty of Southern belles working here, back in the day. Can't say how many of them were actually born in the next county, but the boys did love those accents. During World War II, when the airport was a training center for pilots, Madam Beverly brought in a cook—a widow from one of the local ranches. Every week she'd make a big Sunday dinner, the girls would dress like they were going to church, and all those homesick fly-boys could eat for free."

And come back on Friday to visit those same, sweet girls who'd been waved under their noses. But Wyatt wouldn't spoil the old man's fond memories by pointing out an inspired marketing scheme disguised as patriotism.

"Wow," Melanie said. "That's…brilliant."

Gordon and Louie both burst out laughing.

"Not the sentimental type, I see." Gordon gave her an approving nod. "Or a fool."

Wyatt saw a flash of bitterness before Melanie ducked her head.

"I'll give you the first one. The second…" She shrugged.

Gordon tilted his head, his still-canny gaze taking in her profile. After a moment, he gave a soft *hmmff*. "We've all been fools at one time or another. I tend to be more concerned about a person who makes a habit of it."

"I try to stay in the *fool me once* category," she said with a wry twist of her mouth.

Gordon tilted his water glass to clink it against hers. "That's the best I've ever been able to do."

She shot him a grateful smile, lifting her head and squaring her shoulders. "I am so glad I decided to go for a jog this afternoon. Can we do it again?"

"I would be honored. Give me a call. I don't usually get out of the house until after nine in the morning." He gestured to Louie. "If you'll hand me one of those matchbooks…"

Louie reached into a small cardboard box beside the cash register and pulled out a pen and one of the matchbooks left behind by the previous owner.

Gordon grinned. "Been a long time since I wrote my number in one of these for a pretty girl." He scribbled the digits and presented it to Melanie with a flourish. She clutched it to her heart and fluttered her lashes, drawing a chuckle from the old man, then tucked it into a concealed pocket on the side of her tank top. Gordon slid off his stool and paused to give the bar another once-over. "If you brought back the Sunday dinners, I might be persuaded to share my wife's recipe for Southern-fried chicken."

"I'll put it on my list," Melanie promised.

She and Wyatt both walked with him to the door, and stood just outside watching until he reached the end of the block and turned left onto the paved trail running the length of the dike that protected the downtown area from flooding of the Umatilla River. Melanie leaned against the brick wall and tilted her head back. Wyatt saw her eyes widen the instant she caught sight of the inscription on the building across the street.

Hadrich Blk 1902.

"Is that…?" she asked.

"Yep." Wyatt allowed himself to enjoy her consternation. "They own that whole block. And the next one. Plus various other properties around town, and more farm and ranch acreage in Umatilla and Morrow counties than any other private entity."

Her jaw sagged as she stared at the name, etched in stone. "But I thought…I mean, he's so…he gave me Tootsie Rolls."

"He's a very nice man. He just happens to also be the retired CEO of a multimillion-dollar family corporation."

"Oh my God." She pressed a hand to her heart. "And here I was, feeling sorry for this poor, lonely old soul and wondering if I should have Louie get sandwiches for after our walk tomorrow."

"He is definitely not poor. Lonely? Probably. But he's got eight grandkids playing every sport they offer at school. He never misses a game or a meet, so he's not exactly sitting home alone. And he keeps Grace stocked up on Tootsie Rolls, too."

Melanie rolled her head to look at him, her gaze so intent it made him want to step back. "You admire him."

"Why wouldn't I?" Wyatt had to fight not to break eye contact. The question was like a dentist's probe, poking for tender spots while she measured his reaction. What did she expect to see? "Gordon was—still is—a savvy businessman who has reinvested his money in this community and raised three equally smart and socially responsible children. But he's still a gentleman. And…a gentle man. You don't find many like him."

Melanie studied him for another beat. Then she gave

the slightest nod and went back to staring up at the name chiseled into the building.

When she remained silent, Wyatt angled her a glance. "Did you learn anything useful?"

"From Gordon?" Her brows puckered thoughtfully. "He gave me some ideas, but I can't come up with a plan until I know what *you* want."

"I've already told you."

"Uh-huh." She pushed away from the wall and fished the apartment key from one of those invisible pockets. "Which will require further discussion, but this evening is too gorgeous to waste sitting around town. I'm going to go put on some jeans and drive up to the highest spot I can find to watch the sunset. Want to come?"

He did a double take. "With you?"

"Unless you'd rather head to different places and chat on the phone?"

"No! I mean, with you is fine." He had to pause, unnerved by the invitation. He'd assumed she was being friendly for Gordon's benefit, but the old man was long gone and here she was, inviting him to go for a drive. With her. Alone.

"Is something wrong?" he blurted.

She paused, key in the door. "Nothing new. Why?"

"You're being nice to me." He narrowed his eyes. "What's the catch?"

"No catch," she said breezily.

Too breezy. Too friendly. A thought struck him. He stepped closer, grabbed her chin to turn her face toward him, and leaned in close to stare directly into her eyes. Her pupils looked normal, but still… "Did that cow hit you in the head yesterday?"

Her breath caught, and he realized how close they were. Noses almost touching, his mouth so close—

"*I* am fine," she said, refusing in true Melanie style to pull away. "But if you don't back off, I can arrange for *you* to have a head injury, and I'm not talking about the one on your shoulders."

He dropped his hand and gave her physical space, but kept the pressure on with his gaze. "What are you plotting?"

"Nothing!" She jammed her key in the apartment door and cranked hard enough that he feared it would snap off in the lock. "It has been brought to my attention that my work situation has had a negative effect on my personality. To paraphrase, I'm sort of a bitch, *and* I'm no fun anymore. That is not the person I want to be, so I'm going to change…beginning now."

"With me."

"Might as well tackle the toughest job first." Then she grimaced, recognizing the insult buried in her declaration. "And it's gonna take some work. Old habits and all that."

Wyatt folded his arms over a heart that had accelerated to double time. He could barely keep his hands off her when she was sniping at him. If she started being civil…

He lifted sardonic eyebrows. "I'm supposed to believe that all of the sudden bygones are bygones?"

"I admit, it's a stretch." One corner of her mouth curled. "But like they say, fake it until you make it."

And despite the sexual awareness that crackled between them, she had to fake liking him. He swallowed, the knowledge burning all the way down, landing in his gut where it could eat yet another hole. When would he learn? He and Gabrielle had had enough chemistry to set off an atom bomb, and look how that had worked out. And since she'd been happily remarried for years, it was fairly obvious which of them was impossible to live with.

He turned away abruptly. "Grab a coat. It'll get cold by sunset."

She disappeared through the door, and Wyatt could hear her taking the stairs two at a time, leaving him to cool his heels on the sidewalk. He should walk down to the deli and have them throw together some sandwiches, potato salad…

Three steps down the street, he changed his mind and walked to the trunk of his car instead. Besides the duffel that held his bullfighting gear, he kept a second, emergency bag packed with jeans, a long-sleeved T-shirt and a sweatshirt, all of which had seen better days but were perfect for roadside emergencies—and impromptu hikes. He grabbed the bag and went into the bar to change.

When he came out, Melanie was leaning against the side of the building. She'd pulled a thin, zippered hoodie over her tank top and donned jeans faded to white in places, worn so soft they clung to her butt and legs with the familiarity of an old friend.

Or lover.

She had a jacket draped over one arm and a small, backpack-style purse slung over her shoulder. Her eyebrows shot up when she saw him. "Good Lord. I didn't know you owned clothes that old."

He was unable to stop himself from covering a grease

stain on the sweatshirt with his palm. "There you go, obsessing over my wardrobe again."

"Whatever." She rolled her eyes and straightened. "My car or yours?"

"You have to ask?" Wyatt sneered at her SUV.

She eyed the keys that dangled from his fingers. "Can I drive?"

He turned his hand over, cradling the keys in his palm as if he was considering it. Then he tossed them in the air and snatched them again with a quick, hard laugh.

"You're gonna have to fake it a lot better than that before you get your hands on this baby."

She lifted a brow. "If I was really trying to fake it, I guarantee you would never know the difference."

Then she sauntered down the block to the Camaro, leaving him to scrape his tongue up off the sidewalk.

Chapter 17

DAMN HER SMART MOUTH.

Just because he left her an opening a mile wide didn't mean she had to jump through with both feet. Wyatt hadn't said a single word since they got in the car... thank God. There was no possible segue to that insanely inappropriate remark that wouldn't make matters worse, no matter which of them tried.

Better to bite their tongues and ignore the elephant turning pirouettes on the console between them.

The heat of the sun still lingered in the black leather seats of the Camaro, but the long shadows thrown across Main Street by the lowering sun had cooled the interior to a temperature just warm enough to magnify the scents of warm car and hot man. Melanie caught herself squeezing her knees together in response. Damn Wyatt for being even sexier in faded, grubby jeans that fit his remarkable ass to perfection and, worst of all, made him look almost normal.

Like something she could not only have, but keep.

"We'll have to swing by and feed the horses. And can we hit a drive-through on the way?" she asked as the seductive power of the car vibrated through every fiber of her body.

"I ordered subs. And I had them put the condiments on the side so you could add what you want. Is that okay?"

That was wonderful. Efficient. And maddening, the

way he was always one thought ahead of her. "Great," she said.

The deli was located inside a convenience store. While Wyatt put gas in the car, Melanie wandered the aisles, picking out baked all-natural multigrain chips, then a bag of mini-Oreos so her system didn't go into shock from all that healthiness. She added a couple of bottles of raspberry-flavored sweet tea and a pack of spearmint gum. As she paid the cashier and stashed everything in her pack, Wyatt came in to get his order from the deli. The bag the starry-eyed high school girl passed over the counter looked as if it held enough sandwiches to feed them for a week.

Wyatt handed it to Melanie as they walked to the car. She peeked inside. "Hungry?"

"Yes. And I don't know what you like, so I ordered four different kinds."

Once again, thinking of everything. "Are we allowed to eat in the car?"

"That depends." He shot her an almost-grin as he circled the hood to the driver's side. "How messy are you?"

Her pulse skittered, and she fumbled the bag as she reached for the door latch. If he kept that up, her self-control was gonna end up scattered like crumbs. That would be bad. Very bad. For reasons that got a little vague when she settled into her seat and inhaled another lungful of man-scent.

She tried to focus on the town as they continued east, past the towering concrete silos of Pendleton Flour Mills. "I have to stop by the Pendleton Woolen Mills outlet store. The crib blanket you gave Violet and Joe is amazing."

"The design is called Sons of the Sky. It's Kiowa. The stars and rainbows celebrate the child's birth, and the turtle amulet is for protection. Its hard shell guards the child's spirit and ensures a long, protected life."

"That's cool. My mother has Kiowa blood."

Wyatt gave her face a thorough inspection as he stopped in the turning lane and waited for a grain truck to pass from the opposite direction. "I can see it. You have the bone structure."

"Uh…thanks?"

He turned his attention back to the road. Within a few minutes, they wheeled into the driveway to his acreage. After the practice session that morning, he'd given her the full tour, showing her how to turn on the sprinklers to irrigate the small pasture the two horses now shared with the cows and providing her with a key to the storage shed where they'd stashed her tack.

When they'd tossed hay into the feeders, Wyatt and Melanie climbed back in the car, but instead of turning toward the interstate, he whipped the Camaro onto a highway headed north, his hand loose on the gearshift as he accelerated past a sign that declared they were en route to Walla Walla, Washington.

She leaned forward to scan the road ahead. "I thought we were going up the mountain."

He twisted his wrist so she could see his watch, the hands reading just past seven. "Sunset won't be for another hour and a half, so I thought we'd drive up to Tollgate. You can see some of the countryside on the way."

As they drove, he pointed out anything he thought might interest her. Mile by mile, she relaxed as he carried on a running monologue. The depth and breadth of his knowledge about the area was astounding. He explained how salt brine was used to grade the sweet peas just now flowering in the fields, separating them based on whether they floated or sank, then told how the town of Athena came to be named after a Greek goddess but had a high school band that featured Scottish bagpipes—all delivered with a wry thread of affection.

Wyatt had told her one undeniable truth during their dinner. He loved this place. It shone in his eyes, and made it nearly impossible to tear *her* eyes off of him.

When they turned off Highway 11 toward the mountains, he gestured to the horizontal bands of dark brown that circled their flanks. "That's basalt, laid down by lava flows when the Cascades were full of active volcanoes, then buried in silt by the massive floods at the end of the last ice age. This is some of the richest topsoil in the world. They grow close to hundred-bushel-an-acre dryland wheat here."

Melanie settled in to enjoy the scenery *outside* the car as the highway was quickly swallowed up by a pine-filled canyon that wound into the flanks of the mountains. A creek splashed alongside, over more of the chunky, brown lava rock that the water had cut into sheer walls in places.

"Usually mountains are formed by an upthrust that pushes the rock to the top," Wyatt said. "Here, the layers of soil were so thick it never made it to the surface, which is why they look like big dirt hills sitting on a rock foundation. Because of the sun and prevailing wind, the trees are almost all on the north-facing slopes, in case you need to orient yourself when you're hiking."

She threw him a squinty-eyed look. "Are you

planning to dump me out here to see if the flatlander can find her way home?"

"I don't even have a spot picked out to shove you off a cliff." His voice was laced with exasperation. "It was your idea to drive up to the top of a mountain—and drag me along. If anyone should be paranoid…"

Especially when she'd managed to insult him twice in the process of inviting him. *Fake it until you make it.* Gah.

Since she couldn't seem to open her mouth without something asinine falling out, she retreated back into silence. Eventually, the narrow highway emerged onto a flat where the trees were interspersed with wide meadows. Wyatt turned off before they reached the cluster of buildings that formed the community of Tollgate. In deference to the Camaro, he bumped slowly along the crumbling asphalt and then gravel as their route became less of a road and more of a track. It opened into a turn-around above a maze of canyons even steeper and narrower than the one they'd driven up.

Wyatt parked at the edge of the deserted parking area. "High enough for you?"

"It's stunning." As she stepped out of the car, the breeze caught her hair and feathered it across her face. The view was incredible. Intimidating.

And so *not* Texas.

Without waiting for Wyatt, she ducked her head, slung her pack over her shoulder, and strode off on the beaten dirt path marked *Trailhead*. The tight knot of homesickness loosened at the scent of pine, fresh grass, and damp earth.

Deep breath.

All in all, things were going better than she'd had reason to hope—other than the lack of progress in finding Hank, and it had only been a week since she'd officially put Wyatt on his trail. There'd also been nothing new in the way of communication from Westwind, and Violet had reported that the opinion at the warehouse was generally in Melanie's favor with a sprinkling of derogatory comments from, in Gil Sanchez's expert assessment, "the dickwads she wouldn't sleep with."

Melanie could tick them off on her fingers, which made her smile, just a little.

"How far does this go?" she called back to Wyatt.

"Ten miles."

Oh. She slowed a little, taking stock.

"They call this Coyote Ridge," Wyatt said, so close behind that she jumped and tripped over an exposed root.

His hand shot out to catch her elbow, steady her, then immediately let go before she could shake him off. The path was too narrow to walk abreast. She was so conscious of his gaze on her back—her butt?—that her steps felt jerky, although the stiff muscles from her adventures in cow fighting didn't help.

"Why am I leading the way?" she asked.

"You went first."

"What if I take a wrong turn?"

"Just stay right when the main trail switches back and heads downhill."

Their trail continued along the narrow razorback, with enough holes, roots, and chunky, sharp-edged rock that Melanie didn't dare let her gaze wander from where she was setting her feet. Behind her, the scuff of Wyatt's shoes was barely audible. The man was sneaky quiet.

When the trail dead-ended at the point of the ridge, she paused, studying the two canyons that merged at the bottom of the long, steep hill at her feet, strewn with rock, hummocks of grass, and the occasional scrubby, wind-blown tree. Near the base, the slope ended abruptly in a cliff, the rock exposed and cut through by centuries of floods. The breeze had picked up, making her wish she'd tied her hair back.

Wyatt came alongside and held out the jacket she'd left in the car. "You'll need this before long."

"Thank you." She tied the sleeves around her waist for the moment.

Wyatt had a larger day-hiker's pack and the bag of sandwiches. He waved toward a table-sized flat rock. "We can sit over there."

They did, both facing west but slightly away from each other, and lapsed into a surprisingly mellow silence, content to enjoy the murmur of pine boughs, the calls of birds she didn't recognize, and the distant splash of water from the bottom of the canyon.

She polished off the last bite of her cold-cut combo and stood to brush the crumbs off her sweatshirt before pulling on her coat. As Wyatt had predicted, the air had cooled quickly, although the breeze had also died to a mere rustle in the knee-high bunches of grass. Beyond the broad north-south valley that held the main highway, the sun hung low over a smaller range of hills that would lie north and west of Pendleton. If she remembered correctly from her map, the massive Columbia River must be just beyond that rise, flowing east through the Tri-Cities of Pasco, Kennewick, and Richland, Washington, then making a sweeping U-turn back to the west, forming the border between the states on its way to the Pacific.

Mentally adding the Columbia Gorge to her *must-see* list, Melanie slung her pack over her shoulder and, drawn by what sounded like a small waterfall, picked her way down through the trees on the sheltered side of the ridge, only to be brought up short by one of the thick bands of lava rock. The cliff wasn't high—ten or fifteen feet—but it extended as far as she could see in either direction. The splash of water seemed to be directly below her, so she eased as close as she dared and peered over the crumbling edge of the cliff.

"Be careful," Wyatt said, practically in her ear.

She squeaked, startled, and jumped back, colliding with a hard male body. Her elbow caught him in the ribs. He grunted and sidestepped—directly onto one of the loose rocks. His leg buckled, and he stumbled. For a heart-stopping instant he teetered at the edge of the cliff. Just as Melanie made a grab for him, the unstable rock gave way.

She caught nothing but thin air as he fell. With a curse and a clatter, he was gone.

Melanie listened in horror to a thud, another curse, and the unmistakable sound of a body hitting something solid. And then there was silence.

"Wyatt?" She dropped to her belly to peer over the edge, but couldn't see past the trees and shadows. "*Wyatt!*"

The second was on the verge of a shriek as panic clamped an icy hand on her throat. *Oh God, oh God, oh God*. She scooted along the cliff, squinting into the trees, but in his faded jeans and gray sweatshirt, he was invisible in the shadows beneath the trees.

"Wyatt!" she shouted again. She heard what might

have been a groan—or the wind through the trees. No other sound or movement. She scrambled to her feet, glancing first up the hill, then over the cliff. Did she run back to the car and race into town for help? No. Wait. Wyatt had the keys. She doubted he had a spare set hidden inside the bumper. *He* was smarter than that. She clawed her phone out of her pocket. No signal, of course.

There was only one option. She had to get down there. He could be bleeding. He could be...

Melanie shook off that thought and crab-walked along the edge, looking for a likely set of hand- and footholds. A few feet from where Wyatt had gone over, a large pine grew on the edge, its roots extending down the cliff. Below, the rock face was pocked with holes and jagged points. She lowered onto her belly, took a deep breath, then grabbed the root and swung her legs over the edge. For a terrifying moment she dangled, legs flailing. Then her feet found purchase.

Slowly—*too slow, dammit*—she lowered herself, the rough bark of the root digging into her palms. Her descent was an agonizing crawl, fear and adrenaline pounding through her veins and accelerating her heart rate into the red zone. She had to fight the urge to rush. She'd be no good to Wyatt if she fell, too. The muscles in her toes cramped from grasping at the slippery footholds, testing each before trusting it with her weight.

And wondering—damn her self-centered mind—if Tori knew a good defense attorney, too, because no one was going to believe she'd done this by accident.

She was over halfway down when she heard another groan. Her heart leapt—and her foot slipped. For an instant she hung, cursing as her toes scratched desperately for purchase. Her shoe caught on a lip of rock. She clasped the root to her chest and flattened against the cliff face, panting from terror and exertion.

"Mel—" This groan was louder, but distinctly her name. Wyatt was alive and conscious. Relief blasted through her.

"I'm coming! I'll be there in just a minute."

"No, don't—"

She eased down another step...and the rock beneath her foot gave way. She dropped, hitched for an instant, then the force of her weight snapped the root. There was an instant of *Oh shit, this is gonna hurt* before her butt hit the ground. The impact jarred every molecule in her body and made stars burst behind her eyes. Her legs bounced, flipping her backward down the steep incline. She threw her arms up to cushion the back of her head against rocks and branches, twisting sideways just as she crashed into a huge fallen log—and something that grunted in pain.

She lay on her stomach, eyes squeezed shut, braced for the searing pain of a broken bone. It didn't come. As the universe slowly righted itself, she took inventory. She felt the deep throb of bruises, the burn of scrapes, but when she inhaled, her rib cage expanded right on cue. She let the breath out in a rush and opened her eyes to discover that the log under her cheek was actually a hard, denim-clad thigh.

"Melanie?" Her name was a harsh wheeze.

She lifted her head to meet his gaze. Wyatt was sprawled on his back, struggling to take in air—and her nose was buried in his crotch.

And damn his eternal soul, those blue eyes were laughing.

Chapter 18

MOST WOMEN WOULD HAVE BLUSHED AND SCRAMBLED AWAY. Not Melanie. She just glared at Wyatt as if he'd somehow done this on purpose, then slowly levered herself onto her hands and knees, still planted between his legs.

"If you're gonna scare the shit out of me, you should at least be bleeding." She eyed him balefully. "How bad are you hurt?"

Not as bad as it could have been, considering he'd fallen off a cliff. Well, slid, mostly. He'd managed to throw his upper body onto the edge, scrabbling at enough handholds to slow his fall, but he'd still hit pretty damn hard.

Despite that, he could barely keep from grinning at her irritated reaction to his possible injuries. She was such a cowgirl.

He took a careful breath, the first normal one he'd managed since the log had slammed the air out of his lungs. His side stung, but he'd broken ribs before, and this wasn't that kind of pain. "Just banged up a little."

"Says the guy who worked three more performances at Salinas after dislocating his shoulder. Be more specific."

She remembered his injury from four years ago? Apparently, he wasn't the only one who'd been paying attention. "It knocked the air out of me, I've got a knot on back of my skull, and I turned my ankle. What about you?"

She rocked back onto her haunches and shoved her hair out of her face. "Scrapes and bruises. Can you sit up?"

"Yes."

She held out a hand. He paused a beat, then took it, her grip firm, steady...and all too brief. Once seated, he pulled his knees up and rested his elbows on them.

"Which ankle?" Melanie asked, grimacing as she lowered herself to sit facing him.

"The same as always." He lifted his toes, and a hot shaft of pain shot up his leg. Shit. That wasn't good. "I usually wear a brace when I'm hiking, but I didn't take the time to put it on tonight."

He'd been too busy chasing after a woman.

Melanie's eyebrows drew together in concern. "Are you going to be able to climb out of here?"

"No."

She took a few beats to absorb that, then nodded. "I'll climb up and—"

"No, you won't." He pointed at the cliff. "I explored this canyon last summer. That band of rock runs the full length without a break. I had to go all the way back around the point."

"How long did it take?"

"Over two hours to get to the main trail on the other side of the ridge." Scrambling along the creek the whole way, over deadfall and boulders.

She tipped her head back to gaze at the narrow slice of visible sky, where the last rays of the sun speared through a wispy layer of clouds. In another half an hour, they'd be in complete darkness in the depths of the canyon. "Well...shit."

"Yep."

He studied their surroundings. Below the log that had broken their fall—and he wasn't sure it had done him any favors—towering pines marched down to the creek, the glimmer of water visible between their trunks.

"Looks like tough going," Melanie said, following his gaze. "We probably shouldn't risk it in the dark, especially with you having a bad wheel."

"Nope."

She squinted into the dusk, weighing their options. The ground they would have to traverse to get down to the creek was steep, littered with moss-coated rocks and rotting logs. His ankle throbbed at the sight. The descent was going to be a killer.

"What happens if you don't get home tonight?" she asked.

"No one is expecting me until the eight o'clock practice session tomorrow morning."

Her chin dropped, and she stared down between her knees. "It could be days before anyone realized I was gone."

"I'd miss you." When her head jerked up, he hastily added, "If you didn't wander into the bar some time tomorrow, Louie and I would notice."

Her mouth twisted. "Well, that warms the old cockles. Can you walk?"

"I'll manage."

She gave him a narrow-eyed look, then eased to her feet and over the rocks to where her pack had fallen. Wyatt's was still on his back. He shrugged it off and unzipped the main compartment, cursing when he reached inside and found cold slime. The leftover sandwiches had cushioned some of his fall, but the plastic tubs of mayonnaise and mustard had exploded. The lens on the flashlight in the side pocket was shattered. His aluminum water bottle had survived with only a dent.

He opened one of the side compartments to pull out the ever-present roll of self-adherent bandage. Before he could hitch up the leg of his jeans to inspect the damage, Melanie returned.

She dropped her pack and plucked the bandage out of his hand. "I've got this."

"You know how?"

"In four years of varsity basketball and volleyball you sprain a few ankles, and we didn't exactly have a crack sports medicine team on hand at good ol' Earnest High School."

She grabbed the cuff of his jeans and swung his leg around to prop it on a rock. He had to resist the urge to yank it away, not accustomed to being managed.

Instead, he asked, "You played varsity as a ninth grader?"

"The competition for starting spots isn't that stiff when there's only twenty kids in your grade." She carefully peeled off his sock, then applied an expert figure-eight wrap around his ankle.

"Violet said you could have played basketball in college."

"I got a couple of offers." She finished the wrap, tore off the excess bandage with a practiced twist of her wrist, and smoothed the loose end so it stuck down. "They wouldn't let me rodeo if I was playing ball. And Colorado and Arizona were too far away."

From what? Home? Friends? Or…

"Afraid to let Hank out of your sight?" Then he grimaced. "Sorry. That was uncalled for."

"So was that crack I made about you saving everyone else. Let's just call it even, okay?" Her face was in shadow, her voice neutral as she stood. "If you soak that in the creek, it'll keep the swelling down."

When she held out her hand, he took it, letting her pull him to his feet. Upright, he tested his theory and found that yes, it hurt like a bitch. He'd fought bulls with worse, but he'd also had it both taped and braced and was working on a groomed surface.

They crawled over the log, and then Melanie grabbed his wrist, ducked under his arm, and wrapped it around her shoulders, cinching her other arm firmly around his waist. "Lean on me as much as you need."

His mind blanked out at the unexpected press of her body against his, the wildflower scent of her hair filling his head. He closed his eyes and breathed in even deeper. Maybe they could just stay like this…

She nudged him with her hip. "Ready?"

No, but he took a step…and hissed involuntarily.

Melanie yanked on his wrist. "What part of *Lean on me* do you not understand?"

The part where he had to relax enough to let at least some of his weight settle on her shoulders? He gritted his teeth and took another tentative step. His foot skidded on the slick layer of pine needles, and he swore again. By the tenth step he forgot about pride and lust—mostly—and leaned heavily against her.

They managed half a dozen more steps before she tripped over a rock and pitched forward. Wyatt threw an arm around a smallish tree to stop them both from tumbling face-first down the hill. Grunting from the effort, he hauled her around—and smack up against him. Her startled eyes registered the fact that one of her palms was plastered to his chest, his arm locked behind her shoulders and his hand dangerously close to cupping her breast.

For a few beats they remained motionless, their combined breath a hot cloud between them. He let his hand slide down to her waist, his head bowing in an irresistible urge to taste…

She eased away a few inches. "Whew. That was close."

He wasn't sure if she meant the near-fall or how he'd very nearly kissed her. This was why he'd been insane to bring her here. Well, not specifically *this*, because who in their right mind would have guessed they'd end up trapped in a freaking canyon together?

She angled around, repositioning herself under his arm, and they started again. They were both sweating and panting when they staggered to a stop at the side of the creek. Melanie helped him ease down onto a flat rock, then lowered herself onto a log with a thankful groan. "Are you sure you can walk out of here tomorrow?"

"Yes." He *would* manage somehow. He'd crawl out on his hands and knees before he sent her ahead for a rescue squad and became one of *those idiot hikers*. Wyatt eased off his shoe to run his fingers lightly over the bubble of swelling around his anklebone.

"How bad is it?" she asked. "Honestly."

"About a four out of ten. I'll soak it off and on all night, plus I have these." He unzipped another small pocket in his backpack, retrieved a bottle of extra-strength ibuprofen, and gave it a shake. "Need some?"

"God, yes. I'm gonna have a bruise on my ass the size of Fort Worth." She held out her hand to let him tap a couple of tablets into her palm, then pulled the remainder of a bottle of tea from her pack to wash them down. "You chill…literally." She flashed a quick smile at her own joke. "I'll make camp."

He pulled one of the empty plastic sandwich bags over his foot to keep the wrap dry, scooted over, and lowered his foot into the biting cold mountain water. *Ahhh!* People thought bullfighters were addicted to adrenaline. In reality, they were hooked on ice—the cure for everything that ached.

Beside him, Melanie rustled around in her pack, taking inventory. "I've got another full bottle of tea and a bag of cookies. You've got water and sandwiches. It might not be exactly balmy tonight, but we're not gonna die of hypothermia."

He had nothing to add, so he just nodded.

She pulled something out of her little pack and stuck it in the pocket of her jeans. Then she dug around some more and came out with a set of car keys that jingled and flashed silver in the gloom. An instant later, Wyatt had to scrunch his eyes against a bright pinpoint of LED light.

"Key chain flashlight," she said. "We gave them away to clients at Christmas, and I snagged one for myself."

The beam was small, but allowed her to prowl the immediate area. Twigs snapped under her feet as she pushed through a patch of brush to move down the creek bank. "Anything useful in your pack?" she asked.

"A plastic rain poncho and a butane lighter, but it's full of mayonnaise."

"Damn. A fire would've been—" She stopped abruptly, then the light shot into the air, clutched in her triumphant fist. "God bless you, Gordon. I still have that book of matches in my pocket."

She disappeared for a few moments, then the flashlight swung back toward him. "There's a better spot over here. Nice and flat, and there's even an old fire ring from other campers. I'll gather what wood I can break off those dead trees. You should be good and numb by the time I'm done."

Not to mention exploding from frustration. He'd rarely felt so useless. Worse—a liability. He ground his teeth, swallowing the helpful suggestions that were the only contribution he could make, certain they would not be appreciated.

So Wyatt just sat there, one more lump in the dark while Melanie crashed around in the underbrush, her light bobbing like a firefly among the trees. And dammit, now that the pain in his ankle was ebbing, his body had decided to replay every sensation of rubbing up against Melanie, and the baser parts of his brain were chiming in with all the ways he could keep her warm tonight.

He dumped out his pack and began rinsing mayonnaise and mustard off the contents. Melanie passed by three times, her arms loaded, then returned to squat beside him, propping the light so it illuminated the space between them. "Had enough?"

And more. He pulled his foot out the water and peeled off the plastic bag. She picked up his sock and reached for his foot.

He snatched both out of her grasp. "I can dress myself," he snapped, sounding peevish and ungrateful.

"Fine." She shot to her feet, and for an instant he thought she might kick him. And that he deserved it. "I assume you can also get your cranky ass over to the campsite."

She left him to try. But she also, intentionally or not, left the little flashlight.

Chapter 19

OF ALL THE ASININE, UNGRATEFUL...

Melanie propped one end of a good-sized branch on a rock and stomped on it to break it in half. And then she remembered why Wyatt had needed her assistance to begin with and swore under her breath. Okay, yes, he had good reason to be put out with her. It was just so unlike him to let it show.

Then again, it was even more unlike him to not be in charge.

Her irritation faded, pushed aside by a smile. He was pretty much at her mercy, and he *hated* not being in control. It made him grouchy. And oddly more likable. Human, almost. She cocked her head, listening to the sounds of his painfully slow progress along the creek bank, as she contemplated their accommodations for the night.

Directly in front of her, a shoulder-high wall of rock extended from the hillside almost to the creek bank. Large blocks had fractured off and been pushed aside by either the forces of nature or humans who'd come before them, leaving a ninety-degree niche. They were far from the first to appreciate the natural shelter it provided. The ground at its base was packed almost smooth and cleared of rocks, the ring of stones black with soot.

With the rock wall at her back and the fire at her feet, she might just be able to shake off the prickling sensation of eyes watching her from darkness that became more impenetrable with every passing minute. She crouched beside the fire ring, struck a match, and held it to the bottom of a tripod of tiny, dry twigs, gratified when the flame immediately took hold. One by one, she carefully fed in larger twigs until she had a merry little blaze going.

The sharp crack of a branch made her flinch, and she whirled around as Wyatt emerged from the bushes, a long, straight branch clutched in one hand as a makeshift cane. His face was sheened with sweat from pain and, she suspected, the effort not to let her see how much it hurt. In his grubby jeans and sweatshirt, with his hair rumpled and a streak of dirt down the side of his neck, he was hardly recognizable as the man who'd greeted her when she arrived in Pendleton.

She willed her racing heart to just give it a rest, and gestured toward the pile of pine needles she'd scraped together in the rock niche. "Have a seat on our couch."

As Wyatt hobbled around and sank down with a nearly silent sigh of relief, she laid a larger branch on the fire.

"What time is it?" she asked.

He squinted at his watch. "Almost ten."

"And the sun rises at…"

"Around five. But it's light enough to get out on my bike by four thirty." He spoke with the assurance of a man who had done it. By choice. *Geezus*.

So…seven hours until daylight. Alone in the freaking wilderness with Wyatt and the knowledge that all of those muscles felt just as good as they looked, and his body put off more heat than her slowly growing fire.

That was *so* not going to happen. Thanks to Michael, she was already enough of a cliché. She would not add *We only got naked to stay warm...I swear*.

She started to toss a short, smooth chunk of wood onto the fire, then stopped, turning it over in her hands before eyeing Wyatt's walking stick. "How are you at whittling?"

"What?" He looked at her as if she'd spoken in tongues.

"You know, that thing old men do on front porches while they gossip about the neighbors?" She made a carving gesture before holding up her piece of wood. "This is the right size and shape. Make a hole in the side of it and a peg on the end of your stick, put them together, and you'll have a decent crutch. While you work on that one, I'll find the pieces to make another."

"Good idea," he said, grudgingly, as if annoyed that he hadn't thought of it first.

And maybe, if what the old men said was true, the work would soothe the grumpy beast. She stood, sucking in a breath as her various bumps and bruises made their presence known. Visions of the slipper tub and that sinfully comfortable bed danced in her head, and she nearly groaned.

"Are you okay?" Wyatt asked, his gaze sharpening.

"I feel like I've been beaten with broomsticks, but I'm not hurt." And they both understood the difference between pain and a true injury.

She fished the multi-tool from her pocket and tossed it to him. He plucked it out of the air with one hand and leaned closer to the fire to unfold and inspect the various attachments—four different screwdrivers, bottle and can openers, even a corkscrew—then folded the two halves around and tested the result.

"I should get one of these," he said, opening and closing the pliers.

"You'd be amazed how often it comes in handy. Just last week, I used it to fix a loose handle on my drawer..." On the desk that wasn't hers anymore. She scowled into the fire. "Hank gave it to me. He said I needed to be ready for emergency wine parties."

Wyatt was silent for a long moment. When she looked up, he was staring down at the tool in his hands, and she knew he wasn't thinking about how much he wanted a good Chardonnay.

"Have you found anything?" she asked quietly.

"I know where he's not, and where he hasn't been. And that covers damn near every rodeo from California to North Carolina." His forehead knotted in frustration. "I'm missing something. Another place he could be working that's outside my usual contacts."

Finally, surrounded by black emptiness as deep as a grave, she gave voice to her darkest fear. "You don't think he might be—"

"No." The denial was reassuringly abrupt. "He got himself into some kind of a bind, and he's too proud to ask you for help. Now that the summer rodeos are starting, he'll show up somewhere."

The devil made her point out the flaw in his argument. "Wouldn't you have heard if he'd signed on anywhere?"

"If it was a pro rodeo. But there are all the regional associations, high school rodeos, open rodeos, unsanctioned bull-riding events..." He shook his head. "Even I can't keep track of all of them. There's enough contestant crossover between all the different levels, though…someone will see him."

"While we just wait?"

Wyatt took the time to compose his answer, which meant he was deciding what parts of the truth to tell. "I've made other inquiries. If he's had any issues with his finances, or with the law…"

In other words, if Hank was in jail and hadn't bothered to use his one phone call to ask his sister or any of his friends to post bail, or if he was hiding from debt collectors. Dark possibilities slithered through her mind—a drunken car accident, an enraged husband, a bookie looking to collect on an overly ambitious bet. So many ways a man could get in serious trouble when he had a habit of acting first and thinking later.

"Melanie. Don't." Wyatt's voice was almost gentle. "There could be a perfectly reasonable explanation—"

She jerked her chin up and glared at him. "I know how my brother is. *If* he's okay, chances are he's done something so bad he's ashamed to tell me."

Wyatt didn't bother to argue. She tossed the smaller piece of wood to him, and he began working out how to fit the two together. The fire was burning strong, so she added a couple of the largest logs she'd been able to scavenge. As she started to scoot around to the other side, she belatedly realized just how little space there was in that handy corner. She and Wyatt would have no choice but to sit practically hip to hip.

Or she could stay on this side. She glanced over her shoulder. The darkness pressed down around them, trailing cold fingers across the back of her neck. The weight of it seemed like more than her pitiful little fire could fend off. And here up north there were bears and cougars and even wolves in some places. How many of them prowled these mountains, waiting to leap out of the shadows?

If she asked, Wyatt could no doubt quote the statistics off the top of his head, along with their odds of being attacked.

She hesitated, then started at the hoot of an owl. She slanted a quick glance at Wyatt to see if he'd noticed and caught him looking away. *Damn.* He never missed anything. But at least he hadn't mocked her outright… yet. And if she had to choose her evils, she'd go with the one that didn't have actual claws or fangs. Wyatt looked solid. And warm, tucked back where the rock contained and reflected the heat of the fire. And he could beat off most predators with that stick.

She shuffled around to where her butt was barely on the edge of the mat of pine needles she'd made as a cushion against the hard, increasingly cold ground. If she angled her feet just right, she could keep at least a foot of space between them, with her back slightly toward him. She latched her arms around her bent knees, wincing as the bruise on her butt made its presence felt.

Time slowed to the speed of Wyatt's ancient glaciers. Once, on an impromptu overnight stay in the Palo Duro Canyon, she'd claimed she could stare into a campfire forever. Looked like she was going to get to prove it— minus Shawnee, Violet, the s'mores, and the cooler full of beer. With nothing better to occupy her mind, it danced between being painfully aware of Wyatt's nearness, the ache in her butt, and imagining cunning, hungry eyes watching her from *out there*.

She checked her phone. Three whole minutes had

passed. Only four hundred and twenty-eight to go, and no way she was going to sleep. She pulled her little notebook and a pen out of her pack and opened it to her notes. Her motives for inviting Wyatt along on what was turning out to be their version of a three-hour tour hadn't been entirely about extending the ol' olive branch. She'd also hoped to lull him into a mellow mood before launching her *Who is Wyatt Darrington?* project.

He was *not* mellow. But he was a captive subject, and she would go bonkers if she didn't do something.

She cleared her throat. "As long as we're stuck here, and there's nothing better to do…I might as well go ahead and irritate you some more."

"Are you going to start whistling some non-song over and over?"

She scrunched up her nose. "Who *does* that?"

"Joe. When he's driving, because he knows I can't strangle him while we're doing eighty on the interstate."

"No wonder he and Shawnee get along so well." She shifted, turning toward him. She needed to see his responses, not just hear them. She held up the notebook. "I have a few questions."

"I didn't realize there would be a test," he deadpanned. "I would have studied."

"This is a pop quiz. I want your first, most honest response, not what you think you should say or what I want to hear." She purposely angled her chin. "If you can manage that."

The firelight turned his hair and skin to bronze, accentuating the Greek god effect. He met her gaze without blinking. "I can if you can."

"What?"

"I'll answer any question you ask—as long as you answer them too."

"I…" She stared at him for a few beats. She had nothing to hide…exactly. But every one of these questions had been crafted to scrape away the surface and expose the truer self beneath—or so the original author claimed. On the other hand, she had started this. She could hardly back down now. "Sure. Why not?"

The equivalent of an extended version of Truth or Dare with Wyatt, in a situation where neither of them could walk away. What could possibly go wrong?

Wyatt's mind raced as he fit the pegged end of his walking stick into the hole he'd bored in the crosspiece, then set the crutch and the knife aside. What was she after? He crossed his injured ankle over the other and leaned back against the rock, lacing his fingers behind his head as if the tension wasn't taking tiny, sharp bites out of his gut. "What is the point of this test?"

"Your interest in the Bull Dancer is obviously more personal than financial." Despite her grubby jeans and tangled hair, Melanie had become every inch the professional, her accent fading in favor of more clipped tones. He suspected it was a habit she'd developed on purpose. She would know that there were people outside of Texas who equated a Southern drawl with a dip in IQ, and she wasn't one to put herself at even the slimmest disadvantage. "I've done a fairly thorough analysis of the business climate in Pendleton. This questionnaire is designed to examine your values and goals so I can develop a plan that reflects both."

Ah. He'd suspected as much. Did she realize how many of these questionnaires he'd administered and taken, both in college and in therapy? How much reading he'd done about the underlying principles? He could spin it so she'd never even suspect he was gaming her little quiz.

Or he could play it straight.

His brain stumbled a little over the idea. What if he didn't try to outguess her? What if he just…answered? This could be his chance to tell her—without actually *telling* her—why he'd done what he'd done. Made the choices she might not otherwise be able to comprehend…or forgive.

Hope glimmered faintly in his chest. If there was any path that didn't lead to exile from everything in Texas that had come to mean the world to him, this could be his first step.

She flipped a page forward, then back again, as if debating where to begin in probing his psyche. Finally, she settled on a question. "Let's start with an easy one."

Right. As if anything between them could ever be simple. But maybe, if he took a chance and let down his guard, it could at least be a little clearer.

Chapter 20

ALL OF HER QUESTIONS SEEMED MUCH TOO PERSONAL NOW. She had based the questionnaire on one she'd found on an online dating site that promised to *reveal your inner selves*, but she'd steered clear of anything with obvious romantic intent and adapted the rest to suit a business environment.

This environment was as far from businesslike as she could imagine, but Wyatt's expectant silence was stretching too long.

She cleared her throat. "Okay. First question. If you're at a karaoke bar, what song do you sing?"

"I don't."

She shot him a surprised glance. He tilted his head back and closed his eyes, looking for all the world like he was on a private beach soaking up the sun. "You can't sing?"

"I said don't, not can't. I sang in our church from the time I was eight, and I was a soloist in show choir in high school."

Of course he was. She could picture him center stage in the East Coast prep version of *Glee*. "But no karaoke?"

"Not my thing."

She tried to imagine him belting out a George Strait song to a drunken mob, but even in her mind, he refused to step up to the microphone. He stayed firmly planted with his arms folded and one of those infuriating half smiles, too cool for such foolishness.

Well. She was already annoyed, even if he wasn't. "Fine. Let's say you lost a bet and had to. What song would you pick?"

He hesitated, just an instant.

"First thought," she reminded him.

He opened his eyes to frown at her, then gave a slight shake of his head. "I was going to say the Beatles' 'Let It Be.' But that's hypocritical."

"Why?"

"I don't look to the heavens for guidance."

Rather than argue the existence of God—she was pretty sure he'd done his research and then some—she took a different tack. "That song is about Mary, who was probably a real person, if you consider the Bible as a historical document. Treating the lyrics as purely metaphorical, calling upon her memory is no different than being inspired by say…Martin Luther King Jr."

His thoughtful squint made the crows' feet around his eyes more prominent, and for a moment he looked his age. Nearly forty—and at thirty-four she wasn't so far behind. How the hell had that happened?

"You could look at it that way," he conceded. "But I'd sing something else. Maybe 'Lean on Me.'"

She snorted.

He sliced a glance at her. "What?"

"That's pretty much you in a nutshell…always there to save the day. But you're forgetting the second part."

He frowned again.

"You know. You can lean on me, 'cuz it won't be long until I need someone to lean on too?" She snorted again. "You're all give and no take."

"I prefer to deal with my own problems," he said stiffly.

"No kidding." Oops. She was supposed to be going cold turkey on the sarcasm.

"What's your song?" he asked.

"'These Boots Are Made for Walkin','" she answered promptly. "Shawnee, Violet, and I sang it every time in college."

Wyatt smirked. "Talk about a theme song."

"We liked to think so." She scanned her list and picked the next most harmless question, assuming there was such a thing. "What's one thing you've always wanted to do but haven't?"

He turned his head slowly and gave her a deliberate once-over that made heat flash from her head to her toes. Then he raised his eyebrows. *You really want me to say it?*

She tucked her chin and cleared her throat. "Alrighty, then. Moving on…"

"You didn't answer."

She could have pointed out that he'd covered it for both of them. Instead, she said, "Shawnee and I used to talk about team roping together at the Women's National Finals Rodeo."

"Why haven't you? You're both good enough."

She shrugged. "You know. Time. Work. I had to prioritize."

"And now?"

She glanced up. "What do you mean?"

"You have an opportunity to evaluate your priorities, and thanks to Shawnee, you have the horses. Rodeo was a huge part of your life. Don't you miss it?"

"Of course. I just…" Didn't have an answer. The old urge was an increasingly insistent tug on her sleeve, but she wasn't ready to scrap her career in favor of selling ads for the *Earnest Herald*, and she'd already failed at juggling both.

"Shawnee has Tori now," she said, and picked what she *had* considered to be the most provoking question on the list. "If you could change your upbringing, would you?"

"No."

His immediate answer was the exact opposite of what she'd expected. "Why not?"

"My *upbringing*"—he gave the word a cynical twist—"has given me advantages I wouldn't have had otherwise. I like to think I use them to help as many people as possible."

Oh. Well. She wouldn't have thought of it that way. And she didn't like how his quiet declaration made her heart give a little flutter.

"What about you?"

She did hesitate, but she'd made the rules so she gave him the honest answer. "Yes." Then she hurried to clarify, before he could ask. "For Hank's sake, not mine. I had some really good years with our parents, but by the time he came along…"

"You'd change your parents but keep Hank."

She glared at him. "Yes, I would keep my brother. I know that might be hard for you to understand—"

"I'd trade you in a heartbeat."

She blinked, confused. "Parents?"

"Brothers." His voice had gone flat. "Mine, the pious prick, in exchange for yours, who doesn't know what *manipulative* means."

Yikes. Bitter much? "Hank still manages to do a lot of damage."

Wyatt opened his eyes, and the black void in their depths made a chill shoot up her spine. "You have no idea."

And she wasn't sure she wanted to get one. She fumbled with her list and blurted, "What's one thing about you that most people don't know?"

His smile mocked her as if to say, *Made you blink.* Then he tipped his head back and stared up at the stars. "My given name isn't Wyatt."

"Really?" She did a double take. "What is it?"

"Charles. Charles Stanchfield Darrington."

Melanie choked down a laugh. "Not *the third*?"

"I'm the younger brother. Matthew got the privilege of being numbered. And he's the sixth." His lip curled. "The Darringtons have been a plague on humanity for a very long time."

Double yikes. Even she wouldn't go as far as to call her parents a disease. "How'd you pick Wyatt?"

"It was my nickname when I played lacrosse. I was the fastest shot on the team and had deadly aim."

She knew nothing about lacrosse, other than it seemed like an irresistible temptation to whack opposing players with a stick, but she still got the reference. "Like Wyatt Earp."

"Yep."

And he'd been so determined to leave his past behind that he'd even shed his name. She turned a page in her notebook. "So, Chuck…"

He fired a warning glare at her. "Don't even think about it."

She grinned until he said, "What don't people know about you…other than you're scared of the dark?"

Chapter 21

"I AM *NOT*." SHE BRISTLED ON REFLEX, THEN SCOWLED. Nothing but the truth. "I'm afraid of what's *in* this dark. Prairie girls aren't used to having to worry about large predators." She waited for him to laugh at her. "Aren't you going to tell me I'm being silly?"

"No. Your fears are perfectly valid."

Oh great. "Thanks. You've made me feel ever so much safer," she drawled.

"Better nervous than cougar bait."

Now he was just being cruel. She glared at him, but he ignored her. "I guessed that one, so you owe me another secret."

"Fine." She huffed out a breath. "I can't open canned biscuits."

His face screwed up in distaste. "Why would you want to?"

"Because not all of us are Miz Iris." She rolled her eyes at his uppity attitude, then sighed. "It's the way they explode. Scares the hell out me even though I know it's coming. I spook easily. Loud noises. Sudden movements…as you probably noticed." She pointed her pen at him. "For future reference, you should stop sneaking up on me so I don't push you off another cliff."

"You didn't push me. I fell."

"You wouldn't have fallen if I hadn't pushed you."

"I took a bad step."

She made an exasperated noise. "Oh, for crying out loud. You can't even let me have credit for this mess?"

His eyebrows shot up. "Most people would say *blame*."

"Most people aren't dealing with you," she muttered into her kneecaps.

"I heard that."

"Good." The hell with it. She'd clean up her attitude tomorrow. Or today, but after she had made it back to civilization without any tooth or claw marks in her hide. "Next question. Describe a defining moment in your life."

"That's not a question. It's a prompt."

She gritted her teeth and counted to ten. Forward. Then backward. "I can't imagine how you ended up divorced."

His expression didn't change, but behind his eyes, he shut down. *Bang!* Like a shutter slamming in her face. *Shit.* Once again, she'd gone that step too far. Drawn blood in what had been a friendly sparring match. "I'm sorry. That was uncalled for." She closed her notebook. "That's enough—"

"No." He made an abrupt *bring it on* gesture. Stopping now would be admitting she'd won—and even though she'd started it, she wasn't even sure what game they were playing.

Why was he being so open? What advantage did he hope to gain?

"What was the question again?" he asked.

"The, um, *prompt* was 'Describe a defining moment.'"

"My grandfather's funeral."

Again, he'd caught her by surprise. She'd expected *the first time I worked the National Finals* or *when I was named Bullfighter of the Year*. "You were close?"

"I admired him." He shifted, rolling his shoulders as if the subject had caused the muscles to tighten.

She stayed quiet, waiting for the silent *but*...

He crossed his arms over his chest, tucking his hands in his armpits. Pure defensive posture. "I was seventeen when he died. That day...I looked around, and I realized that out of all the hundreds of people who'd shown up to pay their respects, there wasn't a single soul who'd wake up every morning and feel empty because he was gone."

Melanie thought of the pastor of her church—warm, serene, content—and shook her head. "I don't understand. How can they be clergymen and still be so..."

"Religion and ambition aren't mutually exclusive."

She frowned, troubled. "Is it like that in all the big churches?"

"No. It's not even like that everywhere in *our* church. But my family..." He shrugged again. "For a while, I thought I could fight the good fight from the inside. Open their eyes and show them the way." His voice was ripe with self-disgust. "I was wrong."

Then he shifted again, and in a blink he was once more the lazy beach bum. "What's yours?"

"I, um..." Wow. After that, she felt frivolous even saying it. "Winning the college championship. Not just for myself," she rushed to add. "The individual title was a huge thrill, but I also had to come through for the team. I was the last to go, the only chance we had to outscore Tarleton State...and I delivered. It's the only national team championship our school has ever won."

"That's something to be proud of," Wyatt said quietly. And without a hint of sarcasm.

She could learn from him. The longer they went on, the more she understood just how much she had to learn *about* Wyatt Darrington. She crimped the edge of the notebook paper between her fingers. "What's one thing you would change about yourself?"

"This." He made a circular motion around his head. "Once in a while, I'd like to be able to just take life one moment at a time."

"Have you tried meditation?" she asked, only half joking.

"What do you think?"

That she'd always considered his mental aerobics a choice, not an affliction. Another point to seriously ponder.

"What would you change?" he asked.

"My temper."

He laughed.

She scowled. "I'm serious. Do you have any idea how much trouble it gets me into?"

He raised his eyebrows again.

She sighed. "Yeah. I guess you had a front-row seat for this last round."

"Do you wish you hadn't done it?"

A debate that had been raging inside her skull for a week. "No," she admitted. "I just wish I could've gotten away with it."

"Maybe next time."

She huffed out a laugh. "I'd rather not have a next time."

His silence was answer enough.

"Okay. That's a little unrealistic. How 'bout I shoot for *Next time I won't ruin my life*?"

"You think it's ruined?"

She paused, then hitched a shoulder. "I didn't do myself any favors."

"Don't be so sure," he said cryptically.

She considered asking him to elaborate, but they were supposed to be slicing and dicing *him*. She went back to the notebook and the question she'd been working up to. The man couldn't be a bullfighter forever, but unlike most used-up cowboys, Wyatt had an almost infinite number of options. "Where would you like to see yourself on your fiftieth birthday?"

He took a minute to think before saying, "Involved. Not just the guy who writes the checks. A real part of… something."

A feat he hadn't quite been able to accomplish here or on the rodeo circuit. The sport was a tightly knit fraternity, nowhere more so than in the elite ranks, but despite his success, Wyatt was…separate. One almost unnoticeable step outside the circle, with the exception of his friendship with Joe.

Was that what he wanted to build at the Bull Dancer? A community? Not an unreasonable expectation. Cafés, bars, coffeehouses…they all had a way of bringing people together and forming connections. But how would she go about making that happen?

"What about you?" he asked.

She answered without thinking, her mind whirling with possibilities. "The same, I guess."

"You already have that back in Earnest."

"So do you."

He leaned forward to toss a twig into the fire, a neat little move that put his face in shadow. "I just drop by once in a while. It's your life."

Once again, he was setting himself apart. Or was it possible that, despite the depth and breadth of Wyatt and Joe's friendship, he truly believed he had become expendable the moment his best friend said *I do*?

Surely a man this smart couldn't be that stupid?

"You know, once she lays claim to you, it's not that easy to escape Miz Iris's clutches," she said.

"That would depend on the circumstances."

She sensed something, a shadow moving under the surface of his inscrutable gaze, but before she could make out its shape, he turned those laser-blue eyes on her. "What about your career?"

She made a face. "If I do snag an agency job, I guess I'd want to be a partner by then."

"That doesn't sound very enthusiastic."

She started to shake her head, then realized Wyatt was the one person who not only wouldn't mock, but also would appreciate what had driven her career path. "I want to make a difference," she blurted.

"Like you did at Westwind? You went there because you believed in their products." It was a statement of a truth he'd already observed, and once again, she was uncomfortably aware that, unlike Michael, Wyatt *did* know her. On a level that made her want to squirm.

"I don't sell anything unless I believe in it." She snuck a quick glance. Wyatt was gazing straight up at the stars as if they held his complete interest. "In an agency, it's all about landing the big fish, bringing in the bucks."

"What's the alternative?"

"I'm still working that out." She shook off the gloom of uncertainty. "Last question, and it's an easy one. What person do you admire most?"

"Someone I know personally?"

Geezus, he was almost as anal as Cole Jacobs. "Know *of*. Dead or alive," she clarified, before he could ask.

He paused, and then he said, "Pass."

"*Pass?*" She stared at him in amazement. "This one is a gimme for a guy who memorizes freaking history books."

He slanted her an unreadable look. "You said you wanted my first, honest reaction."

"Well, yeah, but—"

"Then I have to pass…or you have to agree to accept my answer without explanation."

Damn. She didn't like either option. She paused, debated, then nodded. "No explanation required."

"Okay." He still hesitated for a few breaths before saying, "Grace. And you."

She dropped her notebook. It bounced off her shin, landed edge first on one of the fire-ring stones, and toppled into the fire. She made an instinctive grab for it.

Wyatt jackknifed forward. "Don't. You'll get burned."

Too late. The fire popped, and a glowing ember shot up to glance off her palm. She jerked her hand back. Wyatt snatched her wrist and turned her palm up, bending low to examine the tiny black smudge.

"It's fine." There was barely a sting from the hot coal… but the sparks from the gentle brush of his fingers radiated up her arm. The breath that was supposed to steady her was more like a snort of cocaine, his mind-bending scent slamming straight into her heart and sending it racing. The nape of his neck was right under her nose. His hair was trimmed to ruthless perfection, but this close she could see that it curled at the ends, as if rebelling.

The thought made her want to laugh. Or maybe it was the contact high of having Wyatt practically in her lap that was making her giddy. She lifted her other hand, but instead of pushing him away like she was pretty sure she'd intended, her fingertip brushed a golden curl that nestled in the hollow at the base of his skull.

He went utterly still. Her lungs seized up, and neither of them breathed as they remained frozen, his hands cradling hers, her fingers resting on warm, surprisingly soft skin. Slowly, his head came up, and they were eye to eye. And close. So, so close…

The mesmerizing blue of his gaze pulled at her, as powerful as an undercurrent on a hot summer beach. She let it drag her in, closing her eyes as her mouth touched his. The instant their lips touched, he made a low, feral sound deep in his throat, hungrier than anything that might lurk in the night. With a swiftness and power that startled a squeak out of her, he scooped her up, turned, and deposited her safely away from the fire without breaking the kiss. And then he was stretched out over her, his hard weight once again pressing her into the earth, but this time neither of them was pretending they didn't notice exactly how well all of their parts fit together.

Her fingers dug into his neck, urging him even deeper as their tongues sparred. Her other hand slid under the hem of his sweatshirt, only to be frustrated by the T-shirt he'd tucked into his jeans. She flattened her palm and molded the soft cotton over muscle that flexed beneath her touch as his hips rocked into her. He buried his fingers in her hair, tilting her head to a new, better angle.

Her body arched, begging for his touch. Dear God. She was going to explode if he didn't—

He tore his mouth free and shot to his feet, cursing when his weight landed on his sore ankle. Snatching up his handmade crutch, he tucked it under his arm and hobbled to the creek as she blinked after him, too stunned to react. Then she closed her eyes and concentrated on breathing until her lungs took up a reasonable rhythm. The rest of her body took a *lot* longer to recover. Finally, though, the chill worked its way through the haze of arousal.

She shoved herself into a seated position to find nothing but embers in the fire ring. Like their kiss, the flames had burned hot and fast, then quickly died down. There was probably a metaphor in that—something about banked fires, or being careful what you struck a match to. Her brain was too fried to be either witty or wise. Her notebook was still smoldering, half burned. She used a stick to poke it into the center of the fire and watched the pages curl and blacken in the resulting flames.

Her head spun with a whole new list of questions, but the rigid set of Wyatt's shoulders as he sat on his boulder beside the creek didn't invite conversation. She chose not to push it. They had hours of darkness yet to go, followed by more hours of what promised to be tough hiking. Better to retreat to their respective corners for now.

At least until she no longer had the taste of him in her mouth—and the nearly irresistible urge to take another bite.

Chapter 22

So much for *The truth shall set you free*.

Wyatt picked up a pebble and flung it into the black water. More like the truth shall make you an idiot. No wonder his family had avoided undiluted honesty. It was some dangerous shit.

But she *had* kissed him first.

Which didn't excuse going off like a powder keg. He could blame it on lack of sleep, but he knew better. He'd been exhausted for months. Sick of himself and this screwed-up situation. Worn to the bone by constantly guarding every word and lying to people he loved.

He hated the lying…almost as much as he dreaded having to stop. And on the inevitable day of judgment, that kiss would be one more piece of the evidence stacked up to damn him to hell.

He glanced over to check on Melanie, huddled in the glow of the fire she'd rebuilt. Her chin drooped toward her chest, then jerked up as the nearby owl hooted again. If life was anything close to fair, he could go over there, wrap her in his arms, and stroke her hair as she dozed off, her head cradled against his shoulder.

But who was he to complain, considering the good fortune that had been heaped upon him merely by an accident of birth? To assume that he also deserved love and all of its trappings was beyond greedy. He'd never known anyone who'd managed more than an appearance of both.

Then he thought of Gordon, with his gentle smile and pocket full of Tootsie Rolls. Scratch that. He did know one person. But if Wyatt had ever had a chance to be that kind of man, he'd missed the turn.

In his peripheral vision, he saw Melanie do another head jerk. Oh, for crying out loud. He yanked his foot out of the water, peeled off the plastic bag and pulled on his sock and shoe. Then he jammed the crutch under his arm and stomped off into the woods with the plastic rain poncho clutched in one hand and her tiny flashlight between his teeth.

The poncho was basically an extra-large trash bag with a hood tacked onto one long side. He tied a knot in hood and in the two short ends to close the armholes. When he was satisfied, he filled the sack he'd made with pine needles and limped back to drop it next to where Melanie sat.

"What's this?" she asked, eyeing it suspiciously.

"A pillow. Get some rest." His voice was sharper than he'd intended, prickling with all of the things they weren't talking about. He waved his crutch. "I'm going to find wood to make another one of these. I'll tend the fire while I'm at it, and keep an eye out for critters." He pulled his phone out of his pocket and held it out to her. "I downloaded a science podcast earlier. You'll like it. They're talking about how GMOs are developed. And it'll drown out the other noises."

"But your battery—"

"Isn't doing me any good down here. As long as you've got a charge on yours, we're fine." Rather than waiting for her to decide, he dropped the phone in her lap. "At least lie down, even if you don't sleep."

He wheeled around and thumped off into the trees. When he was sure he was out of sight, he turned to see her scowling at the phone. She pushed Play, set it on the ground beside his makeshift pillow, then toppled over onto her side, back toward him and knees curled into her chest—closing him out even as she trusted him with her safety. He choked off a silent laugh. Wasn't that the perfect metaphor for their relationship? She did trust him in certain situations, and respected him up to a point. Wanted him in a purely physical sense.

She just didn't like him much.

He stalled as long as possible, waiting for her to doze off. His teeth were chattering when he crept back to the fire. He fed more sticks into the flames and stood as close as he dared. To the east, the outline of the mountains was beginning to emerge against a gradually lightening sky.

Melanie had one hand tucked under her cheek again, and the other fist clenched loosely under her chin. Again, the likeness was a knife slash to his chest. He jerked his gaze away. Turning slowly, he roasted his body like a chicken on a spit until the last of the shivers subsided. Then he settled down to sit and whittle at his crutches, watching the stars fade and blink out, one by one.

—◆◆◆—

Melanie woke to the sound of her name, spoken softly from a near distance. She gathered her sleep-logged thoughts and oriented herself before responding. *Forest. Cold. Wyatt.* She opened her eyes to find him watching her from across the dying embers of the fire. The sky was a soft iridescent gray, pearly morning light chasing the shadows into the depths between the trees. She pushed up onto one elbow, blinking the grit from her eyes.

"It's almost four," he said, his voice as muted as the colors of the landscape.

She nodded, stifling a groan as she forced her tight muscles to unwind. Wyatt stood and moved as if to offer her a hand, then stopped, thinking better of it. Smart man. If he pulled her anywhere close, she might wrap herself around him like a kudzu vine, seeking heat.

He held up a bottle. "Ibuprofen?"

"Please."

He tossed it to her. She fumbled, her fingers awkward with cold and sleep, but managed to trap it against her chest. While she washed down a couple of tablets with a swig of tea and combed her hair, he used the empty tea bottle to dump water on the fire, poking at the embers until he was sure they were extinguished. She emptied the pine needles from the poncho sack and gave it to him to tuck in his pack.

All the while, he avoided meeting her gaze. Impulsively, she put a hand on his arm. He froze.

"It was bound to happen," she said quietly. "We've always known it would if we got too close."

He stared down at her hand for a long moment. "And that's it? Chalk it up to the circumstances and move on?"

"Do you have a better idea?"

The next silence stretched even longer.

"That's what I thought," she said, even though a tiny part of her had been hoping for…something. She shook off the stab of disappointment, squared her shoulders, and turned to face downstream. "Lead on, Chuck."

—∾∾—

The going was as hard as she'd expected. Wyatt clambered over rocks and fallen logs, through brush and ankle-grabbing grass with amazing dexterity and barely a wince, but it had to be brutal. By the time they stumbled onto the wide, well-worn trail, the sun was full up and she had peeled off both her jacket and her hoodie. She could have cried when she saw the sign pointing up the hill that read *Trailhead, 1.8 miles*.

God. It was never going to end. And if she was dying, she could only imagine how Wyatt felt. He damn sure wasn't going to tell her. Three switchbacks and a wind-sucking climb later, she nearly did weep when they finally topped the ridge and saw the Camaro, gleaming like a red-and-white rescue beacon.

Behind her, Wyatt blew out a long, relieved breath. "Can I borrow your phone?"

"Sure."

She checked the time before handing it over. Today's practice wasn't going to happen. It was after seven, they were over an hour out of town, and he was in no shape to waltz with bovines this morning.

Wyatt dialed, then turned slightly away as he spoke. "Hey, Grace. This is Wyatt." He paused. "Yeah, it's Melanie's phone. Long story. I need to cancel this morning's session. Would you let the guys know? My phone is dead so I don't have their numbers." Another pause. "I will. Thanks."

When he hung up and held the phone out to her, she waved him off. "Hang on to it in case Grace needs to call you. Hand me your backpack."

He frowned, but passed it to her. She unzipped one of the side pockets.

"The ibuprofen is in the other one," he said.

"I know." She plucked out the car keys and tossed the pack at his chest, forcing him to grab it with both hands, dropping one crutch. She was a dozen steps down the trail before he recovered enough to yell after her.

"You are *not* driving my car!"

She lengthened her stride when she heard him stumping along behind her at a faster pace than she'd expected. "That ankle is killing you. Give it a rest."

"I'm perfectly fine—"

"Yeah? Great. Then whoever gets to the car first drives." And she kicked her tired legs into a sprint.

She was already behind the wheel when he limped up to the car. He didn't argue, just tossed his pack into the trunk and climbed in. The silence vibrated with annoyance.

"Don't pout." She fired up the engine, and her heart revved along with its throaty rumble. "I promise I won't even squeal the tires on the curves."

No matter how tempting.

Wyatt folded his arms and stared straight out through the windshield.

"Fine. Be grumpy. Meanwhile, *I* will enjoy the drive." She might as well, considering it might be the last time she was ever allowed anywhere near the Camaro. Or Wyatt.

She got the feel of the manual transmission as she crawled down the pitted gravel road. At the highway she turned right, toward where the signs promised she would find a gas station and convenience store in Tollgate. And most importantly—a restroom with running water.

Wyatt remained stubbornly silent as she parked in front of the rustic log store. She turned off the car and palmed the keys before he could make a grab for them, then made a beeline for the bathroom. The sight in the mirror was enough to make her wince. Her makeup had coagulated beneath her eyes, accentuating the lovely purple bags. Her hair hung lank and stringy, and she was still sporting a few pine needles.

Scrubbed and plucked reasonably clean, she wandered into the store, reaching for a pack of mini donuts, then replacing them with a sigh as she imagined powdered sugar scattered all over the interior of the Camaro. She settled for a crumb-free banana with her cup of coffee.

Out front, she found Wyatt lounging against the car. Her pulse did a big *ker-thump* at the sight. His hair was damp and rumpled, his eyes hidden by aviator sunglasses. With a day's stubble and that grim set to his jaw, he looked lean and hard and a little dangerous in ratty jeans and a faded black T-shirt.

The effect was only slightly diminished by the bag of frozen peas in his hand.

They climbed in the car without a word. Wyatt kicked off his shoe and packed the bag of peas around his ankle. Then he peeled the wrapper off a roll of antacids and popped two in his mouth before tipping back his seat and closing his eyes. Obviously, their adventure hadn't agreed with his ulcer.

She wheeled onto the highway, the big engine chomping at the bit like a horse fresh off spring pasture. The temptation was huge to give the Camaro its head and see what it could do, but she kept it in check. When she'd reached cruising speed without dropping the clutch or grinding the gears, the hands fisted on Wyatt's knees relaxed. Five miles down the road, she heard a soft snore.

She grinned…and hit the gas.

Chapter 23

WYATT WOKE WHEN SHE DROVE PAST THE BAR, CROSSED the bridge in downtown Pendleton, and started up North Hill. "Where are you going?" he asked, his voice gravelly with sleep.

"I'm taking you home." She tapped the phone on the console between them. On-screen, the map function was silently guiding her. "I put your address in my contacts before I left Texas, just in case."

He scrubbed a hand over his face, frowning. "Why didn't you stop at the bar? I can drive across town."

Of course he could—but then she wouldn't have an excuse to see where he lived. "It's not far to walk, and it's all downhill. Plus I can grab some breakfast along the way."

She waited for him to insist that she turn around, but he only reached down to remove his melted pea ice pack and put on his shoe. The navigation system led her to a condo fourplex, all dark wood and high, angular rooflines, fronted with generous expanses of glass to maximize the mountain view.

"I'm in number one," he said—as if there was any doubt—waving her to the far end of the narrow parking lot and a double-stall garage.

He pushed a button on the remote clipped to the sun visor. The right door rolled up to reveal what looked like a sporting goods warehouse. Three bikes, water skis, snowboards, a pair of kayaks, a canoe, a paddle board, and what she thought might be a windsurfing whatever-they-were-called…all mounted on special racks in the extra stall.

Not hard to figure out what Wyatt did in his spare time. Or to picture him racing over the waves in water-soaked spandex. Great. She really needed *that* image stuck in her head. But Lord, it would be a sight to see. He would be good at it. Wyatt was good at everything.

She parked the car in the exact center of the empty stall, pulled the keys out of the ignition, and dropped them into the palm he held out. "Well, it's been—"

"I have bagels," he said abruptly. "And eggs and sausage."

She blinked at him in surprise. "Are you offering to make me breakfast?"

"I have to cook for myself anyway."

She opened her mouth to decline but immediately thought better. Hell yes, she wanted to see the inside of his condo. After all the times Violet had gushed about the granite, the custom furniture, the artwork—how could she resist? And seeing how he chose to live could give her valuable information she could apply to the bar.

Yep. Purely business. Nothing personal, like how the more she learned about Wyatt, the more she wanted to know.

"Thanks. That sounds great."

He did the slightest double take, as if it was another offer he'd made not expecting her to accept. Really, you'd think he'd know better by now. He pushed open his door, swung himself out of the car, and grabbed a pair of real crutches conveniently hanging on a hook right next to a tennis racket. Of all the equipment, they looked the most worn.

"How bad is your ankle?" she asked again as she followed him to the door into the condo.

"Nothing major. A couple days' rest—"

"I mean in general. I know you've had a couple of surgeries…"

"Three," he said. "The last one was to clean up the cartilage inside the joint. It's not pretty in there, but as long as I wear my brace and don't fall off of cliffs, I get by."

Until a bull decided to rearrange his plans. "For how long?"

He reached up to swing the door open before crutching up the two steps into a mudroom. "Cutting my schedule back and being very selective about which rodeos I work has been a big help. I've got a few more years in me."

"Barring another major injury."

He shot her a dry look over his shoulder. "Me and every other bullfighter."

A truth universally acknowledged. Every time they stepped into the arena could be the last. It was a reality they accepted the same as a cop, a firefighter, or a soldier.

She followed him into the laundry/mudroom, closing the door behind her and deliberately not looking at the basket of clothes on the dryer. She did *not* need to know whether Wyatt was a boxer or briefs guy. They passed through a short hallway and into the living room. Melanie had a moment to get an impression of a soaring, vaulted ceiling, gleaming hardwood floors, a wall of shelves packed with books, a pair of waist-high, glossy black abstract figures that curved around each other in a way that was incredibly sensual, and pieces of pottery and glass that were clearly works of art.

Then a woman sprang from the nearest chair—a leather recliner that had swallowed up her slender form. "Wyatt! Where have you been?"

Silvery blond hair, enormous green eyes, and a face... *damn*. She was too exquisite to be real. It was like walking in and finding a...a...unicorn, or some other magical being you assumed only existed on-screen, courtesy of liberal airbrushing.

"Laura." Wyatt had gone stiff as a board. "This is a surprise."

And not a good one. Laura made a sheepish face. "I know. I should have called, but..."

She trailed off, and her gaze locked on Melanie with an intensity that was unsettling. Not angry or jealous. More...excited. And nervous. As if she'd hoped and prayed for this moment and couldn't believe it was happening. She stepped forward and held out a slender hand. "It's so good to meet you."

"I..." Melanie accepted the greeting, feeling like an Amazon shaking hands with a fairy. "Hello."

Laura laughed, a sound like the ring of priceless crystal. "I'm sorry. I'm freaking you out. It's just that I've heard so much about you that it seems as though we already know each other."

"Really?" Melanie shot Wyatt a baffled look. Why on earth would he talk to this woman about her?

His face was utterly blank, but his eyes... "Did you come alone?"

"Of course not. Julianne was bored, so she went downtown to poke around in the antique shops."

At eight thirty in the morning? Melanie had walked by most of those shops during her tour of the bars. None of them opened before eleven. She'd made note because she intended to do some poking around of her own.

The skin on her back began to tighten. Something was off. The way Laura was studying her. Wyatt practically vibrating with...tension, or fury? Possibly both. And Laura lying about her friend's whereabouts. It was just... Melanie couldn't define the feeling other than *wrong*.

She took a step back. Then another. Then waved toward the door. "I don't want to intrude."

"Oh, but I was hoping we could chat," Laura protested.

"I really need a shower. And a nap." Melanie kept backing toward the door. "I'll touch base with you when I have some ideas sketched out, Wyatt."

She turned and bolted, her gut screaming at her to run, the same as when she'd watched a potential tornado cloud bearing down on the ranch. She didn't know what was causing this disturbance in the atmosphere...but she had no desire to be caught up in the storm.

Wyatt waited until the door slammed shut behind Melanie, then let out the curse that had been boiling on his tongue.

Laura made an attempt to look chastised, but her eyes were bright with excitement. "Oh my *God*. The resemblance..."

"Are you insane?" Wyatt snapped.

Laura made an *oh pooh* gesture. "I didn't expect

you to bring her home with you." Her green eyes sharpened as she took in his clothes and the crutches. "What happened?"

"I don't want to talk about it. Where is Julianne?"

Laura's eyes shifted to the window. "I told you. She's—"

"Don't feed me that bullshit. The antique shops aren't open yet." Hell, even Melanie had caught that lie, and she'd only been in town for three days. "Where is she?"

Laura made a face, then sighed. "She's staking out the bar from that coffee shop across the street."

"With Maddie?"

"Of course."

Dammit. He grabbed the phone mounted on the kitchen wall. "We have to get her out of there."

"But if we wait a few minutes, she'll get to see—"

Wyatt jabbed at buttons, cursing when he hit a wrong digit and had to start over. Yes, the coffee shop was right across from the bar, making it the most convenient place for Melanie to grab breakfast. He expected this kind of idiocy from Laura, but Julianne…

Laura clamped her hand around his on the phone. "Relax. It's not like she's going to take one look and just *know*."

"The hell she won't. You have the damn pictures, Laura." Pictures he'd snapped with his cell phone when no one was looking of photos scattered around Miz Iris's living room, some so old the colors had begun to fade. Smiling girls from the ages of two to twenty. And boys. Wyatt ground his teeth, wanting more than he ever had to shake Laura, and that was saying something. He settled for shoving her hand away.

He drummed his fingers impatiently on the handgrip of his crutches as he waited. One ring. Two. How long would it take Melanie to walk twelve blocks downhill?

Laura pushed out her bottom lip, a pouty Tinker Bell. "You're overreacting."

"No, I am not. You, on the other hand—" He cut off when a woman's voice answered. "Get out of there *now*, Julianne."

"Well, good morning to you, too, Wyatt," she drawled.

"I don't have time to screw around. Melanie could walk in there any minute. What do you think is going to happen if she comes face-to-face with Maddie?"

Julianne hesitated a beat, then sighed. "You're right. I shouldn't have let Laura talk me into taking the chance. We're out of here."

Relief weakened Wyatt's knees. Thank the damn stars, one of them had some sense. "Use the back door, just to be safe."

Laura scowled at him as he hung up. "You didn't have to be rude."

"Jules gets it. You—"

"I just wanted to meet her." The pout turned into a whine that set Wyatt's teeth on edge.

"That is *not* in the contract." Another thought slammed into him. "Grace doesn't know you're here."

If she had, she would have warned him when he'd talked to her this morning.

Laura ducked her head, a flush staining her translucent skin. "It was a last-minute trip."

"You're required to give Grace twenty-four hours' notice."

So she could decide whether to brace herself for a

visit…or leave town. If she'd stumbled across Julianne and Maddie unexpectedly…

Wyatt cursed again.

"I just wanted to meet Melanie," Laura repeated obstinately. "It's only a matter of time before you chase her off. Although, since you apparently spent the night together…"

Wyatt fisted his hand and ground it into his forehead, which had begun to throb in counterpoint to his ankle. Laura was the sweetest, kindest, and most impossible person on the continent. Honest to God, there were times he was convinced her brain had an *off* switch. And Melanie thought he didn't understand what it was like with her and Hank.

He let out a low, hard laugh. There was some irony for you.

Laura frowned at him, then at the hallway to the garage. "I don't understand why she ran off like that."

"The way you were looking at her—" He threw up his hands, pushed beyond anger. What if Melanie somehow suspected… "I've told you, she is the most intuitive, observant person I've ever met."

And Melanie had instantly recognized that Laura's interest in her was *way* out of proportion.

"I know. But I didn't think—"

"No. Kidding." The story of her life. Once upon a time he'd thought it was cute. Hell, he'd thrived on it. With Laura, there was always an opportunity to come racing to the rescue, only one of many reasons their relationship had been out of whack from the beginning. And now she was giving him those wide, wounded eyes that made him feel like he'd plucked the wings off a butterfly.

"I'm going to change my clothes." He swung past her to his room, where he peeled off the sweat-dank T-shirt and tossed it in the general direction of the hamper. A shower would have to wait, along with popping a couple of pain pills, crawling into bed, and dragging the covers over his head. First, he had to get two women and a child bundled up and safely out of town—and follow them clear to the county line to be sure they didn't turn back.

He blew out a long, harsh breath. *Stand down.* The imminent danger had passed, and he could trust Julianne. Like a younger Wyatt, she was occasionally too blinded by love to say no to one of Laura's ridiculous schemes, but now that she'd come to her senses, she would take charge. Laura might be stubborn, but she was no match for her wife's iron will.

Most of the time. It was that potential *other* that kept a slight, wary distance between Wyatt and Julianne. They were both all too aware that if the going got tough in Laura's marriage, she might not hesitate to use Wyatt as an escape hatch.

And he might not be able to resist letting her.

He brushed his teeth, popped another couple of antacids, then dug out clean cargo shorts, socks, T-shirt, and his ever-handy ankle brace. As he tightened the last strap on the Aircast, the doorbell chimed. His heart shot straight into his esophagus. What if Melanie had come back—

Then he heard the unmistakable sound of a little girl's giggle.

A reluctant smile was already tugging at his mouth when he came out of his room, leaving the crutches behind. He'd be needing both hands. Julianne straightened, as graceful and lovely as the statues she'd brought back for him from one of her trips to Ghana, her skin and hair as dark as Laura's was light. She offered Wyatt an apologetic grimace. He just shook his head. Lord knew, he understood better than anyone.

Then the child clinging to her leg spotted him and shrieked in delight. She threw out her arms and began to topple forward. With two long strides, he caught and scooped her up, the pain in his ankle a distant second to the aching joy of her weight in his arms, the sweet baby-girl smell of her filling him up and emptying him out at the same time.

"Hey, beautiful," he said, unable to help a smile even if it threatened to crack at the edges.

She pressed pudgy hands to his cheeks, fascinated by the day-old stubble. He kissed a nose that would probably someday be sprinkled with Grace's freckles. Smoothed a hand over hair as dark and straight as Melanie's. Maddie flashed him a carbon copy of her daddy's grin.

The spitting damn image of Hank.

Chapter 24

WYATT WAS TOTALLY, IRREVOCABLY SCREWED. HE HAD been from the moment Gil Sanchez had cornered him during a visit to Earnest and uttered those six fateful words.

"Grace is pregnant with Hank's kid."

The timeline had been simple enough to reconstruct. After Hank had been fired by Jacobs Livestock, he'd sworn he'd show them all they'd made a huge mistake. For the first couple of months, it had looked like he might. According to Wyatt's sources, Hank hadn't been his normal, happy-go-lucky self, but everyone he'd worked with had been impressed by his skill in the arena. Unfortunately, distance and time had not improved his attitude toward the folks back home.

He'd blown into Earnest the weekend before Thanksgiving, pissed off at the world. He hadn't been in town ten minutes before butting heads with his father in the middle of Corral Café, and turning right around and leaving again. According to Violet, he hadn't stopped to see his sister, or answered any of her calls or texts.

But at some point during that visit he *had* connected with Grace. Wyatt had never asked for details, and she'd never offered them.

Predictably, Hank's visit at Christmas had been a disaster, topped off by the scene at the Lone Steer on New Year's Eve. Hank's version of partying had always been dancing and flirting, shooting pool and shooting the bull, not stumbling into the bar already shit-faced and truly *mean* for the first time in his life. No one could have imagined that, even drunk, he would sneer at Grace, mocking her in a voice loud enough to carry over the roar of conversation during the band break.

"Sorry, Gracie. You've already had the only piece a' me you're gonna get."

That weekend, Gil had walked in unexpectedly and found her crying in the office at Sanchez Trucking, where she worked a few hours on Sundays helping with filing. After prying the truth out of her, the bastard had immediately turned to Wyatt.

And any slim chance Wyatt might have had with Melanie had crumbled into dust. He couldn't un-know that Hank had fathered a child. For Grace's sake, he couldn't tell anyone. He was trapped in a continuous lie of omission.

If he was already beyond the point of no return, why not give Laura what she wanted more than anything else?

And now he sat on his couch, cuddling Melanie's niece, torn between strangling Gil and thanking him.

Pointing out that Wyatt wasn't exactly a neutral party, Gil had provided his own attorney to look out for Grace's interests when she'd agreed to the open adoption. The lawyer had done an excellent job, inserting the clause that gave her complete control of when or even if she would have contact with Maddie or her parents.

And insisting on a confidentiality clause. Unless Grace decided to inform Hank, her parents, or anyone else before then, Maddie's existence—and parentage—would remain a secret until her tenth birthday, sentencing Wyatt to a decade of piling lie upon lie. Somehow, though, he had continued to cling to a miniscule grain of hope. He, of all people, should be able to worm his way out…

The moment Laura and Melanie came face-to-face, reality had crashed down on him like the proverbial ton of bricks. There was no finessing this situation. Even if he could tell Melanie tomorrow, if she could set aside her anger long enough to appreciate the impossible position he'd been in, Hank would still be planted firmly between them, and she wouldn't push her brother aside for Wyatt's sake.

He would never ask her to.

But Laura was finally a mother—and Wyatt was a godfather. He had given himself the unexpected gift of Maddie, a piercing joy that he couldn't regret even as it threatened every other relationship in his life—creating an invisible wedge between Wyatt and Joe that neither of them had yet acknowledged.

"Where *were* you and Melanie all night?" Laura asked.

"We went for a hike." Maddie squirmed, and he set her down on the couch beside him. "I fell and twisted my ankle, and we had to wait until this morning to hike out again."

"That's it?" Laura looked disappointed.

No, that wasn't even close to *it*, but it was all he intended to share.

"Have you had any breakfast?" Julianne asked, always the practical one.

"No."

He let his head drop back against the couch cushions

and closed his eyes as Maddie poked inquisitive fingers into the thigh pocket of his shorts. The refrigerator door opened and closed and pans clattered, Julianne making herself at home in his kitchen.

The couch cushions barely moved when Laura sat down. "We've been talking…"

Wyatt opened one eye a slit, caught the quick glance that ricocheted between the two women, and felt the familiar twist of dread in his gut. "No," he said flatly.

"Couldn't you at least talk to Grace? See if she'd be willing to consider—"

"*No.*"

Startled, Maddie flinched away from him, her eyes going wide with alarm. Laura gathered her up and snuggled her close, stroking her back. "It's okay, sweetie. Uncle Wyatt isn't mad at you."

Her tone was designed to inflict guilt, but damned if he would let them wind him up that easily. He focused on Julianne. "You agreed to her terms."

And today, of all days, he couldn't deal with this. His mind insisted on weaving an alternate version of what the previous night could have been, and where that kiss could have led. But that could never happen in this reality, and piled on top of his pain and exhaustion, the overwhelming shittiness of it made him want to howl.

He clamped his hands around his head and dug his fingers into his scalp. "Even if Grace was willing—which I guarantee she is not—we don't even know where Hank is, or what kind of mess he might be in when we find him."

"Are you sure you will?" Laura asked.

Wyatt nailed her with a loaded stare. "I've got my inside man working on it."

"You asked my father to find Hank?" Her eyes went wide with distress. "Does he know Maddie is Hank's daughter?"

"Of course not. I said I needed to find someone. He didn't ask for details. I didn't offer an explanation."

"He's very good at ignoring inconvenient details." Laura's soft lips twisted as she pried Maddie's fingers from around the pendant of her silver necklace. Her father might not have been directly involved in what had been done to her, but all the signs had been right under his nose, if he'd chosen to look. He also couldn't quite come to grips with his daughter's sexual orientation, compounded by her choice of life mate. People in their cloistered world didn't marry outside their lily-white circles.

Laura shrugged off her rare display of bitterness, her voice going airy. "Well, if Hank has so much as cashed a check, my dearest daddy will be able to track him down."

And then he and Wyatt would never speak of it again. Laura's father had fingers in so many financial pies that there was almost no limit to his reach. Wyatt had no desire to know what arms were being twisted on his behalf, but anyone who earned money, filed taxes, or accumulated debt left a trail.

At least, that was Wyatt was banking on. Pun intended.

Julianne dished up scrambled eggs beside a toasted bagel and brought the plate to Wyatt, along with a glass of apple juice for him and a sippy cup for Maddie. She swept the little girl up into her arms and tweaked her chin. "You're right. We made a deal, and we have to stick to it. Maddie will be fine. Won't you, baby girl? You've got two mommies and Uncle Wyatt who love you enough to make up for all the rest."

The perfectly cooked eggs congealed into lumps in his stomach. Yes, Maddie would be more than fine. Laura and Julianne had the means to give her every advantage, and the home full of light and love they all deserved. And Wyatt...

He would be to them what he had become to Joe and Violet—an outer planet in their cozy little solar system, swinging by now and then to soak up a little reflected warmth.

Chapter 25

MELANIE WOKE IN THE MIDDLE OF THE AFTERNOON, STIFF, groggy, and starving.

She turned up her nose at the leftover scone from her stop at the coffee shop that morning. She needed real food, and she might as well buy some groceries and make herself officially at home.

She pulled on shorts and a tank top and grabbed her phone, which advised her that the nearest grocery store was ten blocks straight west. The weather couldn't have been more perfect—the sky a bright, cloudless blue with a warm, dry breeze rustling the leaves of the tree at the end of the block as she strolled around to the parking lot behind the bar. At least a dozen cars passed before she could turn onto the one-way running west, a lot of traffic for a...

Huh. What day *was* it? Melanie counted it out with her fingers on the steering wheel. She'd arrived on Tuesday. Wednesday she'd made her uninvited guest appearance at the bullfighting clinic. She'd spent most of Thursday polishing her résumé and working on that stupid questionnaire before traipsing off to the mountains with Wyatt. Which made this Friday. And the first time in...well, hell, she couldn't remember when she'd last lost track of the day of the week.

Summer vacation, before their senior year of college? Nope, that couldn't be it. She and Shawnee had hit the regional rodeos and team ropings hard that year, so she'd

known exactly when to load up and where they were due
to rope next. She'd roll back into the ranch days later, at
Lord only knew what time on a Sunday night, already
craving the moment when she'd crawl behind the wheel
to head for the next one.

In the beginning, she'd felt almost the same rush
when she walked into her office on Monday morning,
but no honeymoon lasted forever. Even on the rodeo trail
there had been days, even weeks, that had been more
like living the nightmare than the dream. Bad draws.
Lousy loops. Flat tires and one blown transmission.

She wouldn't trade a minute of it.

She'd always accepted that roping wouldn't be her
career. Unlike Shawnee, she wasn't willing to scrape
by training horses. The payoffs weren't big enough
to make a living on the regional circuit, and women's
roping events weren't included in the pro rodeos, where
the real money could be made.

Melanie's first full-time job—assistant to the events
coordinator at the fairgrounds in Amarillo—had seemed
ideal until she discovered—*duh!*—that those events were
primarily held on evenings and weekends, the same time
as rodeos and practice sessions. Every step up the ladder—
first to head events coordinator, then the jump to marketing director at Westwind—had meant more responsibility,
longer hours, until she had to let something go.

Giving up her roping was one thing. Sacrificing her
friendships, though? Losing track of her own brother?
How had she become a person who couldn't make the
time to watch Hank fight bulls at his first major rodeo
in Fort Worth? Who hadn't made it to a single one of
Beni's Little League games this spring?

For what?

The question was wiped away by the sight of a huge bronze statue of a bronc rider on her right, in front of a set of wrought-iron gates and a towering, unmistakable grandstand.

The world-famous Pendleton Roundup grounds.

She hit the brakes. The car behind her honked, so she whipped into a driveway that circled the tree-shaded park adjacent to the rodeo arena and stopped her car at the curb to get out and gape. It was right *here*. Literally steps from the freaking grocery store.

Slamming the car door, she walked past the statue to the gates to wrap her hands around the iron bars and press her forehead between them, frustrated by her limited view. Through the gap beside the grandstand, she glimpsed a slice of the inside of the massive arena, but not the legendary grass surface.

There must be some way to get inside…

The distinctive rumble of the Camaro didn't register until it was too late. She dropped her hands and spun around, but Wyatt had already pulled in behind her SUV, aviator glasses firmly in place and one tanned arm dangling out the open window.

He lowered the phone that had been pressed to his ear. "Paying your respects?"

"It is one of the sacred temples of my people."

He nodded in acknowledgment and pushed open his door. The hum of a motor caught Melanie's attention, and she turned to see a golf cart whizzing toward her on the broad, paved path that curved around the end of the arena, inside the fence. It lurched to stop at the gate, and the driver jumped out. He had the scrawny butt and toed-out

gait of a bull rider, probably retired, since Melanie judged
him to be near her age. His cap and T-shirt were splat-
tered with water, his jeans soaked from the knees down.

He produced a set of keys, unlocked the gate, and
opened it with a flourish and a smile. "Welcome to the
Pendleton Roundup."

Melanie goggled at him. Did they have some kind
of electronic sensor on the front gate to detect tourists?
"Uh, thanks?"

"I appreciate it, Rowdy." Wyatt's voice was once
again so close behind her that she jumped. Even on the
crutches, he'd managed to sneak up on her. And, duh.
Of course the man hadn't magically appeared. Wyatt
had summoned him.

"No problem." Rowdy eyed Wyatt, obviously unac-
customed to seeing him anything less than perfectly
groomed.

But today, he hadn't bothered to shave. He wore
another black T-shirt, this one with *Weather Guard*
stamped on the front, black cargo shorts, and the same
dusty running shoes from that morning. Downright slov-
enly by Wyatt's standards.

Rowdy's gaze slid down to the crutches and the
Aircast. "You take a shot at that school of yours?"

"Something like that."

Rowdy made no move to step aside and let them in,
his gaze moving to Melanie.

Wyatt waved an impatient hand. "Rowdy, this is
Melanie Brookman, my…"

Melanie lifted an eyebrow, curious to see how he
intended to define their relationship, but he seemed to
be stymied.

She stuck out her hand to Rowdy. "Marketing consultant. I'm helping him get the bar up and running. Come down after work, and we'll buy you a beer."

"Nice to meet you." His eyes made no secret of measuring up her assets, and his smile was a little more than friendly. "I'll definitely take you up on that beer."

Wyatt made a noise that was not encouraging, and his voice chilled several degrees. "We don't want to keep you."

"Yeah, I'd better get back to it. I've got a busted sprinkler head over on the Indian Village field. Shoot me a text when you leave, and I'll come over and lock up behind you." Then he jumped into his golf cart and zipped off.

Wyatt made a grand gesture toward the arena. "It's all yours."

Melanie took a few steps toward it, then paused. "What are you going to do?"

"I'll be right there." He pointed with one of his crutches at a square blue sign on the rail at the bottom of the grandstand.

The handicapped section. She couldn't hold back a laugh. They strolled together to the arena fence, where he made a left into the seats and she...just stared.

Green, green grass stretched for what seemed like a mile, the only turf arena in professional rodeo. The grass was ringed by a wide, banked dirt track that the Roundup had used to include a variety of races over the years, most recently the Indian Relays. The roofs of the grandstands towered high above her head, enclosing three-fourths of the perimeter, the effect both intimate and intimidating. *Since 1910.* Over a hundred years of rodeos had happened right here.

"Go ahead." Wyatt propped his crutches against the rail and settled onto the bottom sky-blue wooden bench. "Walk around."

She drew a breath, unlatched the gate, and let herself in. A part of her was braced for someone to call her out for trespassing, but there was only the sound of traffic on the street behind them and the hiss of sprinklers from beyond the north grandstand. The dirt track was like pockmarked concrete, pounded hard by winter rain, and the grass was almost ankle-high. She paused at the edge, looking around, but nothing matched the blurred images in her head.

There was no knee-high white railing surrounding the grass, or rodeo queens who came flying in and jumped their horses over it. No portable fences to create the roping chutes on the west end, with cowboys sprawled in the grass or milling around on horseback.

Not even the bright, primary-colored chute gates, the background in the photo that still graced the mantel at their ranch—two-year-old Melanie in pink cowboy boots and high ponytails, perched in the front of the Hamley's saddle her daddy had just won as the tie-down roping champion of the vaunted Pendleton Roundup.

A saddle that had gone up in flames along with the rest of his rodeo dreams.

"Where are the gates?" she asked, frowning at the blank white bucking chutes.

"They put them in storage to preserve the paint."

She ran her gaze around the arena one last time, taking in the stretch of shiny, new covered grandstand where once there had only been metal bleachers, then turned away. This wasn't the Roundup. It was simply concrete, wood, and empty space, in limbo until that one week of the year when it came to life.

"How old were you the last time you were here?" he asked.

"Six. It was the year before the fire."

The wildfire had roared across the drought-stricken Panhandle, wiping entire ranches off the map...including the Brookmans'. "Daddy was fourth in the world standings at the end of the winter rodeos, the best year he'd ever had. Then the place burned up in April, and he stayed home most of the summer helping Granddad rebuild. Everything was gone. Fences, barns, corrals, the house."

She refused to even mention the cattle. It had been too horrible. Her grandfather had only managed to save half the horses and half the herd—the ones that were too damn mean to let a fire get the best of them, her father said.

They'd also lost the mobile home that had contained all of her family's worldly possessions other than what they'd had with them at the rodeo in Red Bluff. God bless Iris Jacobs, clicking away with her ever-present camera, or there would be no baby pictures of Melanie.

Or of her parents when they were still the couple she'd been born to.

She heaved a sigh. "By the time he could get away again, he was too far out of the running to have a chance at making the Finals, so he didn't even bother to enter Pendleton."

Or any of the other rodeos at the end of the season. Or the beginning of the next. Coming on the heels of her grandmother's passing, the fire had broken her grandfather, emotionally and physically. A bad case of smoke inhalation combined with his pack-a-day habit had damaged his lungs, triggering progressive disease, and he could no longer put in the hard days required to maintain the ranch, let alone bring it back from near dead. Johnny Brookman had had no choice but to park his rodeo rig a dozen years earlier than he had planned, slogging through the ashes while his shot at qualifying for the National Finals slipped away.

He had a right to some bitterness, but in her opinion, he'd used up his quota a long, *long* time ago. And her mother…

"Things have changed a lot since you were here last," Wyatt said, thankfully veering away from the subject. "New grandstands, upgrades to the concessions and restrooms…"

"They needed it."

He nodded, then gave his head a slight shake. "I liked it better before, when it wasn't quite so huge. It was more personal."

Another reference to that connection he seemed to crave. The one he hoped to make via the Bull Dancer. Their enforced proximity had accomplished that much. She knew *what* he wanted from the bar, and had a good idea *why*. The *how* would be another matter.

"Was this your first rodeo?" she asked.

"As a spectator? No. I went to the one in Heppner first. I was at loose ends, so I thought I'd take in some authentic western culture." He hitched a shoulder. "By the end of the weekend, I was hooked."

Literally, if you considered that he'd ended up as a bullfighter.

She wanted to hear more of that story, but her curiosity nudged her in a different direction. She looped one arm over the pipe railing that closed off the end of the grandstand, separating the two of them. "I thought you'd be busy entertaining your guests."

His mouth tightened a fraction, but his shrug was offhand. "They left early."

She studied him more closely, able to see behind his dark glasses from this angle. Violet was right to be worried. There was a near-constant tension about him, a guardedness that went beyond his innate reserve. He was strung together on nerves and Rolaids, only relaxing with visible effort. Melanie couldn't put her finger directly on the problem, but after this morning, she suspected it had something to do with Laura.

And with herself.

Their night in the woods hadn't helped. After all the years of treading so carefully, they'd crossed a line—and not just physically. Yes, the kiss had been exhilarating, unnerving, and most likely unforgettable. Worse, though, her brilliant questionnaire had pushed them treacherously close to what they'd never allowed themselves to be.

Friends.

She could feel him trying to retreat. If he'd known he would see her, he wouldn't have left his preppy-boy armor at home. And it *was* armor. One more way he set himself apart, even as everything he said told her he craved closeness.

She'd have to give that some thought when she wasn't so distracted by the view. This rough-edged version might not be as pretty, but it was harder to tear her eyes off him. His hair was slightly mussed, and that stubble would rasp against her palm. Or her—

"You rock the morning-after scruff pretty well for a blond." She wasn't making any secret of studying him, so she might as well just put it out there. "Maybe you should try going the full Jeremy Buhler."

He gave a half laugh, rubbing a hand over his chin. "No one will ever fear this beard. And they definitely won't mistake me for a world-champion team roper."

"You don't rope?"

"Not even a little bit."

She blinked at him in amazement. There was an athletic endeavor Wyatt hadn't conquered? "Have you tried?"

"Enough." He shifted, stretching his arm along the back of the bench in one of those moves that appeared relaxed and confident, but signaled that he wasn't thrilled with the direction of the conversation.

So of course she pursued it. "By *not even a little bit* you mean…"

"I can't swing the loop." His irritation came through loud and clear as he made a circling motion with his hand. "Whatever it is you do with your wrist to keep the rope from wrapping around your neck…"

"Really?" She cocked her head, honestly perplexed. "It's not that hard."

"Says a woman who's been doing it since she could stand upright."

True. But still… "Can you ride a horse?"

"Of course."

"You don't ride when you're at the ranch with Joe."

"I learned English style," he said, as poker stiff as

those hoity-toity types in their polished boots and stretchy pants. "I'm not comfortable in a western saddle."

Yet another example of how he was not a cowboy. It obviously bothered him…so why didn't he do something about it?

"I could teach you," she blurted.

"To ride western?"

The image that flashed into her mind had nothing to do with horses. *Yeah, darlin', we could get western all right.*

"To rope," she clarified, for him and for her overactive imagination. When he continued to stare as if she'd suggested naked pig wrestling, she indicated his ankle. "I owe you something for that."

He gave an even more offhand shrug. "In that case, you can teach my clinic while I rest up for the rodeo in Sisters."

"Okay."

His head snapped around. "I was just—"

"I know. You were kidding," she cut in. "But I'll do it. You talk, I'll be your legs."

"You can't…"

He trailed off when she folded her arms and arched her brows at him in a silent *Oh, can't I?* She knew she had him when he scowled and snatched up his crutches.

"Fine. Eight o'clock tomorrow at the practice arena."

He hopped nimbly down the two stairs and swung off toward where they'd parked, moving so fast she almost had to break into a jog to keep up. She angled past him and out the gate as he waited in stony silence to slam it shut behind her. What was his problem? She was trying to help, *and* she'd made it through an entire conversation without snarking at him.

And they said women were moody.

Chapter 26

WYATT DIDN'T DROP BY THE BULL DANCER THAT EVENING.

He told himself he was resting his ankle, but the less-appealing truth was he had no desire to watch Rowdy drool on Melanie…and no doubt that the annoying little bastard would show up for the beer she'd offered. The way he'd looked at her that afternoon made Wyatt wish he'd let Joe kick the crap out of Rowdy that night in Redmond, back when he'd been a continual pain in their asses inside the arena.

Of course, Louie had made a point of calling to give him a detailed report. He was like a damn cat, always knowing exactly how to get under Wyatt's skin and enjoying every minute. He went on about how Melanie had charmed Rowdy and the friend he'd brought along so much they'd stayed for a second round. Then Gordon had strolled in with a couple of his cronies, and she'd won their hearts by ordering out for fried chicken with the works.

"We've even got a table full of tourists who wandered in and stayed 'cuz everybody was havin' such a good time. This is more people than have been in this place since you bought it."

And Melanie wasn't even trying yet. She was like Joe. All she had to do was show up.

Wyatt tamped down the surge of envy, declined the invitation to join the fun, and hobbled to bed before the sun fully set. Dealing with Laura on the heels of a sleep-less night was bad enough, but then he'd had to not only explain the impromptu sleepover to Grace, but confess that Laura and Julianne had come to town without warn-ing…and why.

He had to keep secrets about Grace, but he categori-cally refused to keep them *from* her.

She'd sat on his deck, staring down at the Roundup grounds ten blocks below. "I don't trust them."

"I don't blame you." He was pretty damn uneasy himself. Laura was impulsive, stubborn, and extremely good at conjuring up reasons why her needs should take precedence, and today he'd lost some of the faith he'd had in Julianne's ability to resist her.

Grace's fingers curled around the arms of her wicker chair. "Can I trust you?"

"When it comes to Laura?"

Grace's shrug said, *Among others*.

"I made you a promise, Grace. I don't break my promises."

She stared for a few moments longer, then nodded and pushed to her feet. "She's never been good for you, you know."

"Melanie?"

"Laura." For the first time since the conversation began, Grace looked directly at him with a tired, sad little smile. "Thanks to me, Melanie is impossible."

If anything, he was in even worse shape on Saturday morning. His ankle had stiffened up overnight, and his red-rimmed eyes bore testament to a shitty night's sleep despite his exhaustion. He scooped handfuls of cold water and splashed them over his face and hair, which was standing on end, thanks to the stupid natural curl. That, at least, would be taken care of next Tuesday with his regularly scheduled appointment with his stylist.

He picked up a razor, weighed it in his hand, then tossed it down again. He was worn so thin that it would be like dragging the blade over fresh road rash. Maybe the beard would help disguise that fact that he looked like hell, felt worse, and couldn't work up an ounce of give-a-shit. And if he didn't get his butt in gear, he was going to be late for his own class.

He grabbed a pair of jeans from the drawer reserved for work clothes and the black T-shirt from the day before off a chair. A glance in the hall mirror had him grabbing a Cubs cap off a hook in the mudroom and mashing it down over the hair that had sprung right back up again.

Despite his lack of grooming, Wyatt was the last to arrive at the practice arena, parking between Melanie's SUV and the crappy minivan he'd bought for students who didn't own a vehicle. The horses had been fed, and Melanie had set out a hay bale and was roping one end as if it were a calf's head. Scotty and Philip lounged in the shade, watching.

When Wyatt emerged from his car, cap tugged low over mirrored sunglasses, and fished out his crutches, Scotty gave a low whistle. "Holy shit, man. What happened to you?"

"I fell in a hole." He ignored Melanie's snort as he looked around. "Where's Dante?"

Scotty hitched a shoulder. "Some of his Pasco buddies stopped by last night, and he took off with them."

Oh hell. Wyatt knew exactly what kind of *buddies* Dante had in Pasco. "Did he take his stuff?"

"No."

Wyatt inclined his head. "Grab a couple of boxes, pack what's left, and give it to Louie. Dante can stop by the bar to pick it up."

Scotty and Philip exchanged a quick glance before nodding.

Melanie stopped in the middle of coiling her rope to gape at him. "That's it? One mistake and he's out? That's a little harsh, don't you think?"

"No." Even though it tore at his gut, knowing how fast and hard Dante could fall when Wyatt cut him loose.

She shook her head, her mouth tightening. "I always thought you were bluffing when you told Hank you'd blackball him if he screwed up again."

Always? Even when she'd raged at him and about him? His heart bumped, and if he'd had more than one good leg, he would have kicked himself. Geezus, he was dense where she was concerned. With Hank seemingly on a mission to get himself fired, Wyatt had set himself up as a target for Melanie's wrath, to deflect it away from Joe and the Jacobs family. Did he really think she wasn't smart enough to see what he was doing?

Or willing to use him as a sacrificial goat if it saved her relationship with the others?

And now Scotty and Philip were eyeing him, their ever-present distrust rising to the surface. Had they misjudged him? Would he give them the ax for the slightest misstep?

"Dante isn't Hank." Wyatt gestured toward the arena. "When Wild Woman got you down, Scotty and

Philip jumped in without thinking twice. Dante stood and watched."

Understanding dawned, clearing her face. "You would've had to chain Hank to the fence to hold him back."

"Exactly."

She cocked her head, studying him for a beat, then nodded as if something had been settled to her satisfaction. With a few expert flips of her wrist, she finished coiling the rope and tossed it on the bale. "So what's the plan today, boss?"

With Grace off at a rodeo and Wyatt waddling around on crutches, he went back to the wheelbarrow dummy to avoid any injuries. Today, though, he dialed it up a notch, having Melanie and the two men take turns working as pairs, learning to coordinate their movements so they would be in the best possible position to rescue not only the rider, but each other.

"No, no!" he yelled at Scotty, when he and Philip collided and Melanie knocked them into a pile with the dummy's head. "You're attacking too soon. Float around the perimeter when your partner takes the lead, and don't step in unless he gets into trouble or the bull comes unhooked and stops following him. Show him, Melanie."

She did, timing her entrance perfectly. *Damn.* If she'd been twenty instead of thirty-four, he would consider her a serious prospect.

Behind them, someone cleared their throat. "Um... excuse me," a male voice said.

They all wheeled around to find a young man peering over the fence. "Uh, hi. I was told I might find a Melanie Brookman here?"

Her forehead puckered in concern, and Wyatt could see her mind jump straight to Hank. "I'm Melanie. Is something wrong?"

"I can't say." The young man sounded apologetic as he gingerly extended an envelope through the rails. "I'm just supposed to give you this."

Melanie strode over and snatched it out of his hand.

"Oh yeah. I forgot." He cleared his throat again, trying to sound official. "Melanie Brookman, you have been served."

She swore, tearing it open while he beat a hasty retreat to the generic sedan he'd left idling behind the rest of the cars. As she scanned the document, her mouth went slack, and the color drained from her face.

"What?" Wyatt asked, reaching for the paper.

She balled it up, threw it on the ground, and stomped on it before slamming out of the gate and into her car. Her tires spit dirt as she gunned out of the driveway.

Wyatt picked up the letter and smoothed it out. He dropped an f-bomb of his own when he saw the letterhead.

That son of a bitch.

But Wyatt couldn't help a fierce spurt of admiration as he read to the end. Michael had gone back to Colorado and been fired on the spot, thanks to photos of his paint-splattered pickup that had mysteriously been forwarded to his boss's inbox, the return IP address untraceable. The Earnest Ladies' Club had been busy.

Michael had immediately filed a wrongful termination suit against his employer, claiming his relationship with Melanie had been nothing but a mild office flirtation that she'd blown out of proportion. He'd cast her as a desperate, delusional thirtysomething who went ballistic when she learned he was married.

The letter requested her side of the story.

Wyatt folded the paper and stuffed it in his back pocket, then turned to Philip and Scotty, both wide-eyed with curiosity. "Take the rest of the day off."

They hesitated, then Philip said, "Anything we can do?"

"No." Wyatt bared his teeth in what didn't even pretend to be a smile. "I've got it handled."

Chapter 27

MELANIE ANNE BROOKMAN, DO YOU SOLEMNLY SWEAR THAT you did the nasty with Sara Miller's lawfully wedded husband?

Her stomach heaved. She slammed on the brakes, lurched onto the shoulder, and threw open the door to spew coffee and Froot Loops on the side of the highway. Her breath came in gasps as she fumbled for the lukewarm bottle of water in the cup holder. Rinse and spit, rinse and spit, getting the worst of the taste out of her mouth. Then she flopped back into her seat, pulled the door shut, and cranked the AC so cold air blasted her in the face.

Goddammit. She'd reached the point where she could forget that bastard for a whole half hour at a time…and now this. The empty space in her stomach filled with black, slimy loathing, equally divided between herself and Michael. He was a worthless shit, but that letter had hit the nail square on head. She had been the epitome of a woman who was so hard up she that jumped the first likely man who came along.

Now they wanted her to place her hand on a Bible and swear to her stupidity—making it a matter of permanent record.

And damn Wyatt for showing up today looking so…damaged. She needed at least one constant right now, and he had always been the rock she could pound on with both fists. He could *not* crumble on her now.

He also couldn't see her wrecked, so she wiped away the snot with the hem of her T-shirt, put the car in gear, and drove on into town. Up in the apartment, she stripped and took a quick shower. Slapping on the minimum of makeup and yesterday's khaki shorts and tank top, she headed back down the stairs less than thirty minutes after she'd arrived. She burst onto the sidewalk, fully expecting the Camaro and its owner to be parked outside, blocking her escape, but neither was in sight.

Smart man, choosing to give her some space. She used it to jump in her car and get the hell out of Dodge. Or Pendleton, as the case may be.

Past the Roundup grounds, she had to make a choice. Go south toward something called Pilot Rock, or take the interstate? She chose west. It wasn't like she had any particular destination in mind. She just had to move. And keep moving for as long as it took to come to grips with this latest sucker punch.

At the intersection of the west and northbound interstates, she randomly chose north. Within minutes, she was crossing the broad Columbia River and into Washington state—home of Starbucks, basketball powerhouse Gonzaga University, and legalized pot.

Now there was an idea. She could get herself a stash and a cheap motel room and stay stoned until she could face her life again.

She veered onto the first exit ramp north of the river instead, in response to a sign advertising the Columbia Crest winery and the promise of a tasting room. Crackers, cheese, and a few sips of wine poured by a friendly stranger sounded like just the ticket for her now-grumbling stomach. When she laid eyes on the villa-style stone building surrounded by lush gardens, she felt the first trickle of tension leaving her body.

She stayed for over an hour, limiting herself to those sips, letting the sommelier tell her more about the ideal climate for growing grapes than she'd ever thought she'd want to know and talk her into a very nice—if pricey—bottle of late-harvest Muscat Canelli. The woman also gave her a map of Washington wineries. *Hot damn.* There were a couple dozen more within a fifty-mile radius…and she might just hit them all.

Her phone buzzed with an incoming text from Wyatt. Well, that had taken him longer than she expected.

Where are you? he asked.

She could almost hear that patented cool exasperation…layered over well-hidden concern. Took a drive to clear my head.

We need to talk.

I'll be at the Bull Dancer after dinner. She paused, then added, Don't worry. I'm just indulging in some retail therapy.

Probably better not to mention that she was test-driving booze. Before he could respond, she turned off the phone. She wouldn't put it past him to be able to call some crony who could track her via the signal.

The next stop was over a massive ridge—the Horse Heaven Hills, she read, shaking her head at the name as she drove past miles of brown scrub brush—in the small town of Prosser, where she acquired two more bottles of wine. What the hell, call it early Christmas shopping. Or stocking up on survival rations, the way her luck was running.

She also acquired a purple shirt that said *Wine may not be the answer, but it helps me forget the question*. Amen to that, sister.

Her looping route skimmed the southern edge of the Tri-Cities—Kennewick, Richland, and Pasco—where she spotted a sign that promised a mall. *Yes!* Time to do some down-and-dirty shopping.

When she finally parked her car in the lot behind the Bull Dancer, her hair was sleek and shiny from a shampoo and blow-dry, and she'd had her face done by one of the makeup artists at the Macy's counter, the result several degrees more sultry than normal. She had traded her day-old clothes for a sky-blue sundress splashed with vivid red poppies, and a pair of strappy red heels to match.

The color of the day for a scarlet woman.

Instead of hauling her loot up to the apartment, she left everything but her purse in the car and strolled in through the back door of the bar, startled to find the place packed—by their standards.

Half of the tables were full and most of the stools, and the jukebox thumped out unintelligible hip-hop. Wyatt was at the far end, back to the bar and arms folded, face set. When she'd turned her phone on at the mall she'd found two more texts, both demanding to know where exactly she was and when she'd be back. From that look on his face, *When I damn well feel like it* wasn't the answer he'd been looking for.

He had changed into artistically faded jeans and a short-sleeved sport shirt the same sky blue as his eyes, but he still hadn't shaved and his hair seemed to be defying his attempts to tame it. The evidence that he could be messed up should have made her happy. Instead, she wanted to kick him. If anyone got to come undone, it was her. He had to wait his turn.

A low whistle caught her attention, and she glanced over to see Louie grinning at her. "Helllooo, beautiful!"

"Thank you." She twitched her skirt and grinned back at him, then circled a hand in the air to indicate the crowd. "What's the occasion?"

"Your new friend, Rowdy, is throwing a welcome-home party for a buddy who just got back from Afghanistan." Louie ignored a woman who was waving for a refill as he inspected Melanie from heels to newly plucked eyebrows. "What's your occasion?"

She smiled, putting an edge on it. "Looking good is the best revenge."

"Then baby, somebody's gonna die tonight."

She laughed, then stopped abruptly when Wyatt's gaze swung around to meet hers. He did not grin. His gaze took in her dress, the shoes, the *look at me* makeup, and with a slight flick of an eyebrow, he managed to express his disapproval.

Well, screw him.

"Pour me a shot of your world-famous Pendleton whiskey. On second thought, make it a double with a splash of Coke and put it on my tab." She shoved her purse across the bar. "And put that someplace safe, please."

"I've got this round." Rowdy sidled up next to her, his eyes focused somewhere well below her face, which required some imagination on his part. The spaghetti straps of the dress bared a lot of shoulder but not much cleavage, even if she'd had anything to show off. "You look great. Wyatt said the two of you had plans tonight."

Oh he did, did he? She fired another look down the bar at Wyatt. He met it with an impassive stare. She flipped her hair and turned her back on him. Her pride had been run through the shredder, and tonight she intended to allow someone to patch it up. Since Wyatt had made it clear he wasn't up for the job...

She made wide eyes at Rowdy. "He was obviously mistaken."

Louie brought her drink, and she downed half of it before thunking the glass down on the bar.

Rowdy grinned. "This night is looking better by the minute."

Chapter 28

IF ROWDY MOVED HIS HAND ONE INCH CLOSER TO HER ASS, Wyatt was going to grab the knife Louie used to cut up limes and chop a few fingers off.

Not that Melanie seemed to mind, the way she was letting Rowdy lean into her, practically eye-to-eye and lip-to-lip, thanks to the heels on those damn red shoes. Wyatt hadn't failed to notice, though, that she was sneaking glances his direction, measuring his reaction. Did she want to see him stew, or was she hoping he'd intervene?

Or was that just him hoping that she was hoping? He swore silently. If she *was* trying to goad him, he wasn't sure what response she was looking for. That kiss had pushed them into new territory, and Wyatt had no idea what the boundaries were.

He did know that the contrast between the Melanie in pads and cleats from this morning and this woman with her scarlet mouth and dark, come-hither eyes was making his head ache...not to mention other parts of his body. His imagination was having a field day with how easy it would be to slide those tiny straps off her shoulders and feel her shiver when he traced the hollow above her collarbone with his tongue. He knew how she tasted now. How she felt pinned underneath him. He knew...

Too much—and not nearly as much as he'd like. But enough to realize, as he watched her take a gulp from her second double, that he was going to have to put a stop to this, whether it was what she intended or not. She was acting out, hurt and angry, and he couldn't sit by and let her do something she'd hate herself for in the morning.

Wyatt signaled to Louie, who'd also been keeping a concerned eye on her.

"That there is not what she needs," Louie said, scowling at Rowdy.

"I know." And Wyatt could defuse the situation in two minutes if he could get her alone and show her the email from the attorney, verifying that they no longer needed her testimony after Wyatt had passed along the statements he'd gathered at the Waffle House. Then all he had to do was survive her justifiable fury when she realized what he'd done behind her back.

It wouldn't be the first time she was furious at him. He knew for a fact it wouldn't be the last. If he could redirect her anger, he was more than happy to let her take her frustration out on him instead of herself. Under the circumstances, it could be a benefit, reestablishing some all-important distance.

"Bring me her purse," he told Louie. "But don't let her see."

While Melanie was distracted by an introduction to one of Rowdy's friends, Louie slipped Wyatt the purse. He tucked it against his side, keeping it out of sight as he groped blindly for her keys. His fingers encountered a wide-toothed comb, two pens, one of those small notebooks, her multi-tool, and a lipstick. No keys. He unzipped an inner side pocket and found some change, a few thin paper scraps that felt like receipts and…

He froze at the unmistakable shape and crinkle of

a strip of condoms. Son of a bitch. Maybe this wasn't a chance meeting. While Wyatt had been home sulking last night, she could have made a date with Rowdy over that beer they'd shared. Had she walked in tonight knowing he'd be here, fully intending to sleep with him? Or were these a relic of her affair with Michael?

Wyatt crushed the condoms in his fist. Either way, Rowdy would not be trying them on for size.

He was halfway off his stool, propelled by a blast of white-hot possessiveness, when he remembered he still hadn't found the keys. Whatever else, he had to be sure she couldn't go squealing off in her car after downing those drinks. He turned the purse around and checked the outside pocket. There they were—car key, apartment key, and that handy little flashlight key chain.

Now he just had to persuade her to have a few private words with him...and refrain from slamming Rowdy's head into the nearest wall. Wyatt didn't have a lot of experience with insane jealousy—or any right to it in Melanie's case—but he was beginning to understand how so many men ended up in prison in those old country songs.

He took a deep, centering breath before he stood, slow and casual, letting his ankle adjust to his weight. It was feeling much better after an afternoon propped on the end of the couch while he burned up a few phone lines. Not the easiest thing, tracking down a lawyer on a summer Saturday, but it could be done with the proper combination of charm, persistence, and subtly implied threats.

Getting Melanie to hold still long enough to listen would be more of a challenge. Even in those damn red shoes she'd leave him gimping along in her dust, and he'd left the crutches at home, assuming he'd only be taking a few steps from the Camaro to the bar and back again. He would have to stop making assumptions about anything where Melanie was involved, before he sustained permanent physical damage. Emotionally, he'd fallen off that cliff a long, *long* time ago.

He took another deep breath, fixing a slight smile on his face while he consciously shifted into manipulator mode. How did he pry her away from Rowdy? It would be easiest to take unfair advantage of their working relationship. She wouldn't agree to go outside with Wyatt— but she could hardly say no to her employer.

As he worked his way down the bar, Wyatt made a point of pausing to greet the guest of honor at tonight's welcome home party. He borrowed a page from the infamous Madam Beverly's book as they shook hands. "Show your military ID next time you come in, and we'll buy your first drink."

The soldier grinned. "Better not tell my buddies, or they'll drain you dry."

"It's the least we can do in return for your service."

There. See? He hadn't lost his touch. To prove it, he clapped a perfectly timed hand on Rowdy's shoulder, and the dumb-ass obliged by spitting beer down the front of Melanie's dress.

"Whoops." Wyatt plucked a napkin from a stack on the bar and offered it to Melanie. She snatched it out of his hand with a malevolent glare and swabbed foam off her chest. Wyatt gave first her, then Rowdy a bland smile. "I hate to interrupt, but I need a few words with my marketing guru."

"Uh—" Rowdy said.

Melanie's smile was razor-edged. "It's kind of late for business, don't you think?"

"Ah. I didn't realize consultants worked nine to five, or I would have chatted with you earlier." Except they both knew he'd tried to get in touch. He didn't blame her for not wanting to chat, but he'd use it against her if that's what it took. "If you could spare ten minutes..."

Her eyes narrowed with irritation. "I'd be happy to meet with you in the morning."

"No can do. I'm taking off first thing." Which sounded like an excellent idea, now that he'd mentioned it. Once Melanie was done flaying him alive, he'd need to go off and lick his wounds. His cabin on Wallowa Lake was the perfect hideout. "Like I said, I only need a few minutes."

As he'd anticipated, Rowdy puffed up his chest, pretending he didn't consider Wyatt a threat. *Silly boy.* He patted Melanie's hip with the hand he was in danger of losing. "Go ahead. I'll shoot the shit with my buddy for a while."

"Thanks." Wyatt made a *Shall we?* gesture toward the front door.

Melanie gave him a withering look, then shouldered past and strode out, not bothering to see if he could keep up. She was waiting, claws fully extended, when he stepped out into the gathering dusk.

"What would you like to discuss, *boss*? Target demographics? Drink specials? Oh, I know!" She snapped her fingers and pointed one at him like a pistol. "I bet you have a great idea for a catchy new slogan. 'The Bull Dancer Saloon, where we guarantee fantastic customer service, since you'll be the only customer in sight.'"

Wyatt folded his arms and waited for her to finish.

"What's with the rotten prune face?" She did a sassy twirl. "Don't you like my new look?"

"Not under these circumstances."

She cocked her eyebrows, playing dumb. "What *circumstances* are you referring to?"

He gave her another of those hard, deliberate stares. "This isn't going to help. I understand how you feel—"

"Really?" She drew the word out into two long, acid-drenched syllables. "Tell me, Wyatt, what do you hate the most? The dumb blond jokes, or the way they don't even pretend not to check out your ass during your presentations? It must be *soooo* tiring, having to constantly remind everyone who came up with that great idea because they didn't pay attention until someone with a dick repeated exactly what you said. Oh, but wait—" She knocked a knuckle against her temple. "You *are* someone with a dick. So maybe you don't understand as much as you think."

He had to fight the instinct to defend himself. What could he say? *Yes, I was born into unbelievable privilege, but it doesn't count because I ran away?* They both knew it was bullshit. Leaving home hadn't made him not white, not educated, not male, or not rich. "You're right. And it sucks."

"Fabulous. We agree on something. Now if you'll excuse me…"

He put out a hand to block her. "You can't go back in there."

She looked at his arm as if debating whether she should bite it or snap it in half. "You think you can stop me?"

"Yes." He jerked a thumb toward the door and quoted the flyspecked sign posted inside. "I am the proprietor, and *we reserve the right to refuse service to anyone.*"

Hell. That wasn't what he'd meant to say, but the sparks that were flying off of her were burying themselves under his skin, kindling fires that threatened to reduce all of his good intentions to ashes. Her mouth dropped open, and he braced himself for some truly spectacular swearing. Instead, she snapped it shut, whirled around, and strode away, her heels clicking angrily on the empty street.

"Melanie...wait! Could we just talk—"

Her answer was a stiff middle finger shot straight in the air. He took a couple of steps in pursuit, but his ankle made it clear that anything above a sedate stroll was a bad idea, not that he was sure what he'd do if he caught her. Attempting to stop her when she was like this would be like tackling a mountain lion.

If she intended to go to one of the other bars, she was headed the wrong direction. "Where are you going?"

"To the bridge. It'll have to do, since I assume you'll follow me and there's not a cliff handy."

He'd already taken several more steps, but he stopped. "The rail is too high."

"Then I'll knock you over the head with a rock and roll you off the dike."

She wouldn't. Would she? "If you're going to commit assault and attempted murder, you'll need your keys to make your getaway."

She stopped dead and spun around. He held up the keys in one hand and the purse in the other.

She swore and started back toward him. "Don't think

I won't kick you square in the nuts and stomp on your fingers when you fall."

"Not a doubt in my mind." He unlocked the apartment door, yanked it open, and threw both the keys and the purse to the top of the stairs before she could reach him. Then he stepped back, feet braced, ready to dodge or deflect any blow aimed at his groin. If Melanie had said it, she was seriously considering it.

She went for the door instead, but paused with her hand on the knob. "If I go in after them, you won't let me out."

"Nope." Although it would take all of his strength to hold the door shut if she was determined to push it open, and there was the fire escape…

Her hand dropped, and she turned on him. If it were possible for a stare to be literally cutting, his guts would've fallen out onto the street. "What…the hell… is your problem?"

"You." He gestured toward her painted face, her dress, those damn red shoes. "I know what all of that means, but you're wrong. And if you would just let me explain—"

"Yes!" She threw her hands in the air like a Baptist preacher. "Please, oh wise and knowing male, tell me how I'm supposed to feel. Better yet, explain why it is that you could leave this place with any of those women you've never met before and you get high fives, but if I do the same, I'm an embarrassment to your shitty little bar."

Despite his vow to remain calm, his temper began to stir. "I did not say—"

"You don't have to. I grew up in the goddamn Bible Belt. I've heard it all my life." The bitterness in her voice ran generations deep. "Well, sorry, but not sorry. I'm done trying to please anyone but myself. I'll sleep with who I want, when I want, and y'all can just deal with it."

Not fucking likely.

Wyatt's anger boiled up, shooting past the red line and straight into fury. Yes, her rage was justified, but she did *not* get to lump him in with bastards like Michael and her former boss.

He *had* tried to do what he could for Hank. He *hadn't* asked to be dragged into Grace's dilemma. All he'd ever wanted, from damn near the first moment they'd spoken on the phone, was Melanie, but it was as if the entire universe had conspired against him, and he was so damn tired of fighting this bone-deep need…

He took a step toward her. Then another. She didn't budge, but her eyes flicked toward the apartment door as if reconsidering her choices.

He leaned in close, his breath fanning her cheek, his voice low and lethal even to his own ears. "Is that what you want? Just someone with a pulse you can use up and toss out when you're done?"

He heard her swallow, but she didn't flinch. "Why shouldn't I? Men have been doing it forever."

"Yes, we have."

He gathered a fistful of her hair and wound the warm silk around and around his hand until his knuckles were pressed to the nape of her neck. Her breath caught at the electric press of skin against skin, and her eyes went even darker. The line he'd held for so long had been crossed. He was beyond stopping—unless she made him.

"As long as you're determined to do something you'll hate yourself for in the morning, it might as well be with me." And then he kissed her.

And instead of shoving him away, Melanie clenched both hands in his shirt and yanked him closer.

Chapter 29

FINALLY.

The instant Wyatt's mouth crashed down onto hers, Melanie realized everything she'd done—the hair, the makeup, the dress and shoes—had been geared toward this exact moment. She'd thought she just wanted a good fight. To stomp and shout and fling insults that would bounce off of Wyatt the way they always had.

But what she'd really wanted was this. Not just any-*body*. *This* body, hard and unyielding as his hand twisted into her hair and a powerful arm looped around her waist, pinning her to him as he devoured her. Only Wyatt could handle her when she was like this—wild, ravenous, tee-tering on a fine line between desire and rage.

Rowdy had made himself a convenient tool to nudge Wyatt over the edge, but not with anything as simple or petty as jealousy. She'd had to make this the lesser of evils. Wyatt was too damn honorable to *take advantage of her* when she was on shaky emotional ground, but he could be needled into making the sacrifice if he was convinced he was saving her from worse.

Then drown her in wave after wave of sensation.

His mouth possessed her so thoroughly she had to assume he was trying to erase every man who'd ever kissed her before—and he was doing a damn fine job of it. She was dimly aware of car lights passing on the street, a horn honking. Wyatt released her hair to reach for the apartment door, opening it and hauling her through. Their combined weight slammed it closed with enough force to knock dust loose from the ceiling high above.

When he reached up to turn the dead bolt, she knew he wasn't going to change his mind this time.

He wedged his knees between hers and pinned her in place with his hips, his body an iron wall of heat and power. Her breath caught at a sudden awareness of his sheer physical presence and her vulnerability. All that strength was on a very short leash.

But this was Wyatt. He would never allow himself to do her harm.

His hand wrapped around her bare thigh, sending a firestorm of need raging through her as he slid his palm down—knee, calf, then ankle. But he stopped her from wrapping her leg around his waist, reaching instead for her shoe and stripping it off. He tossed it over his shoulder to *thunk* against the wall. The second followed.

"I hate those shoes," he muttered, his breath hot enough to burn the words into her skin.

You were supposed to. But she was quickly losing the ability to think at all, let alone dissect her own intentions.

He ripped his mouth from hers to inflict a series of bites along her jaw and into the curve of her neck, an exquisite trail of tiny pains intensified by the rasp of his beard.

"This shirt's gotta go, blue eyes." She hooked her thumbs inside the front edges and yanked, hard enough to send buttons pinging off the tile floor. He dropped his arms and let her shove it down past his wrists as he caught a spaghetti strap between his teeth and dragged it off one shoulder. He spun them around so he leaned against the door and had access to her zipper. She barely noticed, busy tasting, testing his reactions, her teeth first nipping then skimming his flesh, drawing a deep, rumbling sound from his chest when she found his nipple.

He shoved the dress down over her hips to drop around her bare feet. And then they were flesh to flesh, breasts to chest, her fingers buried in hard muscle as she all but tried to climb him. He peeled her off with a pained groan. "Not here. We're gonna hurt each other if we don't find a padded surface."

"No crutches?" she asked, momentarily surfacing as he dragged her toward the stairs.

"I won't be needing them for this." He flashed her a pirate's smile, glinting with fierce intent in his unshaven face, and again her breath hitched. There was a wildness in him tonight, and it sent a ripple of unease through her. She had expected, even craved, a reflection of her own rage—Wyatt angry *for* her—but when she'd kicked the ever-present embers, they had flared into a wildfire fueled as much by his pent-up anger as by hers.

She had pushed him beyond his limit, tapped into some hidden core of molten fury...and it was both terrifying and thrilling.

He dragged her to the top of the stairs, scooped her purse from the floor and hooked the strap over his shoulder, his bare torso turned to marble by the silvery-gray illumination from the skylight. Clean, hard lines, the curves and angles as sharply defined as if they'd been cut into stone.

But stone wouldn't sear her flesh as he spun her around and took her mouth again, cool plaster at her back and hot male sliding against her front. He cupped her butt and lifted her a few inches, her legs around his waist. His hips pulsed, the hard ridge beneath the fly of his jeans deliciously abrasive through silk and lace. Long, talented fingers slid beneath the elastic, finding, stroking, circling but not quite penetrating. She arched, seeking the perfect alignment as she rocked again and again. If he would just touch her there…there…oh God, *there*.

And she came undone, the climax blasting through her. Before she even stopped shuddering, he pushed open the unlocked door to the boudoir and carried her the few strides into the room to dump her onto the bed. She blinked, trying to focus in the nearly dark room as he dropped her purse beside her, kicked off his shoes, then his jeans, cursing when he had to pause to work one leg over his ankle brace.

Then his hands were on her again, peeling off her underwear and tossing them aside before his mouth found her breasts. She didn't have time to float all the way down before he drove her up again, nipping and sucking, tongue and teeth and the rasp of his stubble bringing every millimeter of her skin to excruciating life.

She twisted away, scrambling to the head of the massive bed, the silk coverlet slick beneath her knees. Wyatt caught her, hitching an arm around her hips and dragging her back against him. His teeth closed on the back of her neck as he slid, hard, hot, between her thighs. She reared up and tipped him onto his side. With a swift twist, she spun around to grab his shoulders and push him onto his back.

He laughed, low and rough, and hitched himself up to

lean against the padded headboard as he reached for her purse. "Mind if I help myself?"

To...*shit*. How did he know about the condoms? Then her gaze moved from his face and down over that lean, breathtaking body, and she forgot to care. As he dug out a condom and ripped it open, she feasted on the sight and the feel of his body, her fingers ruffling the silky patch of hair on his sternum, circling his flat nipples, riding over the subtle ridges of his abs. Muscle and bone as finely tuned as the engine in the Camaro, maximum performance in a heart-stopping package.

He groaned when she skimmed her fingernails lightly down the inside of one thigh and back up the other, then paused to cup and squeeze, watching him twitch in reaction.

His gaze locked with hers as she took the condom, and held as she rolled it into place, then swung her leg over to straddle his thighs. She moved over him, slowly, deliberately, watching his body tighten and his neck bow as she just barely took him, an inch, then two, then up again as his breath hissed through gritted teeth. Again. And again. Drawing the anticipation and ache out until it sang through them both like the hum of a high voltage wire.

Then she drove her hips down, swift and hard, gasping at the shock of him inside her. And suddenly she was a wild thing again, all claws and teeth and hammering need. His hips rose to meet her, their bodies slamming together with punishing force. Her fingers dug into his shoulders, his into her hips, and still they strained harder. Harder. Pounding away at thought and reason until there was nothing left but this moment. This man. This—

She shattered, her body a bright arc of fire and light. He rocked hard into her again, and again, and then made a deep guttural noise as he pulsed hot inside her.

Like every storm, this one left a momentary stillness in its wake as they reeled in the shock of its passing. At first she heard nothing but the thud of her heartbeat in her ears and the harsh rasp of their breathing. Then she became aware of the thump of music from the bar below. The bellow of a train whistle only a few blocks away, where the tracks angled through downtown. The salty dampness of Wyatt's skin where her cheek was pressed into the curve of his neck.

Oh. God. What she'd just done...and with *Wyatt*. She had never felt so raw. Defenseless. As if a storm had raged through the room and left her stripped bare of far more than her clothes. She made a noise, embarrassingly close to a whimper, and his arms came around her. For one breath, then two, she teetered on the verge of burrowing into his chest like a lost kitten.

But this was Wyatt. And he would see...*everything*.

She pushed free of his embrace, rolling onto her side to hug her arms around a chest that felt overstuffed, in danger of flying apart. Wyatt touched her shoulder, gently, tentatively, in such stark contrast to the ferocity of their lovemaking that she nearly crumbled. If she just leaned back, let him spoon all of that heat and strength around her...

But that was another, much more dangerous line, and she knew without question that once she crossed it, there would be no stepping back.

So instead, she retreated. Swinging her legs over the side of the bed, she sat up. "I'm gonna take a shower. I seem to have worked up a lather."

He didn't make a move, not a sound, as she ducked into the bathroom...and locked the door behind her. She braced for a knock as she cranked the taps and drew the curtain around the standing frame with trembling hands. Her legs felt equally unreliable when she stepped into the tub, so she sat down, drew her knees up and latched her arms around them, but it wasn't enough. The trembling seemed to start in her bones, as if she'd been socking away the pain and uncertainty, and now it was all escaping in a series of fine tremors. As she turned her face into the stinging spray, she gave in and let the tears fall.

―――

Melanie stood under the shower until the water ran ice cold. Then, shivering, she wrapped herself in a towel and spent another twenty minutes drying the hair she'd just had done only hours before. When she couldn't find any more reason to hide in the bathroom, she finally opened the door.

Wyatt was gone.

He'd left a single, pink-shaded lamp burning beside the bed, which he'd made. When she stepped closer, she saw that the sheets had been changed, the covers turned down...and her phone left on the pillow like a hotel mint. She picked up the sheet of paper beside it, torn from her new notebook, and unfolded it to read the block-style print.

CHECK YOUR EMAIL.

She sank onto the edge of the bed, tucked the towel

more securely around her, and did as instructed. The
most recent message—with an encryption key to ensure
privacy—had been forwarded by Wyatt, originating
from the same attorney who'd sicced the process server
on her this morning.

> *Dear Ms. Brookman,*
>
> *I am writing to inform you that you may dis-*
> *regard our request for your testimony. Upon*
> *examination of the attached video and signed*
> *statements provided to us by Mr. Darrington,*
> *we are confident that the plaintiff will choose*
> *not to pursue his case...*

What video? And what testimony? She skipped past
a few more lines of legalese and opened the document
file. There, in Wyatt's careful, flowing handwriting, was
a transcript of the telephone conversation between her
and Michael at the Waffle House, minus the part where
both she and Wyatt had threatened to make his life hell.
It had been signed by five strangers, who were identified
as either employees or customers.

Her hands dropped to her lap, numbly cradling the
phone. She didn't need to watch the video. She'd been
there for the performance. And that, she realized, was
exactly what it had been. A show put on for the benefit
of their fellow diners. Her chest constricted again as she
replayed the scene. Wyatt turning on her speakerphone.
Cranking up the volume so the others could hear every
word Michael said. Not to embarrass her, as she'd so
wrongly assumed.

To guarantee there would be witnesses who could corroborate her version of events.

A strangled laugh escaped past the tight band in her throat. *Geezus. Leave it to Wyatt.* Who else would even think…would be so cool-headed and cold-blooded…

And have her back so thoroughly?

She lifted the phone, her thumb hovering over the reply button, then tossed it across the room onto the fainting couch. After tonight, after everything, she had no idea how to respond. Didn't trust anything she might say. Was she angry? Relieved? Grateful? Mortified?

Something…else?

The emotions balled up inside her in an impenetrable knot, and at that precise moment, she had neither the energy nor the fortitude to pick it apart. Instead, she let the towel drop to the floor, crawled between the cool, crisp sheets, and turned off the light.

She squeezed her eyes shut, hugging one pillow to her aching chest and burying her face in the other, trying to ignore the sharp twist in her gut when she found no trace of Wyatt's scent on either.

Wyatt sat on the hood of the Camaro at the scenic pull-out on Cabbage Hill, nursing the one beer he'd allowed himself. From there, he could track the progress of the eighteen-wheelers that made up ninety percent of the traffic in the wee hours of morning, from the first rattle of jake brakes as they crested the summit, passing behind him to glide around the swooping curves of the mountain flanks, accelerate across the flat, then disappear momentarily into the Umatilla River valley at the southwest corner of Pendleton before crawling up the steep incline on the opposite side and fading away into the distance.

He could guess at which of the lights scattered on North Hill was the security light at his condo. He didn't need to see Main Street or the Bull Dancer to imagine Melanie lying alone in that bed. Sleeping? Crying?

Cursing his name?

The phone beside him had remained dark and silent long past the time when she would have read his email. No return message. No text. No call.

By now, he shouldn't be surprised. There might have been a time when her temper had ruled her actions, but it was long past. Her silence told him nothing except that she'd retreated into the emotional space she'd created for the express purpose of absorbing, contemplating…and plotting. An extended version of taking a deep breath and counting to ten. It was, he had decided, the most predictable thing about her.

What she would do when she stepped back out again was anybody's guess.

Call him chicken, but Wyatt didn't intend to be within easy reach when that happened. He couldn't absorb any more of her hurt or anger when his own was already spilling over. Last night had pushed him perilously close to the end of his control, but he'd managed to just barely hang on. God only knew what might happen if he lost his grip. Something bad. Irreversible.

Something like shouting that yes, dammit, he loved her.

He always had.

He rolled up his jacket and propped it behind his

neck, using the windshield as a backrest while the trucks continued to rumble past, one after another after another, until the sky began to lighten. Then he got in his car and drove to the airport.

He took flight just as the sun broke the horizon.

Chapter 30

When Melanie stepped outside for her Sunday morning run, she found her dress hanging on the outside doorknob of the apartment. Her shoes were nowhere in sight. Neither was Wyatt.

Her insides gave a long, slow squeeze that released in a shudder. *Wyatt.*

She could still feel him in all the subtle aches and *ahhs* of her morning-after body. She'd wanted to drive Michael's touch out of her memory, but what had happened last night was more like an exorcism. At one point, she was pretty sure her head had literally been spinning.

She had assumed Wyatt would be good in bed. Wyatt was good everywhere. But she had expected more…precision, like the way he fought bulls. Smooth, graceful, and always in the right place at the right time, with just enough flair to thrill the audience.

Well, this audience was damn sure thrilled, but he'd shattered a whole lot of her preconceptions. Throw in what he'd done at the Waffle House, and it was gonna take a while to put those pieces together into a new whole—and she could *not* do it at the scene of the crime. She had to get out of this apartment. Away from that bed.

Even after the jog and another shower, her mind felt muzzy, like she'd survived a natural disaster and was still in a state of detached disbelief, unable to calculate how much damage she'd sustained. Or inflicted.

When she was dressed, she examined her reflection in the mirror and popped the collar on her sleeveless blouse so it covered most of the telltale red patches on her neck…except a tiny love bite under her ear. She combed her hair around to that side and wove it into a braid that fell forward over her shoulder.

She had no doubt she'd left a few marks on him, too.

She shoved her sunglasses on and studied the result. Better. Now to slip out, feed her horses, and hopefully sneak out of town unobserved. Wyatt did give his students Sunday off…respecting the Sabbath even if he no longer observed it.

When she pulled into the driveway, both horses were loitering near the feed buckets she'd hung from the fence, hips cocked and ears lolling as they drowsed in the morning sun. She scooped sweet feed from the bag she'd bought the day after they arrived. Shawnee had sent her a message saying ol' Roy appreciated a bucket of grain in the mornings. Cole had followed up with photos of the label of their usual brand and the ingredient list, plus exact daily portions.

She leaned on the fence, resting her head against one of the cross braces and breathing the mingled scents of horse, dirt, and molasses as she listened to their rhythmic chomping. It was a gorgeous morning for a ride. Wyatt hadn't said whether the roadside trail ended at the saddle club arena or went on up the valley toward the mountains. Her boots were in the storage shed, packed up along with the rest of her gear…

Her phone trilled, and her pulse along with it. She

fished it out. Not Wyatt. Her heart did a simultaneous clutch and sink, relief warring with disappointment as she frowned at the unfamiliar Oregon number.

"Hel—"

"Melanie?" Grace's voice cut in. "Thank God. I've called everybody I know, and the only one who answered was Wyatt and he's at the lake. He gave me your number."

Melanie's imagination jumped into high gear at the note of panic in Grace's voice. *Car wreck? Appendicitis? Date gone horribly wrong?* "What's the matter?"

Grace's breath hitched, close to a sob. "I can't catch this damn horse."

———

Fifteen minutes later, Melanie braced her hands on her hips and glared into Grace's corral. First the cows, now this. Honestly. It was as if the ghosts of obnoxious animals past had followed her to Oregon.

The horse glared back at her from dead center in the corral, the sun glinting off her silvery-blue roan coat.

"You're twenty-two years old," Melanie said. "I thought you might've grown up by now."

The horse gave a derisive snort. *As if.* This was Betsy—Shawnee's main mount back in high school— who had once escaped at a rodeo and evaded twenty or so people, freight-training at least four parents in the process, until finally Cole Jacobs had said screw it and roped her like she was one of his bucking horses.

Grace slapped at the dust on her jeans. "I always lock her up in the stall when I feed her the night before, but this morning when I opened the gate, she ran me down and got out."

Figured. The little wench was evil right to her core. If she hadn't been such a killer rope horse someone would've shot her ornery little ass by now.

The corral was about twenty yards square and had an open-faced lean-to shed off one corner, with steel portable panels forming the stalls and a hay feeder in the middle. One gate led directly out into a small, irrigated pasture, the other to a graveled driveway where Grace's rig sat, the trailer door open and waiting.

"I'm entered in a rodeo north of the Tri-Cities," Grace said. "If I don't get out of here pretty soon…"

Melanie picked up the rope Grace had flung into the dirt and squared her shoulders. They couldn't lure Betsy into the stalls. *Nice horsey, have a bucket of grain* didn't work with the devil bitch. Chasing her would only end in a lot of sweating and swearing.

"Okay," Melanie said. "Here's what we're gonna do."

Together they dismantled the portable stalls and packed them out to where, using the hay feeder as a center brace, they strung them across the corral to form an alley across the end. Halfway through, Betsy recognized their intention, wheeled, snorted, and blasted past the panels to the opposite corner.

They hauled the last panel out, secured it, and left it cocked at a forty-five-degree angle, forming an entrance to their makeshift alley. Now for the tricky part. Melanie built a loop in the rope and stalked toward the mare.

"We can do this easy, or we can do it hard."

Betsy rolled her eyes as if to say, *Whatever*.

Grace took a couple of practice swings with her loop. Melanie gestured her to the right. "You take that side."

Together they eased toward the mare, watching

every twitch of her nostrils for a sign that she was ready to launch. She let them get within ten feet before exploding out of the corner, aiming for the gap between them. Grace took one swing and threw, the rope bouncing off Betsy's shoulder. Melanie ran after the horse. The mare started to duck away from the entrance to the alley, saw Melanie's loop aiming for her, and dodged through the gap. Melanie and Grace grabbed the end of the last panel and swung it around to close the trap... just as Betsy wheeled around at the far end and came roaring back.

For an instant Melanie thought she would mow them both down, panel and all. At the last second the mare threw on the brakes and skidded to a stop, her nose slamming into the gate, which in turn banged into Melanie's forehead. She let loose a filthy curse, but didn't weaken. They glared at each other, eye to furious eye.

The mare blew snot in Melanie's face, then pivoted on her hocks and trotted off to the other end.

From there, it was simply a matter of folding the panels in, one by one, making the alley shorter and shorter until the demon spawn was pinned in a space only sixteen feet square. Betsy huffed out a loud horse raspberry, then dropped her head.

Fine. You win. This time. But she made a point of stepping on Grace's foot as she tied on the rope halter.

When Grace had latched the trailer door behind the horse, she turned to Melanie with a frazzled smile. "Thank you. I never would've got her by myself." She eyed Melanie's now dust-smudged clothes. "I hope I didn't mess up your plans."

"I didn't really have any."

Grace hesitated, then blurted, "Do you want to come with me?"

"To the rodeo?" Melanie narrowed her eyes. Had Wyatt put Grace up to this? Melanie couldn't imagine why he would, but you never knew with him. Maybe he didn't want her to be alone after...last night. Or he might think watching other girls rope would light a fire under her. Because honestly, Grace didn't seem all that crazy about her company most of the time.

"Never mind. I'm sure it's the last thing you want to do today." Grace knocked her shoulders back, eliminating the slight droop. *Shit*. Melanie was getting way too paranoid. Grace had asked because traveling alone sucked, and it'd taken a lot of nerve for her to extend the invitation. It might mean she'd finally decided they could be friends.

"Wait."

Grace paused, her hand on the pickup door.

"I just...you caught me by surprise." Melanie conjured up a smile that hopefully looked genuine. "I'd love to come. It'll be...interesting."

Fun was pushing it too far.

Chapter 31

MELANIE TIPPED THE PASSENGER SEAT BACK AND RELAXED, letting Grace do the talking. A *lot* of talking. Either Melanie made the girl nervous or Grace was still wound up from the skirmish with Betsy, because there were no uncomfortable silences to fill. By the time they crossed the Columbia River, Melanie knew all about the regional rodeo associations in Washington, Oregon, and Idaho, and Grace's frustration with her own performance so far this season.

Meanwhile, they retraced Melanie's route from the day before, across the Columbia River to the Tri-Cities, but Grace continued on through. North of Pasco, the countryside became progressively more monotonous—huge, rolling farm fields cut by shallow valleys and low, rocky mesas.

"Wyatt said you practice at the saddle club?"

At the reflexive wrinkle of Melanie's nose, Grace's shoulders hunched. "There aren't any breakaway ropers in Pendleton other than the girls on the Blue Mountain College team. Their practices are for team members only, then they all leave for the summer."

So Grace was stuck at the saddle club, which, if it was anything like the one in Earnest, was barely a step above no practice at all. The best ropers had arenas and cattle of their own, leaving saddle clubs to the young and the clueless—both horses and riders. The calves were invariably trashy, ducking, diving crap that knew every dirty trick short of pulling a knife.

No wonder Grace wasn't making any progress.

"He also said you were job hunting," Melanie said. "Do you want to stay in this area?"

"I don't know." Grace pressed her lips together. "I've been here for a year, and as you saw today, I have zero friends outside of Wyatt and Louie. I just can't seem to..."

"Connect?" Melanie suggested.

Grace shrugged. Another mile passed. "After what happened at Westwind...do you think you'll go back to Amarillo?"

"To work?" Melanie shook her head. "Not really an option after the exit I made. Are you thinking about moving home?"

"Maybe. There's a job opening at the high school in Bluegrass, and they want me to come for an interview." Grace's teeth worked her lower lip, as if the decision was more monumental than Melanie would have guessed. Yes, Hank had embarrassed her but...once again, who was Melanie to judge?

Of all the McKennas—mother, father and seven kids—Grace was the only one involved in rodeos. Her father was a school custodian in Earnest, her mother a receptionist at a chiropractor's office in Dumas. Even if her parents had been thrilled with her new hobby, they didn't have the time or means to offer support. She'd worked part-time jobs in college to scrape up the money to buy Betsy—at a considerable discount due to the mare's age and legendary disposition. And then she'd had to find someone to teach her to rope, and scrounge for places to practice.

Suddenly, seeing herself from Grace's perspective, Melanie had to fight the urge to squirm. In rodeo terms, she was everything she'd accused Wyatt of being the night before—a privileged white ranch girl with a father who'd provided her with an arena, practice cattle, expert coaching, and a string of good horses.

Then she'd left, and it had become obvious Hank had no interest in picking up the reins she'd dropped. If she'd become a school teacher, moved back to Earnest, married a nice local boy, and kept roping with her father, would the best in Texas still be coming to Johnny Brookman to buy their horses? Could he have let Hank be, instead of constantly pressuring him, until finally—

Her thoughts slammed up against a terrible realization. *Jesus Christ*. Violet was right.

She'd started with Grace's roping, and in the space of four thoughts, it had become all about Melanie—a blueprint for every interaction with her mother she'd ever cursed.

She clapped a hand over her mouth to cover the breath she sucked in.

"Are you sick?" Grace jerked her foot off the accelerator.

"I…uh…just need some fresh air." Melanie rolled the window down and stuck her head out. The roaring in her ears wasn't entirely from the wind. When…*how* had she let this happen? Image after image from her behavior at Westwind clicked through her mind—muttered insults, unseen sneers, petty little acts of rebellion—to form an ugly whole.

God. *God*. It was exactly what she'd sworn she'd

never be and more. And just like her mother, she'd blamed everyone and everything else for her situation. Leachman. The system.

Michael.

She slumped back in her seat, gulping in deep breaths, not bothering to smooth away the hair that had blown free from her braid to straggle in her face.

"Do I need to pull over?" Grace asked.

"No." Lord, no. The last thing she'd needed was to add *made Grace late for the rodeo* to her list of sins. She waved a vague hand. "Go on. I'm okay."

Or would be, once the horizon stopping wobbling. Everything both Wyatt and Violet had tried to tell her had been right on target. And Fate had obviously thrown Michael Miller in her path for a reason. *If it hadn't been you, it would have been someone else*, he'd said. Well, ditto. The way she'd been going, it had only been a matter of time before she'd done something regrettable. In the pursuit of so-called success, she had lost her bearings. Now she had to find her way back.

And the best way she knew—the direction her friends had been not-very-subtly shoving her—was to start at the last place she remembered truly being herself.

In the arena.

"If you don't mind," she said to Grace, "I'd like to come to the saddle club and rope with you next week."

Grace blinked, considered Melanie's request, then said, "Donetta Jones is in charge of memberships. I've got her number in my phone."

"Thanks."

Grace's reaction was underwhelming, but Melanie supposed she hadn't earned any better. And Grace's muted response was probably part of what made her good at her job—an athletic trainer had to be unflappable in the face of everything from dire injuries to asshole coaches. And someone who might be about to upheave on her floorboards.

"I should ask her about a sponsorship. It would be a good opportunity for the Bull Dancer to make some friends." Both the bar and the man. And on the subject of friends... "Do you know Laura?"

The pickup swerved slightly. Grace steadied the wheel before she answered, her tone clipped. "We've met a few times."

Interesting. Melanie announced she wanted to start roping again and Grace didn't even shrug, but mention Laura's name and she damn near drove in the ditch. How could the two of them possibly be connected, except through Wyatt? But why, when Grace didn't seem to be a part of his life outside of the bullfighting school?

Or was that only since Melanie had arrived?

"She seems very..." Melanie searched for and failed to find a proper adjective. "She's beautiful."

Grace's fingers flexed on the steering wheel. "She and Wyatt aren't a thing."

"I know." Melanie shrugged at Grace's surprised look. "She was wearing a ring. Wyatt doesn't poach on other men's turf."

"Other women. She has a wife."

Well. That put Wyatt's comment about his family's intolerance into a whole different context. And why wasn't Grace surprised to hear that she'd met Laura? Wyatt must have told her. The knowledge gave Melanie that odd, creeping sensation she'd felt at his condo, as if everyone else was playing a secret game behind her back. "He didn't seem thrilled to see her."

Or, more precisely, for her to see Melanie.

Grace used the excuse of passing a truck loaded with what looked like potatoes to delay answering. When she was safely back in the driving lane, she pursed her lips, obviously unhappy about this turn in the conversation. After all the time Melanie had spent lately with Wyatt, reading Grace was like being handed a Dick and Jane book. If she were a better person, she'd let the poor girl off the hook, but since they'd already established that she wasn't, she let the silence stretch to the point of discomfort.

Finally, Grace huffed out a breath. "She's the reason he got in the habit of rescuing people. She needs it on a regular basis."

"They've known each a long time?"

"Forever."

They must have grown up together, in the same social circle, steeped in the same unbending values. Delicate, lovely Laura would have been in dire need of a champion when she came out of the closet, and Wyatt would have leapt to her rescue.

Defying his family in the process.

And then he'd left. But not alone, Melanie guessed. "How did she end up in Portland?"

"Wyatt—" Grace cut herself short and clamped her lips together. "You'll have to ask him."

Yes, she would. This was a story he'd never shared, even with Joe...but he'd told Grace. It made no sense. Grace was smart, and nice enough, and determined. And Wyatt had said he admired her more than anyone except...

Uh-uh. Not thinking about that or Melanie would drive herself crazy with all the questions she'd promised not to ask.

But she couldn't help asking herself, why Grace? She was twenty-three years old, fresh out of college, and to Melanie's knowledge the most exceptional thing she'd ever done was move across the country to start her career. Not easy, but people did it all the time, without a Wyatt to smooth their path. What was so remarkable about her?

Only one of the dozens of questions tumbling around inside her head.

"Are we there yet?" she asked instead.

"Yes."

Grace veered onto the exit to a town that consisted of a gas station and convenience store, a fertilizer warehouse, and a row of sun-bleached houses, all backed up against the side of yet another wide draw. Just beyond, Melanie spotted the cluster of pickups and horse trailers around the rodeo arena. Her pulse bumped, the result of years of conditioning, and she had to remind her body that this wasn't her rodeo.

Her adrenaline glands muttered a few profanities and throttled down, sulking. *We never get to have any fun anymore.*

Soon, she promised.

Grace parked but didn't immediately turn off the ignition, bracing both hands to scowl out the windshield. "Laura isn't the only one. Wyatt lets everybody take advantage of him."

Wyatt? Melanie nearly snorted. He who could manipulate any situation to...

No. Not *his* advantage. Melanie could tick off one

example after another of how he'd maneuvered people into doing what he wanted, but in every case it had been for someone else's benefit.

And just like when he was fighting bulls, he wouldn't hesitate to jump in even if it meant he might suffer collateral damage.

"You, of all people, should be able to relate." The eyes Grace turned on Melanie burned with uncharacteristic intensity. "Laura is his Hank. He's spent his whole life either trying to save her or cleaning up after her, as if it's his fault both of their parents were assholes and she has zero common sense. He can't help himself any more than you can."

She kept glaring as if she expected an answer, so Melanie said, "I see."

"Good. Because you have no idea how much you could hurt him, and he won't stop you." Grace shut off the pickup and bailed out.

Melanie sat, stunned, replaying every detail of the previous night in painful detail. She'd walked into that bar fully intending to pick a fight with Wyatt. Give herself a chance to hiss and spit and curse, knowing he'd let her, pushing back just enough so she could really flex her muscles. But she knew all too well exactly what buttons to push, and she'd failed to consider that Wyatt might also have some anger simmering under that cool surface.

But so what? He was a man, and he was Wyatt the Invincible. Why not use him? What problems could he have that compared with hers?

Melanie tipped her head back against the seat and groaned. She was *such* an asshole.

Chapter 32

WYATT WAS SLOUCHED IN AN ADIRONDACK CHAIR ON THE deck of his cabin, utterly failing to appreciate the startling beauty of Wallowa Lake and the surrounding peaks, when his phone chirped with an incoming text. His heart leapt and jerked like a dog on a chain when he saw it was from Melanie.

Hey, Chuck. I didn't mean to run you completely out of town. You okay?

He blinked, shook his head, then read it again. Run *him* out? By the time he'd landed in Joseph, he'd convinced himself that she'd already be packed and making a beeline for Texas. And asking if he was okay? That was supposed to be his line. She must mean it to be ironic, but the subtext escaped him so he decided to just play along until he got a better feel for her mood. I hate that name. And I'm fine. He hesitated, then added, Did you get my email?

He tipped his head back to watch a hawk circle high over the trees while he waited for the answer.

Yes. The deviousness of your mind never fails to awe me.

She was in awe. Was that good? After the way she'd left him last night, she seemed pretty damn relaxed. Or more likely, that was how she wanted him to think she was feeling. *It's all good. I'm fine. Why wouldn't I be?* The joy of texting. Any emotional context could be easily removed. And compared to coming face-to-face at practice tomorrow with three sets of curious eyes watching every move, the least uncomfortable way to reestablish contact.

She would know. Between her family and her job, this was a woman who'd navigated more than her share of potentially awkward moments. And yes, it smarted to realize he was just another *oops* to be smoothed over, but she was making an effort to get them back on normal footing. Since it was more than he'd dared hope for, he'd quit whining and be grateful.

That's it? he prompted when she didn't elaborate.

I'm still trying to decide whether to kick you or hug your neck. I might have to do both.

He choked out a laugh. He'd take either as long as she'd stuck around to administer them. I get that a lot.

I have no doubt. There was a pause, then his phone chirped again. Do I also have you to thank for the pictures that were sent to Michael's boss?

No. I assume that was Tori, by way of Pratimi. At the urging of the Ladies' Club. Tori's sister-in-law was the same computer-savvy friend Melanie had referred to when she'd threatened to spam Michael's email contacts. Too bad the poor slob hadn't known the kind of people she associated with, or he would have steered clear.

And Melanie would never have come to Oregon. Now there was a bittersweet pill.

Have you taken any other steps on my behalf that I should know about?

He debated confessing that he'd sicced Gil on Leachman, but technically, Wyatt wasn't the one taking steps, and if Violet or Tori hadn't told her yet, they probably hadn't found anything. Yet. Leachman might be smart enough to keep his hands clean until the dust settled from Melanie's bombshell, but he was too conceited to deny his baser needs for long.

I left the rest up to the Earnest mafia, Wyatt replied. And he needed to change the subject before she pried more out of him, so he asked, Did Grace catch you?

Unfortunately for me. I thought I'd seen the last of the mare from hell when Shawnee pawned her off. Now I'm eating a lousy rodeo dog in Podunk, Washington.

Alarm bells trilled in Wyatt's head, and it took three tries to punch in: You went with Grace?

Don't worry—no girl talk. She still thinks you're unsoiled.

He snorted, started to type, then on a whim hit Dial instead. He needed to hear if she was really as fine as she was pretending to be.

"Hello?" She sounded wary. He heard the rodeo announcer in the background, then a burst of rock music.

"You really are at the rodeo. I thought you hated watching other people rope."

"*Hate* is a strong word. And Violet talks too much."

Actually, it had been Miz Iris fretting about how Melanie was straying too far from her roots. "You're avoiding the question."

"That wasn't a question; it was a misstatement, which I refuted. And you avoided first. *Are* you okay? We got pretty rough, and you bullfighters are kinda fragile, what with all the bionic parts."

"I'm fine." And damned if he wasn't, at least for the length of this surreal conversation.

She paused, a listening silence. "Is that a boat I hear?"

"Yes." He watched a water-skier carve a long

graceful turn across the turquoise water. "I flew up to Joseph to spend the day at my cabin."

"Which is lakeside, of course."

"Of course. I make a killing renting it out in July and August, when I'm too busy with rodeos to lounge around on the deck."

"Figures. There's always a business angle with you."

"Not always."

"About that." Her tone went abruptly serious. "Last night…I took advantage of you. And I'm sorry."

He scowled at the wake that slapped against his dock, twenty steep wooden steps below where he sat. "I made the first move."

"Did you? Or did I make you think it was your idea?"

"You did not…" And then he sat bolt upright in his Adirondack chair. "You *sold* me?"

"Right down the river. Or up the stairs, as the case may be." She blew a ripe raspberry into the phone. "And I am a total hypocrite. I've been cursing Michael for exploiting me without a second thought. Then I turned around and did the same thing to you."

Wyatt's mind spun backward, hour by hour, minute by minute, to the moment she'd sauntered into the bar. The red shoes. The lipstick. The dress—with only the flowers in red because all scarlet would have tipped her hand.

She'd painted the picture he'd expected to see, and he'd interpreted every brushstroke exactly as she'd intended. Rowdy was just the not-so-sharp stick she'd used as a prod, even more effective because she'd made Wyatt work at getting her to himself.

Replaying it now, he could appreciate how deftly

she'd scripted their argument. The bitter reference to the bullshit women had to put up with in the workplace, the slut-shaming they had to tolerate, a jab at his white male privilege—she'd nailed every one of his guilt buttons with laser precision. It was manipulative and devious…

And he couldn't have done it better himself.

"Am I fired?" she asked.

There was a note in her voice that went beyond resignation, making all of his protective instincts jump to attention. "Not if you tell me what's wrong…beyond the obvious."

He listened to more background noise—cheering, a buzzer—one of the roughstock events in progress. Finally she said, "I woke up today."

And…

He waited, then realized she'd meant it as a complete sentence. *Oh. Damn.* He'd experienced a few less-than-joyful moments of enlightenment, and even though he knew it was a good thing in the long run…

"Ouch," he said.

"Yeah. Imagine, if you will, looking at yourself and seeing your mother."

Holy hell. That would be a nightmare. Then he winced. "Do I have to replace a mirror in the apartment?"

She laughed. "I don't take my anger out on what I assume is irreplaceable antique furniture."

"Good to know." He settled more comfortably in his chair. "So now you owe me."

The note of caution returned. "What kind of payment are we talking about?"

"Information. I've met your father. Tell me about your mother."

"Oh." She took a moment to compose her answer. "Short version? My dad wanted to be a world champion tie-down roper. My mother wanted to be the woman behind the world champion. I came toddling along a year after they got married, which wasn't exactly the plan, but I took to the rodeo road like a happy little duck to water, so it was all good."

"Mmm. I've seen the pictures." Had several of them saved in an encrypted file on his laptop, in fact.

"What can I say? I was adorable." He could hear her cheeky grin. "I grew up in the living quarters of a horse trailer rolling from one end of the country to the other. Mama was a road warrior, pulling the all-nighters so Daddy could sleep, hauling his horse to California while he flew off to South Dakota."

"That doesn't sound like a self-centered person."

"Only because you were never there if, God forbid, Daddy accepted a trophy or did an interview without giving all the credit to his amazing wife."

"Ah. Now it makes sense."

"Yeah. It was definitely all about her." She heaved an audible sigh. "I guess I wasn't much better. That summer after the fire, I cried when he said he wasn't entering the Fourth of July run. No trick riders waving sparklers? No racing from Cody to Red Lodge to Livingston, trying to make 'em all? It was like they canceled Christmas. And Ma…well, she'd hitched her wagon to a star and ended up parked in the Panhandle instead."

"And she wasn't into being a ranch wife."

"To put it mildly. The day Daddy sold his good horse to buy a tractor, Violet swears they could hear the screaming clear down at their place."

Melanie took an audible slurp from her Coke, the rodeo clown's voice tinny through the phone. Wyatt grimaced at a mother-in-law joke so old it'd probably been told at the Pendleton Roundup back when the cowboys hauled their horses in on the train. Honestly. With all of the Internet at their disposal, was it that hard to come up with new material?

"I'm surprised your mother didn't follow the horse out the door," Wyatt said.

"And do what? She had no job skills other than being a rodeo wife—and those openings are reserved for hot, young things, not women pushing thirty and dragging a kid along. She hung in there, hoping Daddy would change his mind and hit the road again, but Grandad's health went downhill so fast...and then came Hank. Ma decided if she ever wanted to do anything but cook, wipe snotty noses, and stare at the ass end of a herd of cows—her words—she'd have to get an education."

A worthy goal, but... "Why broadcasting?"

"She decided to be a star in her own right. Radio, TV, one of those women who interview the cowboys on the rodeo telecasts..."

According to Miz Iris, the minute Hank was old enough to eat solid food their mother had enrolled in classes at the community college, followed by a series of jobs in larger, neighboring towns with low pay and long, unpredictable hours, leaving her son to be raised by a series of babysitters...and Melanie.

"And in the meantime, you decided to be a roper."

"It was either that or the chute help. Daddy was practicing every day, training horses to make extra money. I got tired of pushing calves and tripping the gate so I started roping in self-defense. Since I was good at it, he decided to use me as an advertisement. He took me to all the junior and high school rodeos, and I can't tell you how many times we came home without whatever I was riding that weekend. I learned pretty fast not to get attached."

Wyatt would've expected a hint of sorrow or bitterness—he'd seen how it was with most little girls and their horses—but she sounded amused. "It didn't upset you?"

"Only when he sold my best mount a week before the junior high finals. The colt he put me on took three strides out of the box, bogged its head, and tried to buck me off. Shawnee edged me out for the championship." She snickered. "I like to remind her she got that trophy buckle by forfeit, just to piss her off."

"And you were how old?"

"Thirteen." She laughed at his incredulous tone. "Hey, one thing about being *my* daddy's girl, I learned to cowboy up and rope off of whatever I throwed a leg over."

The same way she didn't hesitate to step in and fight a few bulls just for fun, or bail over a cliff to Wyatt's rescue. The woman was fearless—except when it came to dark woods and canned biscuits. He realized he was grinning and started to squash it…then didn't. Alone on his deck he could enjoy the vision of a pint-sized Melanie schooling her horse and then going ahead and roping anyway, probably cursing like a sailor the whole time.

"And Hank?"

The laughter drained from her voice. "He is our

mother's son—despises cows and has no interest in roping, which didn't stop Daddy from making him do it anyway and riding his ass the whole time. Hank wanted to ride bucking horses like the Sanchez boys, but that was out of the question."

So he'd hung around the Jacobs ranch as much as possible, where he'd developed a love and a talent for fighting bulls. Potentially one of the best in the business…and a complete waste in his father's eyes. Christ. Why couldn't parents just let their children *be*? A question Wyatt had debated with dozens of therapists— Laura's and his own.

Melanie's Coke gurgled dry. "My father would've loved Michael. I even imagined introducing them—" She cut off with an abrupt curse. "God that's pathetic. Still trying to impress my daddy."

"It sneaks up on you. You think you've escaped their force field, then realize you bought a second-rate whorehouse just to picture the look on their faces." *Shit. Where did that come from?* He imagined her eyes narrowing as she analyzed what he'd intended as a joke.

Then she made a dismissive noise. "Nope. That might be a fringe benefit, but it's not what you want most."

"Really? Do tell."

"There's the East Coast snob. *Rah-lly dah-ling?*" She laughed at her own horrible impression. "I think I've almost got it figured out. I'll let you know when I'm sure."

"To think I wasted all that money on therapy when all I needed was good marketing." He injected a dose of sarcasm to cover the discomfort of knowing that this woman—who'd so effortlessly maneuvered him into her bed—had him under her microscope.

"*Everybody* needs good marketing." Her voice softened. "Hey, Wyatt?"

Her soft drawl wrapped around his name, turning it to sweet, Southern music that made his heart soar and his voice catch. "Yes?"

"Even though I know it was really crappy of me... thanks for last night. I promise not to use you that way again, if you promise not to do things behind my back."

And his idiot heart crashed back to earth, because of course he couldn't make that promise. He couldn't even answer without serving up another lie. "From this day forward," he said, the best he could do.

His phone signaled an incoming call. He glanced at the number and froze. Laura's father—who had only one reason to make contact.

"I have to take this." Wyatt forced himself to sound vaguely annoyed, even as his heart thudded. It was either no news, good news, or bad news. The first would be frustrating, the second a miracle, and the third—well, it depended on *how* bad. And yes, he was already breaking his vow, but only temporarily. He would share what he learned, but not until they were face-to-face. "Tell Grace good luck."

"Too late. She just missed her calf."

Damn. "Well, then, I'll see you tomorrow at practice."

"I'll be there." The snark came back into her tone. "And afterward we can discuss the disappearance of one pair of kick-ass red shoes."

Chapter 33

THEY ARRIVED BACK IN PENDLETON LATE IN THE AFTERNOON, so Melanie drove straight from Grace's house to Wyatt's acreage, saddled up Roy, and, leading the sorrel, rode down to check out the saddle club arena. Afterward, she roped the bale for a while. Her loop felt better than it should have, all things considered. By eight o'clock, she was back at the apartment, still restless. She hit the riverside trail for a long stroll. She had paused to sit on a bench and watch a fly fisherman work his graceful magic with line and lure when her phone rang.

She frowned at the sight of Wyatt's number. What would he—

"How soon can you meet me in the bar?" he asked.

Her heart gave a hard, painful thump at his abrupt tone. "Depends on how long it takes you to fly home."

"I'm already here. Half an hour?"

Shit. This was serious. She jumped up to retrace her steps. "Three minutes."

"I'll be there."

The Camaro rounded the corner and parked in front of the bar as she turned off the path onto Main Street. Wyatt stepped out of the car, an escaped Tommy Hilfiger model in sunglasses, gray jeans, and a red-and-blue-plaid button-down with the sleeves rolled to the elbows. He had a leather portfolio tucked under his arm. She could barely detect a limp as he locked the car and walked around to wait for her under the Bull Dancer sign. He still hadn't shaved.

She should have felt awkward, considering the last time they'd seen each other they'd been in an advanced stage of postcoital shock, but her head and her heart were too full of fear.

"Hank?" she asked.

"Yes."

He unlocked the door and held it for her. The lights were already on inside, even though the bar was closed for the day. Had Louie forgotten…

She yelped as Scotty popped up from behind the nearest booth, spray bottle in one hand and rag in the other. Belatedly she caught the lemon-ammonia scent of industrial-strength cleaner.

"What's up?" he asked.

Wyatt took off his sunglasses, stuck them in the pocket of his shirt, and frowned at the clock. "You usually clean in the morning."

"Me and Philip hit the river today with some friends."

Wyatt's eyes narrowed. "Which friends?"

"Not the potheads, Grandma." Scotty shook his head, disgusted. "We made a deal. You let me into your school, I stay clean. I am a man of my word."

Who looked all of fourteen with his freckles and ginger hair sticking up from the cowlick he'd given up trying to tame.

"Is marijuana legal in Oregon?" Melanie asked.

Scotty grinned. "And Washington."

"*If* you're twenty-one," Wyatt added.

"What are you doing here?" Scotty asked, ignoring him.

"Business," Wyatt said, and gestured Melanie to the far end of the bar.

Scotty shrugged and went back to work swabbing down the booth.

Melanie plunked onto the last stool, waiting impatiently while Wyatt settled next to her. "Well?"

"I have a...contact in the financial services business." He set the portfolio down and smoothed a hand across the engraved leather surface, with the ubiquitous *Let 'er Buck* bronc rider logo in the center and Wyatt's name underneath, probably a token of the Roundup's appreciation. "Money is the easiest way to trace a person...if you can access the right information. Credit cards, bank accounts, bills—"

Melanie slapped a hand down over his...hard. "The longer you diddle around, the more time I have to imagine Hank bleeding out in a ditch."

"He's not dead." She'd barely started to breathe a sigh of relief when he added, "Or at least he wasn't in January."

January? But that was only a month after... "I thought you'd found him."

"I didn't say that, but I'm a big step closer."

"What *do* you know?"

He opened the portfolio and pulled out several sheets of paper. "He has a bad debt that was turned over to a collection agency in April."

"What kind of debt?"

He slid the stack of papers toward her. "A hospital bill."

Fear jerked at her heartstrings as she tried to focus on the lines of medical gibberish, each with a designated dollar amount. Leafing through the bill with trembling hands, random items jumped out at her. *Anesthesia.*

Surgical assistant. Radius and ulna. CAT scan, abdominal. Dammit. Where was Tori when you needed an interpreter? Melanie reached the end and sucked in a breath. "*Sixteen thousand dollars?*"

"He broke both bones in his left forearm, which required plates and pins. That's the internal fixation." Wyatt tapped a line item. "He also had a bruised kidney. And no insurance."

Hell. Hank had always been on the ranch policy, but even if their father had been willing to carry him, their local insurance agent was well aware that Hank was no longer employed at the ranch in any capacity. Melanie had enrolled him in an individual plan…which he had obviously let lapse.

"It could have been worse." Wyatt was cool and matter-of-fact. Heartless asshole, she would've said two months ago. Now she suspected he was muting his own emotion, the better to help her keep a grip on hers. "According to the nurse, he checked out against doctor's orders. They wanted to keep him at least another day to monitor for infection and internal bleeding."

But he'd left under his own power. That was good. Or not, if the feared complications had become reality. "All by himself?"

"No." Wyatt's forehead creased as if the gaps in his information physically pained him. "He left with a woman."

Of course there was a woman. Wasn't there always with Hank?

"The nurse remembered that the pickup had Montana plates," Wyatt added. "And she introduced herself as Bing."

Melanie frowned. "Bing? Like the cherries?"

"Yes."

"Wait a minute." Melanie swiveled to stare at him. "A *nurse* told you all this? Have they ever heard of patient privacy?"

"Have you ever seen a woman who could resist when the Man bats those baby blues?" Scotty asked, making her jump again when his voice came from the booth directly behind her.

Wyatt shot him a withering look. "Eavesdrop much?"

"I didn't realize you were telling secrets," Scotty retorted, unfazed.

Wyatt turned back to Melanie. "I told her it was an urgent family matter, and it was imperative that I find him."

"You pretended to be a lawyer," she accused.

Wyatt's fingers curled as if he wished he had a glass or mug to cradle, his classic defensive move. "I may have implied that if I could locate him, he would come into enough money to pay off his account. And since I already had all of his personal information and the itemized bill..."

Melanie opened her mouth, then closed it again. She'd provided Hank's social security number and birth date. What did it matter how Wyatt had gotten his hands on the rest? Then she realized she'd overlooked the most important piece of information. She searched the top sheet of paper and found the name and address of the hospital. Her jaw dropped. "*Yakima?*"

"Yeah. That's why I was able to speak to the staff personally."

"It's only what...two hours from here?" She glared at him. "He was practically in your backyard."

Wyatt's expression became even more pained. "I

was gone nearly all of January and February working Denver and Fort Worth. If I'd been here when it happened, I might have heard something. And he got hurt at a rodeo sponsored by the casino in Toppenish. I've never had anything to do with the Indian rodeo association and until a few days ago, I didn't know you and Hank were descendants."

"That's one of Philip's goals." Scotty gave up all pretense of working to plop down at the end of the booth. "To work the Indian National Finals Rodeo."

Melanie slapped her forehead. "Shit. Philip. The Indian Rodeo Association isn't that big. If he's been around at all, he might know this woman, or know someone who does."

"I texted him the same time I called you." Wyatt checked the clock. "He was at the gym, but he's coming right down."

Philip ambled in a few minutes later, freshly showered. Free from the usual braid, his hair fell black and glossy to his waist. Either he had great conditioner, or it was like with men and eyelashes—they were just naturally blessed, the bastards.

"Have you heard of a woman named Bing?" she demanded, without preface.

Philip's eyes went wary as he looked first at Melanie, then Wyatt. "What do you want with her?"

"You know her?" Melanie jumped from her stool, barely restraining herself from grabbing him by the shoulders and shaking out the answers.

Philip sank down opposite Scotty and slid back in the booth, more guarded by the second. "Everyone knows Bing. Her grandson was my friend."

Grandson? Melanie had to do a quick mental shuffle. She'd been picturing a girlfriend, or that weekend's fling—a questionable and very short-term source of information. But someone's grandmother…

"Where does she live?" Melanie advanced another step. "Do you know how to reach her?"

Philip folded his arms. "First you gotta tell me why."

"I'm looking for my brother." Melanie forced herself to unclench her fists. "She might know where Hank went after he left the hospital in Yakima."

"Hank?" Philip's face cleared, and his eyebrows shot up. "*That's* your brother?"

Her breath whooshed out like she'd been punched. "You know Hank?"

"I seen him a couple of times. He lives out north of Babb with crazy old Norma." Philip squinted at Melanie. "If you didn't know where he is…did you hear about the other guy?"

Melanie stiffened. "What other guy?"

"The one who's paralyzed. Bull stepped on him and broke his back." Cold dread settled into her gut at Philip's grim expression. "Hank might've been able to stop it if he'd been in position…" Philip gave a shrug that invited them to fill in the ugly blanks. "Hank took it pretty bad."

"How bad?" Wyatt asked.

"Dakota was freaking when they packed him out of the arena, practically screaming that he couldn't feel his legs. Everybody was shook up, but the rodeo must go on, ya know?"

Philip's dark gaze swiveled to meet Melanie's. "When they turned out the next bull, Hank never moved. Just stood right there and let it run him down."

Chapter 34

WYATT HAD TO GIVE MELANIE CREDIT. FOR A WOMAN who'd never been in a small plane, she'd stayed pretty calm, even when the going got rough. With atmospheric wave activity causing turbulence over all four mountain ranges between Pendleton and Babb, Montana, they'd been bounced around for most of the trip, and it was a whole different experience in a six-seater.

Conversation had been nonexistent. There wasn't a whole lot left to add after their text and telephone chat. She'd needed a safe outlet for the emotions she could no longer keep bottled up. He'd provided one. Then he'd removed all traces of himself from the room, as close as he could give her to an anonymous one-night stand.

And once again, they would put it behind them and never speak of it again. It was their way.

Besides, Melanie was distracted enough between worrying about Hank and riding out the periodic bucks and jolts of the small aircraft. It took all of Wyatt's concentration to keep the plane on a relatively even keel—especially when it came time to land. The web page he'd checked had been very generous when they called the scrubby strip of grass an airport. Throw in the gusty crosswind, and their touchdown had been a lot more adventurous than he preferred.

The wind rocked the Cherokee and plastered Wyatt's jacket against his back as he ran a rope through the ring on the underside of the second wing, pulled it snug, and tied it off in two practiced, well-spaced knots. He gave the rope a tug to test that it was secure, then turned to where Melanie stood huddled against the fuselage. His instrument panel claimed it was sixty-three degrees, but the air had a biting edge that cut right through his clothes—and he was a northerner compared to Melanie.

He tapped his fingers on the door. "You can wait in the plane if you're cold."

"No. The fresh air is good."

He studied her face for signs that she might be about to upchuck her breakfast burrito. "Feeling a little green?"

"You think? Between buzzing the runway to chase off the cows, and the holes—" She took a couple of steps to kick dirt from one of the mounds that pocked a runway marked by rows of old car tires painted yellow. "Didn't your plane used to have two engines? It seems like a spare would be a good idea."

"I traded the Cessna in. This one is a lot cheaper to own, and just as safe."

"If you say so." Melanie hugged her ribs, shivering as she scanned their surroundings. The rocky flat was cut off to the east by the river that flowed along the base of a ridge and into Canada, close enough that Wyatt had had to be careful not to encroach on international airspace. Beyond that ridge, they'd glimpsed the plains that stretched east to infinity. To the south, the choppy surface of Lower St. Mary's Lake gleamed an unearthly blue. At their backs, clouds piled up behind the jagged peaks of Glacier National Park. Snow still clung on the highest precipices and in shady niches, contributing to the chill. Fifty yards away, a steady stream of RVs, cars, and pickups rolled by on the highway. Wyatt could almost sort the locals from the tourists at a glance.

"Are we early?" Melanie asked.

"No." Wyatt hesitated, then stepped around behind her, putting a hand on each shoulder to pull her into the shelter of his body. When she stiffened, he kneaded her shoulders gently. "Consider me a human windbreak."

As he continued the massage—purely therapeutic, even if his heart and body wanted to think otherwise—she relaxed enough to tilt her face up to the sun, the crown of her head brushing his jaw, but her muscles vibrated with tension. He ached to wrap his arms around her and hold on for as long as he was allowed.

His phone buzzed, and he checked the text. "Hell. I forgot I had a haircut scheduled today. I won't be able to reschedule before I leave for Reno."

"You'll have time to get it cut while you're down there."

Wyatt scoffed at the suggestion. "I'm not letting a stranger touch my hair."

"*What* was I thinking?" But as snark went, it was far from her best effort.

He tilted his head to scowl at her, dragging out the inane conversation to distract both of them. "Oh, and you would walk into any old salon?"

"Always do." She flicked the end of the ponytail that danced in the breeze. "I never get around to making appointments. I just walk into one of those mall places if I notice the ends are getting fried." When she saw the look of honest horror on Wyatt's face, she rolled her eyes. "As hairstyles go, this isn't exactly rocket science."

Unlike his, which required practice and precision. He'd had enough of the pretty-boy crap when Laura had persuaded him to let it grow out—very temporarily. *My angel face*, she'd called him, toying with his mop of curls. Back then, his future had been laid out like the squares on a Monopoly board—from Connecticut Avenue to Park Place, acquiring the requisite wife, children, and real estate along the way.

Now here he was, standing in the heart of the Blackfeet Nation with the woman who'd ended up owning him.

A black short-box pickup slowed to turn onto the gravel road leading to the airstrip, and Melanie stepped quickly away, as if not wanting to be seen too close to him. He tried to brush off the sting. It was possible Hank could be behind the tinted windows. If he saw Wyatt's hands on his sister, this conversation would be over before it started.

But there was only one person in the vehicle, and the woman who stepped out was, at a guess, around five years older than Wyatt, with smooth, dark skin and jet-black hair cut in short, funky spikes. She wore a summer-weight black sweater, fashionably distressed jeans, caramel-colored suede boots, and a jacket to match. When she smiled, her face transformed from merely attractive to striking.

Wyatt had to force his answering smile past a knot of impatience. Bing had been maddeningly evasive on the phone, refusing to say anything specific about the situation beyond assuring him that Hank had recovered from his injuries, but she had promised to meet them herself. Why had she sent this—

The woman extended a graceful hand to Melanie. "You have to be the sister."

"Uh, yes." Melanie accepted the handshake but shot a quick *Who is this?* look at Wyatt.

He was trying not to gape, having recognized the rich, contralto voice. "And you're Bing."

He managed to make it a statement instead of a shocked question. To have a grandson near Philip's age, she would've had to be…and then her son or daughter must have been… Wyatt gave up on the math, stepping closer to Melanie to give her a subtle nudge with his elbow. She blinked, as if he'd interrupted similar calculations on her part.

"No sense standing out here in this damn wind." Bing gestured to her pickup. "I could use a cup of coffee. How 'bout you?"

Melanie opened her mouth, no doubt to demand to see Hank immediately. Wyatt grabbed her elbow and gave it a warning squeeze as he steered her toward the pickup. She jerked away, but clamped her mouth shut and climbed into the front passenger's seat when he opened the door for her. Wyatt slid into the back seat behind her, where he could see Bing's face and hold Melanie down if necessary. She was in no state of mind to be patient or tactful, which was why Wyatt had insisted that Philip give *him* Bing's phone number, and that he be the one to talk to her.

They turned east on the highway, crossed over the crystal-clear river, and skirted the edge of the lake. Ahead and to the right, the Rockies loomed, row after row of sheer cliffs and razor-edged crests. These were the real deal, not glorified hills like the section of the Blue Mountains around Pendleton.

If Melanie pushed him off one of these, Wyatt wouldn't limp away.

"How far is it to where Hank is staying?" she asked.

"About ten miles up that way." Bing waved a hand over her shoulder, opposite the direction they were traveling. She silenced any protest on Melanie's part with a cool, assessing look. "When he got hurt, I asked if he had family I should call. He said no."

Melanie sucked in an audible breath at the implication. *He didn't want you there. Why is that?*

"Does he know we're coming?" Wyatt asked, carefully neutral.

"Norma doesn't have a phone." One corner of Bing's mouth curled down. "And a call might guarantee he'd be gone."

Melanie thumped a clenched fist on the center console. "*Why?* He knows he can always come to me for help."

Bing gave her an enigmatic glance. "Can he?"

Before Melanie could return fire, Bing made a left into the parking lot of a café housed in a large, purple tin shed with a bright-red door and *Aliens Welcome* painted on the roof in three-foot-high letters. The decor suggested they were referring to the kind who might arrive via flying saucer. Inside, the dining room was a mix of rustic wood and hippie kitsch. At just past eleven on a Monday, only one table was occupied—by a family with Iowa license plates, two squabbling elementary-school boys, and a teenaged girl mesmerized by her phone. The server who greeted them had a man bun and a Swedish accent.

Bing marched past him to the table farthest from the tourists. "We'll take this one. And bring me a cup of coffee and a piece of huckleberry pie."

"Ice cream?" he asked.

"Huckleberry." She nodded at Melanie and Wyatt.

"They'll have the same. And give me two burgers with the works to go. Put it on my check."

"I'll take sweet tea if you have it," Melanie said.

She settled into the chair across from Bing with an expression that made Wyatt feel as if he was taking a seat between two mama bears who'd laid claim to the same cub. Whatever Bing had to say, she didn't expect them to like it. *Damn*. Wyatt wanted to smack himself. He'd been so thrilled to locate Hank that he hadn't realized Bing had never actually agreed to take them to him.

And she was still in the process of deciding.

Chapter 35

WHO THE *HELL* DID THIS WOMAN THINK SHE WAS? IF SHE thought she could keep Melanie away from her brother much longer, she was fixin' to get schooled. Any of the other locals could lead her to Hank, and Melanie would go around, over, or through anyone who tried to stop her.

Bing nodded her thanks to the waiter as he set down their drinks, then waited until he was out of earshot. "You heard what happened in Toppenish?"

"Only what Philip told us."

Bing nodded again and took a sip of her coffee. She spoke with a less-pronounced version of Philip's Native American...did you call it an accent? As when Melanie was using what she called her "professional voice," the words revealed that Bing was educated, but the shapes of vowels and the weight of the consonants were different.

"Was it his fault?" Melanie blurted.

Bing shrugged. "The cowboys know the chance they're taking when they climb on. The bullfighters can only do so much."

"That's not an answer."

Bing looked Melanie straight in the eye. "There aren't many bullfighters who can do what Hank does and make it look easy. Like this one—" She tipped her head toward Wyatt. "The kid got slammed down on his face practically under the bull's nose, and that's a hooky son of a bitch. Even if Hank had done everything right, he might not have gotten there in time. None of our other bullfighters would have had a prayer."

"Does he understand that?" Wyatt asked.

Bing swung her dark eyes over to him. "What do you think?"

Wyatt didn't bother to answer. In the same circumstances, he would never forgive himself. Neither would Joe. They understood the worst could happen every time the chute gate cracked, and they could accept it—eventually—if they'd done everything humanly, and sometimes superhumanly, possible to protect the cowboy. If they hadn't...

They would have to try to live with it.

Melanie shook her head. "He started out so well after he left Jacobs Livestock. I can't fathom what went wrong."

"One of his new Florida friends asked him why he left Texas, and Hank made the mistake of telling the truth." Bing's hand tightened, as if she'd like to have more than words with those so-called friends. "When the story spread, they left out a few pertinent details— like how Hank never did more than kiss Mariah Swift, or that she was from Washington state and had no idea she was two months shy of legal in Texas. Keeping it quiet was as much self-preservation for her as for him. Imagine the guilt if he'd been hit with a mandatory two-year prison sentence, all for a summer fling."

"Hank wasn't just having fun," Wyatt said quietly.

"No." Bing gave a pitying shake of her head. "He fell hard. Understandable if you've ever met Mariah. Hank's not the first cowboy she's blown out of his boots, and she's always liked 'em older. Drives her parents insane."

"You know them?" Melanie asked.

"His mother is Shoshone. They show up once in a while at the bigger Indian rodeos. Mariah is an amazing girl— smart, talented, gorgeous, and very mature for her age. Hank thought they would just let things blow over, then pick up again once she was old enough." Bing's mouth twisted down at the corners. "She had other ideas. Six weeks later, she was posting pictures with her new beau."

Oh God. Poor Hank. He'd tried to tell Melanie how he felt about the girl when she'd charged to the rescue after Mariah's daddy had busted his jaw and Cole Jacobs had fired him. She'd been too busy calling her brother ten kinds of an idiot to listen.

And she wondered why he had stopped coming to her with his problems.

"That's why he didn't go back to Florida for the beginning of the new season," Wyatt guessed.

Bing nodded. "The biggest contractor in that region had asked him to work all of their rodeos for the next year, but he took it back when he heard the rumors. Told Hank flat out that he wasn't bringing someone like him on board when he had a fourteen-year-old granddaughter."

"Four*teen*?" Melanie burst out. "For God's sake. Hank might not've used the best judgment where Mariah was concerned, but he's not a predator."

Wyatt put a settling hand on her arm. "*We* know that, but a bunch of strangers are going to believe what they hear."

"Especially when it's been blown all out of proportion," Bing put in sourly. "That's when it finally hit him. What had happened with Mariah wasn't *no big deal.* The law and the gossips didn't give a shit about his intentions. In their eyes, he was no better than scum-bags who hang out at the mall stalking the teenyboppers. That's when he really started coming unraveled."

"Right around Thanksgiving," Wyatt said.

"Yeah. And then he went home and made it all worse."

Getting into a yelling match with their dad. And sleeping with Grace. His friend. His little red-haired girl. Then getting drunk and expressing his regret in the most humiliating way possible.

Melanie propped her elbows on the table and pressed the heels of her hands into temples that threatened to explode. "God. This thing with Mariah—it's like the gift that won't stop giving."

"She was also at Toppenish," Bing said flatly. "Like I said, they occasionally pop up at the big-money rodeos. Seeing her knocked Hank on his ass. He made it through the rodeo that night—probably on auto-pilot—but the next day...whatever he did overnight to dull the pain hadn't worn off. That would have to be the day some-thing horrible happened. When he needed to be at his absolute best, and wasn't."

"And the bull that ran him down?" Melanie braced herself to hear the worst. "What was that?"

"The beginning of an emotional meltdown. But if you're asking if he was suicidal—I'm not sure even he can answer that question."

"What about now?" Wyatt asked, when Melanie couldn't force out the words.

"He's making progress. But he's got a lot to deal with—the breakdown of his family, the loss of his alternative support structure as part of the Jacobs crew, damage to his self-worth from the thing with Mariah.

And now there's an eighteen-year-old boy in a wheelchair, and Hank's convinced he helped put him there. I don't know many people who possess the coping mechanisms to deal with that much emotional trauma."

At the rise of Wyatt's eyebrows, she smiled. "Did I forget to mention that I'm an addiction counselor at Indian Health Service? I can talk all the jargon."

"You aren't his counselor, or you wouldn't be able to tell us any of this," Wyatt said.

"No. I'm his friend. He needs that right now more than anything."

Even more than his sister?

Bing's dark gaze settled on her, reading the obvious thought. "He needs someone who isn't part of his old life. A person who has nothing invested in anything but him."

"And that's you?" Melanie asked, hurt sharpening the question to a near insult.

"Yes."

They fell silent as the waiter brought slices of pie, the dark berry filling oozing out to pool around generous scoops of paler-purple ice cream. Wyatt ignored his. Melanie picked up her fork and tested the crust, then took a small bite. The intense flavor of the berries exploded in her mouth.

"Good?" Bing asked.

"Excellent." Although the pastry was no match for Miz Iris's, but nothing ever was. Melanie took another bite, this time with ice cream. Even better. She kept eating because she didn't know what else to do. Finally, she paused. "What about now? Is he...safe?"

"As far as I can tell. He's in a situation where, in his words, it's nearly impossible for him to screw up anything else. We have to start there and give him the tools he needs to rebuild."

"How long will that take?" Melanie asked, realizing even as she spoke that it was a ridiculous question.

Bing just shrugged.

"And this…state he's in. I suppose you have a name for it."

"He hasn't been formally evaluated, but I would call it a major depressive episode. I have seen no signs of substance abuse. He doesn't even drink more than a beer now and then. With therapy, time, and possibly medication, he could come out of this just fine."

Could. Melanie lifted her eyes to challenge Bing's steady gaze. "And you think he can get all of that here."

"I do." Bing gave her a long, thoughtful look, then a slight nod, as if she'd come to a decision. "And you need to judge for yourself. Just don't expect him to be happy to see you."

Chapter 36

WHEN MELANIE TURNED SHE SAW THAT BEHIND THE corral, a pickup camper had been set several yards back into the trees on a platform of wooden pallets, with moldy, disintegrating straw bales packed around the bottom for insulation. Lord. The thing must be crawling with mice.

"Hank?" Melanie had to ask because the blade-thin man leaning in the camper door bore almost no resemblance to her brother.

Like Wyatt, he'd given up shaving, but the result was scraggly and uneven, as if he whacked at it occasionally with a pair of dull scissors. The hair he'd always kept short fell well past the collar of a tan canvas chore coat worn through at the cuffs and hem. But it was his eyes that unnerved her, dark and flat in his gaunt face.

"What are you doing here, Mel? And with him?" He jerked his chin toward the pickup.

Wyatt stood utterly still, but Melanie knew he was as cocked and ready as that shotgun—muscles primed to explode into action. It took considerable effort to keep her voice level. "You haven't called, and I couldn't find you. I was worried."

"Yeah? What kind of deal did you make with the devil to track me down?" Then he snorted in contempt. "As if I need to ask."

She bit back the knee-jerk response. She hadn't

really expected Hank to attack. Not like this. Why hadn't she thought to make Wyatt stay...somewhere? Anywhere but here. Why hadn't he offered to stay back? He had probably thought she needed protecting—and assuming that gun was loaded, he might be right—but the sight of him was enough to ruin any chance of a civil conversation between her and Hank.

Ever.

"He's awful pretty." The old woman shuffled out onto the warped wooden step, as hunched and gnarled as the wind-tortured trees. She leered at Wyatt, showing three rotting brown teeth. "I'd do him for nothin'."

Wyatt didn't quite hide his grimace. Norma cackled, leaning on her shotgun as she squinted at them from a face that had collapsed in on itself as if the bones had dissolved along with her spine.

"I s'pose you want to haul that one back to Texas." She waved a bony claw at Hank. "Go ahead. Ain't worth a shit anyway."

"Neither is the pay," Hank retorted.

Norma *hmmphed*, then scowled at Bing. "You bring me anything besides tourists?"

"Always." She held up a carton with the pie Wyatt hadn't touched and a bag with the takeout burgers. "Let's go inside and give them some privacy."

"I'll wait in the pickup. I can use the rest before the flight home." Wyatt climbed into the front seat and closed the door. From there, he could keep an eye on Melanie and Hank without listening in...and avoid being trapped in the close confines of the trailer with a woman who didn't appear to have had her spring bath yet. He tilted the seat back and closed his eyes, but Melanie had no doubt he was still watching.

She stepped over to the corral. The piebald nudged at her with his nose, and she rubbed his forehead, grateful for something to do with her hands. He wasn't much to look at, but he was in excellent shape, his shoulders and flanks thick with muscle. On closer inspection, she could see that at least half of the fence rails had been replaced, the ends freshly cut and smelling of sawdust and pine sap. The dilapidated shelter also sported new brace posts and patches on the roof, and the stack of hay bales alongside was neatly covered with an old truck tarp tied to concrete cinder blocks.

As Hank stepped away from the camper to prop his arms on the side of the corral opposite her, she could see that, unlike Norma, his hair was clean and his clothes, jacket aside, had seen a washing machine in recent memory…and nobody washed their chore coat.

She ran her fingers through the horse's forelock. "Nice spot. What do you do other than keep the place up?"

"She's got a couple dozen cows running around in the hills." His lip curled at the irony. "Yeah. My favorite."

Geezus. Hank was voluntarily herding cattle? This was worse than Melanie had thought. "She owns this place?"

"Nah. It's tribal land, but if they run her out of here, they'd just have to put her somewhere else. And it's open range, so the cows go wherever somebody doesn't fence 'em out."

Which accounted for the cattle they'd seen grazing the road ditches. "Does she actually pay you?"

"Only in beef and venison. She is a damn good shot. I scrounge up enough pocket money to keep gas in the generator and beer in the fridge. Don't need anything else." He made a show of looking around. "Guess we coulda picked up a little, but we aren't in the habit of *entertaining*."

Anger sparked at his snotty tone. "I heard they have a phone at the Babb store. If you'd bothered to call, I wouldn't have had to sneak up on you."

"Sorry." His gaze settled on her, unrepentant as his voice. "Didn't mean to drag you away from work."

The barb struck home, but she refused to let him see her flinch. "No problem. I'm what you would call *between jobs*."

"You finally told the Leech where he could shove it?" For an instant he was startled out of his shell, but she only caught a glimpse before he retreated behind a sneer. "Wonders will never cease."

She shrugged, matching his attitude. "I screwed up. Got involved with a client who turned out to be married. Let's just say when I found out, I didn't take the news well…and now I've got all kinds of time on my hands."

"So you figured you might as well put them on Wyatt."

A denial leapt to her tongue, but she swallowed it. She refused to lie, and she hadn't come here to explain or excuse herself. "I just wanted to be sure you're okay."

"Well, now you've seen for yourself." He spread his arms, inviting her to see that no, he was not okay, or anywhere in the vicinity. But he was alive and physically healthy. For now. He shook his head. "You can stop looking at me like that. I decided not to rid the world of my presence."

"Don't say that!" she snapped.

The horse shied, then ambled off to lip at the remainder of his morning hay.

Hank held up both hands, palms out. "Just kiddin', Sis. You used to have a sense of humor."

I also used to have a bright future and a brother who called me every Sunday. "It's been stretched a little thin lately."

They stared at each other across the corral, each tense second loaded with all the things she couldn't say and didn't want to hear.

She detected a softening in his expression—or manufactured it out of the flickering shadows. "I had a bad moment in Toppenish. It hurt like hell, and I'm literally gonna be paying for it for the rest of my life, so I'm not keen on tryin' that again."

She drew a deep, steadying breath. "How long do you think you'll stay?"

"Dunno." He cocked his head toward the pickup. "How long you plannin' to sleep with the enemy?"

"Wyatt is not—" *Hell.* She didn't even know where to start, and from the way Hank's jaw had tightened, there was no explanation that would suffice. "Could we forget about that? I just want to talk to you."

He squinted, then rubbed his chin, making a show of thinking it over. "You know how Miz Iris always says you can judge a man by the company he keeps?" He jerked his head toward the pickup. "If that's how you want to hang, then we don't have anything to talk about."

"Hank. Wait!"

But he'd already turned his back. He paused only to lift one hand and flip his middle finger. "Pass that along to the condescending prick and tell him 'no' still means '*hell* no.'"

And then he was gone, swallowed up by the shadows beneath the trees.

"I love you anyway," she whispered. The same words she'd said every time she'd bailed him out of whatever mess he'd managed to get into. Hank wouldn't have heard her if he'd been standing three feet away.

Melanie clenched her hands on the fence rail. The rough bark dug into her palms, a counterpoint to the raw ache in her chest. Dammit. *Why* had she brought Wyatt? It would have eliminated any chance at a civil conversation even when Hank was still...Hank. She took a moment to breathe through the worst of the pain, then pushed away from the corral and headed for the pickup. The door swung open, and Wyatt stepped out. Bing must have been watching, too, because she came out of the trailer with Norma stumping along behind. Wyatt watched her intently but didn't say anything, just held the door.

Bing climbed behind the wheel, also silent. No one spoke until they bounced from the dirt track onto the main gravel road.

"Is that an arena?" Wyatt asked, pointing down the river.

"Yes. There's a bar and restaurant up on the hill. They have team roping and open rodeos all summer. Hank comes over and helps out to earn a little spending money."

Melanie's head jerked up. "Fighting bulls?"

"They asked. He said no." Bing's tone implied that his refusal had not been a polite one.

Melanie closed her eyes, slowly shaking her head. "I can't believe he won't even try…"

"*Can't*." Bing corrected. "Not until he makes peace with what happened to that boy."

"How's he going to do that out here all alone, with no one to help?" Melanie demanded.

Bing raised her eyebrows.

Melanie made a frustrated noise. "But he's down there with nothing…"

"Exactly. I found him a place where there are no expectations to live up to. No one to let down." Bing shot her a pointed look. "From what I've been able to pry out of him, that's a nice change."

Melanie felt her face going hot. Yes, she'd lost her temper and her patience at times, but dammit, she'd also been the one cheering him on. She'd paid the tuition for a bullfighting clinic when their dad refused, then driven Hank all the way to Stephenville for the damn thing, missing two good rodeos in the process.

She hadn't fought for him all these years to just walk away now.

Bing heaved a big *I told you so* sigh. "This is why I didn't want to take you down there. You only see what it's not. Did you even notice what *is* there? When he first came, he barely set foot out of that camper. Lately, he's been fixing on the corral and barn, riding that ol' horse for hours through the hills, working over at the arena a couple of days a week. I even got my nephew to drag him to open gym nights at the grade school a few times. It might not sound like much, but from where he started…"

Melanie blew out a long, shuddering breath. "And

I'm supposed to just leave him, and expect a bunch of strangers to care as much about him as I do."

"I doubt we can manage that." Bing's face softened. "You *are* his sister. But I will look out for him. It's what I do."

And it was what Melanie had *always* done. Now Bing thought she could waltz in and do a better job of it?

Melanie stewed all the way back to the plane. When they arrived, she was stunned to realize it was only twelve thirty. They hadn't even been on the ground for two hours, but there was no reason to hang around.

She would be back, though—alone and with a plan.

"Are you sure you don't want to eat before you go?" Bing asked as she pulled to a stop.

"We just had pie," Wyatt reminded her, even though he hadn't eaten any. "And if the trip home is anything like coming over, we're better off on an empty stomach."

Melanie leaned against the pickup beside Bing while Wyatt untied the plane and did his preflight inspection. Satisfied, he came over and extended a hand to Bing.

"We appreciate your help."

"You're welcome." She turned and folded Melanie into an unexpected hug. "I'll keep you updated."

"Thank you," Melanie whispered. "And thanks for everything you've done for him. I don't mean to seem ungrateful. It's just…"

"I know." Bing patted her back, then turned her loose, gave a final wave, and drove away.

Melanie stood watching the pickup bump over the grass and onto the highway, oblivious to the chilly wind that whipped her ponytail like a flag. She started when Wyatt put a hand on her shoulder.

"Do you want to stay?" he asked quietly. "I can arrange a rental car, and we could go back to see him again tomorrow…"

She shook her head, especially at the *we*. "It would be a waste of time."

Even if she went to Norma's alone, in a place like this, Hank was bound to hear if Wyatt was anywhere in the vicinity. She took in the mountains, the river, the lake. It was incredibly gorgeous. And maybe Bing was right. It could be good for Hank. For now.

She turned abruptly toward the plane, shaking off Wyatt's hand when she would rather have curled into the hard, reassuring heat of his body. She'd dragged him along to see Hank without a second thought, a flashing red sign that she was already becoming *way* too accustomed to leaning into his strength.

"Let's get out of here," she said.

He didn't argue. She supposed the gist of her thoughts was obvious to a man who knew her way too well. When they were settled in, seat belts securely fastened, Wyatt handed her an airsickness bag.

She tried to push it away. "I was fine on the way over."

"And you'll probably be fine on the way back." He shoved the bag onto her lap. "But just in case. You are not puking purple all over my cabin."

She didn't have the energy left to fight even this tiny battle, so she kept the damn thing. "Whatever. Take me home, Chuck."

Chapter 37

MELANIE WOKE WITH A VISIBLE START WHEN THE WHEELS touched down. After their night in the woods, Wyatt could tell if she was sleeping…or faking it so she didn't have to talk to him about what had passed between her and Hank. He knew the act had become reality when she started twitching and mumbling.

Was it the stress, or was she like him—incapable of shutting down completely? He wanted to know. Just once, he wanted to be with her for reasons other than crisis control. To hold her, touch her, watch her sleep just for the mutually agreed-upon pleasure of it.

He also wanted world peace and an end to global warming.

She blinked groggily and scrubbed a hand over her forehead. "How did I doze off on that carnival ride?"

"After we refueled, I took a detour and found smooth air over southern Idaho and the low end of the Blues." He turned off the runway and taxied toward the area reserved for private aircraft. "Did you sleep at all last night?"

"Not that you'd notice." She yawned hugely and checked the clock. It wasn't quite five o'clock Pacific time. "Wow. You can cover a lot of territory in a day with this thing."

He nodded, then switched over to the ground frequency and radioed Pendleton Aviation that he was going to tie up instead of hangaring his plane for the night and wanted it fueled for takeoff to Reno the next morning. Heat radiated up through the soles of his shoes when they stepped out onto the asphalt.

Melanie tilted her face into the mid-afternoon sun, soaking it up. "Ahhh! I thought I was never going to be warm again. I don't know how Hank..."

She trailed off with a shake of her head, clearly not ready to discuss her brother. Still in her thinking space. When she emerged, would she jump in her car and drive straight back to Montana? Without Wyatt. He might not have heard what was said, but the gestures Hank had made toward him had been crystal clear.

Wyatt should apologize for tagging along. He'd known what would happen when Hank saw him, but for Maddie's sake—and for Grace's—he'd had to judge the situation for himself. The fact that Melanie had allowed his presence was testimony to how scared she'd been about what she might find out in those woods.

Once again, Wyatt was the lesser of available evils... and pathetically grateful to be even that much to her. Saying he was sorry would be just one more lie.

While Wyatt tied the plane down and went through his postflight routine, Melanie strolled over to a vending machine beside the door to the flight school office. She'd pulled her hair out of the ponytail, and it rippled in the breeze as she sauntered toward him with a Coke in each hand, a leggy, loose-hipped all-American fantasy girl.

He downed half the Coke in the first few gulps. Damn, that tasted good. When he lowered the can, he took the chance of asking, "How are you doing?"

"I'm not sure yet. But I do know I'm starving." She visibly shook off the clouds that darkened her eyes. "Burgers?"

"Race you to the car." And this time, he won.

―⁓⁓⁓―

When they emerged from the drive-through, Wyatt asked, "Home?"

"No." She slid him a considering glance. "I realize you've already done more than enough, but could you manage one more favor?"

"Sure."

Her brows arched. "Not even going to ask what it is first?"

"Not today." Not ever, even if he went through the motions. For an incredibly perceptive woman, she had somehow failed to realize that he was incapable of saying no to her. "What do you have in mind?"

He doubted it included taking her back to the apartment, pulling the curtains, and trying to love her hurt away. After everything she'd been hit with in the past week and a half, how was she even upright, let alone functional?

"Come riding with me. Horseback," she clarified when he blinked in confusion. "I need some fresh air to clear my head after today, and the boys need exercise… if I'm going to rope tomorrow night."

"Really? That's…great."

She scrunched up her nose. "I doubt it after all this time, but I'll get back in the groove eventually. So…?"

She wanted him to ride. With her. *Hell.* Why didn't she just ask him to strip naked on Main Street? He'd be less self-conscious. He sighed. "That'd be great."

He almost managed to sound like he meant it.

She ate in the car—careful not to drip ketchup from her loaded burger, he noticed—then left him to wolf down his two double burgers while she caught and brushed the horses. As she tossed blankets onto the back of the sorrel, Wyatt realized the flaw in her plan.

"You only have one saddle."

She swung it onto the horse and reached under his belly for the front cinch. "You can take this guy. I'll jump on Roy bareback."

Literally. As Wyatt tried to get comfortable in the unfamiliar western saddle, she grabbed two handfuls of mane and vaulted onto the buckskin, then settled on his back as if she was kicked back in a rocking chair.

Gesturing at the trail, she said, "Lead the way."

Damn. He'd been hoping to totter along behind where she couldn't watch him, and he could enjoy the sight of her flowing so easily with every move of her horse. Unlike him. He sighed and nudged the sorrel forward. The horse stepped out eagerly. Wyatt was intensely aware of Melanie's gaze on his back as he tried to focus on the rhythm, the press of his thighs and calves against the saddle, keeping the reins snug to maintain that ever-important contact his riding instructor had drilled into his head.

When the trail crossed the saddle club driveway, she rode up alongside. "Did you ever ride outside the ring? Just meander over the hills or whatever you have out there?"

"No. My family doesn't meander. Our riding was all about discipline."

"Well, this isn't." She poked him lightly in the side.

"Make like Gus McCrae and slouch a little. The judges aren't watching to be sure your horse maintains a perfect topline."

"Habit," he said stiffly. "I was taught to keep my horse between my legs at all times."

She laughed. "An excellent strategy. Things tend to go straight to hell when I fail to keep a leg on either side of my horse."

Wyatt grinned reluctantly. He was aware that he was overly sensitive about the subject, but all of the things that set him apart, his riding style had always felt like the most emphatically *not cowboy*.

"What we need here is to give your brain a logical explanation for why we ride the way we do." She moved a few steps past, then swung Roy around to face him, making a wide, sweeping gesture. "Picture the Panhandle, and how much ground a horse might have to cover. You want him as relaxed as possible to conserve energy on those dawn-to-dusk days—his and yours. And that is one of Cole's horses, so I guarantee he can follow a trail or a cow from here to Texas all by himself. Your job is to leave him alone and let him do it."

Well…okay. That made sense. Wyatt took a deep breath and drew upon his progressive relaxation training to consciously push the tension out of his body with the exhale and allow his shoulders to slump.

"There. That's already better." She swung her gaze around to study the trail, which crossed over the highway and meandered toward the river, skirting a series of large ponds. "How much farther does that go?"

"About half a mile."

She jerked her chin. "Give ol' red there his head."

Wyatt did as she instructed, putting slack in the reins. The horse heaved what sounded like a sigh of relief. For the rest of the way, Wyatt attempted the opposite of contact, imagining himself so light in the saddle that he all but floated. In response, the gelding dropped his head and settled into smooth, ground-eating strides designed to cover a lot of Texas country. The sun was warm on Wyatt's back, the air sweet with the scent of blooming Russian olive trees. He was so lulled by the clomp of hooves and the easy, rocking gait that he was surprised when they emerged from a cluster of trees at the river's edge.

"Much better," Melanie said.

"Thanks." He had to squelch a foolish smile at her approval.

She slid off of Roy, unsnapped one end of the roping rein from the bridle, and picked her way across the stretch of rocky beach, leading the horse. Wyatt followed suit. The horses eased up to snuffle and lip at the river, cold, rushing water being a novelty to creatures of the flat, hot Texas prairie. Melanie crouched to trail her fingers in a small side stream, as graceful as a deer with sunlight striking fire in the chestnut brown of her hair.

Another image permanently burned into Wyatt's brain. Another place—along with the bar, his arena, the Roundup grounds, and especially the apartment—where he would never stop seeing her.

He cleared his throat. "How's the job hunt going?"

"I just finished putting everything together. My portfolio is pretty strong, but the cover letter…" She grimaced. "*I'm eager for new challenges*. Ugh. And I wouldn't ask Westwind for a letter of recommendation even if I thought I'd get one."

"As your most recent client, I'll give you a reference."

"For what? I haven't done anything yet."

"I beg to differ. Our business has quadrupled since you came to town. Louie had to restock the beer cooler a week sooner than usual." A chore most bars performed nightly—at least.

Her mouth twisted. "That's just pathetic."

"Tell me about it." He picked up a small piece of driftwood and turned it over in his hands as he watched her from the corner of his eye, trying to sense her mood, what direction she might swing. He edged back from the side of the river. No sense making it easy if she settled on being mad at him for screwing up her chances with Hank.

"Speaking of doing something about the bar," she said, "I have thoughts."

"I was hoping."

She threw him a mock sneer. "These things take time. I drafted a preliminary plan, but I like to get to know the client, figure out the things they don't want to tell me."

And now she'd reached a verdict. His body tensed, fiber by fiber, as he braced to hear what she'd deduced about him.

"Such as…" She flicked water from her fingers in a shower of sunlit diamonds. "You failed to mention that you'd talked to Hank since Cole fired him. When, pray tell, was that?"

Crap. He'd hoped Hank hadn't got around to mentioning that. Wyatt scored a groove in the soft driftwood with his thumbnail. "About a month after he left Texas. There's a winter rodeo series in Billings, Montana, that needed a bullfighter, and they would have put him up."

"He said to give you this…" She flipped him a middle finger.

Figured, but at least the gesture hadn't been aimed at his sister. Wyatt heaved the driftwood out into the river. "I should have found someone else to make the offer, but I thought it would be worse if he accepted, then found out after the fact that I set it up."

"And his sister was too wrapped up in the big release of our new fly control mineral formula to be bothered."

Oh hell. He grimaced in apology. "I'm sorry. I didn't even consider—"

"You shouldn't have had to! He's *my* brother. *My* responsibility." She stood abruptly, causing the sorrel to jump back a step, rocks clattering under his metal-shod hooves. "I tried so goddamn hard to fill in all the gaps for Mama, did everything I could to keep the peace between him and Daddy, hauled him to practice and rodeo and the ER, and he won't even…" She gulped in a breath, giving her head a violent shake. "No wonder he was hiding. As usual, it's me, me, me!"

Wyatt wanted to insist that she'd been a teenager, for hell's sake, doing the best she could, but she wasn't asking his opinion. She was just thinking out loud, still sifting it all through…

Still in her time-out corner. And she'd invited him inside the space she so rarely shared. He felt as if she'd handed him the key to a secret glade wrapped in sunshine, water, and rustling trees. His heart stumbled, half joyfully, half fearfully.

Don't screw this up. Do not screw this up! He bit back the reassurance that leapt to his tongue and waited.

She wound the end of Roy's bridle rein tight around her hand. "Hank tried to tell me how he felt about Mariah. And I told him not to be stupid. How's that for supportive?"

"Understandable, considering the circumstances. You were trying to protect him."

She hunched her shoulders. "Maybe I should have tried listening instead. Then he wouldn't be…"

She bit her lip and kicked at a rock before turning dark, miserable eyes toward Wyatt. "I know I promised not to ask…but if you could explain what in the *hell* would make you want to be more like this, I could really stand to hear it right now."

"You believe," he said simply. "In yourself, your friends, a greater power…and in Hank. For all of the times and all of the reasons he's given you to stop, you've kept believing in him."

"Have I? Or was I just using him to get back at my parents for leaving me to pick up their slack? Nothing better than helping him do exactly what Daddy didn't want."

"Now you're being stupid." He caught her arms to make her face him. "Tell me…what did you think the first time you watched Hank fight bulls?"

She bowed her head and closed her eyes, as if fixing the image in her mind. And then she blew out a wavering sigh. "I was amazed. He was so *good*. And I was excited, because I'd never seen *him* so excited. He was one of the best players in every school sport, and he liked them all, but the day he made his first save in the arena…it just lit him up." She raised her head to meet Wyatt's gaze. "You know how that feels."

"I do." And it still did, every single time, but this wasn't about Wyatt. "Are you listening to yourself? You watched your brother find his calling, and you were thrilled *for him*. Those are not the words of a self-centered person."

She ducked her head again, pressing a fist to her temple. "I can't tie him up and drag him out of that place, no matter how much I want to. But I can't stand doing nothing. I just…I don't know how to help him. I'm supposed to *know*."

"We'll figure it out." He rubbed her arms, resisting the impulse to fold her close. His body was already trying to misinterpret her proximity. "I've been through worse than this, Melanie. I'm not going to pretend it'll be easy, or quick, but Bing is right. He's showing signs of recovery. And you need time, too. Everything you've had to deal with…most people would be flat out on the floor. Give yourself a break, and a chance to sort it all through."

She tilted her head, considering, then angled a look at him through her lashes. "While you start prodding your contacts for the best treatment options?"

Busted. "I may have made a mental list on the flight home," he admitted.

She huffed out a soft laugh. Then she threw one arm around his neck and gave a quick, hard squeeze before stepping back, turning to toss the rein over Roy's neck and snap it to the bridle.

His unguarded heart gave another of those hopeful bounds before he reined it in. *Stop!* Even if she'd meant it as more than a platonic gesture, he couldn't…*could not* allow her to believe they could be anything more than friends—and even that was unforgivably selfish. His fall was inevitable. Encouraging her to climb onto this crumbling ledge with him would be flat-out cruel.

"What was that?" he asked, lacing his voice with a touch of easy humor.

She grabbed two fistfuls of Roy's mane and vaulted onto his back, then swung the horse around to face Wyatt. "I told you I wasn't sure whether to kick you or hug your neck. I made up my mind."

Without waiting, she pointed Roy toward home. By the time Wyatt climbed into the saddle and caught up, she was almost to the highway.

"Got any plans for the evening?" she called over her shoulder.

"No. Why?"

"No better therapy than work, and no time like the present to get started on my plan for the Bull Dancer. Like I said, I have thoughts. And I have an extra rope."

"A...*what?*" On top of that unexpected embrace, the images that popped into his head short-circuited his ability to process information.

She frowned thoughtfully as she reined up and waited for a car to pass. "I wonder where we could find a dummy steer."

Oh. His lust bubble burst into Technicolor shreds. "There's a farm store on Southgate that carries rodeo gear. They're open until nine, and they probably have what you need."

"Me?" She splayed a hand across her chest and gave him a wide-eyed grin. "*Au contraire, mon ami.* We're gonna teach *you* how to rope."

Chapter 38

MELANIE WATCHED WITH GROWING AMAZEMENT AS WYATT wrestled with a loop that seemed determined to strangle him.

She'd never seen anyone make swinging a rope look quite that difficult, and one year during the Amarillo State Fair she'd taught a Cowboy 101 session to a group of retired insurance salesmen from Cleveland whose idea of athletic prowess was balancing four full beer cups on a paper tray.

Maybe a shot of something from the bar would help Wyatt. It certainly couldn't hurt.

He threw the rope on the ground, grabbed the tail, and began coiling it—the one part of the process he did with his usual ease. He'd probably been handling lines on the family yacht since birth. No wait, they would have a crew for that, but people in his social set would have to have a sailboat, too, wouldn't they?

"This is stupid," he growled.

"You're just saying that because you keep whacking yourself in the head."

He divided his glare between her and the dummy steer she'd also persuaded him to buy. It was lightweight, made of tough plastic plumbing pipe, and built low to ground for roping on foot instead of from a horse. They'd set it up on a decent-sized space behind the bar that might've once been a patio but was now home to nothing but the Dumpster, baking aromatically in the direct glare of the evening sun. Put a high board fence around this, though, slap some patches and stain on the cracked, pockmarked concrete, and it'd make a dandy cowboy playground.

All part of the plan.

Wyatt built a new loop, gritted his teeth, and promptly wrapped it around his neck. Wow. He was actually getting worse.

"No. Watch." She rescued the wadded-up rope, straightened the loop, and demonstrated—again. "You have to rotate your wrist...see?"

His expression went borderline murderous. "Do I *look* like I'm not trying?"

"Honestly?"

He gave another growl and yanked the rope out of her hands. "Explain to me again how this is supposed to help the bar."

"You *are* the Bull Dancer," she repeated, the soul of patience. "It's your brand. You put it on your corporation, your car, and the sign out front. Therefore, people expect you to be the face of this establishment...but that's not gonna work unless you learn to connect with the clientele."

"By connecting this rope with that goddamn steer?"

He was gonna have to get to the point where he could throw it first. She had to bite her lip to keep from laughing. God, it was fun watching him get all cranky. After everything with Hank, this was exactly the kind of distraction she needed. "There is no place better to get to know people than at the ropin' pen. And believe it or not, being bad is good. Team ropers *love* to give advice, even the ones that suck."

Especially the ones that sucked. If you can't do, coach, whether anyone asked your opinion or not. And most of 'em got smarter—and a lot handier with a rope—when they were astride a barstool. Best of all, their version of roping was as much of a social occasion as a competition, which made them prone to stopping for dinner and drinks on the way home from the local jackpot or the weekly team roping practices at the saddle club.

And the Bull Dancer had plenty of parking out back for horse trailers.

She folded her arms and watched him try again. This time, he managed two swings before the loop twisted up and smacked him in the ear. Dear Lord. She couldn't take it anymore. She confiscated the rope, untangled it, then stood with her back to him, holding up the loop in her right hand and the coils in her left. "Here. Put your hands over mine, and I'll take you through the motions."

He hesitated for a beat, then stepped up behind her. His palms were damp, and the scent of hot male enveloped her. She sucked in a breath, and the air stuck in her lungs, as if trying to absorb the essence of him. She forced herself to exhale, then nearly gasped when he flexed his knees to accommodate their height difference, his denim-clad thigh sliding between hers and his cheek so close his breath tickled her ear.

"Okay," she managed. "Here we go."

Her bare arm pressed against his when she demonstrated. His wrist was stiff, resisting the motion as she brought the loop around and tried to roll her palm upward.

She gave their entwined hands a shake. "Relax, and let me move you."

Crap. And her breathy voice made it sound even more suggestive. She felt the reaction shiver through his muscles and heard him swallow. She did the same, then said, "Let's try this again."

She hadn't realized how much hip action was involved in swinging a rope, every swoosh of the loop accompanied by the excruciating slide of body against body. She was so cross-eyed with lust that she gave up and closed her eyes. *Swing. Swing. Swing*. The swaying movement increased the friction and mimicked that age-old rhythm, waking every primordial urge. The temptation to arch her back and press into the hardness she knew she'd find was nearly irresistible.

Swing, swing, swing, swing…

She wasn't sure how much more of this she could take. Had she really thought she could have him once and walk away? Now *that* was delusional.

"There," she said, her voice so throaty it was barely recognizable. "Feel that?"

The noise he made summed up her state of arousal in one low, hot breath—and erased the last of her self-control. She dropped the rope and turned in to his arms. His hands came to rest on her hips, pulling her closer even as he shook his head. "Melanie…"

"Don't." Her gaze followed her fingers over the stubble on his jaw, already softer than the last time she'd touched him. "I listened to more of those science podcasts while I was driving around the other day. Do you know what an event horizon is?"

"The boundary where the force of gravity around a black hole is so strong that nothing can escape."

"That's my walking encyclopedia." She patted his

cheek and lifted her eyes to meet his, losing her breath yet again at pure, hot blue of them. God, he was gorgeous… and she was going to have him, to hell with the consequences. "We have crossed the event horizon, Wyatt. We can't stop this now, no matter how hard we try."

He pressed his cheek into her palm, rubbing like a cat. "What about Hank? You know how he'd feel about this."

"Once or a hundred times…in his mind it's all the same. And this has nothing to do with my brother." She slid her hands down to take Wyatt's and squeeze. "I'm not looking for comfort, or a distraction, or anything else except *this*."

Those eyes searched her face, dark with concern—and tightly controlled need. "Are you sure?"

"That I want you?" She laughed. "Believe me, I've had a year or five to think about it."

They walked around to the door of the apartment, strolling hand in hand as if they were determined that this time would be as slow and thorough as the last had been rushed. When they stepped into the room, Wyatt pulled out his phone, muted the ringer, and set it on the fancy lady's desk. Melanie followed suit, but connected hers to a wireless speaker and started a music app. Lilting Native American flute music floated on the breeze that ruffled the sheer silk at the windows. She also reached into her purse, pulled out the remaining condoms, and tossed them on the bed.

Wyatt stepped up behind her and once again wrapped his hands around hers, then smoothed his palms up her arms. She sighed in pleasure. He nuzzled her hair aside to murmur in her ear. "Do you trust me?"

"If I didn't, instead of crawling into that plane, I'd be hitchhiking back from Montana right now."

He laughed softly, his breath playing across the fine hairs at her nape. "There's my incurable romantic."

"Just statin' the facts." She tilted her head to give him better access. "I've already put my life in your hands. What now?"

He traced a line with one finger from the underside of her chin all the way down to the first button on her shirt. "Take off your clothes."

To his dying day, Wyatt would never forget the sight of her strolling over to the bed and looking him square in the eye as she stripped, then gave a long, languid stretch, arms overhead and back arched, pulling her body into a single taut curve. She smiled at his low groan and draped herself across the bed, head propped on one hand and her hair spilling over her shoulders. "Your turn."

Her eyes shamelessly drank him in as he pulled his polo shirt over his head and then peeled off jeans, underwear, socks, and shoes in one motion, somehow managing not to trip as he kicked them aside. She craned her neck to watch as he picked up one of the condoms and slid onto the bed behind her.

He leaned in to touch his mouth to the corner of hers. "Trust me."

She held his gaze for a moment, then gave a slight nod and let her head drop into the crook of her arm. He lifted her hair, strand by silky strand, until she was totally exposed. Then he began to touch her, learning her textures and tastes with featherlight brushes of fingers and lips, exploring her body with long, deliberate strokes of his hands along her spine, over the curve of her hip, kneading the muscles of her butt and legs until her eyes fluttered closed and she moaned in appreciation.

"Keep that up, I'm gonna slip into a coma."

"That's the plan." But he shifted his attention to her front, keeping the same unhurried rhythm as he stroked her stomach, her breasts, her thighs, searching out her most vulnerable spots and testing to see what made her shift and arch, seeking relief from the need he built, touch by touch. He pulled back to find the condom, rip it open, and roll it into place as he dragged his teeth along the curve of her shoulder, feeling her shiver at the rasp of his stubble.

She moaned when he pushed inside her, then locked his arm around her waist to keep her still. "Shhh. Just let me…"

Her body closed hot around him, pressing into him, begging for speed and power. He held her tight, allowing only the slightest pulse of movement as he continued to run his other hand over her. She squirmed in his grasp, but he refused to cede control as he slowly, *slowly* pushed her up and up, until she reached the peak and tumbled over, shuddering in his arms as he followed her to a blinding climax.

As their pulses hammered in unison, his hands continued to glide over her, bringing them both down slowly while he built the store of memories that would soon be all he had of her.

He'd known it couldn't be more, and had barely hesitated. As she'd said, he'd already crossed the event horizon, and there was no going back. For as long as she was here, he wouldn't think about how, beyond that point, not even light could survive…let alone a foolish human heart.

Chapter 39

WHEN HE'D PICKED OUT THE OVERSIZE BATHTUB FOR THE apartment, Wyatt had fantasized about a moment like this—lolling in the warm, fragrant water with Melanie using his chest as a backrest and his shoulder as a pillow. Her hair was piled in a messy bun, tickling his nose as she tilted her head to study their reflection in the cheval mirror.

"I feel like an advertisement for erectile dysfunction."

He scooped up a handful of water and let it trickle into the hollow of her collarbone, watching it spill over and meander between her small, firm breasts. "I hope you're referring to the bathtub."

"As if you have anything to worry about." She wriggled her butt, making waves in more than the water.

"I *am* almost forty."

She patted his knee. "I could barely tell."

"Good to know," he said dryly. He leaned forward, skin sliding against slippery skin as he retrieved a bar of soap, then settled back again. The light from the single high window had turned to sunset gold, and the soaring notes of a Celtic ballad wafted in from the other room. Damn. He even loved her music. He soaped up his hands and set the bar aside to knead her shoulders and neck.

She let her head tip forward with a deep, contented sigh. "If this bullfighting thing doesn't work out for you, I have an opening for a personal slave."

"You can't afford me." In ways that had nothing to do with money, but he refused to let those thoughts poison this moment.

She was silent for a few moments, and he felt tension gathering in her muscles as her brain kicked into gear.

"What?" he asked, running his thumbs along the inner curves of her shoulder blades.

"You said you'd been through this before."

Wyatt's hands stilled.

She angled a look over her shoulder, eyes searching. "Was it so bad you can't explain, or is trust something you only receive, not give?"

"I...both, I guess." *Could* he trust himself to tell her as much of the truth as possible without somehow bringing the rest crashing down around him? He had never told this story beginning to end, even to Gabrielle. Being so exposed would have made him too vulnerable to attack.

But it also made him...knowable. How could he ask her to understand him if she didn't have all the pertinent information?

"Never mind." She slipped out of his grasp, pulling away.

"Don't." He caught her arms to stop her. "I just need to figure out where to start."

She eased back against him. "At the beginning?"

"Of which life?"

"This one." She ran a finger along his forearm, leaving a trail through the fine, wet hair. "The other belonged to someone else."

He pressed a kiss into the hair at her temple. "Only you would know that."

Only you. Her fingers went still, then her hand flattened over his, pressing down as if to provide support. For him, or did her heart stumble over those words, too?

He drew a deep breath and took the plunge. "For me, it started when Laura tried to kill herself."

He felt the jolt of it hit her body. "How?"

"She overdosed on Adderall...the ADHD medication. It was her prescription, and thankfully she was almost due for a refill. As it was..." He closed his eyes against the rush of memories—Laura pale and still in a forest of tubes, pumps, and beeping monitors. "She had a heart attack."

Melanie folded both of their arms over her chest and squeezed. "How old was she?"

"Twenty. She was in her second year at Trinity College, and I was finishing my undergraduate degree at Yale." Wyatt took another breath. "And we were planning to get married."

Married?

Melanie twisted around to face him. "But she's gay."

Wyatt grabbed her by the waist, repositioning her hip so it didn't crush any vital parts of his anatomy. "How did you know?"

"Grace said she has a wife." Oh crap. Of course that didn't mean she couldn't be into men too. "I just assumed...is she bi?"

"No." He made a pained face. "Laura was...unaware. It's her preferred state. We were thrown together from the time we were babies, practically a couple by middle school. She thought that was why I felt more like a big brother to her than a boyfriend. It was what our families wanted, so she just went along with it and assumed she'd figure out the big deal about sex once we were married."

"Okay. Whoa." Melanie held up a dripping hand. "You dated this girl from the time you hit puberty, and you never had *sex*?"

His jaw went tight, instantly defensive. "I was going to be a priest. I didn't believe in sex before marriage."

"Well, a gay girlfriend must've been a big help with the ol' vow of abstinence." Then she cringed. "Sorry. That was probably a dozen kinds of offensive."

Wyatt smiled slightly. "And true. I was as horny as any fifteen-year-old, but I could count on Laura to put on the brakes. We were the perfect pair of enablers. She was my chastity belt, and I was her excuse not to wonder why it was so easy for her to say no."

"Until…"

"Laura met someone."

Oh Lord. Was this gonna be one of those humiliating *My fiancée left me for another woman* stories? "A girl?"

He nodded. "Her partner on a sociology research paper, who was out and proud. Suddenly, what Laura called her *admiration* of other women was very obviously lust. She panicked." A spark of anger flashed in his eyes. "Instead of talking to me, she went to her mother, who made her swear not to tell her father. They consulted mine instead…their trusted friend and spiritual counselor. With the help of my older brother, they cooked up a plan to *fix* her."

"Oh no."

"Oh yes." Wyatt's smile was a terrible thing. "In public, my father and brother pay lip service to the church's ideology, but privately they are adamant that homosexuality is an emotional disorder manifested as a weakness of the flesh. If Laura would put herself entirely in God's hands and pray for His forgiveness, He would save her."

"How could they force her to listen to that bullshit?"

"They didn't have to." His hands massaged her upper arms, his gaze diamond hard. "The nineties were Tom Hanks in *Philadelphia* and Arthur Ashe dying of AIDS and *Don't ask, don't tell* as official military policy. Being gay in Connecticut meant never getting married, maybe never having children. All Laura ever wanted was a husband to give her kids and the status she'd always enjoyed as her parents' child. Being gay would make her an outsider in that world. She *wanted* someone to tell her it wasn't real, and if she wished hard enough and clicked her heels together three times, she could go right on with the fairy tale."

"And no one bothered to tell you?"

His mouth twisted. "I'd made the mistake of expressing my opinions. They didn't trust me to *do the right thing*. I should have known something was wrong when she moved back in with her parents, started coming up to Yale every weekend and pushing to get married right away. Spending as much time as possible with me and away from other women was part of their *treatment*. I was so focused on graduating with honors that I wasn't paying attention—until she made me."

"By attempting suicide."

He nodded. "Afterward in the hospital, she was hysterical because she'd failed me, failed her parents, failed God. They had to sedate her for her own safety.

My father—this man of our so-called benevolent God—stood outside her room and told me she was better off dead than gay. And my mother nodded along."

"Jesus Christ."

"Was nowhere in the vicinity." One more who'd abandoned Wyatt in his time of greatest need—or so it would have seemed.

"What did you say?"

"To them? Nothing." He hunched his shoulders. "I didn't dare. They would have cut off my access to her. So I told Laura it didn't matter. We would still get married, and we'd work it out together."

Melanie's stomach twisted as she imagined a younger version of Wyatt—scared, betrayed, standing alone against the mob—and still trying to save the day. "You lied to her."

"Not exactly." Melanie wouldn't have thought his expression could get even grimmer. "I had to get her out of there, but I had no legal rights. So I let them think I agreed that our angel had allowed herself to be seduced away from Jesus. Said it was my fault, that I'd neglected Laura and her loneliness had made her vulnerable. Her father stepped in and insisted that I pick her up when she was released from the hospital and take her to their vacation cottage to recuperate. No one dared disagree with him."

And there it was, the springboard that had launched Wyatt out of the family nest. "You didn't go to the cottage."

He shook his head. "I only made one stop...in a small town on the Connecticut border, to find a justice of the peace."

Melanie gaped at him. "You married her anyway?"

"It was the only way I could take care of her." He gave a helpless shrug. "Her father made sure she had access to whatever money she needed. I'd gained full control of my trust fund when I turned twenty-one. We had plenty of cash and no particular destination, so we just kept working our way across the country."

"Did you really only stop here because the car broke down?"

"Not just the car." His hands moved back to her shoulders, massaging gently, but his gaze had turned inward, and it didn't appear to be a pleasant view. "Laura had been coming unraveled for days. When the car blew up, she had a complete meltdown and started defibrillating and had to be rushed to the emergency room. Back then, there was an inpatient psychiatric hospital in Pendleton, so we stayed here. She had to be heavily medicated at first, which left me with nothing to do but drive around—and go to rodeos."

Where he'd found his vocation and possibly his salvation. But... "I can see why you blame your father, your brother, Laura's mother...but why God? He didn't tell them to do this."

"He sure as hell didn't punish them. Laura was destroyed, emotionally and physically. With the damage to her heart, pregnancy could be a life-threatening condition for her." The sadness in his voice was profound. "She lost the one thing she wanted more than anything, and they lost...nothing."

"In this life. We don't know what He's got planned for them in the next."

"We don't *know* anything." His hands tightened on her shoulders. "What if they're right?"

She gently pried his fingers loose to press them between hers. "Then you and I are gonna be ridin' the same train straight to hell, because I'd rather hang out with Satan than their version of the Almighty."

He choked out a laugh, bending until their foreheads touched. "*This* is why I wish I could be like you. Everything is so straightforward."

She had to close her eyes against a rush of emotion so intense it was as if it had scorched her heart. This beautiful, complicated, wounded man had bared his soul to her, but he acted as if his scars were irrelevant. As if only Laura's dreams had been destroyed.

What Melanie felt at that moment was so far beyond anything she'd ever experienced that it was like falling into another, terrifying dimension.

"Are you callin' me simple?" she asked, dry humor being the only cover she could find.

"Good God, no."

She forced a big smile. "There. See? One good chat with me, and you're already back on speaking terms with the Man."

He laughed again and slumped back in the tub, sloshing water over the sides. Instead of crawling into the space he'd made for her, she sat facing him, nearly paralyzed by the vision that was Wyatt, naked, wet, and gilded by the last rays of the setting sun filtering in through the high window. She had to look away in order to do some mental calculations. "You were twenty-two when you eloped. And you were married how long?"

"A little over three years." He stretched his arms out along the sides of the tub and settled himself more comfortably. "Like I said, it wasn't easy or quick, but eventually Laura worked things through."

"And in the meantime, you were…"

He shifted uncomfortably, seeing where she was headed. "Her husband."

"Forsaking all others?"

"It was easier that way."

She doubted that—at least from his standpoint—but she couldn't imagine him disrespecting even vows of expedience. "So you were twenty-five years old…"

"And Laura wanted to move to Portland. This was never her kind of town. I went with her and stayed until she found a great support group and a close group of queer friends. And I…asked a woman out for the first time ever."

"Whoa." Melanie stared at him, flabbergasted. "You'd never been on a *date*?"

"Not with a stranger. I was so clueless…" He made a pained face. "I turned into the reverse of the gay male friend. Her crowd called me their token straight guy, and as soon as our divorce was final, they made it their number one goal to find the perfect woman to *initiate* me."

Melanie's mouth dropped open, but she couldn't make any words come out.

Wyatt glared at her. "Go ahead. Make all the jokes about the twenty-five-year-old virgin."

"I—" She gave her head a shake, trying to rearrange years of misconceptions. "You're gonna have to give me a few minutes here. This is like…like…finding out Mozart didn't actually write symphonies when he was thirteen."

"*Thirteen?*" He stared at her in disbelief. "You thought I was having sex in junior high?"

She threw up her hands, flinging drops of water across the room. "I never drilled it down to a specific age. I just assumed…I mean, look at you, and well…*damn*."

As he continued to stare at her, the irritation slowly faded and his mouth quirked. "So you're saying I do okay for a late bloomer?"

"As if you didn't know." Then another thought struck her. "*Holy shit!* Joe mentioned that you were living in Portland when he met you. Were you still—"

"You *cannot* tell Violet!" Wyatt's eyebrows slammed together. "She'd tell Joe, and I would never hear the end of it."

Melanie grinned at him.

"I'm serious, Melanie. You can't—"

She splashed water in his face. "Cool your jets. Your secret is safe with me. If I did tell her, I'd have to explain how I wrung it out of you."

"And we wouldn't want that," he said flatly.

Hell. So much for lightening the mood. She traced a vein on the back of his hand as she examined her own reaction. Her mind rebelled at the idea of another clandestine affair. *Either own it, or don't bother*, Shawnee liked to say. If Melanie had only stuck to that mantra where Michael was concerned.

She met and held Wyatt's gaze. "I won't sneak around ever again. You can assume that I will tell Violet about this. We're all big girls and boys. We can handle it."

His eyes darkened, a cold shadow falling over blue water. "You can't be sure."

"Yes, I can." She put her hands on his knees and squeezed. "I know you. I know me. And I know our friends. I'm not saying it won't get awkward, but as long as we're honest with each other and them, we can work though whatever happens."

"Then we need to be clear on where this thing is going." His gaze shifted to one of the hands he'd fisted on the side of the tub. "I've been married and divorced twice, and I've learned that I can't sustain that kind of relationship. I won't stop analyzing and second-guessing until I pick it completely apart. And you have to think about Hank. At some point, he's going to be ready to rejoin the living, and he'll need his sister."

And today had proven Wyatt and Hank couldn't coexist in her life.

He leaned forward to run his thumb along her cheekbone, his eyes suddenly burning bright. "I would never willingly do anything to hurt your brother…or you. You know that, don't you?"

"Yes."

She'd always known, even when it was easier to pretend that he was picking on Hank. Even if Wyatt had been willing to take another chance, to put that battered heart of his on the line one more time, he wouldn't ask her to choose between him and her brother.

Damn him.

"So I guess that's settled," she said, remarkably calm considering the howl of pain building inside her chest. "We have our fun until I'm finished here, then we never speak of it again."

His fingers tightened a fraction, as if in protest. Then his hand dropped away from her face. "It's better this way."

In whose godforsaken opinion? She could see no good in ripping apart a connection that was the truest and strongest she'd ever found. But she also couldn't see a future that wouldn't eventually tear them apart.

"I hate this," she whispered.

"I know."

He gathered her into his arms and held on tight while the light faded and the room went cold.

Chapter 40

MELANIE WOKE UP ALONE ON TUESDAY MORNING. SHE had—reluctantly—sent Wyatt home the night before to pack and rest up for the flight to Reno. And to be honest, she'd needed to take a step back, if only to prove she still could.

No matter how much it hurt.

She dragged on jogging clothes, laced up her shoes, and headed outside. As she stepped into the hall, something thumped onto the floor—a box that had been propped against the door, sporting a Justin Boots logo. What the heck? She pried the lid open and inhaled the intoxicating scent of new leather. Peeling back the tissue paper, she sucked in another, even more appreciative breath. She had drooled over this exact pair of boots in the western store a block down the street—plain, brown square toes with a low roper's heel, and tops stitched in an intricate floral pattern of pink, turquoise, and white.

She couldn't resist. She toed off her sneakers and pulled on the boots. Of course they were the right size. She fished out the folded piece of yellow legal paper in the bottom of the box.

These will fit you better than those shoes.

The paper crunched in her fist. *Damn him*. For a guy who didn't think he was good at relationships, he had a real knack for twisting her heart into a corkscrew, even from a thousand miles away.

How much worse was it going to be when she was the one who had to leave—permanently?

————

Wyatt landed in Reno on the heels of a morning thunderstorm. Puddles steamed on the pavement as he walked into the terminal, and there wasn't enough product in the world to squelch the curl in his hair. By the time he got back to Pendleton, it would be totally out of control.

Sort of like his feelings for Melanie. He'd thought it was hard lying to her before, but nothing compared to looking her straight in the eye and insisting he didn't want her to be a part of every minute of his future. Although, there had been *some* truth to what he'd said. He couldn't have her, and he couldn't imagine how he'd ever stop loving her, since he'd already tried every way he knew how.

So no, he would never get married again.

He'd had to say it. The way she was looking at him... Wyatt couldn't take the chance that in her emotionally battered state she might finally give up on Hank and turn to him, if only for consolation. He might not be strong enough to push her away, so he'd had to throw up another block.

Why not the same, old tired one he'd used to screw it up at the very beginning?

The clerk smiled brightly as Wyatt dragged his luggage cart up to the desk. "Welcome to Reno! Here for the rodeo?"

"Yes, and thank you."

Not a question he usually got, but today he'd opted for jeans and worn his belt and National Finals bullfighter buckle, which he usually left in his suitcase unless he was making an official appearance. Also, the rope Melanie had given him was hanging from the cart. With plenty of time to kill at the rodeo grounds and dozens of potential coaches among the roping contestants, he just had to swallow his pride, ask for help…and take a ton of ribbing from them about how terrible he was.

He slid his gold member card across the desk, and the clerk tapped the information into her computer. "I have a Mustang convertible reserved for you, Mr. Darrington. Is that correct?"

It was what he'd requested, but it didn't suit his mood. He leaned across the desk and hit her with his best smile. "It was…but I changed my mind. Could we look at another option?"

He was waiting outside baggage claim when a familiar figure strode out with one battered gear bag slung over his shoulder and another in his hand, weaving through the crowd like there was a prize for who got to the curb first. He stopped dead when he spotted Wyatt leaning against the side of the black short-box pickup.

Joe looked left, then right, then back at Wyatt. "Who are you supposed to be?"

Wyatt bared his teeth. "You're welcome to grab a taxi."

"Oh no. I don't know what's going on, but I don't want to miss it." Joe tossed his bags in the backseat, looking more respectable than usual in a blue Jacobs Livestock polo shirt and starched jeans. His hair was still a straggly mess, but Violet seemed to like it that way. He climbed in the cab and rubbed a hand across his own clean-shaven jaw. "What's this?"

"I forgot to renew my monthly razor subscription."

Something for which Joe had given him no end of grief, gob-smacked that anyone would pay more than five bucks for a six-pack of plastic disposables. "If I can't shave with a decent blade…"

"You don't shave your precious face at all," Joe finished, curling his lip in disgust.

Wyatt shrugged, satisfied that he'd deflected Joe's curiosity. He was not going to admit that he intended to keep the stubble for as long as Melanie was around to appreciate it.

As they eased into the stream of shuttle buses and taxis, Joe twisted around to look into the backseat. "Why are you packing a rope?"

"I bet Melanie I'd be able to catch a dummy five out of ten times when I get back to Pendleton."

"Yeah? And what does she have to do if you win?"

"Kite-surfing."

Joe gave a low whistle. "Do I dare ask what you're wagering?"

The ring of Wyatt's phone through the pickup speakers cut him off. Melanie's name flashed up on the dashboard screen. Before Wyatt could react, Joe poked the answer button, then sat back and looked expectantly at Wyatt, mouth firmly shut.

"Hello? Are you on the ground?"

Wyatt bit back a curse. He'd been trying to work out how to tell Joe about the two of them, and this was not it. "Yes. I just picked Joe up. Is everything okay?"

"Hunky-dory. I just needed to ask…do you trust me, Chuck?"

He winced at the nickname. "That depends on the context."

"We're not standing at the top of a mountain, so you can breathe easy on that account. Which reminds me, if that ankle gets sore, you let Cruz pick up the slack. He's young. He can take the beating."

Ankle? Joe mouthed at him.

Wyatt let a slow breath stream out through his nose. "I'll keep it in mind. What is it you want me to trust you with?"

"Your checkbook. I'm fixin' to spend some money."

"On?"

"The bar."

He wedged the pickup between a tour bus and a white courtesy limousine from one of the casinos. "Louie can write checks on the Bull Dancer account. What are you going to do?"

He heard the grin in her voice. "That's the part where you've gotta have faith."

God help him. Or whoever. Then again, short of turning it back into an actual brothel, how much damage could she do in ten days? "Let me know if I should recruit some new employees as long as I'm in Sin City Junior."

"Nah, I've got the staffing handled. And thank you for your confidence." He started to relax. He might just get out of this conversation without Joe too much the wiser. Then she added, "Oh, and Joe?"

"Yeah?"

"Keep him away from the strip clubs. I've heard he has a weakness, and you know how I am about sharing my toys."

The phone clicked off. Wyatt stared straight down the road, the stream of traffic exiting the airport giving him an excuse to avoid even a glance in Joe's direction.

After several excruciating moments, Joe asked, "Why is she calling you Chuck?"

"*That's* the only question you have?"

"It's the only confusing part. Sounds like everything else is proceeding according to plan."

Wyatt shot him an incredulous look. "Whose plan?"

"Ours." Joe cocked his finger, pointed it at Wyatt, and pulled the trigger. "Gotcha."

Chapter 41

WYATT HAD TO PULL OVER ON THE SIDE OF THE ROAD AND put the pickup in Park. "You expect me to believe you made this happen?"

"Believe what you want." Joe shrugged, unfazed by Wyatt's death glare. "But do you honestly think Violet wouldn't want to kick that shithead's ass, with or without Melanie? Geezus. I had to bar the doors and hide the rifle while I talked her down. And she only gave in after I promised her we could tail you after the science fair."

Wyatt goggled at him. "You were watching us?"

"Yep. Man, we damn near shit a brick when that cop drove by."

"I never saw...how did you..."

Joe snorted. "Dude. We live in a house with two kids and still have sex. We've got sneaky nailed."

Wyatt dug thumb and middle finger into his temples. "I don't understand."

"That's because you make everything too complicated. Otherwise, this would've happened five years ago, like it should have. But no, you diddled around until we thought it was too late. When the shit hit the fan with Michael, we figured it was time to force the issue—so we sent you to the rescue." Joe shrugged again. "Everything after that was pretty much a given."

"You were so sure that Melanie would cause a big ruckus, and I would offer to take her away from it all?"

Joe spread his hands. "Were we wrong?"

No, they were not. He and Melanie had both done exactly as predicted. But Wyatt still couldn't believe...

"If this is all true, why did Violet tell Melanie she thought it was best we hadn't hooked up?" A tidbit Melanie had confessed the previous night.

Joe smirked. "What's the quickest way to get Mel to do anything?"

"Just—" Tell her she couldn't. Son of a bitch. She'd talked to Violet, then she'd invited him to drive up to the mountains, proof she could be civilized to him—and it had snowballed from there.

Wyatt pinched the bridge of his nose. "Did you happen to consider that my marriage to a woman like Melanie was a complete disaster?"

"Nope." Once again, Joe shrugged off Wyatt's withering glare. "Melanie is independent. Gabrielle was pathological, which is understandable considering how she grew up. But Melanie was raised on the rodeo circuit and the ranch, where you don't survive without the occasional handout or hand up. You take it when it's offered and give it when it's needed. Hell, she didn't even blow a fuse when she realized that you'd made that lawsuit go away."

No need to ask how Joe knew. Melanie hadn't been kidding when she'd said she didn't keep anything from Violet. "What about the rest? Do you know what's happening at Westwind?"

"Probably more than Leachman does. Thanks to Gil chatting up the warehouse guys, Violet can tell you damn near down to the fifty-pound bag how much feed has shipped out of the plant since Melanie left, and that the grant application she wrote was accepted—which is a big boost for R&D, whatever that means."

"And what about Leachman? Did Gil find anything…"

Joe flashed an inscrutable smile. "I'm not allowed to share that information due to the manner in which it was obtained."

"Jesus Christ," Wyatt said. "It's like a Texas rodeo mafia."

Joe's eyes lit up. "Violet will love that."

And Shawnee would have T-shirts printed. Wyatt clenched both hands on the steering wheel. "Did your informants also tell you we found Hank?"

"Found?" Joe's grin faded. "Was he lost?"

So Melanie didn't tell her best friend everything. "She hadn't seen or talked to him since New Year's. That's why she agreed to come to Oregon. I promised to track him down."

"And?"

Joe's expression got darker by degrees as Wyatt described Hank's condition. When he finished, Joe swore. "What is she going to do?"

"I'll hook her up with the best mental health professionals I know, but honestly? I don't think she can do anything for now. Hank has dug in, and he isn't going to budge until he's damn good and ready. There's a lot more of Melanie in him than you'd think."

Joe cocked his head. "What are *you* going to do?"

"Try to help her accept it."

"And then?"

Wyatt heaved a sigh. "Listen…I appreciate what you were trying to do, and I love you both—"

"Oh geezus."

Wyatt squeezed a dollop of pleasure out of making Joe squirm, then shook his head. "This is way beyond Hank being an idiot. He's going through some serious shit."

"And you're not?" Joe pointed at the dashboard screen. "What about all that?"

"We're scratching a very old itch. When she leaves Oregon, it's done."

"You're just going to let her walk away because of Hank?"

Wyatt leveled a stare at Joe. "If it's me or him, we all know who she'd choose. Even if it was me, how long do you think we'd last if I was the reason he never spoke to her again?"

Joe swore and slammed back in his seat.

"Exactly," Wyatt said and put the pickup in gear.

Silence reigned for the rest of the drive. When they arrived at the rodeo grounds, Cruz's El Camino was already parked in their designated area. He stepped out of his ancient travel trailer, arms folded and dark eyes inscrutable as he looked from Joe to Wyatt, then back to Joe.

"We're fighting bulls with Justin Timberlake?"

Joe laughed.

Wyatt flipped them off, then grabbed his cowboy hat from the backseat and jammed it on his head. As he slung his bag over his shoulder and started toward the locker room, Joe called after him. "Hey, *Chuck!* You didn't tell me what happened to your ankle."

Wyatt yelled over his shoulder. "She pushed me off a damn cliff."

And he wouldn't stand close to any steep drops if he were Joe or Violet. Regardless of their good intentions, their little scheme was practically a carbon copy of what Leachman had done to Melanie. The damage he and Michael had done was nothing compared to what she would suffer if this tore her and Violet apart.

Wyatt threw his bag down outside the door to the locker room and kicked it for good measure—with his uninjured leg. Then he sank down on a bench and tried to figure out how to break the news without getting anyone maimed.

Himself included.

Chapter 42

AS CREWS WENT, MELANIE SUPPOSED YOU COULD CALL HERS motley, though she preferred eclectic. It sounded more chic and less like a skin condition.

There was Louie, who surveyed the group with his standard air of fatalistic amusement, as if he didn't expect much to come of all of this fuss but was prepared to be entertained by the attempt. Gordon sat at the bar sipping his post-walk glass of ice water and passing out Tootsie Rolls to Grace, Scotty, and Philip, and apologizing to Louie, who wasn't allowed candy—at least while under Grace's eagle eye.

And Grace avoided direct interaction with Melanie whenever possible. It was getting to the point that Melanie wanted to march straight up and demand, "What the hell, Grace?"

But then she would have to deal with the answer, and right now, between Hank and Wyatt and the ever-present doubt about her professional future, she had all the angst she could handle.

It was a relief to focus on the job at hand.

"Grace and Louie, you are in charge of undecorating." Melanie swept a hand around to indicate the walls. "We're leaving all of the foundation elements in place—wallpaper, booths, railings—but the rest has to go. The mirrors, the velvet swags, anything with a gilt frame or a gold tassel is out of here."

"Thank you, Jesus!" Scotty declared. "Do you have any idea what a pain in the ass that stuff is to clean?"

"I can guess. And while we're on the subject...you and Philip are going to scrub every crack and crevice of that kitchen, floor to ceiling, wall to wall. I want that sucker to *shine*."

The boys exchanged dour looks.

"We gettin' a chef?" Louie asked.

"No." Melanie winked at Gordon. "My test group wants *real* food."

Louie grinned and patted his belly. "Now you're talkin' my language."

"And what are you gonna be doin' while we're all bustin' our butts?" Scotty asked.

Melanie offered a crooked elbow, inviting Gordon to take her arm. "We have to talk to a man about a fence. And then we're going antiquing."

They met Rowdy at the Roundup grounds, where he introduced them to a friend who was a fencing contractor. If he was at all upset about being left cold at the bar on Saturday night, he hid it well. The asshole.

Melanie had measured the rear patio area of the Bull Dancer and taken photos. The contractor assured her that he could absolutely have a fence up by the end of the week. He also sketched out a design for a simple, retractable rain and sun shade—wide strips of canvas that slid along metal rails and covered the entire space.

"Perfect!" She shook on the deal and gave him her address so he could email her the specs and a bid.

They had just stepped into a coffee shop right outside

the Roundup grounds when her phone rang. At the sight of the name on the screen, her stomach did a complicated swoop and twist—half thrill, half dread. A call from Wyatt could be anything from *No, really, what are you doing to my bar* to horrible news. Despite Hank's declaration that he had no intention of doing himself harm and Bing's promise to keep a close eye on him, Melanie couldn't let go of the fear.

"I hope you haven't changed your mind about the checkbook," she said. "I've already signed contracts."

"I'm afraid to ask." But his amusement sounded forced. "Are you alone?"

She glanced at where Gordon had struck up a conversation with one of his endless number of acquaintances. She caught his eye and pointed at the phone and then the door. He nodded. She stepped outside.

"I am now. What's up?"

"Joe and I talked."

From the sound of his voice, the conversation hadn't gone well. Damn her smart mouth all over again. She should have let Wyatt find his own way to tell Joe about their…whatever it was. "He doesn't approve?"

"I wish. They honestly meant well, Melanie. They just didn't have time to really think it through."

She listened, stunned, as he told her what they'd done. When he was finished, she sank onto the edge of a concrete flower planter, her skin going cold despite the heat of the midday sun. "How could they do that to me? To *us*?"

"They were trying to help."

"By throwing us together when I was a total disaster looking for another place to happen?"

He sighed. "Like I said, they didn't really think it through."

Her jaw clenched, and she shot to her feet. "They're gonna have plenty to think about when I get done."

"Melanie, don't do anything—"

"Tell Joe thanks a lot. I'll be sure and show my gratitude the next time I see him, so he should probably wear a cup."

She disconnected and paced down the short driveway that led to the back gate into the Roundup grounds, punching in Violet's number as she went.

"Jacobs Live—"

"What the *hell*, Violet? You're supposed to be my friend."

Violet had obviously been warned, because she barely hesitated. "I screwed up. Big time. I was just... shit. I don't know what I was thinking. I was so furious about Michael, and Wyatt was right there." She huffed out a disgusted breath. "It sounded brilliant in the heat of the moment. And then he offered you that job, and you accepted, and I thought, okay, maybe this wasn't the worst idea ever."

"Is this where you tell me all you did was wave him under my nose, but I'm the one took the bait?" Melanie stomped on a weed that had sprouted between the cracks of the asphalt. "Because apparently I'm so desperate I'll jump anything with a pulse."

Violet swore. "Wyatt isn't just any guy. He is *the* guy. You know it. He knows it. Hell, even Hank knows it, or he wouldn't have gotten so pissed."

"Hank never liked him."

"Wrong. I'm not saying they were tight, but they did okay until after our wedding. And honey, with the sparks you two were throwing off that night, even your bonehead brother had to notice."

Melanie snorted. "And what? Hank was gonna protect me?"

"More like he was scared shitless Wyatt would take you away from him." Violet *hmphffed*, sounding exactly like her daddy. "He was a total snot from then on, and he had no other excuse. Joe was the one who was constantly on Hank's ass. And it was Wyatt who convinced Fort Worth and San Antonio and the others to hire him."

Melanie came up short at the wrought-iron gates. "What? I assumed—"

"It was Joe?" There was a rustle, as if Violet was shaking her head. "Wyatt takes care of all the contracts for the two of them, ever since he persuaded Joe to leave Dick Browning. He decided Hank was ready to step up to the big leagues, so he made it happen."

When Hank had been acting like a jerk? "Why would he do that?"

Violet gave a soft laugh. "Do I really have to spell it out?"

"I don't...he did it for me?" she asked in disbelief.

"You had just changed jobs, and you were putting in filthy hours, trying to prove yourself. If helping Hank meant taking some of the weight off of you..."

Wyatt might do that. Or she'd been completely off base when...oh hell. "I accused him of not even trying to save Hank."

"Wyatt didn't want anyone to know. He figured it would only make things worse if Hank felt beholden to him."

He was right. After convincing himself Wyatt had it in for him, Hank would not have been grateful. So

Wyatt had worked his magic behind the scenes, and gotten nothing but grief in return. Just one more reason that she…

"Shit," she said. "I'm in love with him."

Violet gave a little squeal. "Yes!"

"No." Melanie braced her back against the metal bars of the gate, her chin sinking along with her heart.

"What do you mean, no?" Violet demanded, practically singing. "You love him, he's crazy about you—"

"He never wants to get married again," Melanie tacked on, mimicking Violet's tone.

"What? Of course he does. He said so."

Melanie's head jerked up. "When?"

"Back at the beginning, when Joe was being a dumbass. Joe said guys like them didn't get happily ever afters. And Wyatt said the hell with that. He intended to have the works, including a herd of kids and a house full of dogs. Or maybe it was the other way around."

"But he just…"

Lied. He'd barely finished promising to be honest with her before he'd looked her straight in the eye and *lied*.

And it made perfect sense. She thought of the notes she'd made that night in the canyon. *Craves connection. Community. Family?* If she hadn't been on such an emotional roller coaster, she would have seen the inconsistency. Those weren't qualities of man who feared commitment…or marriage.

He just didn't want to marry her.

Why would he, after these past two weeks? Why would anyone? She was a rolling disaster with no end in sight. After Laura and Gabrielle, the last thing he needed was more drama.

As if she could hear the running inner dialogue, Violet said, "There has to be a reason…"

"Like what, Violet? Why would he say that other than to let me down easy? Geezus." She thumped her head against the gate. "A classic, *It's not you, it's me*, and I fell for it."

"I don't believe that. Something is not right. I'll make Joe pry it out of him."

"Don't." Melanie heaved a weary sigh. "It doesn't matter anyway. We already agreed this can't happen. Not with Hank the way he is."

"Yeah. I heard." And her tone said she was not happy that it hadn't been from Melanie.

"I'm sorry. I kept telling myself I was overreacting, and I was afraid you'd say I wasn't. And then I saw him…" She fixed her gaze on the coffee shop, where Gordon was waiting. This wasn't the time or place. "I can't talk about it right now."

"Later," Violet said. "You can tell me everything, and we'll figure out what to do. But I need to know… are we okay?"

Melanie blew out a shaky breath. "We have to be. You're all I've got."

"That's not true. You have the whole bunch of us." Violet sniffed, getting teary again. "I am so sorry, Mel. You gave me a shove when I needed it, and I got Joe. I was trying to return the favor."

"And eventually I might appreciate the sentiment. But for now, you can start making it up to me with a phone number. What I need is a ranch cook, and Joe knows just the person."

"Helen! Oh my God, she will be *thrilled*. She's been working as a lunch lady at one of the grade schools in Yakima and swears if she has to dish out one more Salisbury steak with fake gravy, she's going to throw herself on her spatula."

If, as Joe claimed, the woman could hold her own with Miz Iris in the kitchen, Helen was wasted on a bunch of elementary kids. And Joe should know, since she'd fed him for the entire fifteen years he'd worked for Dick Browning. Melanie jotted down the number and started back toward the coffee shop. "I'll talk to you tomorrow. I'm going to the saddle club tonight."

"You're roping?"

"Yes."

"Well, hallelujah! At least something good has come of this mess."

Melanie thought of Wyatt, wet and slick and insanely gorgeous in that bathtub. Despite the ball of red-hot needles lodged behind her breastbone, she smiled. "Believe me, it has not been all bad."

By the time he came back from Reno, she would have the hurt tucked safely away and be prepared to take full advantage of the time they had left. She'd have to stay long enough to coordinate the initial marketing push and develop a long-term plan based on the results. And where she and Wyatt were concerned, she would have to constantly tread that fine line between too much and never enough.

As she hung up, Gordon stepped out of the coffee shop, the twinkle in his eyes muted by concern. "Is everything okay?"

"Fine," she said, brightening her smile to prove it.

Wyatt Darrington wasn't the only one who could lie like a dog.

Chapter 43

THE SADDLE CLUB WAS EXACTLY AS MELANIE HAD EXPECTED. She eyed the collection of ropers, ranging from around ten years old to one silver-haired gent mounted on the inevitable pink-eyed, broom-tailed Appaloosa that couldn't outrun its own fart. There was at least one in every crowd, along with the cranky part-Shetland that had all of Betsy's attitude and none of her talent.

Several of the ropers fell into the same category.

She waved Grace over as a pair of dads chased calves into the chute and the rest of the riders formed a ragged line down the left side of the arena. "Tie your horse up," she said, stepping off of Roy and wrapping the rein around a fence rail.

"But..." Grace glanced over at the others, waiting their turn.

"Trust me." Melanie backed Roy's cinch off a few notches, then strolled over to the roping chute.

The woman who'd accepted the check for her membership squinted at her from a narrow face, her skin fake-baked to years beyond her chronological age. "Aren't you going to rope?"

"Where I come from, the newbie works the chutes," Melanie said easily. "We'll let the kids go first, then Grace and I will rope at the end."

Donetta Jones frowned, not thrilled with this change in the routine. "There's no need—"

But Melanie had already escaped toward the catch pens, signaling Grace to follow. She plucked the sorting stick out of the hand of the nearest dad. "You go help your daughter. We've got this."

He hesitated, then flashed her a grateful smile and made himself scarce.

"You do realize that we're paying for this?" Grace muttered, as Melanie prodded a potbellied Hereford into the narrow lane. "Including the chute help."

"Who will sort off the best calves for their little darlings," Melanie responded. "And leave us to rope all of the shitters. Besides, standing in line for five minutes between runs is a piss-poor way to practice. You need three or four in a row, minimum, for you and your horse to accomplish anything."

Grace pondered that for a moment, then jerked her head toward the arena. "Donetta is not pleased."

"Should I consider that a problem?"

"I don't suppose it is for *you*. You're not scared of anyone."

"And you are?" Melanie shook her head. "If you let the parents and coaches push you around at the high school, everybody wouldn't be singing your praises."

Grace flushed. "That's different."

"No it isn't. You're just not used to sticking up for *you*. Next time, pretend it's one of your athletes they're messing with and…" Melanie swung the sorting stick like a baseball bat. "*Pow!* They're outta here."

Grace snickered, forgetting for the moment that she wasn't supposed to enjoy Melanie's company. As they loaded the rest of the calves, Melanie kept one eye on the action in the arena, making mental note of whether each calf was fast or slow, ducked to the right or left, so she could plan accordingly when her turn came. Unfortunately, it also meant she had to watch the ropers, which was downright painful. If she made it through this night without shooting off her mouth…

"Get your tip down!" Donetta screeched at a skinny girl. The Paint Horse was ducking left so bad when she tried to throw that it was a wonder the kid hadn't been tossed in the dirt along with her loop. As the girl coiled her rope and rode back up the arena, Donetta stomped out to meet her. She jabbed a lethal fingernail into the girl's thigh as she continued to rant. "How many times do I have to tell you? You have to follow through. I don't know why you're making this so difficult."

Maybe because it wasn't as easy as it looked. Breakaway roping seemed simple enough. Rope the calf. Pitch your slack. Stop your horse. In competition, the rope was tied to the saddle horn with a piece of string that broke when the calf hit the end of the rope, thus the name of the event.

The trick was you had to do it faster than anyone else—and at most rodeos that meant two or three seconds, max. The timing of horse, calf, and rope had to be flawless.

As Donetta continued her tirade, the girl's shoulders slumped a little lower with every word, and her bottom lip starting to tremble.

Melanie clenched both hands. *Shut up, shut up, shut up…*

"But Mom…" the girl began.

"Stop whining." Donetta planted her fists on bony hips. "Do you *want* to be a loser?"

Okay, that's it. Melanie tossed her sorting stick aside and swung over the fence into the arena. "She seems to be having a little trouble with her horse. Maybe if you got on and straightened him out a little?"

Donetta's eyes widened, and she glanced to either side as if she couldn't believe Melanie was talking to her. "I don't rope!"

"Oh. My mistake." Melanie forcibly removed any hint of sarcasm from her voice. "The way you were talking, I assumed you must have a lot of experience."

The leathery skin around the woman's mouth drew into tight creases. "I have been to every clinic with her. I know what she's supposed to be doing."

"At the moment, what *she's* doing isn't the problem. Her horse isn't giving her a chance."

Donetta's mouth pinched tighter. "Who the hell are you to tell my kid how to rope?"

"She's Melanie Brookman," Grace piped up, in a tone that suggested any idiot should recognize her. "She and her daddy have trained some of the best horses in the state of Texas. If you know what's good for Katelyn, you'll listen to her."

The man Melanie had relieved of calf-pushing duty cleared his throat. "Grace is right, honey. Why don't you go on over and sit down while we run this next pen?"

Donetta glared at him, stunned. "You think you know better? Fine. See what you can do with this kid."

She turned on her heel and marched straight out of the arena gate to her pickup. The last they saw of her was the rooster tail of dust as she squealed out onto the highway.

Well, hell.

Melanie's stomach jumped as she tightened Roy's cinches, acutely aware of curious eyes watching her every move. She'd hoped if she and Grace waited until the others were done, everyone else would leave before she backed in the box for the first time in seven years. But no. After her altercation with Donetta, they were lining the fences to watch.

At least she had helped Katelyn make a couple of good runs. That would make it slightly less humiliating if Melanie's own roping was a total wash.

She drew a long, steadying breath and swung aboard Roy. "I've never roped on this horse before," she declared, loud enough for all to hear. "I'm going to just track those four big, black calves. Grace can run the others."

She checked to be sure her rope was tied securely to the saddle horn and adjusted the breakaway hondo that would pop loose when the rope came tight around a calf's neck…*if* she managed to catch anything. Roy ambled into the box as if they were on another trail ride, but as soon as she turned him around, his ears perked and his muscles bunched, ready to launch. Since Shawnee had only roped steers on him for the past few years, he would need a little adjusting.

Melanie tucked her rope under her arm, tightened the reins, and nodded her head. She didn't bother swinging her rope, concentrating on her horse's position. Roy broke wide but moved over easily, tracking the calf as it swerved first right, then left, then back to the right again. Twenty yards off the back of the big arena, she set the horse in a neat, smooth stop and let the calf run on out the exit gate.

She repeated the process on the second, but this time picked her loop up and took a few swings before stopping. By the third run, Roy was back in the groove, arrowing straight out of the corner directly to the calf's hip. She took several swings and threw, amazed when it settled over the calf's head. Roy slid to a stop, and the rope snapped loose.

The sound made her tingle all over. And Roy...wow. No wonder he was the only man Shawnee had kept around until Cole.

The next calf faded to the left and dropped his head so low that Melanie's loop spun around his ears and off. She coiled up her rope, patted Roy on the neck, and rode back, prepared to dismount.

"You take this one," Grace said. "Then it'll be an even split, five for you, five for me."

The calf in the chute was the potbellied Hereford that loped out, straight and slow. No need to chase this one very far. Melanie dragged in air as she built her loop, her mind and body settling into the familiar routine as she rode into the box, cocked her arm back, and nodded.

Swing, swing, throw, snap!

Roy planted his butt a stride from the front of the chute as the rope popped free. The whole thing took maybe two seconds. There was an instant of stunned silence. Then someone whistled, somebody else clapped, and a murmur rippled through the little crowd.

Donetta's husband stepped up and patted Roy's neck, shaking his head in amazement. "That was incredible. I can't believe this horse has never been roped on before."

"What?" Melanie blinked at him, still riding the high of a sizzling-fast run. "I said *I'd* never—"

Then she clamped her mouth shut. What the hell? Let them think she'd trained a horse in five runs. She could make it work for her. "It's all about giving them a good foundation. If you stop by the Bull Dancer during our open house a week from Sunday, I'll show you some roping videos that I think would really help with your daughter's horse."

"Oh, well, I'll have to see—"

One of the other men clapped him on the shoulder. "Come on, Howie. You've got the ol' gal on the run. Don't weaken now."

Howie looked like he might be sick.

"I hope you can make it," Melanie said. *If your wife doesn't murder you.*

As they all bustled off to re-pen the calves, she coiled her rope and sat back in the saddle, soaking it all in.

Grace rode up next to her. "How'd that feel?"

Melanie grinned. "Like Roy and I better find us a rodeo and enter up."

And like she'd come home...even though she was half a country away from the Panhandle.

Chapter 44

When Wyatt arrived at the Bull Dancer a week from the following Sunday, the first thing he noticed was that he couldn't find an open parking spot on the street in front of the bar. He pulled around to the back lot and got his second surprise—an eight-foot board fence around the patio, the formerly barren space covered by white canvas sheets that rippled like sails in the breeze. The noise hit him next—voices, laughter, music, and an odd clattering.

And then he smelled it.

His digestive juices kicked into overdrive at the scent of fresh-baked bread and fried chicken. He had to stop short inside his newly acquired back gate to avoid a wheeled steer dummy that came zipping toward him, pursued by two men with ropes. The first captured the horns and turned left, dragging the dummy like a steer in the arena, and the second scooped up the hinged wooden hind legs. Onlookers hooted and cheered from tables set up against the brick rear wall of the building.

"Five point three seconds," a woman announced, holding up her cell phone to show the timer. "Rowdy and Darrel, you're next."

Rowdy glanced over, saw Wyatt, and tossed him a grin. "Just in time...this is the first round of a three-header. Wanna enter up?"

"Not this time, thanks. Have you seen—"

Melanie strolled out the door in low-cut jeans and a bright-yellow tank top, her hair rippling loose and a drink in each hand. The sight of her was like a flower bursting into bloom in Wyatt's chest. She sauntered up, passed him a whiskey and Coke, and gave him a wifely peck on the cheek. "Welcome home, honey. How was work?"

"Not as busy as you." How in the *hell* had she done all this in ten days? He gazed around in wonder at the worn concrete stained to a rustic brown, the cracks and chips simply adding character. The swivel chairs and glass-topped tables were made from wooden barrels that bore the stamps of local wineries, and were nearly all occupied by people talking with the broad gestures and bursts of laughter that guaranteed tall tales were being told. And on every side, the board fence was plastered with banners he'd collected from rodeos across the country and piled in the storeroom until he could figure out where to hang them.

It was exactly what he'd imagined, even though he hadn't been able to picture it until now.

"Cool, huh? We invited the saddle club members to initiate our new roping pen this afternoon." Melanie slipped her arm through his and steered him inside. "Come and see the rest."

As they stepped into the back hallway, the scent of the food intensified. Wyatt drew a long, appreciative breath. "Please tell me that tastes as good as it smells."

"What do you think?" a new voice demanded.

He stared at the woman who filled the doorway to the kitchen. "Helen?"

"In the flesh, and there's still a whole lot of it." She folded him into a hug that was like being swallowed by

Mother Earth, then stepped back and looked him up and down with a critical eye. "All gaunted up from the road, just like Joe used to be. You go on in and find a seat. I'll fix you a plate."

Melanie tugged on his arm, guiding him past vaguely familiar faces that smiled and nodded in greeting. Wyatt responded in kind as she deposited him in a booth. Gordon grinned at him across the table. Melanie patted Wyatt's head as if she could tell it was spinning. "I'll go get that plate for you."

Wyatt nodded vaguely, his attention caught by the room around him.

"So…how do you like what we've done with the place?" Gordon asked.

"I…wow."

With a few basic changes, she'd transformed a faded bordello into a rustic hotel, replacing gilt and velvet with historic black-and-white rodeo prints and vintage signs. Oversize flat-screen TVs hung on the walls at either end of the room, framed in wood to blend with the decor. On the one directly above his booth, Wyatt saw himself in the arena at the National Finals, waiting for a bull rider to nod his head. The other was showing footage of the recent Oregon State High School Rodeo.

Gordon patted a tablet mounted in a bracket on their table. "Folks can take their pick from a whole list of videos on these gizmos, including every Pendleton Roundup that's ever been filmed. Or they can watch live-stream events." He nodded toward a table full of men around his age. "It's great for guys like that who don't do the Internet. And most of 'em don't get food like this at home."

Melanie slid a plate heaped with chicken, mashed potatoes, and green beans in front of Wyatt, all drowned in gravy. A smaller plate held two golden dinner rolls glistening with melted butter. His taste buds had a minor orgasm in anticipation. It had been a long, *long* time since he'd had the pleasure of Helen's cooking.

Melanie gestured toward a corner, where a steam table had been set up. "We're serving everything buffet-style—one entree, two vegetables, bread, and a dessert. Meat loaf on Tuesdays, pot roast on Wednesdays, chili and corn bread on Thursdays, and fish and chips on Fridays. Saturday is cook's choice, and we're open from one until seven on Sunday for Gordon's Special Chicken Dinner."

Wyatt took a huge bite of a crispy fried drumstick and groaned at the explosion of flavor on his tongue. "Dear God, that's good."

Gordon beamed at him.

Melanie laughed. "I knew we'd make a praying man of you again."

He caught her hand as she started to turn away. "This is amazing. I don't know how to thank you."

"Your autograph on the bottom of my paycheck will suffice. I'm just doing my job."

Her *job*. With all that had happened between them, it was easy to forget she was only here because he'd hired her to fix his bar. She'd succeeded beyond his wildest dreams—and in a fraction of the time. The thought settled over him like a cold, creeping fog.

He'd assumed—hoped—that it would take weeks. Maybe months. And as much as he loved the result, he couldn't help wishing she wasn't quite so efficient.

One of the saddle clubbers poked his head in from the back hall. "Hey, Melanie! Ain't you gonna come out here and show us how it's done in Texas?"

"Nah." She waved him off. "I don't want to crush your manly pride."

He grinned. "I don't mind losing to the woman who helped Howie Jones find his balls."

She laughed, but shook her head. "I have to see if Louie needs help behind the bar."

"What is he talking about?" Wyatt asked, tightening his grip to keep her from escaping.

"I, um, may have had a small disagreement with Donetta Jones." When Wyatt's eyes narrowed, she hunched her shoulders defensively. "She was being horrible to their daughter. All I did was suggest that maybe she could get on the horse and do better. Grace was the one who told her to shut up and pay attention, and when she got all pissy, Howie told her to go sit down."

Wyatt nearly spit up a green bean. "Are you kidding me?"

"Ah. I see you know her."

"*Everybody* knows her. She is the bane of the school board, the Girl Scouts, the city council…" Wyatt settled back in the booth and stared up at her. "I've been schmoozing my ass off at Chamber of Commerce events for over a year and couldn't get a soul into this place. You go pick a fight with the president of the saddle club, and suddenly we're the hottest place in town?"

"I tried to tell you—never underestimate the power of the roping pen." She smiled brightly. "Which is why *you* are going to the saddle club with me next time."

Oh hell. Even after seeing him in action, she was

going to stick him on a horse. With a rope. And an audience. Nothing like total humiliation to ensure that no one was intimidated by what Melanie called his *supercool* image.

On the bright side, if she intended to stick around long enough to make a roper out of him, she might never leave. And there he went again, wishing on a star that he knew full well was just a meteor, destined to burn out and leave only a trail of brilliant memories behind.

⁓

Much later that night, Melanie stretched, enjoying the slide of her well-used body against the lean length of Wyatt's. The north breeze cleared away the usual downtown potpourri in favor of the cool dampness of the river with a hint of sweetness from flowers blooming in the nearby park. She'd offered to follow Wyatt to his condo when they'd closed the bar, but he'd insisted on hauling an overnight bag up to her room.

It made sense, given their mutual determination to keep this short term. Why not use this fantasy room to play out their affair? It was, after all, what the place had been built for, and when they were done, he wouldn't be left with her imprint on his personal space, and she wouldn't have to imagine the life they might have had there. Everything would be contained within these walls, a scene inside a crystal ball that only looked into the past.

She laid her hand over Wyatt's where it was splayed out on her stomach, and his arm tightened in reflex as if his body, at least, didn't want to let her go.

She pushed away the bittersweet thought, determined

to savor this man, this day, and her unequivocal success. Her smug sense of well-being wasn't just about the amazing sex. She'd taken a run-down bar and a handful of vague suggestions and crafted them into the answer to his…well, maybe not prayers, but close. The satisfaction of watching Wyatt's eyes light up when he saw it all brought to life…

That was what she wanted.

She could claw her way to the top of the corporate ladder. She was tough enough, talented enough, and had the kind of connections that could make the ugliness at Westwind irrelevant—Tori's father, Joe's stepfather, even Wyatt. But the thought of the meetings, the travel, the unrelenting pressure and convoluted office politics only made her tired. She'd set out to be a trailblazer, determined to knock down doors and break through ceilings—and that way had led to her own brand of madness.

Imagine, though, if she could do for someone else what she'd done for Wyatt. If she could use the gifts God had given her to help manufacture dreams. Instead of promoting herself, why not use her skills to lift up others? There were plenty of government and private organizations dedicated to helping business startups—especially those whose owners began at a disadvantage. Even better, there would still be room in her life for the pleasure of good horses, good friends, and good roping.

And a good man…if she was ever that lucky.

She wriggled around to get more comfortable, drawing an appreciative sigh. Lifting Wyatt's hand, she brushed her lips over his knuckles. He breathed a sleepy kiss into her hair, and she had to squeeze her eyes tight against the hot rush of tears.

Who was she kidding? No one had ever been able to push Wyatt out of her heart. And nothing would ever compare to this little slice of perfection.

So she would have to be sure that she savored every bite.

Chapter 45

THE KITE WAS A BRILLIANT ARC OF RED AND YELLOW AGAINST the deep blue of the sky as it strained at the lines, pushed by wind that raised a steady chop on the wide expanse of the Columbia River. At Wyatt's command, Melanie brought the kite up to twelve o'clock, almost directly overhead.

"Ready?" he asked, steadying the board in the chest-deep water as she maneuvered her body into a balanced position.

She muttered under her breath in response. "Don't pull the kite; let the kite pull you. Don't pull the kite…"

"You've got this." He let go and stepped out of the way. "Remember, weight on the heel of the board."

She gave the bar a slight tilt, and the kite swooped down to nine o'clock. As it began to drag her through the water, she bent her back knee and straightened the front, keeping her arms straight this time and letting the kite lift her up onto the board.

"That's it!" Wyatt yelled. "Now bring the kite back up…"

She raised the bar and the kite shot into the sky, lifting her almost off the water before a wave caught the front edge of the board and smacked her facedown into the river.

She came up sputtering and swearing, but she did manage to keep the kite from nose-diving, too.

Wyatt swung onto the paddleboard he'd brought along and sat astride to row over and retrieve the board. "Time for a break," he called out. "Body drag back to the beach."

She did as instructed, steering the kite to a three-o'clock position so it hauled her to the sandbar where they'd started. This far up the river and on a weekday, there were only two other windsurfers in sight, both mere slashes of color near the far bank. Melanie found her feet and staggered onto the coarse sand, plopping on her butt and scraping tendrils of hair out of her eyes while she steadied the kite with the other hand.

"Flying this damn thing was a lot easier when we were standing in middle of a hayfield," she said, panting from exertion.

"You're doing great. Most people don't even try a water start until the second or third day." Wyatt beached the paddleboard and walked over to take the bar from her and unhook the line from her harness. "You were up for a few seconds that time, until you oversteered and did the nose dive."

"Nice change from falling on my back." She unclipped her helmet and pulled it off, letting it drop as she braced her elbows on bent knees. "I'm done. My arms and legs are like noodles."

Maybe so, but they still looked exceptionally good in that wet suit, along with the rest of her.

The past week had been a miracle, filled with more joy than Wyatt had thought possible. He'd never imagined any woman could slip so seamlessly into every part of his life—from the training arena to bike rides through the fields and canyons to evenings at the athletic club, where Melanie threw herself into the pickup basketball games with savage glee, while Wyatt and his abused ankle stayed safely on the sidelines. They had long lunches at the Bull Dancer with Gordon and Louie, brainstorming promotions for the bar. Over late suppers, Helen regaled them with stories about Joe's early days on the Browning ranch—providing Wyatt with hours' worth of ammunition to torture him, because what were friends for?

More and more often, ranchers or old rodeo hands would wander over to join their bullshit sessions, or drag Wyatt out back to give him a few tips on roping the dummy steer. As expected, Wyatt's debut at the saddle club had been the source of much hilarity—but he'd grudgingly found himself laughing along. And once he'd even caught something other than his own head.

Melanie's introduction to kiteboarding had been considerably more promising, despite the wipeouts. With her athletic ability and strength, she could be skimming over the waves like a pro given another lesson or two— if they had time to get back out to the river again.

They hadn't talked about the exact date of her departure, but she had provided him a detailed marketing plan, and every part of it that required her presence would be complete by the end of June. Eight more days. And nights. Sweet Jesus, the nights, and waking up with Melanie's hair spilling across his chest as she rolled over at the sound of her phone alarm blasting out Jason Aldean's "Crazy Town," then burrowed sleepily into his arms.

She hadn't said she would leave as soon as her work was done, but she hadn't mentioned staying either—and

Wyatt hadn't asked. By unspoken agreement, they avoided all mention of Hank, or Laura, or Melanie's plans for the future. Other than at his arena or the practice sessions at the saddle club, Grace kept a cautious distance, even though Wyatt knew she suffered from a distinct lack of female friends. He also knew her deliberate standoffishness bothered Melanie, but it was one more of those things they didn't discuss.

Melanie hadn't even asked why they spent so little time at his condo…mostly quick stops to pick up the bikes or a change of clothes for Wyatt. Knowing him as she did, he assumed she understood it was easier to keep reality at bay in the madam's room, a place he'd designed to be a step outside of time.

She couldn't suspect he feared that she would somehow sense Maddie's presence, even though he'd taken care to hide any trace.

He grabbed his own board from the beach, attached the lines to his harness and adjusted them for his size and level of expertise. "I'm going for a spin while you catch your breath."

She flicked a hand in a shooing motion, as if she was too tired to speak. Wading out until he was thigh deep, Wyatt tossed his board flat in front of him, sent the kite straight up so he was plucked out of the water, then with a slight twist of the bar, dipped down to drop onto the board and skip away across the waves.

"Show-off!" Melanie yelled after him.

And because he was, and he couldn't help trying to impress her, he sent the kite high again and took flight.

〜〜〜

She could have watched him all day. Soaring, spinning, swooping on the wind as light and easy as the gulls that seemed to dance with him. What would it be like, to fly like the birds?

If she stayed long enough, he would teach her. He might not want to keep her forever, but he was in no rush to see her gone, and she had no urgent business elsewhere. She'd only found one job opening that piqued her interest, and it was in the Tri-Cities...far too close to Pendleton for comfort or her limited supply of self-control. She couldn't live thirty miles away and not come over to see Helen and Louie, and she couldn't stand to be that close to Wyatt and not be able to touch him.

Worse, they could slip into one of those sporadic non-relationships that left her in constant limbo, waiting for his next call.

No. She had to make a clean break and put a few states between them. Someplace close enough to the Panhandle to spend a weekend at Violet's when the mood struck, but far enough away to minimize the chances of bumping into Wyatt when he was visiting. Like shared custody, only of their friends.

But until she found that place and that job...

She watched Wyatt glide toward the beach and carve a deep, showy turn at the water's edge before bringing the board to a stop and landing the kite in the shallows. Easy peasy.

Not.

"Had enough?" she asked.

"Never."

He radiated pure physical joy as he waded toward her, shaking water from his hair and tucking the board under his arm. Another of a thousand heart-stopping moments she had accumulated over the past week, absorbing every scent and sensation to stash like the letters, photos, ribbons, and trinkets her grandmother had collected in a polished cedar box—the first thing her granddad had grabbed when the fire raced toward the ranch.

She took the kite bar from Wyatt so he could unzip his wet suit and peel it down to his waist, sending her pulse skipping at the sight of all that sleek, sculpted muscle glistening wet under the sun.

He took the kite bar with one hand and used the other to pull her to her feet and into a lingering kiss that tasted of cool river and the exhilaration of the ride. She ran her hands up his chest, over his shoulders, and felt his immediate reaction. His eyes were that hot Caribbean blue when he pulled back to flash her a wicked smile. "I have to be at the Bull Dancer at two o'clock to interview the new bartender, which gives us just enough time to stop by my place, drop off the gear...and grab a shower."

Another of those pit stops where she barely had a chance to admire the view. But then, she had no real desire to wander around, trailing her fingers over the spines of books and admiring the abstracts on the living room walls. Since he'd come back from Reno, she'd consciously retreated to a tolerable level of intimacy—not too close, not too far—and being in his home, invading his most personal space, threatened to upset that delicate balance.

While he packed up the kite, she gathered the rest of the gear, stowed it in wet sacks, and hauled it to the car. She pulled an oversized T-shirt and shorts on over her damp one-piece swimsuit before digging her phone out of her purse to check for messages.

There were three texts, all from Shawnee.

The first was a link to the online edition of the Amarillo newspaper. The second said, Call me. The third said, CALL ME NOW.

Melanie clicked on the link first, and sucked in a breath when she saw the headline. "Amarillo Businessman Nabbed in Prostitution Sting." The picture was of Leachman.

She called Shawnee.

"It's about damn time!" Shawnee said by way of greeting.

"We've been out on the river all morning. Oh my God! I can't believe they actually caught *him*, instead of some trucker from Cleveland."

"Puh-leeze." Shawnee's tone was a verbal eye roll. "You think that was a coincidence?"

"What? But how…"

"You mentioned that he liked to stop by one of the truck stops to get serviced, and you'd told Violet that he and Jimmy Ray Towler had regular *golf* dates. Every time Delon hauls a load of cattle to Sagebrush Feeders, Jimmy Ray insists on buying lunch at his favorite café out on the interstate. He and Leachman being creatures of question-able habit, it wasn't real hard to add up." Her voice went pouty. "I wanted to do a stakeout in one of the Sanchez trucks with a big ol' telephoto lens, but we've got a rodeo every week until the end of September, and Cole refused to hire someone to fill in for me. You know how he is about new people. I swear, I'm gonna be stuck picking up broncs until Beni gets old enough to take over."

And she loved every minute of it.

"How did you get the cops to show up right on schedule?" Melanie asked, still having trouble believing her friends had pulled this off.

"Gil put a bug in a few ears, and all of the sudden, the police were flooded with complaints from drivers about these women banging on their doors when they were trying to get some sleep—which actually is a major pain in the ass for most of them. And if you're the chief of police in Amarillo and you're already planning a crackdown, why not earn some brownie points when a certain former U.S. senator suggests that you send a couple of officers out there on Wednesday around five o'clock?"

Melanie slumped against the side of the car, her already rubbery knees threatening to give out. "Unbelievable. Leachman has been slithering out of trouble for so long that I didn't think his hide would ever get nailed to the wall."

"He never messed with one of ours before. And as a token of our appreciation, we all went together and posted bail for the women they rounded up...*after* Tori sent a counselor from a safe house to give them the option to go somewhere other than back on the street."

Good Lord. They'd thought of everything. "Why didn't anyone tell me about this?"

"Tori called it plausible deniability. She said it was better if you could honestly say you had nothing to do with it when you come back to Westwind."

"Wait. *What?* Come back..."

"They haven't filled your position yet, and the board has already placed Leachman on administrative leave pending the outcome of this unfortunate turn of events."

Shawnee coated the words in a thick layer of false sympathy. "Someone has to take charge, especially with the senator putting together a deal to fund an employee buyout of the company."

"Hold on." Melanie slid down to sit in the dirt, her back against the wheel of the Camaro. "You lost me."

"It's pretty simple. In the process of spying on the place, Violet realized it really is a great investment. She sent her spreadsheets to Tori's daddy, and he agreed. He's presenting their proposal at the next board meeting—including a recommendation that they bring you back to handle the transition. It'll go a lot smoother if it's someone the employees trust, instead of an outsider."

Melanie gave an incredulous laugh. "I…don't know what to say."

"I assumed you'd be jumping for joy." Shawnee sounded annoyed. "Don't tell me we did all this for nothing."

"No." Melanie shook her head, but that only rattled the pieces. "I mean, seeing Leachman get his is more than enough. And I would love to march back in that place and do a victory dance on his desk. I just…well, I've been doing a lot of thinking, and I've sort of decided big business isn't the direction I want to go."

"Are you *kidding* me?"

Melanie scowled at a nearby patch of goatshead weed, its evil thorns still green and clinging to the vines. "Hey, you're the one who dumped a pair of rope horses on me, so whose fault is it if I've lost my taste for eighty-hour workweeks?"

Shawnee's triumphant whoop nearly split Melanie's

eardrum. "Welcome back from the dark side! When's your first rodeo?"

"This weekend," she admitted reluctantly. "There's a jackpot right down the road in Arlington."

"Damn. I wish I could see that. Make sure someone takes video, I miss my Roy. And by the way...I will be collecting the standard twenty-five percent for mount money."

Melanie snorted. "I'll have to win something first."

"Right. You, riding Roy? Oregon isn't gonna know what hit them."

When Melanie hung up, she let her head fall back against the tire, still trying to take it all in. She thumbed the screen of her phone to bring up the headline and the photo of Leachman being led away in handcuffs, taken by a reporter who'd been conveniently on hand, no doubt thanks to a well-timed anonymous tip.

Lord. She was glad these people were on her side.

"Nice," Wyatt said from above her, making her jump as always, the sneaky bastard.

She twisted her head around to find him leaning on the hood, reading over her shoulder. She narrowed her eyes at him. "Uh-huh. Like you had nothing to do with this. I don't recall mentioning the prostitutes to anyone else."

"I may have said something to Gil, but that was all." His proclamation of innocence would have been a lot more convincing if his smile hadn't been quite so triumphant. "I was told to butt out, so I left them to it."

She amped up the suspicion in her glare. "I suppose you also know nothing about the senator, and the employee buyout, and asking me to come back to Westwind."

"Really?" Honest surprise flashed across his face, followed by something more complicated. "That's great. You win on all fronts." He pushed himself upright and dragged a silky, loose-fitting nylon T-shirt over his head, muffling his words—and concealing his face as he asked, "How soon do they want you?"

And there it was. The question they'd been so carefully avoiding. *How much longer…*

"It's only a proposal at this point, so I don't know…a month, minimum? And that's assuming a lot." Like whether she was even interested, which Wyatt seemed to take as a given. Why wouldn't he?

But as he tugged the shirt down to his waist, she saw that slight loosening of his shoulders, the subtle release of tension. When he smiled, the warmth once again bloomed in his eyes. "We should celebrate…and I know just the place."

Wyatt's shower was a miracle of engineering and polished travertine tile, with six adjustable body jets, a rainfall feature set into the ceiling, a multifunction handheld head…and gold-finished grab bars on the walls.

"Luxurious, and yet handicapped accessible," Melanie commented as she stripped off her swimsuit.

Already naked, Wyatt stepped up behind her to nuzzle kisses into the curve of her neck while he removed the hair tie from her still-damp braid and began carefully working the strands free with his fingers. "Ever try to get in and out of the shower on crutches?"

As a matter of fact, she had. "I see your point."

She pulled the remainder of the braid away from

him, the better to free up his hands for other things. He obliged by running them over her, leaving ripples of pleasure in his wake as he revisited all of her most sensitive places…several of which she'd only recently discovered herself. She'd been on a slow simmer since before they left the river, and she moaned as his touch instantly brought her desire to a boil.

"Hold that thought," he said, and stepped around her to adjust the angle and temperature of the jets.

She squeaked in surprise when he turned and scooped her up, his hands gripping her thighs. She grabbed his shoulders as he swung around to press her back against the cool tile, letting her slide down until her butt rested on one of the handrails.

"They also have other uses," he said, and lifted her legs to wrap around his hips, everything hot and wet and hard as the water pulsed over them and he drove into her, pushing them both into an ascent as high and wild as a kite in a storm.

<hr>

Melanie emerged squeaky clean and more than a little wobbly on her feet. Between the sex and kiteboarding, she might not have normal function in her lower limbs for days.

Clippers buzzed to life in the bathroom, Wyatt trimming the stubble he'd apparently decided to keep. She touched one of the tender spots it had left on her thigh the night before, and shuddered. He wouldn't get any argument from her. And in a weird way, it made her feel as if she'd put her stamp on him, a visible change she had wrought.

She unzipped the pack she'd brought along and dug out jeans, underwear and bra, and a tank top. But dammit, no socks, and she'd grabbed her boots instead of running shoes. She wrinkled her nose at the thought of pulling them on over bare, waterlogged feet. Wyatt wouldn't mind if she borrowed a pair. She pulled open the nearest drawer and found a rainbow of neatly folded polo shirts. The next drawer was T-shirts and those stretchy nylon jobs he wore under his pads. Her mouth went dry remembering him in transparent, skintight white. She found underwear next—boxers *and* briefs—and finally his sock drawer.

Wow. She'd never realized they came in that many varieties. The man owned a pair for every possible occasion, from black dress socks to that special shorty kind for biking. Fascinated, she picked through the drawer, trying to match the type to the occasion. Basic white crew socks for jeans and boots days—she tucked a pair of those under her arm—knee-high soccer-style in several colors and patterns for when he was in the arena, and near the bottom—

Her fingers encountered the corner of something hard and square. She frowned as she pulled out a picture that had been buried, as if he'd hidden it. She couldn't imagine why. It was just an eight-by-ten of Wyatt and Laura standing on a stone bridge with a waterfall behind them. A stunning black woman leaned close on his other side, and he held a baby—around six months old, Melanie guessed, although babies all sort of looked alike to her from the time they could sit upright until they got old enough to have a conversation. Judging by her frilly dress, shiny patent leather shoes, and the colorful basket

Laura held, this was why Wyatt had declined Miz Iris's dinner invitation at Easter.

The woman must be Laura's wife. Melanie leaned in closer, studying both her and the little girl. Adopted, she assumed, or a foster child. Wyatt had said Laura didn't dare try to have a baby, and with her feathery brown hair and fair skin, odds were this one wasn't the other woman's natural child. But there was something familiar about that grin and sparkle of mischief in her eyes—

She might never have made the connection if Wyatt hadn't stepped out of the bathroom, seen her with the photo in her hands, and cursed.

Suddenly it clicked, each piece dropping like frozen lead into the pit of her stomach. She saw with horrible clarity what she hadn't been able to bring into focus. The connections that were now so obvious. Laura. Grace. This baby.

Hank.

The confirmation was written on Wyatt's face in stark, devastating lines. He didn't try to speak, just stood there in nothing but a towel, braced like a man facing his executioner.

She lifted the photo. "You...did this?"

He gave a single, barely visible nod.

It all made horrible sense. Grace trying desperately to talk to Hank on that awful New Year's Eve. Wyatt's obsession with keeping track of him. The way Laura had looked at Melanie as if she somehow *knew* her. That part of Wyatt's relationship with Grace she'd never been able to grasp. In true Wyatt fashion, he'd rescued Grace and given Laura her heart's desire in one fell swoop. A daughter.

Hank's daughter. Melanie's niece.

Wyatt's secret.

She moved slowly, deliberately, setting the photo on the bed as if it were a ticking bomb that might explode her hands. She held Wyatt's gaze, her body winding up to flee if he made any move to touch her as she edged around the end of the bed.

His face was so rigid that his lips barely moved when he spoke. "Don't blame Grace," he said. "She did what she thought was best."

Not *I'm sorry*, or *Please let me explain*. That would have meant Melanie mattered at least as much as the people in that photo. Or even Grace. She could only stare at him. That was it? No explanation, no excuses, not even an attempt to apologize?

But then, it would have just been one more lie, so why bother?

She scooped up her boots and her damp clothes and headed for the door on legs that threatened to give out. Hell. She didn't even have her car.

"Are you going to tell him?" he asked in that same flat voice.

She didn't slow down, look back...or answer.

—◈◈◈—

If he hadn't been paralyzed, he might have been stupid enough to try to stop her. Instead Wyatt stood frozen, the edges of his vision going white, all of the color in his world fading and shrinking until there was nothing left but the picture that stared up at him from the bed.

He had played this moment in his head every day, in

a thousand different ways. This was more terrible than
the worst he'd ever imagined.

He had to move. To do…things. His mind creaked,
the gears seized up by a shock so deep the pain couldn't
filter through—yet. But some tiny part of his brain was
still functioning, if only at a whisper. *Not just about you.
Have to tell the others.* The voice nudged at him, becoming more insistent. Grace. He had to warn her.

The realization jolted him into action. He fumbled his
phone out of the pocket of the jeans he'd kicked aside
on the way to the shower and punched up the number.
Answer. Answer. Answer, dammit…

"Hel—"

"Melanie knows."

The silence was an echo of his own shock.

"How?" Grace asked breathlessly.

"Me. I screwed up." In so, so many ways. The brain
that had been stalled began to spin, faster and faster. He
couldn't let Melanie find Grace, for both their sakes.
Words that were said in the heat of this moment could
never be taken back. "Get out of your house, and go
someplace where she can't find you. If she calls, don't
answer the phone."

"Okay." Grace's breath shuddered in his ear. "What's
she going to do?"

"I don't know. She took off out of here, and I…don't
know…" The anguish closed his throat.

"Can't you stop her?"

No more than he could stop an avalanche he'd trig-
gered by stepping onto what he'd always known was a
treacherous slope. His gut clenched, the pain so intense
he wondered vaguely if his ulcer had finally burst. He

staggered over to the bed and sat, his towel falling unnoticed to the floor, beside a pair of socks Melanie must have dropped.

"I'll do what I can." But they both knew that once Melanie was on a tear, that wasn't very damn much. "I am so sorry, Grace."

There was a long beat of strained silence. Then she whispered, "Me, too."

Chapter 46

ONCE AGAIN, WYATT DIDN'T COME AFTER HER. THERE WAS no rumble of an engine coming up hard on her heels as she stumbled down the hill to the Bull Dancer. No knock at the door while she crammed clothes into her suitcases. No one lurking at the foot of the stairs as she propped the boot box outside the apartment door, just as she'd found it. No bright-red Camaro at the curb when she emerged onto the street, or parked behind her car in the rear lot, blocking her escape.

Relief warred with knifing slashes of pain. She didn't trust what she might have done if he'd tried to stop her. But dammit, the son of a bitch could have at least tried.

She wished she didn't understand him so well. Then she wouldn't know that rather than dealing with her, he was on the phone warning Grace and Laura, probably Louie, too. *Red alert. Melanie on the rampage.* While they scrambled out of her path, Wyatt would be waiting at the condo to let her rip him apart when she realized he'd eliminated all other possible targets.

Always the sacrificial lamb, shedding his blood to protect the flock. And he thought he had no religion.

He could choke on his guilt for all she cared. And he didn't have to keep his precious Camaro under armed guard, either. She'd already played that card, and she prided herself on never taking the one-size-fits-all approach. She heaved the suitcases into the back of her car, slammed the hatchback shut, and climbed into the stifling interior. At the west end of town, she took the now-familiar interstate on-ramp.

She'd studied the map. If she passed on through the Tri-Cities and kept heading north and east, eventually she would end up in the vicinity of Babb, Montana. And maybe, by the time she got there, she would have some idea what to do.

―⁓⁓―

Two hours later, Melanie's phone rang. Violet's name popped up on the dashboard screen. So, Wyatt had called in reinforcements. She wondered almost casually what he'd told them. Or had he let them think their relationship had reached what he had led her to believe was its natural conclusion? Only one way to find out. She picked up the call.

"Are you driving?" Violet's voice held a razor edge of fear. "Tell me you're not driving if you're as upset as Wyatt said."

Naturally Violet would be terrified. A car accident had devastated her family, and decades later the scars were still visible.

"I'm fine. Not even going the speed limit." She'd set her cruise control to avoid the temptation to mash the pedal to the floor.

"Wyatt is *not* fine. He wouldn't say what happened, but if you're half as bad as he is, you shouldn't be on the road. Dammit. That will teach me to leave my phone in the trailer while we're meeting with the rodeo committee. You're not in the mountains, are you?"

"Not yet."

"What's the next town? I want you to stop and get a room. We've got a rodeo performance in an hour, but I can be on a plane to wherever you are first thing in the morning."

Now that Violet mentioned it, Melanie could hear music in the background, accompanied by voices and the slam of steel gates—standard pre-rodeo hubbub as the crowd filed in and the stock was sorted for the night's show. The sudden, intense yearning to be there instead of here was one more stab to her heart, the one that drained the last of the frantic energy that had been pushing her forward.

Exhaustion slammed into her. She gripped the steering wheel and shook her head to clear the sudden fog. "I'm not far from Spokane. According to the billboards, there are four or five hotels on the airport exit. I'll stop there."

"Thank you." Violet's relief was palpable. "I'll keep my phone in my pocket, in case you need anything. Text me when you're checked in."

"Room number and all," Melanie promised. Not that she expected to sleep, but she couldn't drive much farther without being a hazard to herself and everyone else on the road. "Don't go buying plane tickets yet. I swear, I won't do anything stupid."

"You expect me to fall for that *again*?"

"I'm telling the honest truth, Violet."

Unlike some people. And the fact was, she was tapped out. As the miles and the initial shock had passed, her mind had cleared, but the rest of her had gone numb. Running from Wyatt and to Hank had been her first instinct. Besides, she'd had to get away, and this direction was as good as any.

She had the list of mental health experts Wyatt had emailed to her from Reno. Maybe in the morning, when she was semi-rested and coherent, she could try to get in touch with one of them. She needed to have some idea what impact the news might have before she went charging into that rat's nest and announced, "*Hey, Bro, guess what?*"

"Just take care, okay?" Violet said.

"I will," she promised.

Just like she'd promised to tread carefully with Wyatt, and look how long that had lasted. She made an ugly sound, too close to a sob for comfort.

Was it still a lie if you'd meant it at the time?

She slept more than she expected, drained past empty by shock, pain—and yes, some extremely energetic shower sex. God, that seemed like a lifetime ago. As usual, her appetite had kicked into emergency overdrive, so she scarfed down sausage, scrambled eggs, and a waffle at the continental breakfast bar, then poured an extra cup of coffee to go. She kept moving by drawing on every ounce of skill she'd acquired at burying her emotions.

Who knew she'd be thankful for her screwed-up parents or that she'd worked for the Leech?

She grabbed her suitcase with one hand, her coffee with the other, and shouldered out the front door of the hotel. Halfway across the parking lot, she stopped so abruptly her hard-sided roller bag ran up the back of her heels. She blinked, shook her head, then blinked again, but he was still there, lounging against the trunk of a midnight-blue Dodge Charger parked next to her

SUV, arms folded and ankles crossed as if he could wait all day.

"What the hell?" she blurted.

Gil Sanchez gave her one of his knife-edged smiles. "Still not much of morning person, I see."

And that was coming from the man Tori called the Lord of Darkness. Even in the crisp, excruciating seven a.m. freshness, the shadows seemed to cling to his raven-dark hair and swirl in the near-black of his eyes. She gave her head another shake. "I always thought 'flummoxed' was a ridiculous word…but damned if it isn't all I've got."

"I'm a little out of my zone, too," he admitted. "I'm usually the guy distressing the damsel, not riding to her rescue."

Her eyebrows shot up. "You're going save me?"

His brows drew together over a narrow, copper-toned face, his striking coloring and bone structure a gift from his Navajo mother. In both personality and build Gil was a honed-down, tempered-steel version of Tori's husband, Delon.

This was not the nice brother.

He tilted his head, giving her question serious consideration. "Nah," he decided. "You can kick whatever ass needs it. I'm just here to point you in the right direction."

"Oh." No one would ever accuse Gil of having a savior complex. And yet, here he was. In Spokane. Waiting for her. "Wanna give me a clue so I know where to start?"

"With me."

A car came around the end of the hotel and slowed, waiting for Melanie to move out of the middle of the driveway. She took three steps, enough to clear the way but still leave several yards between her and Gil. A toddler gawked at them from his child seat as the car eased past, not much older than—geezus. She was an aunt... and she didn't even know the baby's name.

Gil stared down the kid until the car turned out of the lot. "I did this. *I* found out Grace was pregnant, and I dragged Wyatt into it."

Okay. *Flummoxed* wasn't even close now. "Why would you do that to him?"

"Because I'm a thoughtless prick. She was a problem I didn't want to deal with, so I pawned her off on him. Apparently I'm the only person in Earnest who didn't know the poor slob was in love with you."

The blunt words were like a fist driving into her sternum. "He...what?"

"Make that two people." Gil's smile twisted. "I avoid the big family scenes as much as possible, so I didn't see you and Wyatt together. I don't even want to hear your excuse."

Her eyes narrowed. "Wait a minute...you *knew* about Grace and the baby all this time, and you didn't say a word?"

Gil hitched a shoulder, supremely unconcerned. "We were all required to sign a privacy statement when Grace agreed to the open adoption. If she wants, she could sue Wyatt's ass for this. And besides, the *secret* is the whole point to a secret baby. Don't you remember anything from those books you and Violet used to sneak out of Miz Iris's stash?"

Yep. She also remembered how those books ended. "You know, a happily ever after could be problematic since Grace *gave her away*."

"And you think Hank would've fought for her?"

"I—" *Crap*. She shoved her roller bag up against the back of her car and plopped down on it as images swam through her head. Hank as he was on New Year's Eve: drunk and ignorant as Grace begged to talk to him. Hank as he was now: bitter, angry, and on the verge of homeless in Montana. She raked her hair back from her face. "You did. We sure as hell didn't expect that."

He did a touché sort of shrug.

Melanie's temper sparked. "You were in the exact same position. Can you honestly say you would've been better off not knowing about Quint?"

"First off, the situation is not the same. I had a relationship with Quint's mother." He paused for a beat, then added, "And I loved her."

A confession even more wrenching when delivered by a hard, proud man in a voice devoid of emotion—making what Hank had done all the more damning. *Gil* hadn't taken advantage of the remnants of a high school crush to score, then blown the girl off in the worst possible way.

He watched that dart hit home before he launched the next. "I also had a father who supported me a hundred percent, and a job at Sanchez Trucking that allowed me the time to drive to Oklahoma and see my son. Quint's mother is so stinking rich she never had to work at all. Have you thought about the hours Grace puts in? Early mornings, late nights, weekends, sixty or eighty hours a week—how was that gonna work as a single mom?"

She knew that. Sort of. If an athletic trainer had to be available at all of the practices and games for every sport a high school offered all year long, that would be, well…a lot. Not so different from what Melanie had been clocking for the past two years. She tried to imagine how she would have managed a child of any age—and failed miserably. She hadn't even been able to keep a remote eye on Hank.

"He deserves to know," she insisted.

"Why?" Gil's stare pressed into her, relentless. "I just came from Babb, Mel. That's where I was when Wyatt called yesterday." When she gaped at him—*Wyatt* had sicced Gil on her?—he patted the trunk of the Charger. "Ol' Blue has some gas, but it can't actually fly. How did you think I got here so fast?"

"I didn't…" Have enough head space left to cram that question in.

Before she could ask, he said, "Yeah, I talked to Hank. I know where he's at…and it's not pretty. Do you think this is what he needs right now? Or he's what a child needs? Because that's what it comes down to, not Hank or you or Wyatt or even Grace. What's best for the baby?"

"I just…I can't…" She slumped forward and pressed her face into her hands. She'd searched her soul for the answers to those questions, and in the end had concluded Bing was the only one who could help her decide. But still… "How can I *not* tell him?"

"The same way Wyatt has not told you. Or Joe. Or anybody else."

Melanie shook her head. Not tell Violet? No dumping her worries next to the plate of cinnamon rolls on Miz Iris's kitchen table to be sorted out and Melanie was promised it would all be fine, just you wait and see? The existence of this baby was a jagged rock lodged between her heart and her spleen. How could she carry it around, day after day, year after year? Look into her friends' faces knowing this...thing. It would eat her from the inside out—

The same as it had been doing to Wyatt.

Gil's mouth curled as he read her thoughts. "If the two of you pitch in, I could probably get you a major discount on a truckload of Rolaids."

"Thanks. You're a real prince."

"Yeah. That's what everybody says."

She stood, then had no idea why. If she got in her car, she wouldn't know which way to turn. She made a helpless gesture. "What next?"

"Start by crossing Hank off your list. You're no good to him."

Her hands fisted, anger spurting heat into her veins. "How can you say that? I'm his *sister*."

"Exactly. His smart, sensible big sis...the one they wanted." When she sucked in an outraged breath, Gil made an impatient gesture. "I'm not saying he doesn't love you. He just resents the shit out of you...and maybe, if you let yourself admit it, you feel the same about him."

At the sharp jerk of her head, Gil's face softened ever so slightly. "You've done more than most people would, Mel, even when he's tried to make it impossible, but you're gonna have to trust us now. We've got him. Me and Bing. You've never been anywhere close to the place he's in. I, on the other hand, have a standing reservation."

She squinted at him, confused. "Why would you bother? You could barely tolerate him before."

"He's actually less annoying now. I can deal with asshole. Clueless drives me up the wall. Plus..." He drew in a long, slow breath and let it stream out through his nose. "When I was hanging off the edge and about to lose my grip, there were people who hauled me up again and again. It's my turn to pay it forward."

And her time to let go. Accept that she'd done all she could, and the rest was up to Hank. He had to decide when or if he was going to crawl out of the hole he'd dug. It was like contemplating whether to cut off her own hand or leave it stuck in a trap while the gangrene crept up her arm. There was no painless option, just the one less likely to kill her inch by inch.

Gil pushed away from his car and strolled around to the driver's door. It was still disconcerting to see him move so easily, without the limp that had become a part of his persona. "Take a right when you get to the interstate. You'll be back in Pendleton before lunch."

For a crazy instant, she wanted to grab his arm and beg him not to leave her. Only the thought of how he'd react kept her planted beside her suitcase. "I have no idea what to say to Grace."

"Tell her she's a fucking hero." He opened the door, then paused to toss her a caustic smile. "And tell the pretty boy he's not so bad, either."

Chapter 47

MELANIE DID NOT MAKE IT BACK TO PENDLETON FOR LUNCH.

She kept thinking about Grace, imagining what it must have been like, faced with those choices. Grace could have opted for anonymity. Could have delivered the baby and walked away without ever laying eyes on it. No one but Grace, Gil, and Wyatt would ever have had to be the wiser. But she hadn't chosen the easy way, and because of it, that baby would never wonder who her family was, or why her mother had given her up.

Grace had blessed her with that peace of mind—at the cost of her own.

That was when Melanie had had to pull off on the side of the highway to swab at the tears that were streaming down her face. And she'd kept having to pull over as more and more of the ramifications hit her. *God. Poor Grace*. She'd come looking for Hank that night at the Lone Steer—alone, terrified, possibly a little hopeful—and he'd crushed her.

Damn him. Maybe it was unfair to be so furious when he had no idea what he'd done, but that was the problem, wasn't it? Hank had never had a clue, or cared to get one. Even now, when the proverbial pigeons had come home to roost, he chose to wallow in self-loathing and spread the pain as far as possible.

At that moment, Melanie was thankful she'd turned

back, because if she could have laid hands on that old
woman's shotgun…

And Wyatt. What pure hell this past year and a half
must have been for him, holding all of this inside,
not even able to share it with Joe. No wonder he was
single-handedly driving up the price of antacid stocks.
Every moment he'd spent in Earnest, every time he'd
had to see or speak to Melanie, the knowledge must
have been like a hot coal, burning in his gut. The lies
he'd had to tell…

He'd lied to her.

She straightened, her tear-swollen eyes narrowing as
she thought of what Gil had said, and replayed Wyatt's
words that night in the bathtub. That *bastard*. Her teeth
snapped together, biting off a curse as she slammed into
the front seat, shifted into Drive, and hit the gas.

He was going to pay. But first, she had to see Grace.

Melanie found her in the first place she looked—at
the athletic club, pushing Scotty and Philip through a set
of medicine ball drills. Grace made a *Halt!* gesture when
Melanie stepped into the gym. The two men flashed
thankful grins that faded into alarm when they saw
Grace's tight, set face, then got a good look at Melanie.

"Should we…" Philip began, shooting a worried
glance from one to the other.

"Go," Grace said.

Scotty scrambled to his feet, keeping a wary eye on
Melanie. "Are you sure?"

"Yes."

They hesitated for a few seconds, then backed away,
letting the door swing shut behind them but lingering to
peer through the thick safety glass.

Grace held her ground, pale and stiff, but head high. "So now you know."

"Yes."

Every breath seemed to echo in the empty gym. Then Melanie broke. She took two swift strides and wrapped her arms around Grace's rigid body. "I am so sorry."

For an instant, she thought Grace would push her away. The she sagged and let out a choked sob. Melanie smoothed her hand over the springy ponytail, made comforting circles on her heaving shoulders. They stood and clung and rocked for Lord knew how long, until finally Grace did pull back, tears spiking her lashes.

"I was so sure you'd hate me."

"No." Melanie shook her head. "Oh, no. Never you."

"But it was so stupid—"

Melanie pressed a finger to her lips. "It was a mistake…and God knows you don't have the corner on that market. As Gordon was kind enough to point out, it's not the mistake that counts; it's what you do about it. You turned your nightmare into a dream come true for Laura and her wife, and I can only imagine what kind of life they'll give that little girl."

"Maddie," Grace said softly. "Short for Madeline."

Melanie swallowed hard. "That was my grandmother's name," she whispered.

"Oh my God." Grace blinked away a fresh spurt of tears. "I had no idea."

Melanie rolled her eyes heavenward. "Apparently someone did. So now she's triply blessed—an incredible birth mother, lovely parents, and her great-grandmother's name."

"You act like I'm a saint, and I'm not." Grace bowed

her head and laced her fingers together. "They paid me. Enough to cover all of my student loans and put something aside."

"Good for you."

Grace's head jerked up, disbelief puckering her brows.

"I'm serious. You gave them a priceless gift. You deserve something in return. Especially knowing that by doing it the way you did, the truth will eventually find its way back to Earnest."

"We have a deal. In writing. They agreed to respect my privacy until Maddie's tenth birthday. Until then—" She shook her breath, tears welling again. "This has been so hard on Wyatt, all because I'm too scared…my parents…"

Melanie hugged her again, quick and hard. "I understand. And maybe they will too, eventually."

"No." Grace's soft mouth twisted. "They might try to forgive because their Bible tells them so, but they will never, ever understand." She bit her lip. "Are you going to tell…anyone?"

Melanie shook her head. "You've had to make all of the hard decisions so far. You don't deserve to have this one taken away from you. If you want Hank to know, you say when and how that happens."

"You can live with that?"

"For as long as I have to…or ten years. Whichever comes first." She reached out and squeezed Grace's cold, interlocked fingers. "It's entirely up to you."

"Thank you," Grace whispered.

"You're welcome. And I mean that literally. If you take that job in the Panhandle, prepare to be initiated into the Earnest Ladies' Club, and brace yourself, 'cuz you're gonna be roping with Shawnee. As of now you are officially one of the family, even if I'm the only one who knows why."

Grace flashed a watery smile. "Plus Wyatt."

"Oh yes. We can't forget Wyatt." Melanie's jaw set, and her eyes went squinty.

Grace's chin dropped. "You can't be mad at *him*."

"Can't I?" She spun on her heel and saw Scotty and Philip dive for cover in the thicket of exercise machines. "Just watch me."

Chapter 48

WYATT SAT AT THE END OF THE BAR AND SCOWLED INTO the glass of straight Coke in front of him. Louie had refused to serve him alcohol before five in the afternoon. For Wyatt's own good, he declared solemnly, taking an obscene amount of pleasure in turning the tables. Wyatt could have walked a block down the street to Hamley's or the Rainbow, but that would have required more initiative than he possessed at the moment, and there was something even more pathetic about having to get drunk in someone else's bar.

At least he knew Melanie was safe—or had been first thing this morning. Goddamn Gil. What kind of asshole drove away without knowing for sure what she intended to do?

Beside him, Joe sat silently watching the Mariners validate Wyatt's decision to continue being a lifetime, card-carrying Mets fan even though he'd moved to the Pacific Northwest. Wyatt had obviously done a piss-poor job of pretending that yes, really, he was fine, since Joe had caught the first flight to Pendleton. Melanie hadn't told them about Hank, though. Joe would have said so. And he wouldn't be here.

Another fight between Melanie and Wyatt? Nothing their friendship couldn't handle. But a betrayal of this magnitude? When Joe learned the truth…

Behind them, the room buzzed and clattered with

a decent-sized lunch crowd, evenly divided between first timers and return customers, who Louie and Helen greeted like old friends. Already today, three people had asked if they took reservations for Sunday's chicken dinner. Wyatt smiled and nodded in the appropriate places and registered none of it. Words ricocheted off the shell that had closed around him, and he was only vaguely aware of the occasional clap on the shoulder, accompanied by a comment about his lack of roping prowess. He should keep going out to the saddle club, if only because they felt so sorry for him that they came and spent their money at his bar.

Melanie would have made him go.

He caught the fresh bubble of pain, cradling it close to his heart before he tucked it in beside the others. If this was all he had left of her, he intended to hoard it for as long as possible. At least he would feel something. He didn't glance up when the door opened, or when the new arrival paused only a few feet away. It took a hard jab from Joe's elbow to make him raise his head.

And there she was, a wavering image in the antique glass mirror behind the bar. The bubbles in his chest burst into a thousand shimmering points of light. He wondered—in a remote, out-of-body way—if they would simply fade away or transform into drops of acid rain. He stared at her reflection, not entirely convinced that it wasn't a mirage.

The door burst open, and Grace, Philip, and Scotty piled through, then skidded to a stop in the entryway, eyeing Melanie as if she were one of devil cows turned loose in the bar. Joe's stool screeched on the wooden floor as he jumped to his feet. He took a single step that put him between Melanie and Wyatt, his hands closing into loose fists and his knees flexed as if prepared to block her charge.

Wyatt swiveled to stare at him. "What are you doing?"

Melanie smiled cryptically, directing her answer to Joe. "For an extremely intelligent man, he can be pretty dense. He actually thinks you'll automatically take my side, just because you're married to my best friend. Even after you dropped everything to be here."

"He's done the same for me."

"But he doesn't expect anyone to return the favor." She folded her arms and tipped her head in exaggerated thought. "I assumed it was a general lack of faith in humanity. Now I'm leaning toward abandonment issues. What do you think?"

"Guilt." Joe said without hesitation. "And a sense of unworthiness. He can't stop punishing himself for the sins of his forebears."

"You've actually *thought* about this?" Wyatt asked, gaping at him.

Joe made a pained face. "I'm married now. I don't get to just leave shit alone anymore. We've gotta pick, pick, pick—"

"Well, you can stop now," Wyatt snapped.

"Oh no. Not just yet." Melanie shifted her gaze toward Wyatt. "I would have been here sooner, but I stopped to see Grace." She flipped a *cool your jets* hand when Wyatt stiffened. "She and I are fine. Right, Grace?"

Behind her, Grace nodded, eyes huge.

Melanie smiled grimly. "*You* and I, on the other hand…"

And of course Joe chose that moment to abandon him. "It looks like you have plenty of backup. I'll just go check on the Camaro."

"Honestly." Melanie scowled at his retreating back. "It's like people think I have no imagination. And you..."

Wyatt flinched at the fury blazing in her eyes. "I'm sorry. If there had been any way—"

"*Five. Years.*" She punctuated each word with a sharp jab of two fingers into his sternum. "You've been feeding me that *It's not you, it's me* bullshit since Violet's wedding—and for the record, every woman in existence assumes *Oh, yeah, it's definitely me*...so thanks for that."

He sucked his arms up over his chest and twisted on his stool to take the next jab in the shoulder. "How long?" she demanded. "How goddamn long have you been in love with me and lying your ass off?"

"Not...*ouch!*" He grabbed her wrists before she could inflict any more pain. "Four years, max. The lying, I mean. I was serious at first. The other..." He could only shrug helplessly. "Always."

She hissed a curse when he refused to let her yank her wrists free. Every conversation in the room had stopped, and every eye and ear was glued to them, but she didn't lower her voice. "That's forty-two months of dating losers and having mediocre sex when I could have had you!"

"They must have been losers if they managed to have mediocre sex with *you*." And what the hell was he saying, in front of all these people?

She bared her teeth. "I didn't say *they* had lousy sex. But imagine what *we* could have done with all those nights if you hadn't been such a damn coward."

Wyatt had to work at taking a breath because his lungs had done a full stop. "I didn't think—"

"Don't even *try* that line." She gave her arm another yank, then settled for kicking his shin. *Shit*, that hurt. "All you do is think! If you'd stopped analyzing and just looked, maybe you would have noticed that I was in love with you, too, you stupid jerk."

Damn. There went his heart. If something didn't kick back into gear, he was going to pass out from lack of blood and oxygen to his brain. He managed to stutter, "I…you…really?"

"Oh, for God's sake." She fell in to him, forcing him to drop her arms and grab her waist as she kissed him.

Lights burst behind his eyes, neurons exploding like transformers during a lightning storm. For what may have been the first time in his life, Wyatt stopped thinking altogether and dragged her even closer. At some point in time that was both an eternity and hardly more than a microsecond, she pulled back, but left her arms linked behind his neck.

"Are we clear now?" she asked.

"Crystal. But what about—"

She cut him off with another quick kiss, then glanced around the bar, pausing to smile at Gordon, who was taking in the show from what had become his booth. "Hey, everybody. As you can see, Wyatt and I have a few things to discuss. So if you'll just excuse us…"

Grace and the boys plastered themselves against the wall as Melanie tugged Wyatt off the stool and out the front door. A single, long wolf whistle followed them.

Damn Scotty.

———— ∿ ————

When they were inside the apartment, she released him

and tucked her fingers into the front pockets of her jeans, suddenly subdued, her eyes uncertain.

"You shaved," she said.

"I didn't see any reason not to."

"Mmm." She wandered over to the window that looked down onto Main Street. "I came to proposition you."

He'd only just regained basic life-sustaining functions, and there she went, knocking the air out of him again. Wyatt plopped onto the edge of the bed. Less likely to suffer a concussion that way, if he did fall over. "What did you have in mind?"

"I'm going to apply for a job with a nonprofit in the Tri-Cities that helps women and minorities start their own businesses." She fiddled with the latch on the window. "They can always use someone with marketing expertise."

His heart stalled again. She wanted to stay? "What about Westwind?"

"After my experience with the Bull Dancer, I realized I wanted to go the small-business route. It's where I hope I can make the most difference." She hitched a shoulder, her gaze still fixed on the street below. "The new job wouldn't eat up my entire life. I can do a lot of the planning work from home, and the schedule is flexible, which will make it easier to rodeo."

"It sounds perfect."

She flicked him a smile. "The pay is crap, but I was hoping I could hook a rich husband to keep me in the style to which I am not accustomed."

Hell. There went his lungs again. "What..." He had to stop, take a gulp of air, and start again. "What about Hank?"

"Gil has relieved me of my position as guardian."

Her hand dropped to her side. "He tells me I lack the necessary experience to deal with the current situation. And"—her breath hissed as she sucked it in between gritted teeth—"now that I know exactly what Hank did to Grace, it may take a while before I can see him without wanting to throttle him."

Wyatt almost smiled, but the pang in his chest canceled it out. She was hurt and angry right now. Once her temper faded…

She shook her head. "Yes, I'm pissed, but it's more than that. Whatever he needs, I obviously can't give it to him—or force it on him—or it never would have come to this. Gil's right. I'm more of a problem than a solution…which I assume you've known all along."

"I…yes," he admitted. No more lies. No more evasion. They'd reached a place where he could—and would—deal in nothing but the truth. "I gave you that list of therapists hoping I could persuade you to talk to one of them."

She gave a shaky laugh. "Always the man with a plan, and that's a good one. I have some serious issues to work through. But I do know one thing for certain. I have to do what's best for me…and as hard as we've tried to deny it, that's always been you. It won't be good for anyone if I spend the next fifty years resenting my brother for keeping us apart."

Emotion slammed into the back of his throat, blocking his airway. She would do that? Choose him over Hank?

"Did you say…*husband*?" he asked, the words just now sinking in.

"We can start by living in sin." She didn't quite pull

off the flippant tone. "I totally understand why you'd rather not rush into anything, although as Violet pointed out, we've diddled around long enough that if you don't know what you're getting into by now…" She turned to brace her back against the window frame, tucking her hands behind her hips. "I won't even make you set foot in a church…but there is a catch."

Of course there was. "Isn't there always?"

"This one is a doozy." Her eyes were dark with regret. "I can't see her, Wyatt. Maddie, I mean. I realize that's what Laura wants—a big, happy dysfunctional family—but as long as Hank doesn't know, I just…can't." She hunched her shoulders. "I can justify knowing about her and not telling because it won't help either of them. But getting to really *know* her—and love her, I'm sure—that goes way beyond Hank. My parents have a granddaughter. Maybe they'll care, maybe they won't, but either way they might never forgive me if I kept them in the dark while I played Aunt Melanie."

Realization washed through him, numbingly cold, and he bowed his head. "Which means I can't play Uncle Wyatt."

She shook her head vehemently. "I wouldn't do that to you. I have no doubt you're crazy about that little girl…and I'm sure she adores you. Laura and Julianne have been your family for a very long time. I won't force you to give that up."

He raised his confused gaze to meet hers. "I don't understand. How would that work with you and me, never talking about Maddie…"

"The same as it's worked up until now. It won't be easy. And I'll probably give in to the temptation to ask a few questions, or peek at your pictures, but that's as far as I can go."

Still, it would leave a huge obstacle between the two of them. Or rather, a very small one.

"It won't be forever," Melanie said. "Grace told me about the ten-year clause. And she could decide to tell Hank before then."

But there was no conviction in her voice. They'd both seen Hank. Hell, even before, when he'd just been oblivious, why would Grace have trusted him with a secret that would almost certainly alienate her entire family? In her place, Wyatt would wait as long as possible.

"There's something else. And this might be the deal breaker." Melanie laced her fingers tightly in front of her. "You have to lay down some serious boundaries with Laura. She can't come running here every time she stubs a toe. I know you feel responsible for her, and that you care about her but..." She waved a hand toward the floor. "There are three people downstairs who raced across town to throw their bodies between us if necessary, and a man who should be getting ready to fight bulls at a rodeo in Texas right now, but he's here instead because you needed him. *Those* are friends. Not just someone who lets you take care of her. I think it's time Laura learned the difference."

Wyatt sat there, stunned. She was right. So was Julianne, even though she'd never said it in so many words. And Laura wasn't entirely to blame. He'd enabled her for too long. And she was the only thing he had left of the first half of his life. He'd clung to that connection, as warped as it was, because he had never been able to believe that, if worst came to worst, anyone else would choose him. But Joe had—no questions asked. And Melanie would, if he gave her the chance.

"You need time to think," she said, and strode across the room.

As the door started to swing shut behind her, Wyatt lunged for it. "No, I don't."

Even he couldn't think himself out of this one. Melanie wanted to stay. She would always stay, because she believed. In herself. In him. In *them*. And he would eventually learn to take as well as he gave because he'd found a woman willing and able to bear his burdens.

The abrupt sensation of release was so powerful he had to grip the door with both hands to keep from losing his balance. Melanie wrapped her arms around his waist, solid and steady.

"I thought you'd never forgive me," he said.

She pried one of his hands off the door to lift it to her lips. "Because of you, my brother didn't destroy Grace or her career. And you had no choice but to keep it from me and everyone else. Did you really think I couldn't appreciate that, or how much it has cost you?"

There was no way to express what he was thinking or feeling, so he scowled. "I also thought you were never coming back."

"There's that *I'm not worthy* crap again." She gave his cheek a patronizing pat. "Have you considered therapy?"

He made a strangled noise.

She laughed, then leaned in until their noses touched and he was drowning in the warm brown of her eyes. "I can't promise I'll never leave you again. There may be times when it's the only way we both survive. But I will always come around sooner or later."

He gave her a suspicious squint. "How will I know whether I'm forgiven or you've just finished plotting your revenge?"

"You won't. But at least you'll never be bored. And I love you too much to do permanent damage."

Love. Marriage. His world did what felt like a full spin. She tried to drop a quick kiss on his mouth, but he hauled her close, shoved the door shut, and pushed her up against it. They were both breathing hard when he tore his mouth from hers to scatter kisses down the side of her neck while he tugged at her shirt. They left a trail of clothes as they worked their way to the bed.

Her stomach gave a deep growl, and she laughed. "I haven't had lunch."

"Luckily, I know a place close by."

"It's Thursday," she said, then gasped as he nipped the tender skin below her navel. "Chili day. I love Helen's corn bread."

"You can have a whole pan, once we're done with the appetizer course."

Handy, having good food in the bar. They could stay up here for days while he made sure this woman understood that he worshiped her with all his heart, body, and soul, and let her return the favor. He was still amazed she would let him foot her bills, given that powerful streak of independence. But this was Melanie. She was too secure to feel undermined because he wanted to buy her a pickup and trailer to relaunch her rodeo career.

He tipped her onto her back to give her a mock frown. "That thing you said about me supporting you…are you sure you're not just after my money?"

She arched and twisted so she was on top. "The cash

is nice. Your incredible good looks don't hurt. And I intend to take full advantage of all those connections of yours on behalf of my clients. But I could have all of that without a ring. The truth is…" She traced a line along the top of his shoulder with her tongue, then nipped his earlobe and whispered, "I'm marrying you for permanent custody of that kick-ass shower."

Epilogue

WYATT HAD NEVER BEEN SO NERVOUS AT A RODEO IN HIS life. Not even the first time he'd fought bulls. Having to step up and perform under pressure was his version of crack. But this…being forced to stand by and watch, with no control over the outcome…

"Next up is Melanie Darrington, from Pendleton, Oregon," the announcer declared. "She didn't join us until almost halfway through the season, and it's taken a while for her to get on a roll. The rodeo here in Colfax is her last chance to qualify for our regional finals, but she'll have to place deep to do it."

As always, Wyatt's chest got tight and achy at the introduction. He'd never thought he'd be proud of the Darrington name until Melanie had decided to wear it. Wyatt had offered to marry her in a church but she'd refused, insisting on cramming their friends and most of their regulars onto the patio of the Bull Dancer. Helen and Miz Iris had sniffled together in the front row until it was time to dish out the massive amounts of food they'd cooked up in the bar kitchen. And Louie—who had been ordained via an online ministry in order to perform his niece's wedding ceremony—had presided over the festivities.

The bride wore Wyatt's favorite sky-blue sundress with scarlet poppies—and white peep-toe pumps. The groom wore cowboy boots.

Tonight she and Roy both appeared to be totally relaxed as they strolled into the arena. His coat gleamed golden under the lights, and his black mane and tail matched the shirt and hat that made her look lean and deadly—like a gunslinger about to step into the street for a showdown. She took a couple of easy practice swings. Wyatt gripped the fence rail so hard his fingers went numb. As she backed Roy into the corner of the roping box, both of their gazes fixed on the calf in the chute. She cocked her arm back and nodded her head.

Swing, swing, swing...zap!

The loop curled around the calf's neck, and she ripped the slack out as Roy slammed on the brakes. *Pop!* The rope snapped free from the saddle horn, the loose end flying in a high, graceful arc under the lights.

"Two point eight seconds!" the announcer shouted. "That'll put her in second place for the moment, with only one roper to go. Now there's a lady who really knows how to come through in the clutch."

Yes. Melanie would always come through, one way or another.

Even for people who hadn't stood up for her. She had ultimately gone back to Westwind Feeds, but only long enough to establish order in the aftermath of Leachman's arrest. She'd also assisted in choosing and training an interim CEO—Anna from the lab, who had a business degree along with her master's in biotech. She still called or emailed Melanie at least once a week, and between them, they had persuaded the board to add scientific credentials to the list of requirements for CEO candidates.

With Melanie's help, Anna was making it very difficult to choose anyone but her.

A pointed elbow dug into Wyatt's ribs. "Dude. You can take a breath now."

Glaring at Scotty, Wyatt peeled his fingers off the rail and shook the feeling back into them. Honest to God. This wasn't even for the big money. He had a whole new respect for rodeo wives who had to sit in the stands and watch their husbands duke it out for world championships. Tori had had to suffer through four National Finals with Delon in gold buckle contention every time, twice successfully. Maybe she could teach Wyatt some breathing exercises. Or share her tranquilizers.

On the return trip from retrieving the rope her calf had dragged to the catch pen, Melanie swung by and held out a hand for Wyatt to slap in congratulations. Her smile shimmered with triumph. "Now you can concentrate on initiating your babies."

As the final breakaway roper exited the arena—she hadn't come close to beating Melanie's time—the music made the familiar switch to a deep, ominous bass riff. All of the sudden, Scotty wasn't quite so cocky, his freckles standing out against his paler-than-usual cheeks as he danced from foot to foot. Philip's face looked like it had been carved from brown basalt stone. Wyatt rubbed his hands together in anticipation as his pulse revved up from long habit.

Time to have some fun.

The announcer's voice rang out above the music. "As some of you know, tonight's performance is very special for two young gentlemen...and for those of us who get to be here to watch. This was the very first rodeo Wyatt

Darrington ever worked as a bullfighter, and as a nod to that tradition, each year he brings his latest protégés here to make their official debuts. Keep your eyes open, folks, because you may be about to meet future legends. But first, please welcome the man himself, seven-time professional bullfighter of the year, Wyatt Darrington!"

The roar as he stepped away from the chutes and saluted the crowd nearly drowned out the remainder of the introductions. He was pretty sure neither Scotty or Philip noticed. Wyatt strolled by and slapped Scotty on the back. "What was that you said about breathing?"

Scotty flipped him off. Wyatt laughed.

And then they all moved into position as the first bull rider climbed down into the chute and took his wraps. He nodded his head, the gate swung open...and two more careers were born.

Half an hour later, Melanie was waiting for them behind the bucking chutes as they shouldered their way through a flurry of backslaps and handshakes. Both Scotty and Philip were grinning so hard they were going to have permanent creases—with good reason. They'd made a couple of nice saves, their timing perfect as they leapt in front of fallen riders and lured the bulls away. Wyatt hadn't had to do anything but hang out on the perimeter and watch as all the hard work they'd done over the summer came to fruition.

There were moments that Wyatt wondered if he'd fallen into a coma and this was just an extended dream. Everything was going so well, it was almost frightening. Laura had pouted for a while after they'd had their

long-overdue talk, but when she'd stomped off to their
room, Julianne had hugged Wyatt and quietly thanked
him. They were disappointed that Melanie had chosen
to keep her distance, but again Julianne had understood,
and Laura would just have to deal.

Wyatt had stayed behind when Melanie went to tell
Hank that she was getting married, but both Bing and Gil
had been with her when she went to see her brother. Hank
hadn't said a word, just stomped off into the woods. This
time, Gil had gone after him while Bing hugged Melanie
and told her she was doing the right thing.

Melanie hadn't tried to see him since. As promised,
though, Bing kept her updated. Most recently, she'd
called to say that Hank had been roped into coaching
a flag football team at the elementary school and was
amazingly good with the kids. Maybe because he'd been
one for so long, Melanie had said, her dry humor a sign
that Hank wasn't the only one on the path to recovery.

Grace was back in the Panhandle, whipping the
athletic training program at Bluegrass High School
into shape and, whether she liked it or not, becoming
Shawnee's protégé.

"That girl needs to acquire some attitude," Shawnee
had declared. "And I happen to have plenty to spare."

Heaven help them all if she succeeded in passing it
along.

Melanie sauntered over to give Scotty and Philip a
hug and an attaboy before she slid an arm around Wyatt's
waist and held up her cell phone. "Check this out."

The text included a photo of a familiar bronze Ford,
a slender blond leaning on the bumper with a triumphant grin and her arms spread possessively across

the grill. I got the pickup. I thought you'd like to know. Best wishes.

It was from Michael Miller's newly ex-wife.

Wyatt laughed. Damn, karma was a beautiful bitch.

"Celebrations are in order." Melanie gave him a squeeze. "Whaddaya think, cowboy? Wanna get lucky?"

He inhaled the heady aromas of rosin, bull manure, and man sweat. A haze of dust floated under the lights on a background of velvety-black sky, and the woman he craved more than the adrenaline that still pulsed in his veins was tucked close against his side.

"I can't imagine how a man could be any more blessed."

She poked him in the belly. "Careful, there. Someone might hear you."

He tilted his head back to smile straight up into the heavens. "In that case, I'd better say thank you."

Rodeo 101

Professional Rodeo: Also known as pro rodeo, refers to rodeos that have been approved by the Professional Rodeo Cowboys Association. The PRCA sanctions around 600 rodeos each year across the U.S. and Canada, establishing the rules for competition, requirements for membership, and standards of care for livestock. Money won at rodeos throughout the season is tracked via the World Standings, and at the end of the season the top fifteen money winners in each event qualify to compete at the National Finals Rodeo.

National Finals Rodeo: Also referred to as the NFR or just the Finals. It is the culmination of the rodeo season, and qualifying is the goal of every full-time cowboy. The nationally televised NFR stretches over ten days in early December, with the money won during the ten rounds of competition added to a contestant's season earnings to determine the World Champion in each event. Since 1985, the NFR has been held in Las Vegas, and is contracted to remain there through 2024.

Circuit: A large percentage of cowboys and cowgirls who compete at pro rodeos are not able to travel extensively due to work or family commitments. For their benefit, the 600+ rodeos of the PRCA are divided into twelve regional circuits (e.g., the

Texas Circuit, the Montana Circuit, the Great Lakes Circuit). Money won by members within each circuit is tallied in a separate set of standings, and at the end of the season the top contestants qualify for their regional circuit finals. Champions of the twelve circuits then qualify to compete in the **National Circuit Finals Rodeo**. Usually held in April, the National Circuit Finals Rodeo provides an opportunity for these skilled part-time cowboys to win a national championship.

Would You Like to Know More?

For more information on the sport of professional rodeo, the events, athletes, stock contractors, and the rodeo nearest you, visit **prorodeo.com**.

And for live streaming action online from some of the biggest events of the rodeo season, visit **wrangler network.com**.

Acknowledgments

A big thank-you to June and Janet Yearwood for lending me their business expertise, and to Tom Weeks for helping me fill in the gaps in my eastern Oregon memories. I'd also like to thank my latest laptop for predictably dying in the midst of the last week before my deadline, and Visions Electronics in Lethbridge, Alberta, for saving the day. My editor, Mary Altman, deserves huge credit for bringing clarity and focus to what arrived on her desk as a meandering mess, and my agent, Holly Root, for being the voice of calm and reason when I lose all vestiges of both.

And to the Pendleton-Hermiston-Tri-Cities area of Oregon and Washington—thanks for letting us call you our home for a decade. We miss you, especially during watermelon season and when it's twenty below and snowing sideways here in Montana.

About the Author

Kari Lynn Dell is a ranch-raised Montana cowgirl who attended her first rodeo at two weeks old and has existed in a state of horse-induced poverty ever since. After ten years in eastern Oregon, she now lives on the Blackfeet Reservation in her parents' bunkhouse along with her husband, her son, and Max and Spike the Cowdogs. Oh yeah, and the cat. There's a tipi on her lawn, Glacier National Park on her doorstep, and Canada within spitting distance. Visit her at karilynndell.com.

RECKLESS IN TEXAS

First in a contemporary Western series featuring
the exciting world of Texas rodeo from author
Kari Lynn Dell

Outside the rodeo ring, Violet Jacobs is a single mom
and the lone voice pushing her family's rodeo production
company into the big time. When she hires a hotshot rodeo
bullfighter, she expected a ruckus—but she never expected
her heart to end up on the line.

Joe Cassidy is the best bullfighter in the business. But what he
finds with Violet is more than just a career opportunity; it's a
chance to create a life of his own, if he can drop his bravado-
filled swagger and let her see him for the man he really is.

"Real ranchers. Real rodeo. Real romance."

—Laura Drake, RITA award–winning author

TANGLED IN TEXAS

It took 32 seconds to end his career...but it only took 1 to change his life

One minute, Delon Sanchez was the best bronc rider in the Panhandle. The next, his knee was shattered. Now all he can do is pull together the pieces...and wonder what cruel trick of fate has thrown him into the path of his oh-so-perfect ex, Tori Patterson.

It's just Tori's luck that Delon limps into her physical therapy office, desperate for help. All hard-packed muscle and dark-eyed temptation, he's always been a bad idea. And yet, seeing him again, Tori can't remember what made her choose foolish pride over love...or why the smartest choice would be to run from this gorgeous rodeo boy as fast as her boots can take her.

"When it comes to sexy rodeo cowboys, look no further than talented author Kari Lynn Dell."

—B.J. Daniels, *New York Times* bestselling author

For more Kari Lynn Dell, visit:
sourcebooks.com

TOUGHER IN TEXAS

He's got five rules, and she's aiming to break them all

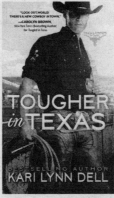

Rodeo producer Cole Jacobs has his hands full running
Jacobs Livestock. He can't afford to lose a single cowboy,
so when Cousin Violet offers to send a more-than-capable
replacement, he's got no choice but to accept. He expects
a grizzled Texas good ol' boy. He *gets* Shawnee Pickett.

Wild and outspoken, Shawnee's not looking for anything but
a good time. It doesn't matter how quickly the tall, dark, and
intense cowboy gets under her skin—Cole deserves something
real, and Shawnee can't promise him forever. Too bad Cole's
not the type to give up when the going gets tough…

"A fun, wild ride! You need to pick up a Kari Lynn Dell."

—B.J. Daniels, *New York Times* bestselling author

ROCKY MOUNTAIN COWBOY CHRISTMAS

Beloved author Katie Ruggle's new series brings
pulse-pounding romantic suspense to a cowboy's
Colorado Christmas

When single dad Steve Springfield moved his family to a
Colorado Christmas tree ranch, he meant it to be a safe
haven. He quickly finds himself fascinated by local folk
artist Camille Brandt—it's too bad trouble is on her trail.

It's not long before Camille is falling for the enigmatic
cowboy and his rambunctious children—he always seems
to be coming to her rescue. As attraction blooms and
danger intensifies, this Christmas romance may just prove
itself to be worth fighting for.

For more Katie Ruggle, visit:
sourcebooks.com

DO OR DIE COWBOY

Here in Texas, we grow all kinds of heroes, but the best ones are cowboys!

First in a heart-pounding cowboy romantic suspense series from author J.D. Faver

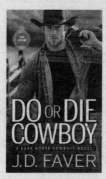

The Garrett brothers are working cowboys with callused hands and soft hearts. This family saga reveals what they'd fight for, who they'd die for, and the risk they'd take for those they love.

When cowboy musician Tyler Garrett encounters a beautiful woman on the run, his life changes forever. He'll put it all on the line for her love—but first they'll have to escape her dangerous past.

For more J.D. Faver, visit:
sourcebooks.com

NAVY SEAL COWBOY

Three former Navy SEALs injured in the line of duty, desperate for a new beginning…searching for a place to call their own.

By Nicole Helm

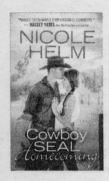

Cowboy SEAL Homecoming

When a tragic accident sends Alex Maguire home, he's not sure what to make of the innocently beguiling woman who lives there. He'll need to keep his distance, but something in Becca Denton's big green eyes makes Alex want to set aside the mantle of the perfect soldier and discover the man he could have been…

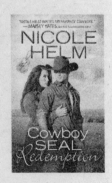

Cowboy SEAL Redemption

Jack Armstrong figured he'd never recover the pieces of his shattered life, but when he and local bad girl Rose Rogers pretend to be in love to throw his meddling family off his trail, he discovers hope in the most unlikely of places…

Cowboy SEAL Christmas

Gabe Cortez doesn't need to talk about his feelings, thank you very much. But when the ranch's therapist, Monica Finley, tempts him with all the holiday charm she can muster, it's hard to resist cozying up to her for Christmas.

For more Nicole Helm, visit:
sourcebooks.com

Also by Kari Lynn Dell